THE SWORD OF GOD

A John Milton Novel

Mark Dawson

AN UNPUTDOWNABLE ebook.

First published in Great Britain in 2014 by
UNPUTDOWNABLE LIMITED

Ebook first published in 2014 by
UNPUTDOWNABLE LIMITED

This ebook published in 2014 by
UNPUTDOWNABLE LIMITED

Copyright © UNPUTDOWNABLE LIMITED 2014

Formatting by Polgarus Studio

The moral right of Mark Dawson to be identified as the author of this work has been asserted by him in accordance with the Copyright, Designs and Patents Act 1988.

All the characters in this book are fictitious, and any resemblance to actual persons living or dead is purely coincidental.

All rights reserved. No part of this publication may be reproduced, stored in a retrieval system or transmitted in any form or by any means, without the prior permission in writing of the publisher, nor to be otherwise circulated in any form of binding or cover other than that in which it is published without a similar condition, including this condition, being imposed on the subsequent purchaser.

To Mrs D, FD and SD.

PART ONE

Chapter 1

SHERIFF LESTER GROGAN saw the man on the shoulder of the road, hauling a heavy pack in the direction of Truth. He was a hundred yards away when he noticed him for the first time, so he slowed the cruiser in order to take a better look. From behind, he looked just like any other hiker who passed through the hills in this part of Michigan's Upper Peninsula. He was a little over average height, and he looked lithe. He looked strong, too, judging by the amount that he was carrying without appearing to struggle. There was a large backpack over his back with several smaller bags lashed to it and, carried on a strap so that it crossed diagonally across his bag, there was a rifle.

Grogan drew up alongside and slowed the car to his pace. He reached for the button to slide down the electric window.

"Hold up there, partner?"

The man stopped. He looked across to him. "Yes?"

"How you doing?"

"I'm fine."

Grogan quickly assessed him. He was dirty and dishevelled, with long dark hair that reached down to his shoulders, matted and twisted at the ends, and a thick, shaggy beard. His clothes were dirty, too. His jeans were frayed at the cuffs and patched in several places, and his hiking boots were caked with mud. He had the bluest, coldest eyes that Grogan had ever seen. They burned out from beneath heavy brows with an icy fire, and as the man turned to look at him in return, he felt momentarily disconcerted.

"Lester Grogan," he said by way of introduction. "You're just coming up to Truth. Couple of miles up the road."

"I know."

"And I'm the sheriff."

The man just nodded.

"And what's your name, friend?"

"John."

"John?" he said, pressing for something that he could run through the computer.

"That's right."

"You got a second name?"

"Sure."

Lester started to feel irritated. "You want to stop giving me attitude and tell me what it is?"

"Have I done something wrong?"

"Not that I know of. I just like to know who's coming into my town."

"Milton."

"All right then, Mr. Milton. Good to make your acquaintance. What you out here for?"

"Just walking."

"Just walking?"

"That's right."

"From where?"

"Trout Creek."

"And where are you headed?"

The man shrugged, the backpack riding up his shoulders a little as he did so. "I don't know," he admitted. "Wherever I end up, I guess."

Lester Grogan had been a policeman for twenty years, and he hadn't lasted as long as that without having learned to trust his instincts. And, right here, this guy was pressing all kinds of the wrong buttons: he was evasive, he had an attitude on him, he looked like a bum. None of those characteristics made him feel a whole lot better about him, or the prospect of him coming into his little town.

"You planning on staying in Truth?"

"Thought I might."

"You want a ride?"

The man shook his head. "No, thanks. I'm good."

Lester reached across and opened the passenger door. "Seriously," he said. "Let me give you a ride. Take the weight off."

"I'm fine, Sheriff."

"Get in the car, John."

The man fixed him with those cold blue eyes again and, for a moment, Grogan thought he was going to call his bluff. That might have meant it would get interesting. But just as he was sliding his right hand down to his holster and his pistol, Milton shrugged the pack off one shoulder and then the other, opened the rear door, and slung it inside. He unslung the rifle and placed it carefully next to the pack, shut the door and got into the front next to him.

"All right," Lester said. "Let's go."

LESTER DROVE west, following the long straight line of Highway 28, crossed the bridge over the Presque Isle River, and continued to Truth. They passed the mailboxes of the big houses on the edge of town and kept going, passing the sign for the KOA Indoor Playground and the strip mall with the gas station, the ATV rental shop, and the Pizza Hut that had only recently been opened. He had lived here ever since he had come back from the Gulf, and every little detail about it was familiar to him, from the wide-open spaces between the businesses to the ever-present green of the forest on the fringes of town. There was the four-way junction where old man McDonald had crashed his pickup into the UPS van last week. Johnny's Bar where, last night, he had been forced to stop a fist fight between Thor Bergstrom's boy and a couple of hikers who had been a little too enthusiastic with their drinking. He knew it all.

It was a peaceful, pleasant town. Small, just over a thousand residents, never too busy and it rarely presented any kind of challenge when it came to policing. Lester liked to think of himself as a modest man, but he was quite sure that the firm way that he went about his job was one of the main reasons for that. He kept on top of things, never allowing problems to develop, stamping them out quickly and decisively. That was what he was paid to do and he took pride in his job.

The man sitting in the car next to him could become a problem. Lester was able to read the signs. He was going to make sure it didn't happen that way.

They reached the junction with Falls Road, the main drag that led into the centre of town. There was a blue sign for the state police and another for Big Trout Falls. The lights changed to red and Lester drew up to a stop.

"So," he said as he waited for the lights to change, "where are you from?"

"Here and there," the man, Milton, said.

"You don't say much, do you?"

"I don't have much to say."

"What about that accent? What is that, English?"

"That's right."

"That's not an accent we hear all that much up around here."

Milton said nothing. The longer Lester was in his company, the more uncomfortable he became. His initial impression, as he had watched him on the side of the road, had been that he was a vagabond, a drifter. The kind of man who, in his experience, only brought aggravation to a place. He wasn't so sure about that now, but, after talking to him, the initial reason for his reluctance to allow him into town had been superseded by something else. It wasn't fear, because it took a lot to frighten Lester, it was more of an apprehensiveness that this John Milton was trouble. He was closed off, opaque to the point of being unhelpful, and it made Lester nervous. He acted like he had something to hide. The reasons for his unease might have changed, but his initial conclusion was the same: this was not the sort of man that Lester wanted in his town.

The lights changed to green. Instead of taking the right that led into Truth, he drove on. Milton turned his head to watch through the window as the glow of the town disappeared behind them, and then, when he turned back, he almost started to speak. Lester stiffened in anticipation. But Milton changed his mind, and, with a thin smile breaking across his face, he stayed quiet yet again.

Lester kept on driving west. They passed the sign that said YOU ARE NOW LEAVING TRUTH – COME BACK SOON and then, at that point, there could be no further doubt. Still Milton said nothing. Lester drove on another mile until the blue expanse of East Lake was visible on the left, and there he slowed the cruiser and pulled into the lot that served the campsite beyond. He turned off the road and crunched across the stones and gravel until he came to a stop. Dusk had fallen fully now, and beyond the wooden guard rail and the gentle slope of the terrain lay the wide tract of the water.

He switched off the engine. "I hope that was helpful."

Milton opened the door and got out of the car. He opened the rear door and took out his gear.

"There's a campsite over yonder." Lester pointed down to the shore. "It's ten bucks or something to stay the night. But if that's a problem, you let them know that Lester Grogan sent you. They'll look the other way."

Still Milton did not reply.

"Goodnight, then," Lester said, reaching across for the door handle. He pulled it shut and lowered the window. "Look after yourself."

Milton put his right arm through the straps of his big pack, hoisted it off the ground, and settled it across his shoulders. He picked up his rifle and turned back to the cruiser. "I'll be seeing you around."

Lester's hand hovered over the start button. He looked back at him with a smile on his face, but he made sure there was steel in his voice when he replied, "No. You won't."

He stared out at the man, saw him looking down at him, felt that same jolt of disquiet and, hoping that he had just misinterpreted his meaning, pressed the button and put the cruiser into reverse. The night was drawing in quickly now, and the lights flicked on automatically, the beams sweeping out over the still water, catching the insects in the bright shafts. The gravel crunched beneath the tyres as Lester put the car into drive, rumbled away to the road, and turned right to head back into town.

Chapter 2

MILTON WATCHED the lights of the cruiser as it headed down the half mile of straight before the road bent to the left and was swallowed up in the dark embrace of the tree line. That, he thought, had been almost comical in its unexpectedness. He looked down at himself. He supposed he did look a little rough and ready, a little ragged around the edges, but he had been living off the land for the past few weeks, and modern amenities had been few and far between. What did they expect around here? A haircut and a manicure? A lounge suit?

He had started out in Ohio. That had been where the trouble had started and where he had decided that the best way to insulate himself from temptation was just to put as much distance between himself and it as possible. He had bought the things that he needed in Akron and then set out into the wilderness, skirting the southern shore of Lake Erie, turning north at Toledo and then following the water north into Michigan. He had walked most of the way, occasionally breaking up the journey by hitching or, on one occasion, smuggling himself into the empty boxcar of a freight train that rumbled north out of Flint. He stayed away from towns, skirting them when he could, and had found quiet spots to sleep in his tent. It had been peaceful and calming, exactly what he had needed to quieten the clamour in his head.

It reminded him of his time in the regiment, and especially the training in the Brecon Beacons, long days and nights living off the land even as other soldiers were trying to track him down. He had been good at it then, and he had been pleased to find that his skills had not atrophied from lack of use. His previous life, in the Group, had often occasioned a life of ease and comfort in the lulls between assignments. On other occasions, he had been required to stay in high-end hotels so as to present the right impression to the targets he had been sent to eliminate. He had never been comfortable with conspicuous excess, and he had found these last days, with their simplicity and honesty, to have been exactly what he needed.

But as he had trekked northwest through the Straits State Park, the rains had come. He had been caught on the road during a particularly heavy downpour. The rain had lanced down so hard that the noise was loud enough to obliterate the sound of the engines of the cars that had ignored his outthrust thumb. He had quickly been soaked to the skin and the rains had been constant, more or less, ever since. He had put up his tent and sheltered for a day. But when it became obvious that the weather had settled in for the long haul, he had struck camp and set off again. He needed to keep moving and if a little discomfort was the price that he had to pay, then so be it.

The rains had continued as he headed north. The tracks that he followed became muddy quagmires, and he had to be wary of flash floods, previously empty riverbeds that became rushing torrents with frightening speed. His clothes were permanently sodden, his hair and beard streamed with water, and the cold started to leech into his bones. He had not intended to stop in a town until he crossed into Wisconsin, but the more he mused on it the more he figured that he could adapt his plan. His time in the wilderness had weakened his urge to drink, and he felt strong enough to resist the temptation again. He saw from his map that the town of Truth was on his route, so he had decided to stop. A warm meal, a hot bath and a clean bed suddenly sounded particularly attractive.

And then this.

You really couldn't make it up.

He glanced around at the parking area, the path that led down to the lake and, on the shore, the open space that was reserved for campers. There was a tent there, the beige canvas just visible in the dying light. It was a big one, pitched next to a four-wheel drive. Fishermen, Milton guessed. And as he paused there, he heard the sound of voices blown up to him by the breeze that came off the water.

He could pitch his tent down there, he supposed. The site was big enough that he could put enough distance between himself and the fishermen so that he wouldn't be disturbed. He remembered from his map that the town of Wakewood was twenty miles to the west. He usually covered around three miles an hour and, if he stayed close to the road, the terrain wouldn't slow him down too much. He could camp here overnight, set off early in the morning, and be in town in time for lunch.

He almost resolved to do that when the sky cracked with a deep, booming roll of thunder. He looked to the south and saw a huge jagged fork of lightning that lit up the water. The first spatters of moisture fell to earth, splashes that burst on his face as he looked up to the swirling dark clouds that were sweeping to the north. The lightning flashed and the thunder boomed again, closer now, and Milton changed his mind. He didn't want to wait until he got to Wakewood. Damned if a prejudiced hick cop was going to tell him where he could and couldn't go.

He rolled his shoulders to settle the straps of the pack, picked up his rifle, and crunched across the gravel to the hardtop. He turned to the east and started to walk the mile back into town.

IT TOOK him twenty minutes. The rain fell heavily, another drenching deluge that defied all logic by the way it seemingly grew in intensity the longer it went on. He passed the WELCOME TO TRUTH sign on the edge of town and kept going until he reached the crossroads where they had briefly stopped for the red traffic light. He had kept a close watch as Grogan had driven him through the town and knew which direction he would need to go in order to find the centre. The rain washed down, slicking the asphalt so that the red, amber and green reflected in long, painterly streaks. He waited for the traffic to clear and then crossed over the road and headed north. It was another two miles to the town proper and, by the time he got there, another half an hour had passed.

As Milton came into the town proper he thought, with a smile, that it was pleasant not to have to concern himself with the procedures that he had lived by for so long. Normally, on arrival in a place like this, he would have conducted an SDR—a Surveillance Detection Run—a routine designed to flush out anyone who might have been following him. That was ancient history for him now, although old habits died hard.

Truth looked like a small kind of place, the kind of town that had most things that you needed, but only a few of each: a couple of hotels, a few restaurants, a few bars. Down on its luck, too, from the looks of the faded and peeling paint on the buildings and the cheap neon signs that fizzed and popped. It was the kind of town Milton had gotten used to seeing. This part of Michigan was a poor country of poor people. The young men he saw on the street corners flashed him threatening looks, crippled by divorce and schools that had failed them, driving rusting jalopies or chopped motorcycles that spluttered and coughed. Drinking beers and smoking cigarettes they couldn't afford, snorting Mexican dope, waiting to commit the senseless crimes that would lock them away. Properties were put up for sale with no hope of selling them, faded memories and broken dreams recycled like the counterfeit shoes and knock-off DVD players that filled the second-hand stores and pawnshops. Milton had walked hundreds of miles and had not seen a Lexus or a Mercedes. Instead he saw dented Fords and Chevys left in front of Laundromats and convenience stores. Scattered homesteads were named Hope Ranch and Last Chance without a trace of irony.

He stopped at a late night Laundromat and asked for directions to the nearest hotel. The attendant directed him up the road and then to the right and, after a short walk, Milton reached it. An old neon sign, with some of the letters unlit, announced it as Perkins Village Inn. Milton went inside, wiping the water from his face.

The teenage girl behind the counter looked up at him with distaste. Milton frowned and then remembered what he must look like.

"Hello," he said. "I need a room."

"How long for?"

"One night."

The girl chewed gum with lazy insouciance and radiated disinterest. She pecked her fingers against the keyboard in front of her. "Yeah," she said. "We got a room. Fifty bucks. You pay up front."

Milton reached into the waterproof belt he wore around his waist, unzipped it, and took out his roll of money. He peeled off two twenties and a ten and laid them on the counter. The clerk took them, slid them in the till, and fetched a key from a rack on the wall behind her.

"Room twelve," she said. "End of the corridor, turn right, on your left."

Milton thanked her, collected his backpack and rifle, and followed her directions. The hotel was old and down-at-heel. The carpet was stained in places, and the furniture in the communal areas had seen better days. Milton didn't see any other guests and, as he looked out of the window onto the parking lot outside, he saw that it was empty. It didn't matter.

He found room twelve, although the "1" had dropped off, and he could only be sure it was the right door because it was between "11" and "13." He unlocked the door and went inside. The room beyond was tired. There were holes in the plaster, and in one corner a leak from the roof had discoloured the paint in a wide downward splash. The carpet was damp, with mould clinging to the skirting board in places, and the curtains had a tear all the way down the centre. The bureau was propped up by a folded cardboard coaster beneath one of the legs and the bed felt lumpy and uneven. The sheets were clean, though, and there were no signs of bugs. That would be good enough.

He had to fight another old urge, to sweep for cameras and bugs. That, too, was old thinking. No one was looking for him now. He was just another drifter, hardly worthy of a second glance. That, at least, was what he was aiming for, although the fuss with the sheriff suggested that he needed to work on that a little.

Milton dumped the pack and his rifle and stripped off his wet clothes. He would take them to the Laundromat to be cleaned tomorrow. There was a shower attachment fixed to the taps, but the bracket that would have supported the head had been snapped off, and there was no curtain to stop the water splashing onto the dirty tiles. Milton stepped into the bath, turned the faucet, and directed the lukewarm spray onto his body. It grew warmer the longer the tap was running and, within two minutes, it was piping hot. Milton emptied the complimentary bottle of soap into his hands and rubbed himself all over before taking the shampoo and washing his hair and beard.

He turned off the tap, stepped out of the bath, and dried himself in front of the mirror. He felt cleaner and fresher than he had for days. He reached up and stroked his whiskers. They were already thick, two inches of growth that was soft to the touch now that they had been washed. He had worn a beard before, when he was in the regiment. Most of the men had grown one. He didn't mind it, but he knew that it was his appearance that contributed to his treatment from the sheriff earlier.

No sense in courting trouble.

He went to his pack and took out his straight razor and then worked the soap into his beard until he had a decent lather. Then, using careful downward scrapes, he cut off the first patch of whiskers. He rinsed the razor and repeated, again and again, until he had removed most of the hair. He was right handed, so the place he was most likely to cut himself was beneath his left ear because it was awkward to see. He saved that until last, applying the blade with just enough pressure and scraping it down. He left a small cut, a shallow trench that quickly filled with blood, but it would coagulate quickly, and since he kept the blade clean, there would be no chance of infection.

He examined his handiwork. It was a half decent job, and it would suffice for now. Maybe he would find a barber's shop, have a professional do it properly, and have his wild hair tamed at the same time.

Perhaps.

He had a change of clothes in his pack. The bag was expensive, the waterproofing was good, and Milton's experience had made him fastidious when it came to packing carefully. The fresh T-shirt, jeans and socks were dry, and, as he dressed, he felt his mood improve. Only his boots were dirty, but he spread out the copy of the complimentary newspaper that had been left on the bureau and cleaned away the worst of the mud.

He pulled them on, laced them up, and started to think about what he would have to eat. A steak and all the trimmings. His mouth watered at the thought of it.

THE BORED clerk was watching *The Simpsons* on a blurry portable TV that looked like it was a survivor from the eighties.

"Where can I get a decent meal?" Milton asked her.

She pointed out the door. "Johnny's. East Helen Street, five minutes that way."

"Thank you."

Milton set off. The rain had stopped, although the clouds overhead were thick and disinviting, promising more to come. He followed the girl's directions into a district that looked like it had, years ago, been the home to Truth's light industry. There were several derelict warehouses, most of them empty with hopeful Realtors' signs that had been etiolated by long exposure to the elements. One lot had been cleared entirely, the old foundations a ghostly tracing visible beneath the street's single streetlamp.

Milton knew a little about the area. It had been the seat of the region's mining community. The deposits of tin and copper in the mountains had invigorated the local economy for years until the seams had grown too expensive to mine and foreign imports had undercut the price so that it had become uneconomic to continue. The area had fallen back on tourism as its main industry, but that was seasonal, fluctuating and, ultimately, unreliable.

He walked until he found the place that the girl had recommended. It was a one-storey structure with wooden siding, a slate roof and leaded windows. A sign above the door, a halved rectangle, white over red, announced that it was Johnny's Bar.

He paused on the threshold. He had known, of course, that there would be alcohol involved. He had decided that he could handle a restaurant. He would concentrate on the food, eat it, and then get out. But he had expected that it would be a *restaurant* rather than a bar in which food was obviously an afterthought. All the old adages he had heard in the Rooms now came back to him, the ones about temptation and why an alcoholic couldn't prosper if he kept putting it in his way.

Unless you're a lion tamer, you've got no business in the lion's den.

He thought back to what had happened in Ohio. About how close he had been to taking a drink. He had found himself in a bar, and it had seemed like the most natural thing in the world to order a whiskey. He remembered, with vivid clarity like it was yesterday, the tumbler on the bar, the ice revolving in the warm brown liquid and clinking up against the glass. It had been almost impossible to resist.

You go into a hairdresser's, eventually you'll get a haircut.

He stopped to assess himself. He certainly felt stronger. He had been vulnerable before, but the time he had spent alone had repaired and reinforced the buttresses that he had erected against his compulsions. It had, for a while at least, allowed him to smother his ten years of guilt without the help of the bottle to do it.

And he was hungry.

If he wanted a proper meal, there was no other choice.

The thunder boomed again, directly overhead and powerful enough to tremble the light fitting in the porch of the building. That was all the encouragement Milton needed. He took the final three paces, reached for the door, pushed it open, and went inside.

Chapter 3

LESTER GROGAN pulled away from the school forecourt with Billy, his oldest son, in the passenger seat next to him. They were in the scarlet Chevrolet Silverado that he drove when he was off the clock. The boy slouched down, poker faced, looking for all the world like his problem was his father's fault. It wasn't, Lester knew, although there were moments when he wondered whether it was.

Lester had received the call an hour ago. Billy and some of his friends had been caught breaking into the high school science lab. Lester's deputy, Morten Lundquist, had been called out. He would have dealt with things discreetly, ensured that he could deal with disciplining the boy at home rather than something public that would go on his record and stain his character.

That wasn't going to be possible.

Problem was, the principal at the school had been the one to find the boys and call the police.

He was called Peter Lyle and he was in the habit of beating his wife. Lester had been called to a disturbance at their house six months earlier. He found the woman with a bloodied nose in the back garden. A case with her half packed clothes flew out of the back door as he checked that she was okay. If there was one thing that Lester couldn't stand, it was a bully. He could not abide bullies. Lester kicked the door down and hauled the man out. There might have been a couple of punches to the side of the head when he had cuffed him. And his report might have mentioned that he had resisted arrest when, in all truth, he had been pretty compliant. But the way Lester read the situation, a thick lip was the least a douchebag like Peter Lyle deserved.

Lester had been disappointed when the wife had refused to press charges.

He had been more disappointed when the local school board had refused to give the man his pink slip.

Because, as his wife quickly pointed out, his oldest boy was about to start at the school.

It had turned out exactly as she had predicted. Principal Lyle was doing everything he could to settle the score with Lester. Billy's grades had suddenly dropped off, and there had been detentions for what had seemed to be the smallest transgressions. Lester had been ready to visit Lyle, either to try to make peace with him or to explain how difficult he could make his life, he hadn't decided which, but now Billy had presented his adversary with his best chance yet to drive his advantage home.

"What were you doing there?" Lester started when he couldn't stand the silence any more.

"Nothing," the boy muttered.

"You broke the window."

"Wasn't me."

"Someone did."

"Joey."

"You know he'll say that you are all responsible, though, right? That you just being there is enough?"

The boy gave a tiny shake of his head and kept staring straight ahead.

"What about the joint? Was that you?"

"Not mine."

Lester sighed. "Whose was it, then?"

"Come on, Dad, have a wild guess how it got there."

He took his eyes off the road and turned to look at the boy. "You're kidding?"

Billy met his eyes and raised his eyebrows in an expression of ineffable cynicism.

Lester gripped the wheel tight.

"Fuck!" he shouted, crashing his fist against the dash.

Billy flinched and turned his face back to the windshield.

"You know you've given him the chance he's been waiting for. How could you do something so stupid?"

They drove the rest of the way in awkward silence. The problem had been on his mind all afternoon. He knew that it had made him crabby and short tempered.

He pulled up outside their modest two-storey house.

"Tell your mother I'm going out."

"That's right," he said. "Go and get drunk. Solves everything."

Lester started to berate him, but the boy slammed the door, turned his back on him, and stalked up the drive to the front door.

Lester put the car into gear and drove back into town, angry.

LESTER MET Leland Mulligan, one of his deputies, at Johnny's Bar. They took stools at the bar, drinking from bottles of Budweiser and watching football. Leland was trying to get him to talk about the new quad bike that he was thinking of buying. The bar was busier than usual tonight: there were the regular drinkers, the old-timers who had nothing better to do than to gradually pickle their livers and bemoan how the country was turning to shit. One table was occupied by the four hunters he had noticed when they had driven into Truth that morning. Another held three people: the two FBI agents who had been nosing around for leads on the bank robbers who had been busy hereabouts, and Mallory Stanton, the sister of the half-witted boy he'd had so much trouble with five years earlier. That table, in particular, was distracting his attention from Leland's attempts to have him weigh in on the respective merits of the Kawasaki and Suzuki ATVs that he was considering.

"And, yes, I *know* they're Japanese," he was saying, "and I *know* you'll tell me I'm crazy, that they'll turn out to be shit and expensive to maintain and I ought to get something American, a Polaris, maybe, but the price they've given me is so good I got to think about it, right?"

Lester grunted in response, fading him out again and watching the two agents. They had come to see him when they had arrived and had explained what they were here to do. It had been last week, the two of them pulling up in a big GMC Denali, fifty thousand dollars' worth of luxury SUV about as useful up here on these roads as tits on a bull. They were based down in Detroit, and they had flaunted the big-city attitude that Lester had grown to resent from the tourists that had come up here to hunt and fish, that unsaid assumption that they could get Lester to do whatever they wanted him to do just by asking.

He was still thinking about those agents and how angry they made him when the door opened and John Milton stepped inside. He didn't recognise him at first. He had cleaned himself up pretty good, shaved off his beard and changed his clothes. But there he was, right as rain. Those same blue eyes scanned the room and settled on him for just a moment before they flicked away again. Lester felt the roil of anger in his stomach. The man had ignored him. He was the sheriff, a man of the law, and this drifter had thumbed his nose at him. Maybe he hadn't been explicit, laid it out clearly enough so that there was no possibility of him being misunderstood.

Or maybe the guy just had a hard time doing what he was told.

Didn't matter either way. Lester knew that if you wanted to be an effective policeman, you couldn't have a situation where your instructions were ignored. He didn't know Milton, but he sure knew the type. A bad attitude, the kind of man who thought he could do whatever he wanted to do and damn what anyone else had to say. You give someone like that an inch and chances are they'll end up taking a mile.

Lester couldn't have that.

He was about to go over to have a word with him when one of the agents, the male one—Wilson? Carson?—came over and took the seat to Lester's right.

"Evening, Sheriff."

He sipped his beer and looked at him with wary regard. "Evening."

"Just thought I'd let you know that we're leaving in the morning."

It was Clayton, he remembered. Special Agent Orville Clayton. Older, moustache that was greying a little around the edges, could stand with losing a few pounds here and there. "You had enough?"

"We've done all we can."

"You finally agree those boys aren't here, then?"

"It doesn't look like it."

"I won't say I told you so."

"We get a tip, Sheriff, we have to check it out."

Lester looked over his shoulder. Milton had taken a stool in the area of the bar that was reserved for those who wanted something to eat and the waitress, a pretty thing called Clementine, was taking his order.

"I got to say something before we clear out," the agent was saying.

"Yeah? And what's that?"

"We never really felt all that comfortable up here, Sheriff. Seemed to us, to both of us, that you weren't all that pleased to have us around."

Lester took his eyes off Milton for a moment and, after finishing a sip from his beer, said, "Well, that's because you didn't listen to me when I said you were wasting your time. I don't have a beef with you or your friend over there, but the way I see it, the way my men see it, too, the federal government getting involved in something like this is a waste of everyone's time. If those boys were hiding out in the hills like you seemed to think they were, well, we'd have found them. We could have saved ourselves a whole lot of time and energy if you people had listened to me right from the outset."

"That may be, but the bottom line as far as I'm concerned is we're all on the same team. I think it'd do you well to remember that."

Lester rolled his eyes. Jeez, the attitude on this prick. *It would do him well to remember?* He was half tempted to give the man a piece of his mind, unvarnished, but he fought against it. What was the point? Him and his pretty sidekick would get into that shiny car that had cost fifty grand of his tax dollars and scoot back down to the city tomorrow and that would be that. What would it achieve?

Nothing, that's what.

It wouldn't achieve a damned thing.

But it didn't do anything for Lester's mood and, as he turned his attention back to Milton, he felt like he would have to do something tonight to help people remember that, around these parts at least, Lester was in charge. That boy, dumb enough to ignore his clear and reasonable instructions, he was going to find that he was in the wrong place at the wrong time with the wrong lawman.

MILTON KEPT his eyes off the bottles behind the bar as he ordered a steak and fries and took his orange juice over to the spare table in the eating area. He had seen the sheriff, and he knew that the sheriff had seen him, too. He wondered whether it might not be more prudent to turn around and find somewhere else. He wasn't in the business of causing unnecessary trouble for himself. Indeed, for most of the recent past he had done everything that he could to stay off the grid: no fixed abode, no records, no credit cards. The risk to his safety had been mitigated by the death of Control and his replacement by Michael Pope as the new head of Group Fifteen, but old habits died hard, and Milton had made a successful career in operating beneath the surface. Antagonising the sheriff had all the hallmarks of being a really dumb move. A man like that, so obviously plumped up with the sense of his own authority, wouldn't take very well to the feeling that Milton was thumbing his nose at him. There would be consequences.

But so what?

What had he done wrong?

Nothing.

He was just passing through town, and he wanted something to eat and a place to lay his head. That was all.

His table was next to another that accommodated four men. Milton gauged them automatically, like he did with everyone. They were dressed in expensive outdoor gear that would, he assessed, have been out of the reach of the local hunters and fishermen. Their hands looked clean and smooth and free of the calluses that he had noticed on the hands of the drinkers at the bar. Their table, away from the regulars, marked them as from out of town, too. Milton had seen an expensive Jeep in the parking lot adjacent to the bar, and he pegged it now as theirs. They were drinking heavily, finishing a round of beers before, one of them, a big blond man with a soft gut and mean eyes, called out to the bar that they wanted another. His voice was loud and unpleasant, slurred from all the drink that he had evidently consumed. The barman exchanged a look with one of his regulars and Milton wondered whether he would refuse to serve them. That might have been interesting. He didn't, though, bringing over another four pints and taking away their money.

The blond man was sitting next to a redhead wearing a black and red chequered lumberjack shirt. The shirt was fresh and laundered, probably bought for a hundred bucks from Macy's. He was skinny, his skin a brilliant white, and his skin was marked with a constellation of freckles. "I've got to piss," Milton heard him say.

He watched as he slowly raised himself to his feet and began to negotiate the short distance from his table to the restroom. Milton's table was between the man and his destination. The man rolled to the right and then to the left, as if he was on the deck of a ship in high seas, and then tripped, stumbling forwards two steps before falling onto Milton, bouncing off his shoulder and falling across the table.

"Are you all right?" Milton asked, reaching out a hand to help the man to his feet.

"You fucking tripped me," the man drawled, his eyes unfocussed through slit-like lids.

"No," Milton said. "You fell. And now I'm helping you up."

He left his hand out. The man swept it away.

Milton told himself to be calm. "All right," he said. "No problem."

"No problem?" The man pushed himself onto unsteady feet, swaying from side to side. "I haven't got a problem, friend. You've got a problem."

Milton stood and took a careful step back to give himself a full range of movement.

He saw, through the corner of his eye, that the sheriff was watching.

He raised his hands. "I don't want any trouble," he said. "All right? It was an accident. You're fine. I'm fine. No harm done. Let's just leave it at that."

The man squared his shoulders, still rolling. "What if I don't want to leave it at that?"

"It would be better if you did."

"Is that a threat?"

Milton watched the man's friends behind him. The blond man, the biggest, had pushed himself to his feet and had taken a step away from the table. He was even bigger than Milton had initially assumed: six foot six and surely three hundred pounds, as big as an offensive lineman, a little blubbery, but that cruel streak in his eyes was unmistakeable. A bully, used to dominating others because he was bigger than they were. The other two looked less interested in getting involved although they, too, had risen to their feet. One for all and all for one, Milton guessed, especially when they were drunk.

"I said, is that a threat?"

"No. It's not a threat. I just don't see why this needs to go any further."

Milton knew there had been moments in his life where, when presented with a choice of direction, the other route would have led to an easier path.

A career in the law rather than in the army.

Staying in the infantry rather than applying to join the SAS.

Staying in the SAS rather than accepting the offer to join the Group.

Staying at the campsite down by the lake rather than coming into town.

He would have avoided the possibility of antagonising the sheriff and, more pertinently, he would never have been sitting at the table into which a drunken out-of-town hunter was to fall. Some of the consequences that followed his decisions could have been foreseen and avoided. Others could not. But Milton was a stubborn man, that was one of his many faults and, sometimes, knowing that one path was likely to be more difficult than another was all the reason he needed to follow it.

"You're a supercilious prick, aren't you?" the man asked.

He telegraphed his right handed punch so far in advance that it was a simple thing for Milton to step back and avoid it. It was a wild haymaker and, once it had missed, the momentum overbalanced him and turned him a quarter to his left. Milton allowed him to fall away and then dropped a little and drilled him in the kidneys. The man arched backwards, clutching at his back, and collapsed to his knees.

Milton turned back just in time to duck as the blond man fired out his own punch, his huge fist scraping against the top of his crown, but doing no damage. The man had been coming at Milton, his impetus impossible to arrest, and he blundered straight into his right knee, raised with sudden and vicious force, sinking into the man's groin. His mouth gaped open as his diaphragm contracted, the air punched out of his lungs, and Milton put him down with a short left cross that connected flush on the side of his jaw. The man was unconscious before he hit the floor, his left leg pinned awkwardly beneath the bulk of his now starched body.

Milton opened his fist and flexed his fingers. That had been a harder shot than he had intended to throw. He wouldn't have been surprised if, upon waking up, the blond man discovered that his jaw was broken.

The other two men had backed right away, no longer interested in him after they had watched what two of his punches had done to their friends.

Milton picked up his overturned glass and, intending to have it refilled at the bar, turned straight into the raised barrel of Lester Grogan's gun.

"Get your hands up," the sheriff said.

"Come *on*," Milton began.

"Hands up now."

The sheriff was toting a Sig Sauer P226 .40 calibre semiautomatic, and from his easy, balanced stance, it looked like he knew how to use it.

"That's not necessary," he said, indicating the gun.

"I won't tell you again."

He raised his hands. "What was I supposed to do?"

"Turn around."

Milton did as he was told, lowering his arms and extending them behind his back.

The sheriff fastened cuffs around his wrists. "You're under arrest. You have the right to remain silent and anything you say can be used against you in court. You have the right to an attorney. If you can't afford one, I'll see that one is appointed for you. You understand your rights, Mr. Milton?"

"You're overreacting," he said. "They both attacked me. Everyone saw what happened."

He leaned closer to him. "You should've listened to me earlier. I knew you had the look of a troublemaker, and my gut's usually right. Turns out it was right this time, too."

Chapter 4

LESTER HOLSTERED his weapon and pushed John Milton in the back, impelling him to start walking to the exit of the bar. The rain was crashing down outside, and Lester cursed at it. He was going to get wet. He reached down for his keys and blipped the lock of the Silverado. He opened the rear door and helped Milton to slide inside.

He opened the door to the front and climbed into the cabin. He looked back at the bar. A small audience had gathered to watch the show. Both FBI agents were there. Mallory Stanton was standing alongside and slightly behind the female agent, frowning at the scene with an inscrutable expression on her face. The regulars from the bar were there, too, although they quickly went inside when they realised it was wet and that the show was over. It wasn't as if a brawl was an uncommon event in the bar, after all. It happened most every Saturday.

He heard the siren of the paramedics and saw the blue flash against the buildings at the end of the road as the truck approached.

"That was one hell of a punch," Grogan said.

"Yeah, well."

"You broke his jaw, I'm guessing."

"A bit harder than I intended."

"You could've picked someone better to hit. Those four are lawyers, up from Detroit. They come every year, hunting and fishing. Can't say I think too highly of them, the attitudes they've got on them. Dollars to doughnuts they'll press charges, especially if you *did* break his jaw."

"Come on, Sheriff," he said. "I wasn't in there for trouble. I just wanted something to eat. You saw it the same as I did. They threw the first punches. I was defending myself."

"Maybe," Lester allowed as he started the engine and put the car into drive.

Milton sat quietly in the back, and Lester shot the occasional glance into the mirror to check him out. He didn't seem particularly perturbed, his demeanour just as blank and inscrutable as when he was in the back of his cruiser earlier that afternoon. He had his right leg crossed over his left, and his hands were behind his back as if it was a perfectly natural thing to sit like that. Milton was a strange one, that much was for sure. Lester thought he was pretty good at reading human nature, but he was striking out here.

He couldn't work out Milton at all.

THE SHERIFF'S Office was on West Harrie Street, a five-minute drive from the bar. Lester slotted the Silverado into the lot, crammed his cap down on his head in the vain hope that it might offer a measure of protection from the rain, got out and went around to the back. Milton was compliant, shuffling across the seat, stepping out and then hurrying ahead of Lester, as he directed him to the rear entrance at the back of the building. Lester took the keys from his pocket, unlocked the door, and gently nudged Milton to step inside. He followed, reaching out for the light switch. Then he took off his sodden jacket, shaking it out and draping it off the back of the nearest chair.

It was a small building with four rooms. There was a central reception area with a desk and a row of metal folding chairs against the wall. A picture of the president hung on the wall next to posters with home security tips and outdated mugshots of wanted fugitives, some of whom had been captured months ago. A door off this room led to a short flight of stairs and down there, in the basement, was the facility's single cell. A third room was fitted out as a unisex toilet, and the fourth was Lester's office.

"In here," he said, leading the way.

He switched on the light. It was a simple, almost ascetic room. Lester was a plain-spoken and tough man, like the long line of hard men who had kept the peace before him. Photographs of his dour predecessors covered the walls of his office, along with the double-barrelled shotgun one of them had felt it prudent to carry. Lester liked there to be a clear distinction between his home and his office, so he hadn't bothered to do very much to imprint it with his own personality. There was a picture of his wife and another of his kids on his desk, but that was the only concession to family that he made.

Lester went behind Milton and unfastened the cuffs.

"You know, if you looked the way you do now when I saw you on the road, chances are I wouldn't have given you a second thought."

Milton stretched his arms and then massaged his wrists. "That's not particularly helpful now, is it?"

"No. I suppose it isn't."

"You thought I was a vagrant?"

"Yes, and I don't like to rush to conclusions based on the way that a man looks, but we've had problems in the past with folks walking in and stealing things from other folks' houses. And I'm not the sort of man who likes to take chances."

Milton didn't reply to that. Instead, he looked up at the framed picture on the wall.

"You served?" he asked.

Lester looked behind him. There, on the wall, was his only concession to ego. There was a line of shooting trophies on the top of a low bookcase and above that was a framed medal.

"Sure I did," he said.

"That's the Navy Cross."

Lester nodded, surprised that he was able to recognise it.

Milton rose and took a step up to it. "You mind?" he asked.

"Knock yourself out."

The citation was framed beneath the medal. Milton read it aloud: "'The Navy Cross is presented to Lester H. Grogan Jr., First Lieutenant, U.S. Marine Corps, for extraordinary heroism while serving as a Platoon Commander with Company D, First Battalion, Fifth Marines, First Marine Division (Reinforced), Fleet Marine Force, in connection with combat operations against the enemy in the republic of Iraq.' You were out there?"

"Did three tours."

Milton kept reading. "'On July 10, 2003, while participating in a company-sized search and destroy operation deep in hostile territory, First Lieutenant Grogan's platoon discovered a well-camouflaged bunker complex that appeared to be unoccupied. Deploying his men into defensive positions, First Lieutenant Grogan was advancing to the first bunker when three enemy soldiers armed with hand grenades jumped out. Reacting instantly, he grabbed the closest man and, brandishing his .45 calibre pistol at the others, apprehended all three of the soldiers. Accompanied by one of his men, he then approached the second bunker and called for the enemy to surrender. When the hostile soldiers failed to answer him and threw a grenade that detonated dangerously close to him, First Lieutenant Grogan detonated a grenade in the bunker aperture, accounting for two enemy casualties and disclosing the entrance to a tunnel. Continuing the assault, he approached a third bunker and was preparing to fire into it when the enemy threw another grenade. Observing the grenade land dangerously close to his companion, First Lieutenant Grogan simultaneously fired his weapon at the enemy, pushed the marine away from the grenade, and shielded him from the explosion with his own body. Although sustaining painful fragmentation wounds from the explosion, he managed to throw a grenade into the aperture and completely disabled the remaining bunker. By his courage, aggressive leadership, and selfless devotion to duty, First Lieutenant Grogan upheld the highest traditions of the Marine Corps and of the United States Naval Service.'" Milton nodded in appreciation. "Very impressive, Sheriff."

"What did you do out there?"

"The kind of things I can't really talk about."

"Special Forces?"

"Mmmm."

"Shit," Lester said, his cheeks beginning to flush with embarrassment. He thought of his English accent and made the connection. "SAS?"

Milton nodded.

"Now you're making me feel stupid."

"Why? You thought I was just a vagrant."

Lester started to speak, but found himself tongue-tied. He really *did* feel stupid.

Milton waved it off. "What happens next?"

Lester didn't know what to say.

"Don't worry about it. Let's just get it over with."

"I've got to book you," he said. "What's after that will depend on the guy you punched. If he's injured, maybe you're looking at a felony, but for now I'm going to write it up as a citation. That's just a written notice to appear in court on a specific date and time. And I have to keep you in overnight."

"And if it is a felony?"

"Then you have to make bail or go in front of a judge within forty-eight hours. But maybe it doesn't come to that. I can encourage him that it's not a good idea. He was drunk, like you say. And he threw the first punch. I was a witness to that."

"Shame you didn't arrest him instead, then."

"Yes," Lester said. "It is." Milton wasn't giving him an easy ride, but that was fair enough, maybe he deserved it. "I'm sorry, Milton. It's not your fault, but I've had a lot on my plate these last few days. My boy, Jesus, I've got more trouble with him than I know how to deal with, and then we've got a couple of FBI agents in town, and they've been making things difficult for me. I think, maybe, I let that get on top of me, and then I saw you in the bar, after what we'd said on the road… Shit, just explaining this is making me feel worse. Look, I'll do whatever it takes to make this go away."

"I'd appreciate that."

"Sure." Lester looked at his watch. It was ten o'clock. "It's late," he said. "Let's get you booked in."

He led the way back into the reception area. Morten Lundquist was just arriving through the rear door.

"Evening, Lester," he said.

"Evening, Morten. You okay?"

"The same tired old bullshit with the wife, but, apart from that, yeah, I'm all right."

Lundquist was in his early sixties and had been a deputy in Truth for thirty years. By rights he should have been made sheriff years ago, but he had never really shown any interest in the post. He was a solid, dependable man, apparently happy with his lot as he approached his retirement. A little too religious at times for Lester's tastes, but he had still been a father figure to him, and over the course of the years they had worked together they had become close. Lundquist had recently started to complain that his wife, Patti, was becoming cantankerous at the prospect of having him around the house full time, but Lester knew that he was exaggerating the reports for comic effect. The old man was planning on spending his autumn years outdoors; he was a keen hunter, and he had been out shooting with Lester many times before.

"Who do we have here?"

"This is John Milton. He got into it with those four out-of-towners at Johnny's."

"The blond one, looks sort of like a big fluffy bear?"

"But still big and nasty enough to play on the line for the Lions? Yeah, that one. Put him down with one punch. Bang."

"Ouch," Lundquist said. "Remind me not to get on your wrong side, Mr. Milton."

"Don't worry," Milton said. "I'm nothing to worry about."

"What do you do?"

"This and that."

"Used to be in the military," Lester said.

"Good for you."

"Morten was in the army, too. Vietnam."

"Long time ago."

"Maybe so. But that was quite a war."

"It was that. Good to meet you."

Lundquist offered Milton his hand and he took it. He pumped it like he was his long-lost brother or a customer in a used-car lot.

"I'm going to book him for a citation, keep him in overnight, and then let him out tomorrow. I think I can persuade the others that it'd be best if they just let this one go."

Lundquist took off his coat and hung it on a peg fixed to the wall. "You sort out the trouble at the school?"

"No," he said. "Not even close."

"You want, maybe I could have a look at Lyle, see if I can dig anything up?"

"I don't know, Morten. I can't think straight about that at the moment."

"Well, whatever, you go on home. I'm on the clock now. I'll take care of the paperwork."

"You sure?"

"Definitely. Go on. Get. I've got it."

Lester shrugged. He wasn't of a mind to look a gift horse in the mouth. He collected his damp coat from the back of the chair and shrugged it on. "I'm sorry you have to stay here tonight," he said to Milton. "It's not too uncomfortable down there and, you ask nicely, Morten will probably make you a cup of coffee and see to it that your clothes are dried for you tomorrow."

Milton nodded.

"And I'm sorry about… well, about earlier. I was out of line."

"Forget it. Just a misunderstanding."

Lester felt like a heel as he opened the door and jogged across the yard to the Silverado. He opened the door, slid inside, and started the engine. He flicked the air to high to heat the cabin and picked the Bob Dylan CD he had loaded earlier. He put the stick into reverse and rolled out into the road as "Subterranean Homesick Blues" started to play. The rain lashed into the windscreen as he put the car into drive and started for home.

Chapter 5

THE MAN the sheriff had introduced as Morten Lundquist opened the door that led down to the cells. It was made from metal, had bars in a little window at the top, and it opened onto a staircase with an iron banister, concrete steps, and fluorescent strip lights overhead. As soon as Milton was inside, Lundquist shut and locked the door behind them.

They went down the stairs. The basement was simple, with a cement floor and plain plastered walls. There was one cell, a small adjunct to the corridor that was separated by a wall of floor-to-ceiling bars. There was a camera fixed to the wall, its lens trained on the cell, and a chair with a collection of hunting magazines splayed out on the floor beside it. The artificial light was harsh, bouncing back up off the smooth floor and glinting against the iron bars.

"Take off your boots, your pants, and your jacket," Lundquist said.

Milton did as he was told, folding the garments and leaving them over the back of the chair. Lundquist opened a closet that Milton had not noticed and brought out an orange prison-issue jumpsuit marked MICH. DEPARTMENT OF CORRECTIONS. He handed it over and, as he bent to step into the legs, the deputy whistled in surprise.

"Goodness," he said, "that's some tattoo."

Milton had a pair of angel's wings inked across his shoulders and all the way down his back. He shrugged.

"Must've hurt, up on your shoulder blades like that. Close to the bone and all."

"I was drunk at the time. Didn't feel a thing."

Milton pulled the jumpsuit up to his waist, slipped his arms through, and pulled it up past his shoulders.

"All right. In you go."

Milton stepped into the cell and moved aside as Lundquist closed the door and locked it. Milton looked around: there was a cot with a thin mattress and a toilet. Previous inmates had gouged out their initials in the mortar between the blocks in the wall.

"You eaten?"

"No," he said.

"Rules say we got to get you a meal. Three squares and a cot, that's the deal. We don't have enough guys staying overnight for us to have a kitchen, plus there's no way you'd want me cooking for you, but I can order takeout. You like burgers?"

"Sure."

"They do a good burger at Johnny's. Bacon and cheese, all the trimmings. You want, I'll get them to bring one over."

"Thanks."

"You want a cup of coffee while you're waiting?"

"Please."

"How do you take it?"

"White, one sugar."

"Make yourself comfortable," he said. "I'll be right back."

Milton sat down on the cot and stretched his shoulders. This would be fine. At least it was clean, maybe even cleaner than the hotel. And he had stayed in far worse places.

That's right, he thought.

You got lucky. This could have been a lot worse.

You go into bars and bad things happen.

He sat back, pulled his legs up onto the cot, and leaned against the wall. He would stay here tonight, and, with luck, the sheriff would be able to see to it that he could leave tomorrow morning. He would go to the hotel, collect his pack and his rifle, and set off again, back towards the west. He had been working his way to

Minneapolis. Morrissey was playing a gig there in a couple of weeks. He was a fan, and it immediately conjured memories of the time he had spent in the regiment. Music had always been a trigger for his memories, and, as he sat in the cell, miles and years and a hundred murders away from that time, he remembered the tunes he had listened to on that old battered Walkman: The Smiths, his solo stuff. He remembered sitting on his bunk in the barracks, not so different from this, treating the blisters that he had collected during the brutal Fan Dance across Pen y Fan, the highest peak in the Brecon Beacons, and listening to his music.

Selection. Five months of Hell. Ninety percent of the men failed. Two of them died.

Milton had been one of the ten percent.

Milton heard Lundquist coming back down the stairs. He backed through the door, two mugs of coffee in his hands. "White with sugar," he said, handing one of the mugs through the bars of the cell. "Burger's on its way. Twenty minutes."

"Thanks. Good of you."

He waved that away. "'Do not neglect to show hospitality to strangers, for thereby some have entertained angels unawares.'"

"I'm sorry?"

"That's Hebrews."

"Oh—the Bible?"

"That's right. Pretty good rule to live your life by."

"I'm not really a Bible type," Milton admitted. "And you don't need to worry about entertaining an angel. I don't think anyone's ever called me that."

Lundquist laughed. "I'm sorry. Lester's always telling me to dial down on the scripture. I know it's not for everyone."

The man paused on the other side of the bars, bringing his mug to his lips and taking a sip.

"What part of England are you from?"

"The south."

"I went over there, five years ago."

"Really?"

"Uh-huh, trip to Europe. My ancestors are Danish. Came over here in the last century, thousands of them, thought they could make a fortune working the mines. Cornishmen, then the Irish, Germans, French Canadians, Finns, Danes, Swedes. You know, turn of the century, three quarters of the families here were born overseas. How about that?"

Milton sipped the hot, sugary coffee.

"How'd that turn out for them, though? Maybe good enough at the time, but now, everything's closed, and all we got's the tourists. And when we get ignorant types like those city boys you taught a lesson, well, I gotta ask myself is it really worth it. You know what I'm saying?"

Milton shrugged.

"What do you make of it, John? What's happening to the country?"

"What do you mean?"

"You look at those government types in Washington, getting fat off the federal teat; they don't give two shits about what happens to the people here. Look at Detroit, last time I went down there the place was dying on its feet, and they don't do nothing about it."

He flashed with a sudden anger that cut through his amiable exterior. Milton finished the drink and handed it back through the bars. "I don't know, Deputy. Don't know if I'm qualified to comment."

"Sorry, I know I'm going on about it again. My wife, Patti, she's always telling me that I'm stuck in the past like I'm some kind of dinosaur. Maybe she's right, I don't know. All I can say is that you work as a policeman as long as I have and you start to notice how things are getting worse. But I'll leave it there." He flicked two switches, and the strip light cut out to be replaced by dim lights that were set in sconces in the wall. "You want anything, you just need to holler. I'll be upstairs. I'll bring your food down when it gets here."

Lundquist shut the door behind him, and Milton listened to the sound of his footsteps as he climbed the stairs. He heard the ground floor door shut and the sound of the key as it turned in the lock.

Chapter 6

SPECIAL AGENT Ellie Flowers rode back to the hotel with her partner, Orville Clayton. She got out of the Denali and ran across the parking lot with a copy of *USA Today* held over her head to try to shield herself from the rain. It didn't work, the newsprint going soggy within seconds and then little rivulets running through the creases and folds and dripping down onto her.

Orville ran after her. She waited until she was inside and then she turned. There he was, dodging the puddles in those ridiculous five-hundred-dollar shoes with the lifts in the heels that were made for him especially. Back in the office, Joey Trimble said Napoleon used to wear shoes with lifts in them like that, so Napoleon had quickly become his nickname. Orville hated it, hated everything that reminded him that he was five eight and not the six foot he listed on his profile at Match.com. Ellie had never cared how tall he was, but she had learned quickly that he was touchy about it, so she never brought it up. Didn't mean that she didn't find the sight of him as he splashed through the water amusing, especially since they had just had an argument.

She was tempted to just go back to her room, without saying goodnight, but her father hadn't brought her up to be petty, so she waited for him in the lobby.

"Fucking rain," Orville said, the water plastering his thinning hair to his crown. "The sooner we get out of this place, the better."

"Goodnight," she said.

He looked confused, as if he had already forgotten that they had argued and he had expected her to come back to his room like the night before like nothing had happened. "You don't want to come in?"

"Not tonight," she said. "I'll see you in the morning."
"This is about what you said?"
"No, it's about your attitude."
"What about it?"
She was tired. "Forget it. It doesn't matter. I'm tired. I need to sleep."
"What's wrong with my attitude?"
"Goodnight."
She reached across and touched him on the shoulder. She thought about kissing him on the cheek, decided against it, and then smiled a little sadly at him and went back to her room.

SHE LIT a cigarette and dialled a number on her phone.
"Hi, it's Ellie Flowers, just leaving a message to say that I won't be coming back to the office tomorrow. I know, yeah, that's what I said. Orville's coming back. I'm going to stick around for a couple days extra. Okay?"
She pressed the remote to switch on the TV, flicked through the channels, but couldn't find anything she liked: ads, a show about monster trucks, a comedy that had stopped being funny about six seasons ago. She took out the phone again and dialled another number.
"Ellie?"
"Ryan. You busy?"
"Never too busy for my little sister. Where are you?"
"Up in Michigan. The Upper Peninsula."
"With the Yoopers? Too much fun."
"This weather's nuts. It's hardly stopped raining."
"What you doing up there?"
"Those boys who've been robbing banks? There was a potential lead. Just a maybe, not even that, but Orville wanted to check it out."
"You up there with him?"
"Don't start."
"What you call him again?"
"Napoleon."

"That's right, Napoleon. He's up there, too?"

"Yes, he's here. Mostly why I'm in a bad mood."

"He still married?"

"Don't."

She finished the cigarette and fished another from the pack. The sign on the door said there shouldn't be any smoking in the room, but the place was a dump, and she doubted that anyone had ever taken any notice of it.

"So what's he done?"

"I think he's got it in his head that I liked him because he was older, like it was some kind of father-figure thing, except it wasn't, never was anything like that. Problem is, now he's got that fool idea in his head, and he thinks he can dispense advice like he really is my old man. He's been doing it tonight, and I've had just about enough of it."

Her brother's tone changed, becoming less frivolous. "You know what I think about that whole thing."

"Don't…"

"I'm not lecturing, Ellie. Just saying."

She sucked down the smoke, listening to the rain beating on the motel window. "Fuck it, what does it matter? I've kind of decided it's all over."

"Seriously?"

"Yeah. It was a dumb idea."

"You know what I think about that."

"Yeah. I know."

"Keep your chin up, little sis."

She inhaled and exhaled again, blowing smoke up at the ceiling. "I saw a hell of a thing tonight. We were in the local bar, talking to the girl who brought us up here, and these two guys got into a brawl with one of the other guys there. One of them was as big as a bear, mean looking, but this other guy kicked the shit out of both of them."

"Sounds like my kind of bar."

"I'm serious, Ryan. Two punches—one, two—they're on the floor. Sheriff arrests this guy, though, but doesn't do a thing about the others even though they started it."

Headlights from a car, pulling into the lot, glared through the open curtains and painted a narrow stripe across the ceiling. She heard passing traffic on the call, too. "So what are you doing?"

"I'm in the car. Outside the apartment of this shit-bird a client's had me tailing for the best part of a week. You wouldn't believe this guy. He's a serious douchebag. She thinks he's been messing around with his secretary, and she was one hundred percent right about that. Thing is, he's been schtupping the Pilates instructor from his gym at the same time as the other one. She's with him now. I'm just waiting for them to come out so I can snap them. Then I'm going home to drink some beer."

"Sounds delightful."

"Like I said, the bureau ever gets to be too much, you know I could always use an extra set of hands down here."

"Tempting."

"I'm serious."

She took a beat, not wanting to sound like she was dissing the business that he had built down there. "Thanks, but, you know… no. This is nothing with Orville. I should never have let it happen, but now that it has, I'm just going to have to put on my big girl pants and get it over with. And I will. Soon as we get back into Detroit, it's done."

"When are you going back?"

"He's going tomorrow. I'm going to stick it out another couple of days."

"Why? You think your boys are up there?"

"I don't know," she said. "Probably not. Almost certainly not. But there's something I can't put my finger on. I need to dig around a little."

"Well, if you want a little distraction right now, the Steelers kick off the second half in ten minutes."

"Shit. I totally forgot." Ellie had been a Browns fan when they had been little kids while Ryan had always pulled for the Steelers. Ever since college, they always had fifty bucks riding on those two divisional matches each year. "Score?"

"Browns are trailing ten-zip. Big Ben's carving them up. Double or nothing, make it interesting?"

"Fuck it. Go on."

"Later, sis."

"Later."

Ryan was thirty-three, two years older than her. He had been an all-state linebacker in his teens, and there was talk of a full scholarship to Penn State until a defensive lineman rolled up his knee and tore all sorts of ligaments that were never meant to be torn. He'd bummed around for a couple of years, worried Ellie with a string of unsuitable women and what was pretty obviously a drinking problem, until he'd accepted that digging his nose into other people's affairs was his family inheritance and set up Ryan Flowers Investigations, Inc., working out of Melvindale, just south of Detroit. It was a solid business, doing work for insurance companies for the most part, getting evidence on drivers who arranged to have someone crash into the back of them and then claimed for whiplash or other injuries that couldn't be disproved until Ryan snapped candid pictures of them shooting hoops, out for a run, or picking up their little girl and flinging her into the air. The claims were always dropped pretty quickly after that, and Ryan pocketed a nice percentage of what would have been paid out. He'd made enough for a down payment on a two-bedroom apartment in Riverview, a second-hand Lexus, and cable TV. He appeared to be happy with all of that.

Ellie had never fought her genes. She'd always known that she would end up working for the government. She'd wavered about which branch she might go into for about six months, had even considered the Secret Service until she had figured out that it was full of wannabe jocks, who got off on wearing black sunglasses and running beside limos, until she eventually accepted that she was always going to follow her old man into the bureau.

Ellie was five eight, the same height as Orville, and knew that she was something to look at when she bothered to make an effort. She had a small, delicate face, smooth white skin with a scattering of freckles, thick hair that she had to work on all the time, and hazel eyes that sparked with life. But she hadn't been bothered tonight, and then she had been half drowned by the rain; she caught sight of herself in the mirror on the back of the bathroom door and grimaced. She unbuckled her belt with the holstered .40 Glock 22 and rested it over the back of the chair. She removed the pistol and laid it under the second pillow on her bed. Strange town, strange people, she didn't take chances.

They had more hardware in a locked rack under the pad in the rear cargo area of Orville's car: a pump shotgun, an M4 carbine, two ballistic vests, leg irons with chains, and four sets of cuffs. Orville was very particular about making sure they always had all the armaments they might need. He never tired of reminding her about the case down in Miami in 1986, the two Vietnam vets who had been turning over banks. Eight feds found them, but all they were packing were handguns and the robbers had AR-15s. Two of the agents had been killed and five injured. The bureau wasn't shy about going in heavy now.

Ellie slumped back against the stained headboard. Had they really thought that they'd use them on the trip, that they might find something in the tip-off, more than just another example of someone blowing smoke up their asses? Maybe, maybe not. Ellie was young for an agent, but she had inherited her father's instincts and wisdom. There was enough about the girl's story that she couldn't just forget about it and walk away. Orville could; that was what they had been arguing about, although that was a useful cover for all the other things that they had been arguing about, too.

Orville.

Fuck.

She switched channels to the game and watched as the Steelers kicked off. The return guy fielded the ball at the two, danced up to the fifteen, and then got crumpled by the gunner who had come down the field at a hundred miles an hour. He ended up on his back, the ball popped up, and the gunner scooped it up and waltzed into the end zone for the easy score.

Sixteen-zip, and tack on another for the PAT.

Ellie thought of Ryan listening to the game on his car radio, and allowed herself a smile. They usually arranged for the loser to buy dinner. She would gladly pay for that to spend an evening with her brother.

Who was she kidding?

Things weren't so bad.

Chapter 7

MILTON SLEPT well and woke at six as the sun rose. He rolled off the bed and, stripping off the jump suit, worked through his usual routine of sit-ups and press-ups. He would normally have stopped with five hundred of each, but he still felt ready for more, so he pressed his back against the bars, reached up to grip the horizontal bar that joined them and, by raising his knees to his chest, added two hundred crunches. By the time he was finished he was slathered in a fine sheen of sweat and his muscles were afire.

Lundquist must have seen that he was awake in the feed from the camera. Milton heard him as he came down the stairs, muttering to himself, as he struggled with the door handle and, after managing to open it, backing into the room with a tray. It held a plate of toast and two mugs of coffee. The bread smelled wonderful.

"Morning, partner," Lundquist said. He balanced the tray on the chair and passed one of the mugs through the bars of the cell. "White, one sugar."

"Thanks."

"And I thought you might appreciate something to eat." He slid the plate with the toast through the space between the bars and the floor. "It's *korppu*. Cinnamon bread. You dip it in your coffee. It's Finnish. My grandpa used to eat three slices every day, and he lived to a hundred and three, so I guess there must be something in it, right? Patti heard you were in here overnight, and she brought some over for you. We don't get many in overnight. Patti thinks we should be hospitable."

Milton took a bite of the toast. It was hard, almost burnt, and yet still sweet. He finished both pieces quickly.

"Thanks."

"Sleep good?"

"Like a baby."

"I'm pleased to hear that."

Lundquist went back to the door and reached down for the bundle of clothes that he had left on the stairs. He placed them on the chair.

"Left them on the radiator last night to dry them out," Lundquist explained. He took a key from his belt and unlocked the cell door.

"Thank you."

Milton dressed. The clothes were warm. He pulled on his boots and laced them up.

"The sheriff's upstairs. He wants to see you before you go."

LESTER GROGAN was sitting at his desk. He was in uniform this morning: khaki slacks and a dark blue shirt with his badge pinned just below the left tip of his collar. It didn't fit him particularly well. He had allowed himself to become a little overweight in recent years, and the shirt was stretched tight over a generous belly that sagged out a little over the belt line. He greeted Milton warmly and invited him to sit in the chair opposite. Milton did.

"You sleep okay?"

"I did."

"And Morten got you something to eat?"

"A burger."

"From Johnny's? They're usually pretty good, right?"

"It was fine."

The sheriff didn't fit the usual profile of the rural lawman. Milton had met a few of them over the years, and Lester was different. Milton expected sheriffs to be the kings of their counties, with comfortable offices, secretaries and deputies. Their walls would be heavy with awards, photos and plaques, the sheriff grinning alongside politicians and business leaders, always thinking ahead to next year's re-election. A display case for school kids and their mothers to gawk at, filled with hash pipes and confiscated marijuana cigarettes, guns and rusty knives. Lester Grogan had nothing. Just a crowded desk and some cardboard cartons piled on top of file cabinets in a dingy room.

"Well, Mr. Milton," he started, "I got some good news and some bad news for you. The big man from last night, his name is Alan Hooper, and he works in corporate law down there in Detroit. He's a big wheel, so they say. I went to the Emergency Room on the way home last night. The bad news is you gave him what they tell me is a mandibular fracture. Broken jaw is what I call it. Two places. Wire mesh, eating through a straw for a week, the whole nine yards."

"The good news?"

"The good news is I went to see Mr. Hooper again this morning. He was burning right up to have me throw the book at you, telling me how he'd bring a civil suit against you if I didn't have you on a felony. I explained to him how that wouldn't be wise for him to do that because, if he did, I'd have no option other than to bring him into it, too, since he punched first, like we said last night, and how could that be good for his career and all? He fulminated about that for a good thirty seconds, got pretty agitated about it until I told him to calm down or should I take out my cuffs, and that seemed to do the trick. Bottom line, Mr. Milton, is that he's happy that we leave this as a citation only. So you're free to go."

"Thank you," Milton said. "I appreciate it."

"Least I could do after we got off on the wrong foot like we did, wouldn't you say?"

"Nevertheless… you didn't have to…"

"No, I did." He got up from his chair. "Where you staying?"

"The hotel."

"Want a ride over there?"

"Seriously? After the last ride you gave me?"

Lester smiled. "This one will be different."

"Sure."

Milton and Lester rose. Lundquist put his head through the door. "Good morning," he said.

"Thank your wife for the toast," he said.

Lundquist waved it off. "It's just toast. You want to try her roasts, you won't be so complimentary. Ain't that the truth, Lester? Patti's roasts?"

Lester smiled again. "Come on," he said.

THEY CAME out of the rear exit, and Lester led the way to the Ford Taurus he used as his police cruiser. He indicated that the doors were open, and Milton got into the passenger seat next to him. He reversed and turned around, and as he nosed carefully over the sidewalk and onto the road, Milton noticed the old Pontiac Catalina that was parked opposite them. It was a four-door sedan, at least thirty years old, dinged up in several places and with a replacement wing that was brown where the rest of the car was dirty white. Milton wouldn't have given it a second thought, but he had noticed the girl in the woollen beanie who was half slumped in the driver's seat. She was watching them, her eyes following the car as Lester paused for a space in the traffic, pulling away and heading to the middle of town.

The sheriff hadn't noticed, but he didn't have Milton's experience, hardwired into him over a decade's service when a missed detail like that could easily mean his death.

Milton watched in the mirror as the Pontiac jerked out into the road, one car behind them. Lester drew up at the stop sign and turned to the right. The Pontiac indicated in the same direction and, as they set off down Falls Road back to the Village Inn, it turned with them and followed, keeping back at a discreet distance.

"What are you going to do?" Lester asked him.

"Get my gear and set off. I only really came into town for a shower and a warm bed."

"Where you headed?"

"West. I take it day by day. I reckon I can get across to Wakewood if I get away quickly."

"Twenty miles? Stay to the road and you'll have no problem. There's a campsite just on the edge of town. Wandering Wheels, I think they call it. You got Sunday Lake down there, too. Very pretty. And after that?"

"I'm thinking about going to Minnesota."

They passed Truth Motors, Holiday Stationstore, and a Michigan correctional facility, and still the Pontiac followed.

"You had a rifle yesterday."

"Back at the hotel."

"You do any shooting?"

Milton nodded.

"What have you got?"

"Ruger Hawkeye."

"All weather?"

Milton nodded.

"I got one, too. You want to try it with the .243 Win. Goes together like apple pie and ice cream."

Lester kept talking about the rifle. Milton kept enough of his attention on the conversation to know when he had been asked a question, but most of his intentness was on the Pontiac behind them.

It kept coming.

Milton kept watching.

Chapter 8

ELLIE FLOWERS woke late, at eight. She had stayed up to watch the second half of the ball game, the Steelers winning at a canter, and started to think of a shortlist of places where she could take Ryan for dinner. Applebee's, maybe, they had that nice place that just opened downtown. When that was over, she had watched hockey for twenty minutes, then flipped channels to watch late night chat shows and trashy TV until she looked over at the clock, saw it was two in the morning, and finally acceded to sleep.

When she got out of bed, she discovered that she had come to a decision about the situation with Orville. She often found that problems that vexed her would be resolved while she slept, and it seemed like that had happened again. She would have the conversation with him now, right this morning, rather than wait until they got back to the city like she had told Ryan last night. That was cowardly, putting it off, and she knew that she would feel better as soon as it was done. So why wait?

She showered, dressed with purpose, and hurried so that she could find him and get it over with before she lost the conviction and put it off again.

Orville was reading something on his phone when she came into the breakfast room, toast crumbs on his plate and a half cup of coffee cooling on the table. She went over to the breakfast bar and decided on a bowl of fruit and yoghurt from the meagre selection.

The trouble with Orville was that he seemed to have a sixth sense about difficult conversations that he would rather avoid. If he got that premonition, and she knew that he would since she practically radiated discomfort, then he would put up his defences and it would be almost impossible to get started. She knew how he would play it: he would pretend that they hadn't argued last night, that she hadn't turned him down, and act like everything was fine in the garden.

She carried her bowl across to the table.

She said, "Morning, Orville—"

She got that far before he said, without looking up, "Ellie, you have to listen to this."

She felt her stomach go tight and tense. She was right; he was going to pretend that nothing was wrong.

"I was reading this story"—he tapped his finger against his phone—"right, about Julius Jenkins, this old black dude down in Florida, down Jacksonville way, about how he's been charged with knocking off a payroll run. Says here he went up to the two ex-marines who were transferring the cash from the van to a warehouse, pulled out a sawed off out from underneath his coat, puts them on the ground, and makes off with the cash. Can you believe that? This guy—"

"Orville," she said.

"—this guy, says here he's in his fricking *eighties*. He puts these two thirty-year-old goddamn *marines* on the ground and robs them blind. Gets better, too: says one of the marines saw a disabled parking sticker on the dash. I tell you what, Ellie, this world gets crazier and crazier—"

"Orville."

"—would never have happened ten years ago."

"*Orville*," she said harshly, "will you just shut the fuck up and listen to me?"

He stopped mid-sentence, his mouth hanging open.

"Thank you. Jesus."

"What is it?"

"Look, there's no easy way to say this. But this thing with you and me, I've been thinking on it, and I've decided that it's come to the end of the road. If you're honest about it, you know it hasn't been fun for weeks. Not for you and not for me. We're always arguing—"

He somehow managed to look shocked, like this wasn't a conversation he had already seen coming for days. "This about last night?"

"No. Yes, partly, but no."

"Because last night, maybe I went a little far. Throwing my weight around a bit, like you said, and maybe you were right. I been thinking, too. You want to stay up here and nose around a little more, you go for it. Knock yourself out. I can give you a couple days. You speak to that girl again, and if you think it's worth it, you can go up in those woods and have a look. A couple days, three days, maybe, no problem."

"Orville," she said, "it's not just about last night, and anyway, I already spoke to Dillard and told him I was going to stay."

His mouth gaped. "You spoke to Dillard?"

"Yes."

"You went over my head?"

"You and I were never going to agree."

"But that—"

"Let's not get sidetracked by what we said last night. That was a symptom of the problem, and treating the symptom isn't going to cure the sickness. Fact of the matter is, I've made up my mind, and there's nothing that's going to change it. We've come to the end of the road. That's just all there is to it."

"All right," he said. "I hear you. This is what we're going to do. You go up into the woods and do what you've got to do. I'll go back to Detroit this morning. When you're finished, you come back, and we'll go out and talk about this properly, like adults. I'm not going to talk about it here." He waved a dismissive hand at the shabby room, the peeling wallpaper, the folding table with the breakfast things.

His voice was firm and patriarchal, as if he was addressing a rebellious teen who was insistent that she was going to leave the house in *that* dress. It was as if his way of dealing with it was to try to ignore everything that she had said. It made her grit her teeth with frustration, but there were other people in the breakfast room now, and she didn't want to cause a scene.

"All right?"

She really couldn't be bothered with it. She didn't have the energy, and as far as she was concerned, what was done was done. He could continue on with his own deluded version of the truth if he wanted to. It made no difference to her.

"Ellie?"

"Fine, Orville. That's what we'll do."

Chapter 9

MALLORY STANTON kept to a careful distance. She knew Lester Grogan just like everyone in town knew him. He wasn't a bad man, but he could get so that he was intoxicated with the idea of being sheriff, drunk with the notion of his authority, thinking that everyone else ought to have respect for his office. Mallory didn't hold all of those views. Truth be told, she didn't believe in any of them, especially not since Arty had disappeared into the woods and Sheriff Lester Grogan and all of his cronies in the Sheriff's Office had been about as useful as lips on a chicken.

No, she thought. *You boys aren't going to help me out one bit.*

The cruiser's brake lights shone bright red through the misty morning, and it turned off into the parking lot of the Village Inn. Mallory wasn't sure what the protocol was to follow someone, but she figured that it wouldn't do to turn into the parking lot too, so she drove on another quarter mile, turned in the forecourt of Pizza Place on Truth Road and came back up on them again.

The cruiser was pulling away, headed back into town, and, for a moment, Mallory wondered if she had lost her chance. She followed, driving past the inn and staring hard at the Ford Taurus until she was as sure as she could be that the passenger side was empty. She turned around again in Woodland Road and, as she approached the Inn for the third time, she slowed and drove into the lot.

She had just reached down to turn the ignition when the passenger door opened and a man slipped into the seat next to her.

She mishandled the door handle in her panicked attempt to get out.

He reached across and fastened a strong hand around her right shoulder.

"Easy," he said.

Her heart thumped as she turned her head and looked over at him. It was the man from the bar, the man Lester Grogan had arrested.

The man she wanted to speak to.

"Why are you following me?"

He had clear blue eyes, and there was steel in them. She had noticed that at the bar last night. Those two men, especially the big one, would have given most people pause for thought. But he had been implacable, steady, as if possessed of an unshakeable confidence that this was nothing that he couldn't handle.

Turned out he had been right about that.

It had been one hell of a demonstration.

Mallory had decided she had to speak to him.

She remembered what she was here for and found a little composure. "I need to talk to you."

"And so you followed me all the way here? What was wrong with the Sheriff's Office?"

"Grogan thinks I'm nuts. I can't speak to you when he's around."

"Did it cross your mind that *I* might think you were nuts?"

She found herself smiling at that: the absurdity of the situation, despite the desperation that had driven her to it. "You don't know what I want to talk to you about yet."

"No," he said, removing his hand from her shoulder. "What's your name?"

"Mallory."

"Mallory?"

"Mallory Stanton. Who are you?"

"John Milton."

She put out a hand uncertainly. "Good to meet you, Mr. Milton."

He took it gently. "You mind me asking how old you are, Mallory?"

"Nineteen," she said, the forced categorical answer coming across as unconvincing.

"How old really?"

"Sixteen," she said.

He stared at her, hard.

"Fifteen."

"And you're driving this bucket?"

"You can drive when you're fourteen in Michigan," she said indignantly.

"With an adult."

"Yeah, well… like I said, I'm fifteen, okay? Have you finished questioning me? You're not my father, Mr. Milton."

He regarded her again shrewdly, and then a little forbearance broke across the impassivity of his face. "Go on, then, Mallory. Why don't you tell me what you want to speak to me about?"

"Here? In the car?"

"Where else?"

"I bet they didn't give you breakfast in jail, right? I thought maybe we could get breakfast. There's this place down the road a ways… anyway, I thought we could do that. And, like, I'm paying."

"I'm not a vagrant, Mallory. I can pay my own way."

"So you'll come? You'll listen to me?"

"Sure," he said. "If you give me a ride back here afterwards, we can have breakfast."

THE CAFÉ was on Main Street and was famous locally for its grits. Mallory's father had been friendly with the proprietor, and she gave her a nod as she led Milton inside. Mallory ducked her head, not because she was ill-mannered, but because she didn't want to answer the inevitable questions about how she was doing. There had been sympathy in the aftermath of his death, but now, the questions and the comments just raked up the memories that she had tried so hard to bury with him when they laid him in the ground. Others were worse, the religious types who she knew were thinking that because he had done it himself that he had damned his soul to Hell, or purgatory, or wherever it was that people who killed themselves went to suffer. Mallory had no time for any of that nonsense. She was a practical girl, and there were practical things that she needed to deal with.

The most pressing issue, the one that stopped her sleeping at nights, was Arthur.

They went to a table in the window and sat down. Mallory took the menus and passed one to Milton.

The waitress came across. "What can I get for you?"

"Pancakes, eggs, sausage, potatoes and bacon, please."

"How'd you like your eggs?"

"Over easy."

"And to drink?"

"Coffee and orange juice."

She turned to Mallory. "What you want, sugar?"

"A cup of coffee, please."

"You're not going to eat?" he asked her.

"Not really hungry," she said, although that wasn't true. Her stomach was empty, but the roiling sensation was more from nerves.

The waitress went to the back with their order. Mallory knew why she was nervous: this man was likely her last chance, and she didn't want him to think that she was crazy, like the sheriff and some of the others she had mentioned this to so clearly did. There was a lot riding on this conversation and on the first impression she gave him.

She summoned up the courage to begin. "Thanks for this, Mr. Milton," she said, waving her hand vaguely. "For coming, I mean."

"Call me John," he said.

"I'd rather call you Mr. Milton, if that's okay?"

"You can call me whatever you want."

"I know you probably think I'm weird, following you and all that, but I'm not. Weird, I mean. This, what I'm about to tell you, this is all straight up."

He nodded. He was paying attention, apparently taking her seriously. That was good.

She took another breath. "I live out on the edge of town. We've got an RV. It's me and my brother, Arthur. I call him Arty. He's what you'd probably call simple. There were problems when he was born, the cord got wrapped around his throat, and he didn't get enough oxygen until they were able to get it cut away. He got brain damage because of it. It's not terrible, I'm not saying he's a vegetable or anything like that, but he's slow. He's twenty years old, but he acts like he's a big kid most of the time. But he's sweet and honest and trusting, and he's my brother, you know?" She swallowed. "Yeah, he's my brother, so I love him."

Milton was still looking at her. "Okay," he said, encouraging her on.

"Last week he went out into the woods north of town, and he hasn't come back. And I need someone to help me find him and bring him home. That's why, well…" She gestured towards him. "That's why I need your help."

"How many days has he been away?"

"Four."

"What about your parents?"

"My mother died when I was little. The cancer got her. My daddy died six months ago. It's just me and Arty now."

"The police?"

"They won't do a thing. They say he's a full-grown man and that means he can come and go as he pleases. But he's not an adult, least not in his head. He can barely look after himself most times. He's not fit to be out there in the woods." She felt the tears come and furiously fought them back; she had promised herself that she wouldn't cry in front of him. "It's on me, Mr. Milton. I have to look after him."

"It's all right," he said, smiling at her.

She stiffened her lip, determined not to show weakness in front of him.

The waitress came back with Milton's food and her coffee, and the pause gave her a moment to compose herself again. Milton sprinkled salt and pepper over his eggs and cut his bacon into smaller pieces. He put one of them into his mouth and chewed.

"You know where he is?" he asked between mouthfuls.

"I'm pretty sure."

"And the sheriff won't go up there and get him back?"

"If he's in the woods, he's right out in the woods. You'd have to trek to go find him. It's not as simple as driving up there."

"So why me?"

"You're an outdoorsman, right?"

"I suppose so."

She shrugged. "So that's what I need."

"There are others, though, right? There are dozens of people here who know what they're doing out in the woods. People who know *these* woods. I don't know them at all. Why don't you ask one of them?"

"I didn't tell you all of it yet. Not the worst part."

He started on his eggs. She found that she was clenching her fists, her fingers curled in so tightly that her knuckles were raised and red.

"About six months ago, after my daddy died, these four young men came into town. I hadn't seen them before, and none of the kids I went to school with had, either. Then, maybe a week after they showed up, they vanished just as fast as they arrived. Then we started hearing the rumours. People were saying that they were part of the gang who've been robbing banks around here, Michigan and Wisconsin, and over in Canada. Do you read the newspapers, Mr. Milton?"

"Not for a few weeks."

"There was a robbery three months ago; a gang of four men went after a bank in Marquette. Took fifty thousand dollars, they were saying, but, this time, instead of getting away on motorbikes like they usually did, they had a problem. This security guard came out of the bank with a shotgun and told them to stop except they didn't stop, they shot and killed him stone dead."

"And you think the men in town were the same as the men who've been carrying out these robberies?"

"I don't *think* it, I *know* it." She paused to make sure it all came out right. "Arty has a job in the gas station. Well, he *had* one, before he went off up there, I doubt he's got it now. There's a store, a little one that sells things for cars, drinks and candy and stuff like that, and he's in the booth serving people. One day he came home, and he told me that these four guys had come into the place to get gas for the car they were driving. He said that they started to talk to him and, the way he said it, they treated him like he was their best friend in the whole world. The thing with my brother, people normally just make jokes about him, try to make him look stupid, and so if anyone is even halfway decent to him, then he thinks that they're going to end up best friends. He's trusting, Mr. Milton. He doesn't see the bad in people even when it's obvious to everyone else."

"What does that have to do with them being the robbers?"

"The day after he first started out with this, he came home again, and I swear, he was drunk. He doesn't ever drink because he says he doesn't like the way it makes him feel, but when you lived with someone like my daddy, then I promise you that you get to know the signs when someone's drunk pretty quick. He was slurring his words, and he couldn't hardly stand straight, so I got him into bed and told him we'd talk about it in the morning. But before I could get him straightened out, he told me that he had a secret and that he'd tell me if I swore to keep it between us. He said that one of them said his name was Tom Chandler. He told Arty that him and his friends were the robbers. Arty said he told him that they'd been hiding out in the woods, up at one of the empty copper mines near the lake where no one goes nowadays."

"He was drunk, like you said. People say all sorts of things when they're drunk."

She felt her anger flash. "I know that," she snapped. "My daddy was a drunk, I told you. I know you can't trust drunks for shit." She stared down at her mug until she composed herself and then, frowning, looked back at him again and said, "I got him to sit down and talk to me about it the next morning. He denied it at first, denied even telling me it, but I wouldn't let him out of the door until he said it all again. And he did. Every word and then he told me some more. He said that they had a trailer on the back of the truck that they brought to the gas station, and they had a couple of motorbikes on it."

"So they were four boys out riding their bikes in the woods. I expect that happens a lot around here."

She felt a knot of frustration in her gut. He was going to disbelieve her, just like everyone else had disbelieved her. She shoved her hand into her pocket and pulled out the crumpled page of newsprint that she had torn from the *Truth News*. She smoothed it out and spread it on the table. It was a police mugshot of Thomas R. Chandler Jr., taken by the state police in Wisconsin, after he had been arrested for assault six months earlier.

"This was in the paper," she said. "I showed it to Arty and asked him who it was. He said it was the man called Tom he had met."

"That doesn't say very much, Mallory. Maybe he said it because he wanted you to believe his story."

"He can't read, Mr. Milton. How would he know who it was?"

Milton paused, looking at the picture, thinking. She found that she was holding her breath.

"All right. Let's assume that he did see them. Why is that relevant?"

"Because we had a big argument about it. I told him he mustn't speak to them if he saw them again. He was to call the sheriff as soon as he could. He said I was a stooge, that what they were doing was right, that they were taking money from the people who could afford to lose it and giving it to those who needed it more. He loves myths and legends, see? DVDs and books and games, he loves it. They've got it into his stupid head that they're something like a modern-day Robin fucking Hood!"

The curse was fast and unbidden and it even surprised her.

"You think he's gone to find them?"

When she spoke, it was with quiet abashment. "I said he wasn't to leave the RV. We argued about that, too, but then he went to bed, and I thought the worst was over. But then I heard him talking to someone on his cell, and he wouldn't tell me who it was. Then, an hour or so after that, I heard a motorcycle engine from outside. He was on the back of a bike as it drove away. And that was four days ago. I haven't seen or heard from him since."

Milton placed his knife and fork neatly on the table.

"Those people I was talking to last night, at the bar, you see them?" she said.

"I did."

"They're FBI. They've been in town a week because they heard that the four boys were up here. I explained to them what happened, but they didn't really believe me, either. They won't help me. I've struck out. That's why I need someone like you."

"You still didn't tell me why you think I can help you."

"I'd go out there on my own, Mr. Milton. I know the woods a little. My daddy used to take me up there. But I know you need to know what you're doing. I mean, *really* know. People go missing up there all the time, and there's no point pretending, I can't follow a map. You can get lost if you go five minutes off the trail."

"I don't know…"

"And these boys are murderers, Mr. Milton. They know the FBI is after them. Let's say I could find them. What would I do then? It's just me. How am I going to do anything? But I saw what you did last night to those two men. You know how to look after yourself. You could handle them, I know it."

"No," he said.

"Please."

He shook his head. "I can't help you, Mallory. You need to persuade the police or the FBI to listen to you. If those are the four men up there, and maybe they are, and they know they're wanted for murder, the odds are that they're not going to be well disposed to people going out and sticking their noses in their business. But the agents can send an armed team up there and round them up. And if Arthur is up there, they'll bring him home."

"You haven't been listening to me. Sheriff Grogan thinks I'm a troublemaker. He said he doesn't want to hear another word about it from me."

"I could talk to him?"

"He arrested you last night. Why would he believe you any more than me?"

"The FBI, then."

"They're going home today. That's what they were telling me last night. You, or someone like you, you're my last chance."

He shook his head. "It's not something I can help you with. I'm sorry."

She took a crumpled ten-dollar bill from her jeans pocket and dropped it on the table.

"I told you…" he started to protest.

She stood up with a suddenness that put surprise on his face.

"Come on, then," she said in a flat and emotionless voice.

"What?"

"I said I'd take you back to the hotel. Let's go."

Chapter 10

MILTON WENT to his room. He collected his razor from the bathroom and took the bottles of shampoo and soap that he hadn't used in the shower, putting them into the toilet bag and shoving that into his pack.

He was troubled.

He needed the comfort of an old routine.

He took his rifle, laid it on the bed, and then found his cleaning kit from the pack. It had gotten wet yesterday and, besides, he hadn't cleaned it properly for a couple of days. Milton was fastidious about making sure his weapons were always clean. That was another habit he had learned in the regiment and, after that, while he had worked in the Group. A misfire when you didn't need it could very easily turn out to be fatal. Milton had always considered himself a craftsman, and any good craftsman treated his tools with respect. He was no different.

He put a cotton ball on the end of his chamber rod and slid it into the chamber. He rotated it left and then right, working methodically to remove any brush bristles that had been left behind and excess solvent that had gathered between the rod guide snout and the end of the chamber. He made sure that the chamber was dry, and then he moved on to the lug recess area, usually the place on a bolt-action rifle that was the dirtiest. He took out a recess tool, wet both ends with solvent, and rotated it in the recess area, moving it in and out, so that he cleaned the breech face, too.

The process was habitual and, over the years, it had almost become meditative. As he worked on the bolt and the action of the rifle, he thought about the things he had done since he had fled from England, the people he had met along the way. He thought of Caterina and Beau in

Mexico, and Eva in San Francisco, and then what had happened with Michael Pope and Beatrix Rose in Russia. He thought of the hours he had spent in the Rooms, listening to other drunks baring their souls, scouring their testimonies for a palliative that would ease the clamour of the voices in his head. Something that would ease his guilt, the never-ending, brutal, discordant blare of his guilt. He thought about the meetings and the people who had offered to be his sponsor and how he had declined them all. He knew that they would eventually press him on his Fifth Step.

We admitted to God, to ourselves and to another human being the exact nature of our wrongs.

That was something he would never be able to do. He heard the others, about how they had cheated on their husbands and wives, ignored their children, hid bottles of booze around the house, soiled themselves or wet their beds, and he knew with the perfect grandiosity of the inveterate drunk that his sins were of a different magnitude altogether. But the thing was, they *were*. He had mentioned some of it to some of them, but only in the vaguest terms. The classified, horrific details he had bottled up and stored away. And that was how it would have to stay.

My name is John Milton, and I am an alcoholic. I am also an assassin. I killed one hundred and thirty-six men and women in the service of my country.

It meant that the meetings would only ever be able to offer him partial solace.

The program had been good for him, but there were moments when the deep well of his shame had risen up and overflowed, breaching his makeshift defences. It had been that way in Ohio, only this time his defences had failed. He didn't feel the guilt when he was drunk. He could drown the reproachful voices with booze, obliterate them for as long as he had a bottle in his hand and, like a sailor hearing the beauty of the siren's song, he had almost submitted.

He had gone into a bar, ordered a whisky and stared at it for what felt like hours. He watched it for so long that the cubes of ice had dissolved into slivers, and then the slivers had dissolved into nothing. *What harm could it do?* he asked himself. What harm? Just one, that would be all it was.

But it wouldn't be just one. Never was. Never would be.

He had tossed his money on the bar and left, taken a bus to a mountain sports shop, bought everything he thought he would need, and had set off that same day.

The journey had brought him here.

He thought about Mallory.

He began to worry that she might have been brought to him for a reason. Drunks in the program were urged to believe in a Higher Power, but Milton had seen too much death to believe in God or Buddha or Mohammed or anything else. Those men and women with no time for religion interpreted GOD as Group Of Drunks and used the Rooms as their Higher Power, but that needed absolute honesty, and Milton couldn't do that. He had tried to fill the void in his soul with a spiritual outlook, and there had been moments where Providence had seemed to play a role in bringing him to a certain place at a certain time to take advantage of an opportunity that, eventually, brought him peace. Coincidence, probably, for he would always fall back on the rational, but a part of him couldn't discount the possibility entirely.

Maybe Providence was at play here.

He had been too hasty. The chances were that Mallory's brother had just gone out to camp in the woods. Kids ran off all the time, it would be something as simple and innocent as that. It was no skin off his nose to divert north for a day or two. He had plenty of time to get to Walker. And if he missed Morrissey, so what? There would be other gigs. He had no itinerary. He would go wherever the wind blew him.

He finished cleaning the firing pin, replaced the spring with a new one, and put the rifle back together again. He slung it over his left shoulder, swung the heavy pack across his right, and went to check out.

He stepped out into the damp morning. The sunlight sparkled off the pools of water that had gathered across the pocked asphalt of the parking lot.

The Pontiac Catalina was still waiting in the same space. He saw the wide blue and white stripes of Mallory's woollen beanie through the dappled glare on the windshield.

Yes, Milton thought. *Providence.*

Tenacity and determination, too.

He would help her.

PART TWO

Chapter 11

ELLIE WENT back to reception.

"Yes?" the girl asked, her eyes flicking up from the show she was watching.

"I need the room longer."

"How many nights?"

She thought about that. How many would she need? Two? That would be enough. How long would it take to hike up north where the girl thought the men were hiding out, check out the area, then come back again? Maybe it would be better to get three, just in case it took longer. Three would be plenty.

"Three," she said.

The girl clicked her mouse, tapped on the keyboard and said, "Done," before she looked back down to the TV.

Ellie heard the sound of a wheeled suitcase approach from around the corner and, before she could take evasive action, Orville came out of the corridor, tugging his little Samsonite behind him.

"Ellie," he said awkwardly.

"Orville."

"Just checking out."

"Yeah."

"You sure you still want to stay up here? Last chance. You want, I could wait for you. You could—"

"No, I'm staying."

"There's this thing," he said distractedly, tapping his finger against his cellphone, "just heard about it. Dillard just called. The VP's due in Minneapolis in three days, right, campaigning through the state this week? The bureau office picked up a threat against him. Probably wack-jobs, probably nothing, but he's sending resources over there. You don't fancy a trip to Minneapolis?"

"No, Orville. I'll see you in Detroit."

He nodded, just once, and pulled his case around her so that he could get to the desk. Ellie felt a little shiver of revulsion, the sheer ludicrousness of the affair coming home to her like a slap in the face. Ryan had been right. *What* had she been thinking? It was the most childish—no, the most *infantile*—thing she had ever done. She made her way out of the lobby and into the foyer. She needed to rent a car, and then she needed to go and get the equipment that she would need for the trip into the woods.

MILTON APPROACHED the car.

Mallory saw him and cranked the window down.

"I can stay here all day," she said, and he could see that she meant it. He had been right about her tenacity, but wrong to underestimate just *how* dogged she was prepared to be. He could see that she was possessed of a single-minded focus so absolute that it allowed her to simply ignore anything that conflicted with her plans. She would badger him until he either relented or fled the town, possibly with her in pursuit.

"You think that'll make a difference?"

"I can be persuasive."

"It's okay. There's no need to wait."

"You'll do it?"

He nodded. "Against my better judgment."

Her face broke into a childish grin, and Milton was reminded of how young she really was. "Thank you." She beamed at him. "When?"

"This afternoon."

"Great. I can do that."

Milton frowned. "What do you mean?"

"What do you mean, what do I mean? I'm coming, too."

"No, you're not."

"I am."

Milton stared squarely at her. "I don't need you to come with me, Mallory."

"I have to come."

"No, you don't. You'll slow me down, and the slower I am in getting up to your brother, the slower I'll be in bringing him back to you."

"I'm sorry. It's not negotiable."

"Well, that's lucky, because I'm not negotiating."

"Then I'll just follow you. What are you going to do about that?"

"I'll tie you to a tree."

"I'm serious."

"So am I. I'm not going to put myself in front of four armed men while I look after a child at the same time."

"I am *not* a child," she said indignantly.

"You are, and you're staying here."

She pouted at him, unbowed.

"Have you thought about this, Mallory? There are no hotels between here and wherever they are. There won't be any warm beds and, tasty though it was, there will be no bacon and eggs on the table. I'm going to travel quickly, eat light, and what little sleep I get is going to be on the ground. And," he said, looking up at the sky, "I don't think it's going to stay dry for very long."

"I've slept on the ground before, Mr. Milton. I told you: my father used to take me and Arty out when we were little."

"It's not really the same thing."

"I've shot whitetail deer before."

"This isn't going to be like shooting deer, Mallory."

She refused to give up. "You've never met my brother. You don't know what he looks like."

"You can describe him to me."

"He doesn't know you, though. I told you, he's simple. He gets frightened easily, especially when he doesn't know someone. And if things don't go the way you think they will, he'll run. If he sees me, he won't. If I tell him to come back with us, he will."

Milton looked at her hard face and the determined frown that was visible below the bottom of her beanie and sighed. It would probably be easier to concede. There was some truth in what she was saying, too, he supposed. It probably would be useful to have her around if the boy got spooked. He would just have to make sure she knew to stay a safe distance behind him if it did get difficult. He wouldn't be swayed on that much, at least. He had made mistakes before and people had paid the price for them. He had sworn to himself that there would never be a repeat.

"Fine," he said. "You can come. But there are some rules and these are not open to debate. First, you do as I say at all times. I don't want any lip. Second, you stay with me. Third, if we find them, you let me handle getting your brother. Are those all clear?"

"Crystal."

"What equipment do you have?"

"Sleeping bag in the trunk."

"Anything else? Ground sheet? Compass? Water filter? Flashlight? First-aid kit?"

She frowned. "Not with me. Just the bag."

Milton sighed, doubting himself afresh.

"Is there an outdoor store in town?"

"Morrisons." She reached down and started the engine. "Shall we go there now?"

"Why not." Milton sighed, settling back into the seat and closing his eyes.

THE STORE was well stocked with everything they would need. Milton was already equipped, but he took the chance to replace some of his older gear and replenish his supplies. They took a shopping cart and worked through the aisles. Milton picked out a backpack and had Mallory try it on to make sure it fitted her comfortably. He dropped the things he thought they might need into the cart: water filter and purification tablets; a map and a compass; a headlamp; two fresh boxes of matches and a backup fire starter; a simple first-aid kit; sunscreen and insect repellent. Mallory already had decent boots that he thought would be up to the job, and she had a fleece jacket that looked like it would be warm enough. He picked out polypropylene underwear, a hooded rain jacket and pants, and a pair of Gore-Tex gloves.

He only had a one-man tent with him, but she was small, and he thought that there would be enough room for both of them. Her sleeping bag was old and primitive, so he bought a new one with a foam pad so that she would be as comfortable as possible.

He wheeled the cart to the checkout and waited as the clerk rang it all up. It cost three hundred dollars. He took out his money roll and counted it out. He had a thousand left. That ought to be enough to get him across the country if he was careful.

"I'll pay for it," Mallory said.

He doubted that she had the cash and, if she did, he guessed that she would need it more than he would. "Don't worry. We can settle up when we get your brother back."

Milton was arranging the gear in Mallory's new pack when he noticed that the girl had walked away from him and had approached the woman who had just entered the store. He watched as the newcomer turned to her, the concentrated expression that Mallory had worn as she scouted the shelves changing into a smile that Milton thought bore a little awkwardness, too.

He hoisted the pack onto his shoulder and walked over to them.

"Ready?" he asked her. "We should get started."

"Mr. Milton," Mallory said, "this is Special Agent Flowers."

The woman turned to him and extended a hand. "Ellie Flowers."

She looked familiar.

"I've seen you in town, haven't I?"

"In the bar last night."

He remembered: she had been talking to Mallory. "Sorry about that," he said.

"What's your name?"

"John Milton."

"Nice to meet you, Mr. Milton."

"Likewise."

"Mallory says you're going to go up into the woods with her."

"That's right. She said the FBI wouldn't."

"My partner didn't want to, no. There's just the two of us and he's not convinced that they're out there."

"But you are?"

"I don't know."

"Where's your partner now?"

"Probably halfway back to Detroit by now."

"And you're staying here?"

"No," she said. "I'm going into the woods."

Milton fought the urge to let out a long, impatient sigh. "You know what you're doing?"

"I've hiked before. Camped a few times when I was younger."

"You got equipment?" He looked down at her feet, shod in plain leather flats.

She followed his gaze. "I'm not an idiot," she said indignantly.

"I was just saying—"

"Well, don't. I'm a federal agent. I know what I'm doing."

He let it ride.

He had riled her up. "What's your involvement in this, anyway?"

"Mallory asked me to go up north and look for her brother. I said that I would help."

"I don't know about that. This is a federal matter. I don't need your help, and I'm not sure it's even appropriate, especially after what you did last night."

Milton snapped, "After what I did? You saw what happened just like everyone else. They went after me."

She shrugged. "You have a temper. If Mallory's right and those boys are up there, what's to say you wouldn't just make things worse?"

Milton started to snap back a retort, but caught himself, took a deep in-and-out breath, and managed a tight smile. "All right, then. Fair enough. Good luck."

Mallory turned to him. "What do you mean?"

"Like she says, she's a federal agent. You don't need me. I'll see you around. I've packed your gear for you. You've got everything you need."

The girl's face fell. "No. I want you to come."

"I don't think so."

He started to leave, but the girl reached out and grabbed him by the wrist.

"Please," she said. Still holding onto him, she turned back to Ellie. "Please, let's all just relax and start over, okay? Agent Flowers, Mr. Milton is an experienced outdoorsman. You said to me yourself last night that's not what you're good at. Doesn't it make more sense for him to come with us up there?"

"This is a federal—"

"Yes," the girl said, interrupting her, "the thing with the men is a federal matter. But Mr. Milton is going to help me get my brother back. That's a family thing. Totally different."

The woman started to retort but stopped herself.

"And, Mr. Milton, if they are up there, isn't it better that the FBI is involved?"

Milton drew another breath. He had already entertained doubts that this was a foolish idea, that agreeing to help the girl was pandering to his ego as much as thinking it was the right thing to do, but he relented. Grandiosity was not something that a drunk could afford. Humility was better. Healthier.

"I don't take orders from anyone except myself," he said. "And I'm not a tour guide."

"I don't need you to guide me, Milton."

Humility was better. But not easy.

He picked up Mallory's pack again and slung it across his shoulder. "Get the stuff you're going to need and meet us outside. We've only got eight hours of daylight left before it starts to get dark. I want to get as far north as we can by the time we have to stop."

Chapter 12

SPECIAL AGENT Flowers had rented a Cadillac Escalade from the place in town, and Milton quickly decided that it made more sense for them to travel the short distance to the place where they would start to hike in that rather than in Mallory's tired old Pontiac. He opened the rear door and found the button to fold down the third-row seats, the motors humming quietly as they doubled over into the floor. He transferred his gear into the SUV, laying his rifle down in the space between the pack and the back of the second-row seats, and then collected Mallory's pack and slotted that alongside. Flowers was struggling with her own pack, catching the strap on the door as it closed behind her, and he crossed the sidewalk towards her with his hand out to help.

"I got it," she said tetchily.

She freed the strap and hauled the pack to the back of the Cadillac. Milton watched her as she muscled the bag across a wide puddle. She was medium height and elfin, with brown shoulder-length hair and exquisitely delicate bones in her face. Her eyes were grey, and her lips, which were full, were set in a severe expression that matched her frown. She had bought more appropriate clothes in the store and had changed into them in the changing rooms out back. She had transferred her suit and work shoes into the car already. The waterproof jacket and leggings and the walking boots were much more suited to the terrain, although Milton was sure that her feet would blister as she broke the firm leather in. Knowing that, and not wanting her to slow them down, he had returned to the counter and bought zinc oxide tape, antibacterial ointment and a sterilised needle.

"This isn't what I had in mind," Milton said to Mallory when Flowers was out of earshot.

"Give her a break," she said. "It makes most sense for us to go together, right?"

"We'll see."

The rear door slammed, and Flowers came around and opened the driver's door.

"Ready?" she said.

Milton opened the rear door for Mallory and followed her inside.

MILTON OPENED out the map that he had bought in the store and spread it across his knees. Ellie turned around in her seat, and Mallory leaned in closer.

"Where did your brother say they were hiding?" he asked her.

She studied the map, gaining her bearings, and then pointed to the Lake of the Clouds, right up on the southern shore of Lake Superior. She pointed to a spot on the southern shore.

"Where?" Milton said. "I don't see anything."

"It's not marked on the map," she said.

"What isn't?" Ellie said.

"There's an old copper mine up there. It's been abandoned for years. That's where they are."

"But you're not sure where it is?"

"Not exactly. Up by the lake."

"Mallory—" the agent began.

"It's all right," Milton interjected. "If they're up there, I'll find them."

"You sure about that?" she said dubiously.

Milton ignored her. He studied the map. "It's twenty miles from here. We follow this road out of town, go over the railroad, and then we can get into the forest from there. We'll hike the rest of the way."

Ellie turned back to the wheel and started the engine.

Milton leaned back in the comfortable leather seats and tried to dislodge the nagging doubt that this whole enterprise had the potential to be a big, expensive mistake.

THE RAINS came again as they drove out of town. The clouds had rolled in with startling speed, and the patchy blue that had been overhead after lunchtime was replaced by an angry churn of inky blacks and greys. As they drove along the narrow blacktop, pressed between the shoulders of fir trees that loomed close on both sides, a tremendous boom of thunder ripped down from the sky, and the rain hammered down. The light vanished and it was quickly almost as dark as it would be at night. The automatic lights flickered on, but the rain was so heavy that Ellie had to drop her speed right down.

He wondered whether it might not make more sense to turn around and go back to Truth, take another night in the hotel, and then start again early tomorrow morning. He was about to broach the suggestion, but when he looked across at Mallory she was so intent and so buried in concentration that he changed his mind. She wouldn't want to take anything that might be construed as a backward step. She would have seen a delay as an opportunity for Ellie and himself to reconsider their involvement. He was sure that she would resist if he tried and, after a moment's thought, he allowed the thought to pass.

They might get a little wet, but at least they would be on their way.

They turned north and kept driving for another mile, passing tiny one-track service roads and fire breaks that branched out to the left and right. They passed two other vehicles during the short drive: a truck laden with logs, so wide on the narrow road that Ellie had to drive halfway onto the shoulder to let it pass them, and another SUV, its lights glowing like golden bowls in the seemingly solid wall of water.

The northern boundary of the town was delineated by the railroad that ran from east to west. They crossed the track and reached a narrow road on the other side that skirted the southern boundary of a farmer's field. Corn was growing in the field, stalks as tall as a man swaying in the strengthening breeze. The four-wheel drive kicked in as the wheels slipped across the slick surface, and Ellie switched to high beams to paint light in the gloom as far ahead as she could. She stopped and switched off the engine, the courtesy lights shining warm and cosy as a perverse counterpoint to the torrential deluge drumming against the roof and cascading down the windshield.

Milton looked at the map again. The farmer's field was perhaps a mile long and a mile wide. They would need to head north, crossing the field before getting to the start of the woods. He had no idea how fast Mallory and Ellie would be able to travel with their packs, but, assuming a decent pace, he figured they would be able to make a good start into the woods by the time they had to camp. Three or four miles ought to be possible today.

"This will be fine," Milton said. "You might as well stay inside while I get the gear ready."

Milton reached behind him for his pack and took out his waterproof trousers and jacket. He pulled them on.

He opened the door and stepped out into the rain. It was as heavy as he could ever remember, save the storms he had suffered through the Asian monsoon season, and he was grateful for his waterproofs. His boots sank down an inch into the quagmire and the mud sucked hungrily as he lifted his feet to step around to the back of the Cadillac. He opened the back and, after taking out what he needed from his pack, he attended to his rifle. He fitted the scope cap tightly to the sight and wrapped the muzzle with electrical tape, sealing it, so that it was reasonably watertight. He wasn't keen on the rifle getting wet, but there was nothing that could be done about it in weather like this. As long as he maintained it carefully when they got under cover again later, he was happy enough that the gun would fire reliably when he needed it to.

He prepared the packs for Mallory and Ellie and called for them to come around.

"I'm just going to call the bureau," Ellie called back. "Two minutes."

Mallory struggled through the slop and came to stand beside him. Milton took her pack and worked it around so that she could easily slip her arms through the straps, but rather than do that, she paused. She opened the ties at the top and then reached into an inside pocket of her jacket. He watched dumbly as she withdrew a .45 calibre pistol from her pocket and slipped it into the mouth of her new pack.

"What is that?"

"What does it look like?"

It was a Ruger P90 with a custom grip, and it looked enormous in her small hand. "What are you doing with a pistol like that?"

"My father had lots."

"You're not taking it."

"Mr. Milton, those boys are murdering dirt bags. What if I need to defend myself?"

"That's what I'm for, Mallory. Me or your FBI friend. Give it to me. I won't go out there with you if you're taking a gun."

"I'll go with Ellie, then."

"I'm pretty sure she'll say the same thing. You want me to ask?"

She looked at the gun, then at Milton, and, seeing that he was not bluffing, she held it by the barrel and passed it to him. It was the stainless manual safety model. He popped the magazine and checked it, seeing the full seven-shot load. He pushed the magazine back into the gun, equipped the safety, and put it into his pack. He didn't have a handgun with him. Maybe it would come in useful, but there was no way he was going to let her anywhere near it.

Ellie stepped out of the Cadillac and shut the door behind her. She grimaced up into the slanting rain as she came around to the back. "Everything all right?"

Mallory looked at him, her eyes expressive.

"We're good," he said. "Speak to them?"

"No signal," she reported. "This weather, I guess."

"We get storms like this," Mallory said, struggling to make herself heard over the rain. "It's not unusual that it takes the network down."

"Is it important?" Milton called.

"It'll keep."

He held up her pack for her to slide her arms into the straps.

"Ready?" he asked them both.

"Yes," Ellie said.

Mallory nodded, still a little sullen at the confiscation of her weapon.

"This way," Milton said, pointing to the field. "I reckon we've got three hours before we need to stop."

He led the way.

Chapter 13

ELLIE FOLLOWED at the rear of their small little convoy. Milton was at the head, setting a brisk but not hurried pace. Mallory was in the middle, bent over a little. She reached up to the straps of her pack with a frequency that suggested she was struggling. Ellie wasn't surprised. Mallory was smaller than she was, and she was finding the pack difficult to carry.

They left the car behind them and started into the field. The crop reached well over her head, but there were narrow paths through it that had been left to allow access for the farm's machinery. The path was rutted, the trenches filled with water and mud, and the ridges slick and treacherous underfoot. By the time they were halfway across the field, it felt as if they had been cut off from Truth and the rest of the world. The stalks bent down at them as the wind whistled around, and Ellie began to feel her mood change, an oppressive atmosphere taking hold. She thought of Orville, the way he would have driven back to Detroit in his Denali, listening to his god-awful country and western, drumming his fingertips on the wheel in that annoying way he had. She started to wonder. Had she done the right thing when she put the hammer down on him like that? He was still her supervising officer, after all. There would have been better ways to let him down. She could have stomached one more dinner with him.

The rain kept falling, and the thick clouds piled up overhead. Ellie's boots were watertight, and she was thankful for that. But the leather was stiff, and she could feel it as the upper on her left foot began to abrade the skin. God, a blister, and they'd hardly started. That was going to be embarrassing. She pulled the peak of her hood as far over her face as she could, rubbed the water from her eyes, and continued on, following Mallory deeper into the field.

They reached the northern end, stepping out from between the high shoulders of the corn. The track at this end had been bolstered with a top layer of asphalt for the first few yards, but then, as that petered out, it became a sodden, waterlogged mire. They followed it for a hundred yards until they were at the start of the trees. Milton stopped in the limited shelter of an oak to consult his map. He seemed satisfied with their progress, considered his direction, and then shouted over the roar of the deluge that they needed to follow the animal trail that had been beaten into the undergrowth towards the northwest.

Ellie pressed on. This was not what she intended to do today. She thought of Orville again. He would already be back in Detroit, maybe even home with his wife. She could have been home, too, at the little apartment she was renting. She could have drawn a bath and submerged herself in it for an hour with a glass of wine and a book. A good long soak would help to drive away the chill that had seeped into her bones even before they had set off on this pursuit. Orville had confided in her that he couldn't stand Truth or the Upper Peninsula, that he had no time for the people, and that the sooner he could get back to civilisation, the better. Ellie told him that she thought he was being condescending. That had started another argument, and he told her that she could do as she liked. He added that she had been gulled by a little girl, that the trip would be a wild goose chase, and that he was still going home.

Milton allowed them to stop at five o'clock, but only for five minutes. He had identified an area on the map that he wanted them to reach by sundown.

Sundown, she thought. *How would they tell?* It was already dark with the thunderclouds overhead.

Milton forged on, picking a path that led them around the fallen boughs and the worst of the vast swathes of nettles and bracken and, very soon, the track was invisible behind them. All they could hear was the sound of the rain on the trees.

Ellie thought of Orville again and her mood began to curdle. She thought of the four boys that they had been chasing for the last six months. They were young and reckless, but they weren't stupid. They had been the subject of a full-court press from the bureau after the security guard had been murdered in Marquette, but they had seemingly just melted into thin air. She knew that they had been in Truth, there was too much independent corroboration of that for it not to be true, but she had no idea where they were now. No one did, unless Mallory was right. She looked up, rain smearing into her eyes, and stared out into the gloom between the trunks of the trees. Was she right? Were they in these woods? It was possible, she supposed. Possible enough for her to have agreed to come and tramp out here in this godforsaken weather, anyway.

Ellie thought about Mallory's story. It was possible, although they had looked into her brother's history and discovered, with very little effort, that his was not the most reliable testimony they would ever hear. The locals they spoke to about him all said the same thing: sweet boy, simple and trusting, but prone to making things up. He was clearly something of a local institution, and Ellie had detected cruelty in the anecdotes about the things that he had done. Some of the locals had told them jokes, bitter little punch lines that said more about them than they did about him.

Orville had allowed himself to be swayed by the prevailing opinion, that he was not to be trusted, and had effectively drawn a line through the middle of his testimony.

Ellie had not been so hasty.

How had he been able to identify the picture of Tom Chandler if he was unable to read? Orville dismissed that, too, saying that someone must have told him who it was, but as she spoke with Mallory, Ellie couldn't bring herself to do that. There were a lot of what-ifs that needed to be tested. If the only way to do that was to follow her up to the Lake of the Clouds, then that would be what she would have to do.

THEY TREKKED north through the trees for another two hours. The terrain sloped gently upwards, and Milton explained as they walked that they would need to ascend around a thousand feet to get up to the lake. The trail widened a little as they worked their way along it, thick banks of ferns on either side before the tightly packed trees. Ellie recognised beech, scrub oaks, and maples. They forded narrow streams of crystal clear water, and then they emerged from the bush just a little way downstream of a shallow collection of falls. It consisted of a half dozen chutes arrayed across a rocky ledge that spanned the width of the stream, sending the water crashing over a shallow drop into a wide pool at its foot.

"How much farther until we can stop?" Mallory complained.

"Another mile."

They climbed the gentle face at the side of the falls and continued ahead, back into the dense foliage. The path drew in tight and then disappeared altogether. Milton retraced his steps, found a suitable alternative route, and followed that instead.

After another thirty minutes they broke through the wet ferns and stepped into a small clearing. The space was littered with discarded machinery and equipment: a coil of heavy cable, chains, pulleys, a large wood stove, assorted cast iron fixtures, and parallel runners for a horse-drawn sled. A huge eastern white pine stood sentry over the junk.

"What's all this?" Ellie said.

Milton rapped his knuckles against the upturned stove. "My guess is that this is an old logging camp. I doubt any of this has been moved for fifty years."

"Can we stop here?" Mallory asked. "I'm exhausted."

Milton paused, took out his compass, and cut an azimuth up to another big tree a mile or two distant. He looked up into the dark sky.

"It'll do," Milton said. "We camp here for the night, get up early tomorrow and press on."

"How have we done?" Mallory's beanie was sodden with water, and she looked miserable, like a drowned rat.

"Not too bad. We're about a quarter of the way there."

Ellie looked around. She had no real experience, but it looked like a good place to bivouac. She removed her pack from her shoulders and stretched.

"How many miles?" Ellie asked Milton.

"About four."

It felt like more. Ellie was fitter than most of the other agents that she worked with, and she was certainly fitter than Orville, but pounding a treadmill in an air-conditioned gym was one thing and struggling across rough terrain in weather like this was quite another. Moisture had seeped into her expensive boots, she had been bitten by chiggers, her legs were slathered with claggy mud, and she was cold.

Milton took out his tent and moved across to a patch of higher ground, avoiding the dips and depressions that would be more likely to gather water. He stretched out the flysheet and then fed the poles through the appropriate sleeves and bent them into the shape of the tent. He pinned them into place, pegged out the structure with tent pegs, attached the guy lines, working at one end and then moving quickly around to the other. He kept the tension as equal as he could as he battled the wind.

Ellie took out her own tent and got most of it up by the time Milton had finished with his. He came across and helped her to secure the inner skin and the attachable groundsheet, then went around and knocked the pegs more firmly into the wet earth.

It took twenty minutes to erect both tents.

"I'm just going to get some firewood," he said when he was done.

Mallory frowned dubiously. "How are you going to make a fire when it's as wet as this?"

"You'll see."

There was a fallen tree at the edge of the clearing. Milton took a small bag from his pack and walked across to it.

"Are you all right?" Ellie asked the girl.

"Wet and cold."

"Me, too."

Ellie's tent was larger than Milton's. "You want to crash with me?" she asked her.

"Sure."

They hauled their packs inside and sat down, watched the rain as it dripped over the lip of the door and listened to it as it drummed against the outer skin. Milton was crouched next to the fallen tree and, using a utility knife that he had taken from his pocket, he started to scrape the blade up and down on the underside of the trunk.

"You think he knows what he's doing?" Mallory asked.

"He knows about being outside."

"What about when we find them?"

"You saw what happened last night. He knows how to handle himself. More than that? I don't know."

"What do you think he does?"

"I've no idea. Why don't you ask him?"

They kept watching. Ellie could see that the tree had been infested with termites. Milton used the blade to dig out the sawdust that had been left behind, scooping it into the bag and then adding dry leaves and grass. He went back to the trunk, snapped off a thin branch, and then stripped off the wet bark. He cut thin grooves into the dry wood beneath and then pried them back until the stick was feathered.

The dead tree provided a little shelter from the rain, and Milton started to build the fire there. He created a pile of tinder and used the fire steel that he wore on a chain around his neck to strike sparks onto it. The tinder started to smoke, and then tiny pinpricks of heat could be seen. Milton crouched there in the rain for thirty minutes, nursing the sparks into a small flame until it was established, then carefully added larger pieces of kindling. He added strips of pine wood that were saturated with resin. The flames took hold, devouring the wood hungrily.

When he was done, the fire was crackling with a healthy zeal.

"You've done this before," Ellie said.

He smiled. "A few times."

When he was finished, he lashed three sticks together to form a tripod, took a small saucepan from his pack, and rested it over the flames. He took a packet of franks, sliced them, and fried them in the pan. He opened two cans of beans and emptied those into the pan, too, stirring until the mixture was hot. The smell was appetising, and Ellie found her stomach grumbling.

He brought the pan across to the tents. "Here. Sausage and beans."

"Not over here, English," Ellie said. "Dogs and beans."

"You want some or not?"

"Give it here."

"I don't think so." He smiled, took out a folding fork, handed it and the food to Mallory and then sheltered in his tent. The openings faced each other.

"Mmm," she said after she had taken the first mouthful. "This is good."

Milton shuffled back until he was sheltered from the rain. "Sausage and beans. I've been living off that for the last few weeks."

"There's something else in here, too, though."

"Wild onions. I picked a few on the way. You snap off the stems and cook the bulbs. Wild garlic, too."

"How do you know all this?" Ellie asked him.

"Just picked it up on the way."

"Come on…"

He shrugged. "I used to be a soldier. I've been trained to live off the land."

Ellie raised an eyebrow. "What kind of soldier?"

"Just a soldier. Infantry. A bullet catcher."

Ellie's curiosity was piqued, and she wondered whether she should press for more information, but he was gazing out at the fire with an abstracted look on his face, and she decided against it.

Ellie took the pan after Mallory and, when she had eaten her fill, she passed it across to Milton to finish off. When they were all done, Mallory opened her pack and took out a bag of marshmallows.

"When did you get those?" Milton asked.

"At the store."

"I don't remember buying them."

"So you don't want one?"

He smiled widely enough so that his white teeth shone, the first proper smile that Ellie had seen from him. "I didn't say that."

She skewered three of the marshmallows on a stick, hurried out into the rain, and held them in the flames.

"This the kind of thing you thought you'd be doing when you joined the bureau?" he asked her.

"It's what I hoped it might be like."

"Riding a desk more than you expected?"

"I guess. I was naïve when I signed up. I knew there'd be some, but it's more than I expected. Sometimes it feels like all I'm doing is pushing paper from one place to another."

Ellie started to feel comfortable in his presence. There was something about him that said he could be trusted.

He was gruff and severe, and there was a restlessness that he did a poor job of hiding, but at the same time he projected a sense of complete proficiency. She would not have described him as reliable, for that was too staid a word, but she believed that if she invested a little faith in him, she would not be disappointed.

She thought back to what he had said earlier. "What kind of soldier were you?"

A moment of unease passed across his face. It would have been easy to miss, but Ellie was good at reading people. "All sorts," he said.

"Did you fight?"

He smiled thinly. "I did."

"Where?"

"Can't really say," he said, closing the conversation.

Special Forces, she wondered? She had met men from Delta in the bureau, and they had been reticent about what they had done before they joined. But those men wore suits and had jobs. They weren't trekking across America on their own, spending weeks in their own company, with no obvious plan for the time ahead. Milton was different. There was something else with him.

He gazed over at her, maybe saw the inquisitive glint in her eyes, and changed the subject. "What about you? What's your background?"

"Bachelor's in Law and then a master's in Criminology at Emory in Atlanta."

"And why the bureau?"

"Why not?"

"You could make more money as a lawyer, right?"

"It's not all about money."

"So what is it about?"

"My father was an agent," she said. "Down in the Tampa office."

"Following in his footsteps?"

"Something like that."

"What does he think about it?"

"I couldn't tell you. He's dead. He died fifteen years ago. Shot by a suspect as he came out of a bank in Jupiter."

"Oh," Milton said.

"I remember the stories he told me. Bank robbers, kidnappings, criminals that made the news before terrorists and cybercrime changed it all into something else. He wouldn't have recognised it today."

"If you don't like it—"

"It's not that I don't like it. It's all right. But I've been thinking about it lately, why I did what I did. You're right. I could've earned a hell of a lot more if I'd taken a job as a prosecutor."

"So?"

"That felt like selling out to me. And my father always said to me that I should do what I wanted to do. And I wanted to do this. I was just a little naïve, is all."

The rain kept coming down, rattling against the canvas. Mallory came back with the marshmallows.

"What about your partner?" Milton asked her.

It was her turn to feel a little defensive. "What about him?"

"Well, he's not out here with us, is he? Why? He didn't think this was a good idea?"

"He wouldn't even listen to me," Mallory interjected bitterly.

"He did, Mallory," Ellie said, immediately annoyed with herself for defending him; why did she still feel the urge to do that?

"He wasn't interested."

"He just doesn't think that the men are in the woods."

"But you do?" Milton asked her.

"I think it's worth a look."

"Yes," Milton said, smiling with gentle sarcasm. "And you thought it would be fun to see what a lawman's job used to be like in the old days."

Ellie raised her middle finger, but she wasn't offended. He was right. There had been an element of that. Even so, the mention of Orville made her feel uncomfortable. She tried, once again, to forget about him.

Mallory used her fingers to carefully pull the marshmallows off the stick. She handed one to Milton and one to Ellie, and they ate them.

Milton sucked his fingers. "You bring anything else in that bag you didn't tell me about?"

"No," she said, grinning. "Just that."

Milton leaned all the way back, supporting himself on his elbows. He stayed like that for five minutes, just staring out into the rain, and then he sat up and told them to give him their boots. He took off his own, and his socks, collected the two other pairs, and hurried back to the fire. He lashed together a screen of leaves and left them beneath it to dry, not too close to the flames so as not to crack the leather but near enough to warm.

Ellie breathed out contentedly, enjoying the sensation of a full belly and the residual taste of their meal in her mouth.

She found that she was pleased that she was here.

ELLIE ZIPPED her sleeping bag up to her neck and stretched out. The rain had eased off, and Milton had gone outside to build up the fire again. The flames were rising high, crackling as they consumed the wood that he had found. The mouth of her tent was still open and she could see him sitting by the fire on a waterproof sheet, his knees drawn up to his chest, lost in thought as he looked into the orange and red flicker of the flames. He had taken an MP3 player and a pair of headphones from his pack, and he was listening to music now, the faint beat of a drum audible over the snicker of the flames.

She was a good judge of people, but there were layers to John Milton's personality that she could only hazard a guess at. He was quiet and brooding, and obviously most happy in his own company. Something had happened in his life that had made him that way. She wondered if she would ever find out what that was.

She sighed and arranged herself so that she was more comfortably spread out across her sleeping mat. Mallory was beside her, her eyes closed, maybe asleep already. She looked up at the roof of the tent, the flames casting dancing shadows across it.

She heard the raucous chatter of coyotes and then the sound of cracking twigs and looked outside as Milton got to his feet. She watched him as he laid more firewood across the fire. He took the pack with the food in it, looped a rope through the straps, tossed the rope over a branch, and then hauled the pack up so that it was fifteen feet above the ground. Bears, she thought. He was putting their food out of reach.

He tied off the rope around the trunk of another tree and turned back to camp.

"Milton," she called out quietly so as not to wake Mallory.

He crouched down at the entrance to her tent. "Yes?"

"You think those boys are out here?"

He looked down at Mallory and mouthed, "Asleep?"

She nodded.

"Probably not," he said quietly. "But she does, and I don't mind going out to take a look."

"Why are you helping her? You never said."

"It's the right thing to do."

The fire burned on brightly behind him, casting him in shadow.

"You warm enough?"

She felt a surprising burn of attraction for him. It caught her off guard.

"I'm fine," she said.

"Stay in the tent. I've cleaned the camp, but there are bears in the woods. I saw one earlier."

"Where?"

"Just inside the tree line. Half an hour before we stopped."

"You didn't say."

"Didn't want to panic you."

"Who said I'd panic?"

"No, you probably wouldn't have. But it's best not to meet one at night."

"I'm staying right here."

"That would be best," he said. "Night."

"Goodnight, Milton."

Chapter 14

IT TOOK Ellie a moment to remember where she was when she awoke the next morning. She had expected to have a difficult night's sleep, but she had been wrong about that. She hadn't stirred once, and now she felt refreshed and reinvigorated. She opened her eyes and turned her head. Mallory was still asleep beside her, breathing gently through her mouth.

She unzipped the tent and looked out. The rain had stopped overnight. A ghostly fog had rolled in, and now it lay on top of the underbrush, thicker the further away it was from the campsite.

Milton was already outside. He had built the fire up into a warming blaze, and he was kneeling before it, topless, his shirt warming on a makeshift clothes line that he had fashioned with a length of string. He had boiled water in the saucepan and was washing his face with a small sliver of soap. He had his back to her, and Ellie saw the tattoo of the angel with the wings that stretched across his shoulders and torso that went all the way down his back. He wasn't big, but he was muscular, without an ounce of fat on his body. Ellie saw scars beneath the ink. She recognised the puckered lips of stab wounds and the circular discolouration where bullets had punched through the skin.

A soldier?

No, she thought. *Not just.*

There was definitely more to him than just that.

She made a little extra noise as she clambered out of the tent.

Milton turned, soapsuds on his face. "Morning," he said.

"Morning."

He took a straight razor and started to shave, drawing the blade down his cheeks and throat in a long, even stroke. He flicked the knife to clear away the suds and whiskers and then repeated the action.

"You sleep well?"

"Like a baby."

He took a double handful of the warm water and dunked his face in it, scrubbing with his fingers until the suds had all been washed away. He stood, revealing yet more scars on his torso.

"Fresh air," he said, his chest rising as he took a deep lungful. "I never sleep as well indoors."

She looked down at his torso, at the tightly packed abdominal muscles, and quickly looked away, colour flooding her cheeks. Milton noticed her discomfort and smiled at it. He reached up to collect his checkered shirt, and dressed.

Ellie smelled cooked bacon and saw the frying pan sizzling happily on its tripod, the flames licking beneath it. She was about to comment on it when Mallory put her head outside the tent. She was still bleary eyed, her hand absently rubbing her scalp.

"Morning," Ellie said to her.

"Did you hear it?"

"Hear what?"

"Last night. Grunting. There was something out here."

"It was a deer," Milton said. "It was snorting. I heard it, too."

"Didn't sound like a deer."

Milton flicked his eyes at Ellie. What? A bear?

He was completely unperturbed. "Hungry?"

THEY SAT around the fire and ate the bacon with bread rolls that Milton took out of his pack. It was surprisingly tasty, and Ellie found that she was hungrier than she expected. Milton boiled more water and used it to make coffee, the three of them sharing his tin mug. Ellie held it in her hands before setting it to her lips, letting the warmth permeate her skin. It was a cold, damp start to the day, and the fog that had fallen like a shroud over the woods did not look like it was ready to shift. Mallory was quiet, almost as if she was feeling trepidation at what the day might deliver. She would find her brother, or she would not. There would be issues either way.

Milton took his map from his pack and unfolded it, spreading it out across his groundsheet so that they could see where they were and where they needed to go.

"All right," he said. "We're here." He pointed at a spot on the map four miles to the north from the spot where they had entered the woods. He traced his finger up the map and settled on a spot three inches up and to the right. "This is where Mallory thinks they are. That's a little over fourteen miles. The terrain is level for the first three, and then it'll be hilly before it levels off again up by the lake. The climb is going to be hard work because I don't want to follow a settled trail once we start to get closer. If there's anyone there, we have to assume that they'll keep an eye on the obvious ways in and out."

"They'd be that careful?" Mallory asked.

"They haven't been found this far."

"We don't use the trails, then," Ellie said. "That's fine."

"Once we get within a couple of miles of the lake, we're going to move more slowly. I'd like to arrive as the sun is going down, so I'm thinking of stopping here"—he indicated a spot halfway between their start and finish points—"for an hour or two in the early afternoon."

"Fine."

"One other thing. If we come across anyone while we're out here, we're a family out on a hike up to Lake Superior. Father, mother and daughter. All okay with that?"

They nodded that they were.

Milton started to break camp, packing away the tents and then burning their rubbish. Ellie and Mallory went a little way into the woods to relieve themselves, and when they came back, the clearing had been returned to the state it had been in when they had found it. The only sign that they had been there were the smouldering remains of the fire and the blackening scorch marks on the underside of the fallen trunk that had nurtured and then sheltered the flame.

Milton was at the highest point of the clearing, his compass in his hand. He double-checked the azimuth that he had cut last night to the next landmark on the trail north.

Ellie picked up Mallory's pack and helped her to settle it on her shoulders. The girl returned the favour, and they waited for Milton to join them. He reached a hand down and heaved up his pack, the heaviest of the three, and slipped his arms through the straps.

"Ready?" he said.

They nodded.

"We'll stop for lunch at one. But we push hard until then."

THEY SET off in the same formation as yesterday: Milton led the way, then came Mallory, with Ellie bringing up the rear. They had only been on the move for ten minutes when they came across what was left of a pine tree. The trunk had been badly clawed; great scrapes covered it from nine feet above the ground all the way down to the bottom. Clumps of black hair were stuck in the gobs of pitch that were still oozing from the tree.

"See that?" Milton said.

"Bears?" Mallory said.

He nodded. "A big one, too."

He looked at Ellie and winked.

They bushwhacked for two hours straight, following the same animal tracks as yesterday. They passed a beaver pond, with two rusting steel leg traps that must have been left behind by a trapper years ago. They forded the main branch of a creek, climbing up an extremely steep razorback ridge that split the two branches of the watercourse. Milton led the way along the top of the ridge. It was precipitous, and Ellie's boots slipped more than once, sending little avalanches of loose pebbles and scree down into the water below. They were up above the tree line now and the views were clear all the way to the taller peaks of the Porcupine Mountains. Nevertheless, she was pleased when Milton saw a suitable path down below and indicated that they could descend.

After an hour they came across the remnants of an old railroad grade and spurs.

"What is this?" Ellie asked.

"Railroad," Milton said. "An old one."

"There are railroads all the way through here," Mallory said. "All the mines, they had to get their silver and copper out."

"How do you know so much about it?"

"My father. He was out here a lot."

They kept going north, following a muddy, practically overgrown two-track, and passed into the foothills of the Porcupine Mountains Escarpment.

Eventually they crossed another railroad that would, at one time, have run east to west. Milton looked at the map and decided that they should turn to the northeast, and they followed the overgrown track until it ran up against a river. They could see where the rail line must have crossed the river on both banks. On their side of the water was an elevated earthen grade that led up to a large eroded pile of fieldstone that apparently served as an abutment. Next to it were the remains of a trestle, with several huge, vertically arranged timbers that would have supported the elevated line until it reached the earthen grade visible some distance away.

They followed the river upstream until they reached Mirror Lake. It was a wide body of water, perhaps half a mile long at its widest point. The waters were perfectly clear, reflecting the fringe of pine and spruce on the far bank and the scuds of clouds blowing overhead.

"We'll stop here," Milton said, pointing to a pleasant spot beneath two huge eastern hemlocks.

The sun had burnt through the mist and, as it reached its zenith, it was strong enough to make for a warm day. It had been a hard morning, and Ellie was grateful for the chance to rest. She unslung her pack, propped it up against the roots of a tree, and then lay down against it. Mallory did the same, dropping to her knees beneath two shade trees leaning over the shore.

Milton took off his pack, dropped it behind him, and removed his shirt and trousers.

Mallory stared at him as if he had gone mad. "What are you doing?"

"I'm hot. Going to freshen up."

She pointed to the lake. "You're going in there?"

"Just for a quick swim."

"It'll be freezing!"

"Suits me."

Ellie watched through the slits of her half closed eyes as Milton launched himself into the water, cutting beneath the surface and then striking out to the middle.

"You don't feel like joining him?" Mallory said.

She did, but she shook her head. "I think I'll stay here."

The sun was warm on Ellie's face. She was slowly drifting into sleep when she heard a strange call and, opening her eyes, she saw a mature bald eagle cruising above the lake. Its sharp beak twisted left and right as it stared down into the water for trout.

AS IT turned out, Milton allowed them to rest on the lakeshore for two hours. He examined his map again as he lay drying in the sun. He concluded that they would reach the mine in three or four hours, perhaps five if the terrain was more difficult to ascend than the contour lines suggested.

He disappeared for ten minutes and came back with a big double handful of enormous blueberries. They gorged on them, wiping the juice from their lips.

They set off to the north again, following the eastern edge of the lake and then fording the Little Carp River where it fed into it. They discovered another old railway grade that ran north. It was lined with pine trees and overgrown with weeds, but it was as smooth as the day it was graded, and they made good time. Milton surmised that it might be the line that had serviced the mine that they were looking for and made a corresponding reduction in the time he thought it would take them to reach their destination, presuming the track continued.

They passed a vertical mineshaft in a ravine at the base of a ridge and quickly glanced into it to see that it had collapsed and was now stuffed full of rocky debris. After that they came across an ancient, wrecked car that had been left to rot. It was upside down on its roof beneath a canopy of hemlocks, the trunk of a paper birch shoved up through the space where the windshield would have been.

"Look at that," Milton said.

"What is it?"

"That's a Model A Ford. You ask me to guess, I'd say that was left there when Teddy Roosevelt was president."

The track ended as it ran up against a tall ridge. They climbed, using their hands to secure themselves as the gradient grew steeper and steeper. Milton reached down to clasp Mallory's hand and dragged her up as they neared the crest. Then he reached down and hauled Ellie upwards. His grip was strong, and he managed her extra weight without trouble.

"All right?" he asked her.

"Fine."

There was a logging road along the top of the ridge. Milton crouched down next to a large pile of timber wolf scat and looked out over undulating terrain. The views were long from the overlook of bedrock, and they could clearly see the vastness of Lake Superior beyond Cloud Peak and Cuyahoga Peak. The leafy canopy in the valley below them was a multicoloured array of sugar maple, eastern hemlock, yellow birch, and patches of eastern white pine, red maple, basswood, oak and cedar. Two miles away, in a wide depression, they could see a large body of water glistening in the late afternoon sunlight.

"That's where we're headed," Milton said. "The Lake of the Clouds."

"How far?"

"An hour from here."

Ellie squinted into the sunlight. "You see that?"

Milton nodded. He took out a pair of binoculars and pressed them to his eyes for a moment. He nodded again and handed the glasses to Ellie. She gazed out through them.

"What is it?" Mallory asked impatiently.

Ellie handed her the glasses. The girl put them to her face and stared out. "Is that smoke?"

Milton nodded. "That's what it looks like."

"A campfire?"

"Maybe."

THEY SCRAMBLED down the ridge, and Milton picked up an almost invisible trail that cut through the trees to the northwest. They walked in silence. For Mallory, at least, Ellie guessed it was a combination of anxiety and anticipation. Their trail led down to the banks of Scott Creek. They discovered a single cable that had been strung across the water with a rotten plank seat attached to it with a pulley. A thick retrieval rope was still fastened to the plank.

Mallory stopped and looked up at it.

"Is that—?"

"No," Milton said. "That's been there for years, probably for the miners to get across. If they're up at the lake, they didn't make that."

They set off again, listening to the plaintive bleating of an animal in the brush. Milton said that it was a bear cub, and that they should keep moving. They did and, after another ten minutes, they came upon the entrance to an active underground den. Milton kept them fifty yards away from it and upwind, pointing out the freshly harvested vegetation and the recent bear tracks that led away down the slope. Ellie was not of a mind to dawdle and she was relieved that Milton was of the same mind.

As they set off again, he dropped back so that he could talk to Ellie privately. Mallory, who was struggling with the weight of her pack, walked on ahead of them.

"Do you have a weapon?"

"Sure I do," she said, opening her jacket to show him the .40 Glock 22 that she wore clipped onto her belt. "FBI standard issue."

"You any good with it?"

She bristled at the perceived slight. "Top of my class."

"Top?"

"Top half."

"Okay," he said. "Top half."

The expression on his face told her that he was only pretending to be impressed.

"You won't need to worry about me if they start to shoot at us."

"I'm not worried."

"What about you?"

"I've got my rifle," he said, indicating the long gun that was slung over his shoulder.

"You any good?"

"Not too bad."

They walked on a few paces.

"Why do you ask?"

"I like to know everything before I get myself into something. The capabilities of the people on my side especially."

"So you think they are up here?"

"I didn't say that. But fail to prepare—"

"—and prepare to fail. Yes, I know, I've heard that before."

Milton looked ahead, checking that Mallory was still trudging along a few paces ahead of them. "Before we set off, I found a gun in her gear. For all I know, she might be the state sharpshooting champion, but I do know that she's fourteen or fifteen years old, and I am not comfortable with a teenager running around with a loaded semiautomatic. Do you agree?"

"Of course."

"Good. I had a little chat with her about it, and I think I persuaded her that it wasn't a good idea. It's in my pack now in case we need another weapon. But I also know that she's more cunning than a lot of people have been giving her credit for, and I wouldn't put it past her to have managed to smuggle something else with her that I haven't seen. What I'm trying to say is, if you see her with a piece, it wouldn't be a bad idea to try to take it away from her. Yes?"

She nodded. "Sure."

"Hey!" Mallory called out. "What are you talking about?"

"You, Mallory," Milton said. "Who do you think we were talking about?"

"Well, don't. I'm right here."

Ellie looked the girl over. She was working hard with her pack, an expression of discomfort on her face that she quickly hid when she realised that she was being assessed. "How are you doing?"

"I'm fine."

"You want to stop for ten minutes?" Milton asked.

"Only if you do."

"I do," he said.

They were atop a beautiful knoll that prickled with huge eastern hemlocks. Milton helped them both to take off their packs. Milton shucked off his own pack and then rather absently stooped down to pick up a three-foot-long snakeskin. He tossed it into the trees.

"We're nearly there," he said. "No more talking when we set off again. If they're down by the lake, we don't want them to know we're coming."

"Agreed," Ellie said.

"And keep your eyes open. It's not impossible they've set something up to warn them if someone is coming. A tripwire, maybe. Something like that. Watch where you put your feet and you'll be fine. It doesn't matter if this last bit takes twice as long. We've still got plenty of daylight. We're not in any rush."

Chapter 15

MILTON LED the way down the descent as quietly and carefully as he could. The hillside was rugged and densely forested, and his warning that they should be on their guard had slowed them all down.

The sight of the campfire had persuaded Ellie that Mallory now stood a very good chance of being right. It was possible that the smoke was from a legitimate source, a party of hunters, perhaps, but that suddenly seemed like a long shot. It would be a big coincidence. She was operating on the assumption that they were going to come upon the fugitives. She had already decided what she was going to do. She was going to call for help. She knew that Mallory would be impatient and determined to continue, but Ellie didn't think that would be the most sensible course of action. Mallory was a girl, strong willed, but very young, and Ellie was confident that she would be able to bring her around to her way of thinking.

Milton, though? She didn't have the same confidence. She found him very difficult to read.

Milton stopped. There was a vertical shaft, flooded and rimmed by square berms of fractured rock. He suggested that the shaft had been constructed to access the same seams of copper as the ones on the shore of the lake.

"We're close," he said.

They carried on, slowly descending through the tree line until the hardwoods started to thin out and Lake of the Clouds became visible. It was a large expanse of water situated in a valley between two ridges. It was fed at its eastern end by the Carp River Inlet and the outflow, to the west, was the Carp River. It was staggeringly beautiful, a wide sheet of blue that glimmered in the early evening sunlight. The slope that they were descending would deposit them on the southern shore of the lake if they followed it to its end. The land rose up on all sides, with a narrow shoulder of flat terrain to the northwest. There was perhaps two hundred feet of gentle slope before them until the water's edge. To the left the cliff reared up sharply, too steep to climb or descend. Milton took out his binoculars and glassed the cliff face and the flat ground from left to right.

There was a collection of tumbledown shacks at the side of the cliff. The huts were heavily screened by ferns and dug into the side of the rocks that overlooked the water. One of them was in the water itself, the gentle flow lapping around its foundations. Behind them, set into the rock itself, was the darkened maw of an adit that must once have entered the mine. The entrance was open, accessed by a flight of stairs that had been carved out of the stone.

"See it?" Milton said, passing the binoculars to Ellie.

"It's the mine," she said.

Milton said that he had come across a few similar places as he had trekked across the Upper Peninsula. The mines had been sunk to bring out copper, for the most part, although some had accessed veins of silver and gold. Almost all of them had been abandoned after the easier seams had been stripped; the ones that were left could not be reached economically. This one must have been the same.

"Look!" Ellie hissed.

Milton took the glasses from her and gazed down at the shore again. There were three men emerging from behind one of the ramshackle huts. As he watched, another two emerged from the tree line, each of them carrying an armful of firewood. They took the wood to a cleared spot that looked as if it had been furnished with a fire pit, and dropped the timber onto a woodpile.

Mallory grabbed the glasses from him and stared. "It's Arthur," she said in an urgent whisper. "You see? At the back."

Ellie focussed on the man to the rear. He was laden with the most wood, so much that it looked as if he was struggling to carry it. He was a few steps behind the lead man and, as the others joined them, he stayed on the periphery.

"We need to call the bureau," she said.

"No," Mallory said. "We can't."

"Mallory, there are four of them down there. There's only three of us."

"Two of us," Milton corrected. "Mallory's not getting involved."

"You knew that before we started," the girl protested.

"I didn't know they'd be here," Ellie said.

Milton asked, "How are you going to call them? There's no signal."

"We go back to Truth. I'll call my partner and he'll bring reinforcements with him."

"No—"

"It'll be a delay of two days, Mallory. Maybe three."

"And where do you think they'll be in three days?" she argued.

"Here."

"No, they won't. They already think the FBI's given up on them. Someone in town knows they're here, and I guess they've already told them you've gone. Maybe they feel safe. It's been a month since they robbed a bank. Why wouldn't they go and do another one tomorrow?"

"Or maybe they don't."

"What if they do? They've already shot one man. What if they kill someone else? Are you okay with that on your conscience?"

The girl had a quick temper and it had tripped.

"Quiet," Milton said sternly, his finger to his lips.

"We can't go," Mallory went on in an angry whisper. "That wasn't the deal."

"No," Milton said. "The deal was I bring you out to see whether your brother was here—"

"I can't just leave—"

"—and now that I see that he *is* here, I'm not happy leaving him any more than you are."

Her anger drained away as she realised that he was on her side. "You'll help?"

"Come on, Milton," Ellie protested. "You can't be serious?"

"I am. This doesn't have to be difficult."

"What do you mean? There are four of them. They're armed. They've already killed a man. They're not going to put their hands up and surrender."

"Yes," he said. "They will."

Ellie turned away from Mallory, putting herself between the girl and Milton. "I can't let you do anything stupid," she said to him. "You might be good in the woods, you look like you know how to look after yourself, but that does *not* mean I think you're capable of going down there and making four fugitives, men with a very good reason not to be caught, surrender to you."

"You should have more faith in me. That's exactly what I'm going to do."

ELLIE ARGUED against Milton's proposal for another five minutes until she realised that he had made up his mind and there was nothing she could do to dissuade him. Her options were limited: she could leave and make her way back to town, but Milton made it clear to her that he wouldn't wait to collect the fugitives. It took a little effort to persuade her that he was serious, but once he had succeeded in that, she couldn't very well abandon him to do it alone. That was her second option: to help. She frowned her disapproval, but signalled her acquiescence.

Milton handed her his rifle. "What are you like at medium range?"

She looked at it a little reluctantly. "I can fire it."

"Top half of your class?"

"Not with a rifle," she admitted.

"It's all right. I don't want you to hit anyone. We're going to bring them back alive. I just want you to give them something to think about."

"How?"

"Distract them. You need to watch me get down there. My guess is as soon as they think they're in trouble, they're going to make a run for their bikes. I can't see them, but there's a track at the back of the huts and, I expect that's where they are, hidden by the trees. If they run, I want you to shoot at them without hitting them."

"So you want me to *miss*?"

He smiled. "Well, yes, if you put it like that, I do. Can you?"

"Of course I can," she said indignantly.

"Good."

"What about you?"

"They've got no idea what they're doing," he said. "Look at them. They've got no security, no lookout, they don't have their weapons with them. My guess, they've left them in the hut. I'm going to walk into camp and suggest that it is in their best interests to give up. If they have a different opinion, I'll persuade them otherwise."

"And if you can't?"

"It's not going to be difficult, Ellie."

"What if it is?"

"If it is, then you go back to Truth. Take Mallory with you and head south. You'll want to trek through the night; don't stop. You'll be back there tomorrow. Then you call in the cavalry. I should think I'll still be around by then."

She sighed and shook her head, ready to try to persuade him again that this was foolish.

"But it won't be necessary." He took off his jacket and laid it out across a branch. "I tell you what: if I can get them to surrender before"—he looked at his watch—"eight o'clock, you can buy me dinner when we get back into town."

"What time is it now?"

He smiled at her. "A quarter to."

"All right," she relented, shaking her head with exasperation, but unable to suppress her smile. "But you don't have to do anything crazy to ask me out."

"No?"

"You could've, you know, just *asked* me."

Milton took Ellie's Glock and ejected the magazine. He nodded in satisfaction as he slotted it back home.

"You have any restraints?"

"Just these," she said, reaching down into her bag for a collection of cable ties.

He took them. "They'll do." He checked his watch. "Better get a move on." He crept through the brush to the camp. Their fire was brighter against the approaching gloom. "Keep your eyes on me."

And, with that, he was gone.

Chapter 16

MILTON STAYED in the cover of the trees and the scrub that provided a thick fringe around the perimeter of the camp. The area was ringed with wetlands and, as darkness fell, the lake and its chain of smaller ponds erupted in a din of peeps and croaks. Milton didn't mind at all. Anything that helped to mask his approach was welcome.

He thought about Ellie. He had surprised himself back there. He hadn't thought too hard about women ever since he had left San Francisco, deciding once again that he wasn't in the business of making attachments. He liked to stay on the move, flitting from place to place, and a relationship would make that kind of flexible lifestyle impossible. Normal people wanted normal lives. They wanted mortgages, regular jobs, fifty-inch televisions, and big washing machines. They wanted a dog, holidays, health insurance. They wanted kids. Milton didn't want any of those things, and he couldn't imagine circumstances where he would. He had been on his own long enough so that the logic that said those items—those *things*—were desirable was beyond him.

It made much more sense for him to be alone. He was fine with that. He didn't want pity, nor did he pity himself. Solitude was an acceptable substitute for the program, at least it was for him, and the possibility of long stretches of time where the only person he had to speak to was himself was a form of meditation that had allowed him to understand himself better.

So why had he asked her out?

Because she was cute and sassy?

He had been thinking about her all day. He kept seeing her in different ways: lying in the tent last night, the firelight dancing in her eyes; her face up close, the freckles that you couldn't see unless you were really looking hard; the way she eyeballed him when he hauled himself out of the lake; the way her chest filled her shirt when she worked the straps of her pack over her shoulders; and watching her from behind as they were climbing the ridge. Those images kept popping into his head, one after another, distracting him, when he needed to keep his focus clear. He dismissed them, but then he would remember the way that her hand had felt in his, the warmth of her body as he had reached down to drag her up the slippery scree. He heard her voice, too, the confident tone, the attitude that almost dared him to argue with her. The way she had said, "I'm staying right here," as he prepared the camp for the night yesterday, the way she'd said it and the way she'd looked at him, making him think that she was inviting him to take her to his tent. He heard that again and again and wondered what would have happened if he had made a pass at her.

An FBI agent.

With his history?

What was he, crazy?

Never mind. No sense thinking about any of that now. He needed a clear head. He would address it all later, once he had taken care of business.

He stayed low, hurrying from cover to cover, breaking into the spaces between the trees and brush only when he was sure that he wasn't observed. As he got closer, he could begin to make out scraps of conversation floating to him on the breeze. He was still too far away to pick out the words, but he could tell from the raucous, bawdy atmosphere that the four of them were drunk. Arthur Stanton was sitting on the edge of the fire, his knees hugged against his chest. They would occasionally gesture in his direction. He would smile or say something, but Milton could tell that all they had for him was ridicule. He was nothing more than their entertainment. A court jester.

He crept closer, sliding into the cover of an oak and then peering around the trunk. He was twenty feet away now. There was a large jug on the ground, and they passed it between them regularly. Milton guessed that they had a still somewhere close, and that they were passing the hours by brewing their own hooch and then getting drunk on it.

Amateurs.

They had no idea what they were doing.

That was good.

He hunkered down behind the trunk of the last large pine before the clearing. The four fugitives obviously felt comfortable enough to set a large fire, and they were gathered around it, passing around the jug of moonshine. Arthur Stanton looked miserable. He was closest to Milton. He would pass him first. He didn't expect that to be a problem and, if there was any shooting, he was far enough away that he ought to be safe.

Milton held Ellie's Glock in a loose grip, composing himself, running through his plan one final time so that it was clear in his mind.

First impressions were going to be crucially important. He needed those boys to be in no doubt that he would shoot them if they didn't do what he told them to do.

He took a deep breath. He looked back up the slope, into the tree line. Ellie and Mallory were hidden amidst the foliage and he couldn't see them. He hoped that Ellie could shoot the rifle, but, if she couldn't, it was too late to worry about now.

He took another breath, stood, stepped around the tree trunk, and walked to the campfire with a confident, authoritative gait.

Three of them had their backs to him. The other one, a weasily, buck-toothed man who looked like he was a hundred and fifty pounds dripping wet, saw him coming. His face changed from drunken confusion to fear. "Hey,

hey," he called out to the others, stabbing his finger at Milton even as he tried to scramble backwards. "Look!"

The others turned.

Milton raised the pistol and aimed it right at them.

"Don't do anything stupid," he said, his voice level and even.

One of the young men had bleached blond hair and tattoos down both arms. "What you say?" he said.

"Lie face down on the ground, hands behind your head."

The man got to his feet, opening and closing his fists. "Ain't gonna happen, partner. There's four of us and one of you. How you think that's going to play out?"

Milton aimed a fraction above the man's head and pulled the trigger. The pistol barked and the sound of the shot reverberated back at them from the cliff face. The round whistled a few inches above his bleached hair. He jumped from the shock of it.

"There might be four of you, but you've been foolish and left your weapons inside."

"You ain't going to shoot us," he said, although his tone did not suggest much confidence.

One of the others, pasty white with a shock of red hair, had started to get to his feet. Milton slowed the pace of his advance, keeping all of them within easy range.

Milton switched his aim, going low, and squeezed the trigger again.

The bullet thudded into the ground in front of the man's feet.

He jumped back, stumbling into the fire.

The one with the red hair bolted for the hut.

There came a loud crack from up the slope as Ellie fired the rifle. The round landed between the man and the door of the hut, sending up a small detonation of pebbles and rocky shards. He stopped suddenly, losing his balance and skidding down onto his behind.

"Let me set this out for you so you know what's going on. There's a sniper up the hill. Probably has one of you in her sights right now. You try to run again and you might find your head gets blown clean off your shoulders. And I'll shoot you, too. I can take all four of you before you get ten feet in my direction. The game's up, boys. It'd be better for you if you figure it out now."

Milton heard the scramble behind him and caught the flash of motion in the corner of his eye. It was Arthur. He spared him a quick glance, his gun arm held steady and aimed at the bleached blond man's head. The boy ran for the entrance to the mine, his feet sliding on the loose scree.

"Who are you?" the blond man asked.

"My name is Milton," he said. "And you're all coming with me."

THE BLOND MAN did as Milton instructed, lying flat on the ground, face down, and lacing his fingers behind his head. It was obvious that he was in charge because the other three quickly followed his example. Milton took Ellie's cable ties from his pocket and fastened their wrists behind their backs, one at a time.

There came the sound of a frantic descent down the slope, and Milton paused cautiously, his pistol waiting, until he saw Mallory crash through the underbrush, a small avalanche of pebbles and scree following down after her. Ellie came behind her, the rifle held muzzle down.

"Good shot," Milton said.

"They give you any trouble?"

"Not really. They're drunk. They just needed to see we were serious."

"She's desperate," she said, gesturing at Mallory. "She saw him run. It was all I could do to get her to wait until you had them cuffed."

The girl was halfway to the entrance of the mine.

"Keep the rifle on them. All right?"

"I've got it. Go."

Milton jogged after the girl. "Mallory," he called out. "Wait."

She ignored him, slipping and sliding down the wet steps and into the dark mouth of the mine.

Milton followed. The opening was rough-hewn and dripping with moisture. He descended carefully, feeling the slickness through the soles of his shoes.

The tunnel was about six feet square, cut into a reddish brown rock. Along the ground was a shallow river of water, running from somewhere in the interior of the mine and draining into a natural vent behind the entrance. It was unlit, and Milton saw Mallory's back just as she disappeared into the darkness.

"Arty," he heard her call out. "It's me."

He stepped out carefully. If he tripped and turned an ankle, broke something...

"Arty!"

"Mall?"

There was a flash of sudden light as a flashlight was snapped on. The beam swung across the walls of the corridor, sparking against his eyes. He blinked to clear them, and when he did, he saw that Arthur Stanton was holding the flashlight, aiming it straight up at the roof. He was at the far end of the tunnel, up against a thick concrete block wall that was topped with a grated opening. Moisture seeped through the cracks in the concrete, and Milton presumed that it had been placed there to hold back a body of water.

Mallory hurried forwards to her brother.

"Jeez," he said. "Jeez, Mallory. It's sure good to see you."

He bundled her into his arms, the beam of light swinging around. Milton walked another two paces and paused, aware that the boy was liable to be frightened by someone he didn't know, especially since that someone had a pistol.

Arthur saw him and recoiled. "Who's that, Mall?"

"It's Mr. Milton," she said. "He's a friend."

"Hello, Arthur," Milton said, smiling.

"It's Arty," he said, still dubious. "No one calls me Arthur no more."

"All right then, Arty. Are you okay?"

"I'm good," he said, looking back at his sister for confirmation.

"You're better now," she said. "Why don't you give Mr. Milton your flashlight?"

"Okay."

He did. Milton took it and flashed it around the tunnel. The water was deeper here, running around the uppers of his boots, and the block wall behind them had been defaced with graffiti. There was nothing else of interest.

Milton led the way outside again, Mallory following with her brother's hand holding hers tightly. The sun was low in the sky, the fading light shining into their eyes as they emerged. Milton let them pass him. They started in the direction of the camp as he shoved Ellie's pistol into the waistband of his trousers. Two shots fired, that was all, three if you counted the rifle. No one hurt. It had been a simple enough thing to subdue them. But Milton couldn't relax. He was experienced enough to know that when things were too good to be true, they usually were. He would only be comfortable when he had delivered them to Lester Grogan back in Truth.

And they had a long day ahead of them tomorrow before he could do that.

MILTON TOLD Mallory and Arty to stay with Ellie and then left them to conduct a careful survey of the camp.

He found four dirt bikes just inside the woods, propped up one against the other. The tracks suggested that they got in and out of the camp by riding along the beach to the east. Milton supposed that there was an easier path in that direction that would allow them to climb the ridge and then give access to the old railroad tracks that crisscrossed the terrain beyond. It would be a reasonable ride to reach civilisation from here, but that was to their advantage. They would be able to traverse the ridges and valleys a lot more quickly than a pursuer in a jeep.

Milton returned to the camp and approached the larger of the two cabins. It was the one that the lake had surrounded, water gently lapping up against the wooden piles that had been sunk into the ground. He splashed through the water and went inside. One wall abutted the rock of the cliff face that stretched overhead. The other three walls were constructed from corner-notched logs, and the roof, panels of corrugated steel, was supported by log rafters. It was dry inside, the water below the raised level of the floor. There were four bedrolls, and an array of empty beer bottles lined the north wall. Milton moved inside and idly flicked the nearest bedroll with the toe of his boot. This was their accommodation, then. He noted that there were only four bedrolls. It didn't look like Arthur Stanton shared the hut with them. That didn't surprise him at all.

He went back outside and approached the second cabin. It was dilapidated and looked like it had been constructed years before. A bank of sand had gathered up to the height of his knee against the walls, and there was evidence that it had been shovelled away from the door. A network of roots had also been cleared away, the remnants still bearing the jagged edges from the serrated blade that had been used for the task. He went inside. Milton saw a ripped canvas cot along the south wall, a fifty-year-old military stove along the east wall, and a folding chair along the north wall. An assortment of cooking utensils and pots were arranged around the stove. There was trap-rigging wire, ammunition, firewood, cans and tools scattered about the floor.

There were three shotguns propped against the wall, and, hanging from a single nail, was a lightweight compound bow and a quiver of arrows. Two handleless shovels were near the entrance. A small shelf held more boxes of ammunition and a combat knife.

The carcass of a big roe deer had been hung from a hook that was screwed into a roof beam. Milton inspected it, rotating it left and right. It looked fresh. Tins of beans and dried food were stacked up across two shelves. Large paper bags were full of vegetables and other groceries.

Milton went over and looked at the cot. It was in bad shape, the tear almost all the way across. If Arthur had been sleeping here, in what was obviously the food and gear store, then it couldn't possibly have been comfortable. And, he thought, if that deer wasn't dressed soon, it was going to start to smell pretty awful.

He went outside, turned, and looked back at the lake and the huts. The sun was dipping down to the horizon. Milton did not wear a watch, so he held up his hand before his face, testing how many fingers he could fit beneath the edge of the sun and the start of the horizon. Each finger meant fifteen minutes until sunset, and he could manage three. Forty-five minutes left.

Mallory and Arty were sitting near the water's edge. Ellie was standing over the four men, the rifle steady in her cradled arms.

"How are they?"

"Plenty of threats," she said, "but nothing to back it up."

"Who's who?"

She pointed at them one after the other. "Blondie is Michael Callow. Red is Tom Chandler. The skinny one is Eric Sellar. Black hair, Reggie Sturgess. They've given the bureau a lot of trouble."

"And you can claim the credit for bringing them in," he said.

"Hardly."

"It's got nothing to do with me. It's all on you."

"We'll see," she said, handing him his rifle. He returned her Glock to her.

Milton was about to say that as soon as they got back to Truth he would be off again, headed west, a job well done. But then he remembered that they were going to have dinner, and he allowed himself a moment to reflect upon whether he might be able to change his plans, just a little, to see what happened. He had no itinerary. He was as flexible as he wanted to be. What harm was there in a little delay?

"What are we going to do now?" she asked him.

"We'll camp here tonight," Milton said. "It'll be dark soon. I don't want to be out in the woods then."

"Fine," she said.

"If we get up early enough and the weather holds, we should be able to make it back to Truth by the time it's dark tomorrow. You'll take them to the sheriff?"

"I need to get them to the marshals in Lansing, really, but I'm already so far from official policy on this I doubt it makes too much difference. Nearest law enforcement official I can find."

"Okay," he said. "It won't be a problem."

"What do we do now?"

"You hungry?"

"Very."

"*I'm* hungry," Arty called out.

"You like venison?"

He got up and came over to them; Mallory followed. "I sure do."

"Then why don't you build up that fire? Nice and big, Arty. I'll fix us something to eat."

MILTON WENT to his pack and collected his big hunting knife.

"The deer in the shed," he said to Arty. "When did they kill it?"

"Today. Michael and Tom went out hunting this afternoon. Shot it with an arrow."

"Two hours ago? Three hours?"

"Just before you got here."

"Alright. Good. Can you build the fire up for me? Nice and hot."

"Sure."

Ellie followed Milton as he returned to the second hut.

"We're going to eat *that?*" she said, pointing at the carcass. The upside-down buck was slowly rotating on its hook.

"We're lucky. It's still fresh, although they should have taken the offal out by now. You had venison stew before?"

She looked a little incredulous. "In a restaurant. Not like *this*."

"Trust me, it's good. You got a strong stomach?"

"I guess…"

He took his knife and found the joint of each elbow, working around it with the flat of the blade until he had removed the hooves. He cut through the skin at the base of the animal's skull and around the neck towards the breastbone, then cut down to the stomach, pelvis and forelegs. He pulled the skin from the shoulders and neck, working downwards towards the chest. It came away clean. He cut the ligaments above the shoulders and twisted the head sharply to break the neck and remove it. Ellie groaned but she didn't turn away. He broke down the carcass, separating the chuck meat from the round, and then ran his knife along the inside of the backbone until he had removed all the tenderloins.

Ellie was pale and wan when he was done. "Jesus."

He grinned. "Trust me, it'll taste amazing." He nodded over at the supplies. "You see what they've got over there?"

She wandered over. "Potatoes, mushrooms, garlic, peppers…"

"Bread, too. And I doubt any of it is more than two days old."

"So they either went down to Truth and picked it all up, or someone's been keeping them well stocked."

"Exactly."

"I've been in Truth for longer than two days. We would've seen them."

"I think they've been getting help. Look at them. They're idiots. They would've been caught weeks ago if they were up here on their own."

"So we're careful when we go back down with them, then."

"Yes. Very careful."

There was a blackened Dutch oven in the shed, and Milton took that and the tenderloins outside. The fire was burning brightly. Milton spread the logs out and pushed the pot into a pile of glowing embers. He poured in a good lug of vegetable oil and, when it was hot, he dropped the meat inside. It hissed and fizzed and spat. He covered the pot with the lid and went back to the shed to chop the vegetables for the gravy.

AFTER THREE hours the meat was blackened and practically falling apart. Milton had wrapped baked potatoes in tin foil and dropped them into the ashes an hour before and then he had warmed the bread, rubbing it with garlic for extra flavour. All of that, together with the meat and the thick gravy, was enough for a hearty meal. The smell was delicious, wafting over the dark camp, and it grew even stronger the moment he removed the lid from the pot.

He took the plates he had found in the shed, doled out generous portions for Ellie, Mallory, and Arty, and then served himself.

"This is really good," Ellie said between hungry mouthfuls. "Where'd you learn to cook like this?"

"The army."

"What were you," Mallory asked, "a chef?"

Milton laughed. He was sitting with his shoulders propped up against a large rock, gazing out over the surface of the lake. He loaded his fork and put it into his mouth, enjoying the smoky flavour of the meat and the rich taste of the gravy. He felt relaxed and contented and, because of that, less reticent than he would usually have been.

"What are you laughing at?"

"I wasn't a chef."

"What were you, then?"

He searched for the right words. "A problem solver. The government would find that there was a situation that couldn't be handled through the normal channels, so me or a colleague of mine would be sent in to try another way."

"Another way?" Ellie said, teasing. "Mysterious."

"That's all you're getting out of me."

It was more than he had told anyone for a long time. He felt a shudder of discomfort, for it was only a skip and a jump from that bland little euphemism to what he had done in the Group, and there were no circumstances where he would have been prepared to discuss that, especially not with civilians who couldn't possibly understand.

And certainly not with civilians of whom he was growing fond.

How did you tell someone you drew a salary for being a killer?

"Is it all right, Arty?" Mallory asked.

"Mmmm," he said, tearing off a hunk of bread and dragging it through the remnants of his gravy.

The girl turned to Milton. "What about them?" She nodded in the direction of the four men watching them with baleful eyes from down by the shore.

"What about them?"

"You going to give them anything to eat?"

"I made enough for everyone."

"I wouldn't," she said indignantly. "Not after what they've done."

"We need to be practical, Mallory. They're going to need fuel for tomorrow. It's going to be a long day. Hard work. If they're hungry, it'll take us longer."

"He's right," Ellie said.

Mallory shrugged, reluctant to admit that he was right even though she knew that he was.

THE ROBBERS were unable to feed themselves with their hands tied, so Milton released them, one by one, directed each to help himself to the food from the pot, and then allowed five minutes to chow down. It was almost midnight by the time that Sellar, who was last, had cleared his plate. The pot, too, had been scraped clean.

Milton was covering them with his rifle. Ellie came alongside him.

"What do we do with them now?"

"In the shed."

"And then?"

"I'll stay up and keep an eye on them."

"All night?"

"It's fine."

"Don't be crazy. We'll split it. You go first; I'll do second shift. You need sleep as much as the rest of us."

"I can manage." He could see from her face that he was wasting his time. "Fine. We'll split it. But I'll go first."

She agreed, heading away to set up the tents with Mallory and Arthur. Milton gestured for the four robbers to get up, and he led them to the hut where they had their bedrolls. They went inside, one after the other, Michael Callow at the rear.

"You're going to regret this," he said.

"I doubt it."

"Who are you?"

"I told you. My name is Milton."

"But you're not with the FBI."

"No, I'm just a concerned citizen."

"Bullshit."

"Go to sleep. You've got a long day tomorrow."

"You here because of Arty, ain't you? How'd it go down? His kid sister ask you to help her come get him?"

"Get inside," Milton said, shoving him firmly in the back.

"I knew I should never have allowed that retard out here."

"So why did you?"

"For the laughs. That boy's entertaining, the things you can get him to do. Still, I know I fucked up. I should have shot him, been done with it. He ain't good for nothing else. I should've done him like a rabid dog. Maybe that's what I'll do, right after I do you."

"Goodnight, Mr. Callow."

"You don't know what you've gotten yourself into, you know that? You fucked up more than I have. Just remember that. You'll see I was right."

Milton let the invective wash over him, ignoring it, and closed the door. There was no lock, but he took out the rest of his rope, looped it around the handle, and then knotted it around a tree to the rear. It was taut, and although it would be possible to force it, it would not be possible to do that without making noise.

Milton went back to the shore. It was a clear night and a little cool, so he built the fire up with the logs and branches that he had seen them bring back into the camp earlier. It wasn't as dry as he would have liked, and it hissed and spat for a few minutes, but the fire was established enough to cope, and the flames were soon leaping high into the air, a wall of radiant heat washing out.

He went around the fire, on the side next to the shore, and sat with his back against the blackened stump of a tree. He could see the hut and the door from here. He had his rifle laid across his lap. There was no way for them to get out.

Ellie and Mallory had erected both tents. The Stantons had gone into one of them and zipped up the door.

Ellie came over to him.

"Are they okay?" he asked.

"Fine. She's relieved."

"I'm not surprised."

"And he's pretty oblivious to the fuss."

"He's a nice lad."

Milton got up, took a long branch and stirred up the fire. He sat down again next to her, closer than before.

She looked over to the hut. "What about them?"

"They're not getting out, if that's what you mean."

"Turned out easy, didn't it?"

"I told you it would be."

"You did." She shifted, just a little, so that her shoulder touched his shoulder and her thigh brushed his thigh.

"Was that the dinner you were talking about?" she asked.

"I was thinking of something a little different."

"I don't know. That was pretty good. You're versatile."

"Don't know if I've been called that before."

He stretched out his legs, flexing his aching muscles, and then he found himself reaching across to her, brushing the hair away from her forehead. Ellie leaned up close against him, her legs tucked beneath her.

"You're very mysterious," she said. "I don't really know anything about you, do I?"

He let his fingers fall down her face, touching the line of her cheekbone and then her jaw, saying, "There's not much to tell."

She said, "I don't believe you," touching his cheek with her hand, then kissed him, very gently, and said, laughing, "You taste of venison."

He felt her fingers brush through his hair and reach around to the back of his head as she kissed him again, a little more firmly, and he had to tell himself to wait. Her lips tasted sweet and her small, slim body felt good against him. He put his arms around her, drawing her even closer, feeling her body in his hands, and she brushed his mouth with hers, saying, "What's the big secret, John? What happened to you?"

He pulled away a little, reflexively, and she looked at him with concern.

She laid her hand on his arm. "I'm sorry."

"It's okay."

"You don't have to—"

"Ellie." He looked for the words, setting aside the reticence that was so practiced it was almost automatic, looking for something more real, more honest. "There are some things in my past that I don't like to talk about."

"You don't—"

"I did some things, after the army, some work for my government. Ten years' worth of it. I regret all of it, every day I spent working for them. It's not something I can talk about, for a lot of different reasons. Shame is one of them."

"John—" she began.

He cut her off gently. "It doesn't matter."

"—you have the saddest eyes."

She took off her jacket and then her sweater, just a bra beneath, and then she took that off, too. Her body was lit by the flicker from the fire, oranges and yellows and reds, and he felt a catch in his throat. She had the most perfect skin, and as he reached across, it felt as smooth as silk. She reached for his jacket, pushing it off, and worked her hands beneath his sweater. They made love on the shore, in the firelight, both of them quiet because they weren't alone, but neither of them able to stop. She remained silent when they were done, just the in and out of her breathing, until she said "John?" and he asked her what. But she didn't say anything else, and Milton covered her with his jacket and lay down with her on the grass until she was asleep.

Chapter 17

DAWN BROKE at a little before five. Milton had carried Ellie to the empty tent and laid her gently inside. She hadn't come to relieve him and, when he took a slow tour of the camp to reassure himself that all was well, he saw that she was still inside, breathing deeply and with a peaceful expression on her face. Mallory and her brother were sound asleep in the other tent. The four men were sleeping too, the sound of their snoring audible over the crackle of the fire. Milton had been the only one left awake. He could have woken Ellie, but he didn't have the heart. He knew he would be fine to make the walk back into Truth without sleep and, besides, he would be able to catch up back at the hotel.

It had been a beautiful, peaceful night. He had heard the sound of trout splashing in the lake, a beaver's tail slapping against the water, and owls hooting in the trees. The stars were spread out above him in a breathtakingly beautiful celestial display that had reminded him of his walk into Texas across the Mexican border, not so long ago. He sat back against the stump with his rifle laid out across his knees, taking it all in. He let his thoughts wander, thinking on all of the big skies he had slept beneath since he had fled from London, the corrupt members of Group Fifteen hard on his tail. That situation had been resolved now, but he had no desire to return. He wanted to see more skies like this one.

He thought of Ellie.

Milton went to the camp store, collected breakfast, and set about making it. They had bacon, tins of beans and a jar of coffee, so he built up the fire again and started to work. When he returned to the fire, she was standing there.

"Morning," she said, rubbing the sleep from her eyes.

"Morning."

"I didn't wake up."

"I know."

"I'm sorry."

"It's all right."

"You should've woken me."

"No," he said. "It was quiet. And I thought you needed the sleep more than I did."

There were spare baked potatoes from last night, and Milton turned those into hash browns.

"About last night," she said.

He stopped what he was doing and looked at her, aware that he cared very much about what she was about to say.

Mallory and Arty emerged from their tent.

He felt his stomach turn over.

"It was good," she said, rubbing her hand up and down his arm.

He dished up a plate of bacon and beans and gave it to Ellie. He smiled at her.

The Stantons approached before he could say anything. Arty was a big man, a good deal taller than him and significantly heavier, too. Mallory, never far from his side, was a wispy little thing in comparison. Yet, where he had an expression of peaceful simplicity in his large eyes, hers burned with sharp intelligence. She might have been triumphant to have been proved right, and Milton wouldn't have begrudged her that, but it appeared that she was more concerned to make sure her brother was content.

"You hungry?" he asked her.

"Yes," Mallory said. "Arty?"

"Very," he said.

"Like beans and bacon?"

"Sure I do."

"Hash browns?"

He nodded, hungrily.

"Sit down, then. I'll bring it over."

There came a banging against the side of the log cabin. It started with one man, and then the others joined in.

Arthur shrank back against Mallory.

"It's all right," Milton said. "They're locked up tight."

He dished out two generous portions and handed over the plates. They wandered down to the shore, sat down and started to eat.

Ellie brought her empty plate over to him. "You think we can get the men back into town?" she asked quietly when she was sure that the Stantons couldn't hear.

Milton looked over at the cabin. The banging was louder and angrier now. He picked up his rifle. "We can."

"You've got more confidence than I do."

"It won't be a problem."

He splashed through the water to the cabin and unknotted the rope, letting the span fall loose. He stepped back and raised the rifle, aiming at the door. "Out you come," he called. "One at a time."

The four of them came out in single file, the morning sun bright in their eyes after ten hours in the gloom of the windowless cabin. Their hands were still trussed up, and any thoughts of escaping into the tree line would have been squashed by the sight of the rifle, aimed dead ahead, close range, a shot that would be impossible to miss. That was before they looked into the face of the man wielding the rifle, saw his implacable blue eyes, and realised that he wouldn't hesitate to take the shot. Even Callow, who came out last, swallowed down the abuse that he was ready to deliver.

Milton directed them down to the fire. He unfastened them, one by one, allowing each of them to eat breakfast, drink a mug of coffee, and then relieve himself in the underbrush before he secured him again and moved on to the next man. The routine was laborious, and it took half an hour, but he knew that it would be a lot easier to transport the prisoners south if they had full bellies and empty bladders.

He observed them carefully, assessing them, trying to work out the hierarchy that existed within their group. Callow was obviously in charge, with Chandler his deputy. The other two were just lackeys.

He noticed one curious thing as he undid and then refastened the cable ties: they each had a tattoo inscribed on the inside of their wrists.

The tattoos were identical. Two numbers separated by a colon, "1" and "3."

"What does that mean?" he asked Chandler, the last to be attended to.

He turned his wrist over so that the tattoo was hidden and said nothing. Milton didn't press.

MILTON HAD the men sit back down in front of the embers of the fire and then called Arty to come over to him.

"Could I have a word with you, Arty?"

"Sure, Mr. Milton."

Michael Callow stared at Arty with unveiled hatred, and Milton saw how badly it frightened him. His hands were shaking as he took him by the arm and led him away from the fire.

"I found their shotguns last night," Milton said to him. "In the shack. The FBI will need them for evidence, but I don't want to bring them all with us, and I don't want to leave them here, ready to be fired. It's not safe. Could you get them for me?"

"I sure can."

"I saw three. Do you know if there are any more?"

"I don't think so."

"Could you have a look?"

"Sure."

He hurried away, and Milton walked across to where Ellie and Mallory were finishing their coffees.

"Are you ready?" he asked them.

"I think so," Ellie said.

Mallory nodded, her mouth full.

"Mallory, you'll need to keep an eye on your brother. Those boys have scared him."

"I know," she said, her eyes flinty. "You don't need to worry about him."

"I don't want them talking to him. If they start, we'll get them to stop."

"How are we going to do that?"

"It's difficult to speak with a rag in your mouth."

She grinned at the thought of that, and Milton was almost tempted to gag them anyway, just to keep her happy.

"They're going to go up front, and I'll come behind them. I'll have a shotgun on them. They'll know not to do anything rash. If I fire, it'll make a mess of all of them."

"What about me?" Ellie asked.

"You're with me. Let them know that you've got your pistol and you'll use it if you have to."

They turned as Arty came out of the store with the three shotguns clasped to his chest.

"Is that it?"

"There's no more."

"Good work."

One of the shotguns was double-barrelled. He wanted that one for himself, far better for suppressing a group of men than his rifle. It was loaded with two shells. That was all he wanted. Two shells ought to be enough for him to put down any attempt to escape but, if it wasn't, if he was overpowered and they confiscated the gun, then they would have two trigger pulls and that would be that. He wouldn't have to face an enemy with an even more serious advantage.

He set the other two down on the ground and, taking out his Swiss Army knife, opened one of the smaller blades and took up the first gun. It was a Mossberg 500

Series, nice and new, certainly not cheap. He checked the magazine tube and the chamber and removed the ammunition, then opened the action halfway, using the blade to turn the takedown screw counterclockwise. He pulled forward on the barrel, separating it from the receiver. He removed the barrel from the other shotgun just the same and slipped both of them into his pack. He gave the receivers back to Arty and asked him to take them back to the store.

He went back to the fire and used a long stick to break it apart.

The four young men looked up at him with hatred in their eyes.

"Ready, boys?" he said. "We've got a long walk ahead of us."

MILTON CUT an azimuth to a tree on the top of the ridge, intending to pick up the old railroads that they had used to traverse the back country as they headed up to the lake yesterday. The weather was clear and bright, and looked set to stay that way for the rest of the morning, although Milton looked at the high, scudding clouds borne along by strong winds, and he wondered how long it would take for the rain to return. They left the campsite much as they had found it. Ellie would return with the FBI in due course. The motorbikes and the shotguns would yield useful evidence in the proceedings that would be brought against the four suspects.

Milton took his rope and looped it around the waist of each man. He refastened the cable ties so that their hands were in front of them rather than behind their backs. The first couple of hours would involve a challenging climb up steep terrain, and if one of them lost his balance he might bring the others down with him.

"All right," Milton said. "Let's get started. Up to the ridge."

They set off in formation: Eric Sellar, Reggie Sturgess, Michael Callow, and Tom Chandler, then Milton with the shotgun and Ellie with her pistol, then Mallory, and Arthur. Milton had slung his rifle across his shoulder, beneath his pack, and held the shotgun in a loose and easy grip, his finger just outside the trigger guard, two cartridges loaded and ready to fire.

They started the climb up to the top of the ridge. The four young men tramped up the slope with sullen dispositions. Sellar tripped halfway up, his right foot sliding through a patch of loose gravel, and he dropped to one knee, cursing as the sharp stones cut through his trousers. Milton held out an arm, holding Ellie, Mallory, and Arthur behind him, wary of a ruse to bring him in close enough so that the others could try to overpower him. There was no attempt, though, and, as Sellar clambered back to his feet, Callow cursed at him for nearly bringing him down, too.

They crested the rise after an hour and found the remnants of a gravelled road that they had missed on the way to the lake yesterday. It was heavily overgrown with evergreens and tangles of alder, and Milton was glad that the moose and bear had preserved something of a trail through it. Eventually, the gravel petered out, and they bisected the ancient railroad. Milton told the men to follow it, their course changing by twenty degrees, as they headed southwest to Mirror Lake.

The railroad descended at a gentle slope, passing through pleasant meadows full of lacy ferns and long grasses. They stopped for ten minutes, and Milton cut a fresh azimuth to bring them right up to the southeastern edge of the lake. They reached the water's edge at lunchtime and stopped for thirty minutes to refill their canteens. Milton took out the PowerBars that he had bought in Truth and handed them around. They all devoured them hungrily. Milton had enough for them to have another bar each, and that would have to be enough. He had no intention of stopping again if he could avoid it.

Ellie, Mallory, and Arthur sat away from the others, talking quietly amongst themselves and staring out at the pair of loons that were floating quietly on the lake, the birds stabbing down into the water with their sharp beaks to catch the minnows that were drifting in the clear waters beneath them.

Milton looked down at his map and cut a fresh azimuth. They had made good time. It was twelve miles back to Truth from the lake. He would have been able to make that at a forced march pace in three hours. He figured that the others would slow him down by half, perhaps even three quarters. Even if it took them twice as long, they would still be in Truth by nightfall.

"Everyone up," he said. "Let's go."

THE PRISONERS began to complain soon afterwards. It started as grumbling and bickering between the four of them, with Callow making dark suggestions that Chandler was responsible for what had happened to them by persuading him that it would be entertaining to bring Arty Stanton up to the lake. Chandler was defensive, responding tetchily that Callow had needed little persuasion.

Milton listened to them argue and wondered how they managed to stay out of sight for so long. They were unprofessional and unprepared, and it had been child's play to apprehend them. If the roles had been reversed, Milton would have established a permanent watch up on the ridge, he would never have allowed a campfire during the day, there would have been no alcohol, and he most certainly would not have allowed an outsider to be brought into the camp for something so trivial as a means to alleviate the boredom. And yet, with all their inexperience and immaturity, they had managed to hide out from the local police and the FBI for weeks. Milton could barely credit it.

They were skirting the boundary of an old cedar swamp festooned with ferns, skunk cabbage, and a carpet of viridescent moss, when Callow turned his head.

"So, who are you?"

"You don't need to know that."

"Why? Frightened what I might do to you when I get out?"

Milton allowed himself a chuckle. "Do I look frightened?"

"No. You look like you're hiding behind that shotgun. Why don't you put that down, untie my hands, and see how tough you are then."

Milton smiled at him, easy and confident. "You're going to have to try a lot harder than that."

"Yeah, bitch? You think?"

Milton jerked his head forwards. "Keep walking."

"You think I'm going to get locked up?"

"I know you are."

"Fuck that shit. I ain't getting locked up for nothing, brother."

"You killed a man. You're going away for a long time. I think you're lucky that they don't execute their prisoners in Wisconsin."

Callow hawked up a ball of phlegm and spat it noisily at the side of the road.

"He don't know shit," Eric Sellar said, with confidence he shouldn't have felt, a smile curling his lip. "He's got no idea."

"Shut up, Eric," Callow warned.

"I was just saying—"

"You were just saying nothing. You just keep walking, that's all, all right?"

Sellar glowered at Callow, but did as he was told.

"You sure you don't want to show me how tough you really are?"

Milton jabbed him in the shoulder blades with the muzzle of the shotgun.

Milton stretched his fingers and then curled them back around the stock and the fore-end. Something was making him unsettled, and he knew what it was: Callow was full of piss and vinegar when he really ought to have been anxious. He was trussed up and forced to march at gunpoint back into town, where he would be handed over to the FBI and swallowed up by the legal process. Milton could tell that he wasn't the sharpest knife in the drawer and that he was young and dumb enough to think that making threats in front of his friends equated to leadership in testing circumstances. But there was something about it that didn't chime for him. Something wasn't right.

"I need a piss," Callow said. "I need to stop."

"Going to have to hold it in. We're going to stop in an hour."

"An hour? You're fucking kidding me, right?"

Milton jabbed him in the back again with the shotgun.

"Shut up, Callow. Keep walking."

MILTON LED them off the track as the sun showed three in the afternoon. There was a quiet hollow with a small lake in the middle, sandhills calling in the distance. Milton distributed the remaining energy bars and said that everyone should refill their canteens for the last push into Truth. Then he released them, one at a time, and accompanied them into the underbrush so that they could relieve themselves. Ellie covered the others while he was away.

"Stop looking at me," Callow said when it was his turn. "What, you some kind of faggot, getting your kicks looking at me going about my business?"

"That's right, Callow. I find you very attractive."

"You sound like a faggot, that faggoty accent you got."

"Have you finished?"

"No."

"Yes, you have. Zip it up. Back to the others."

He prodded him between the shoulders, and he set off to where Ellie was standing guard over the others. They had been ragging on her, and she wore an expression of ineffable irritation as Milton nudged Callow into the circle with his friends.

"You all right?" he asked her after they backed out of earshot.

"They're full of it," she said quietly. "I'm going to enjoy watching their faces when they get dropped into Jackson."

"What will happen to them?"

"I'll call my partner, and he'll send a team up. They'll be taken to Detroit, processed, and then they'll be looking at a cell for the next few months while we finish up the case against them."

"No bail?"

"For them? No chance."

Milton heard the sound of an engine as he stood and cut another azimuth, and as he looked for the source he saw an ATV laden with fishing gear race along the old railroad on the embankment above them. He paused, listening for a variation in the sound of the engine that might suggest that the driver had seen them and was slowing down to come around for another look, but the noise stayed constant. The chug became a whine, and after five minutes, everything was quiet again save for the peaceful chatter of the wildlife.

Milton looked back to the group, his attention snagged by the thick, angry margin of black clouds that were massing on the horizon.

Mallory and Arty made their way alongside them.

"Storm's coming," Mallory said.

"Again?" Ellie said. "I've never seen so much rain."

"Time of the year."

Ellie shielded her eyes and looked out at the growing darkness. "Think we can beat it?"

Milton looked at it, looked down at his map, tried to assess the speed the storm would likely close on their position and the distance they had still to travel. "No," he said. "I don't think so. I think we might get wet again."

THE RAIN came when they were still an hour out of town. It fell lightly at first, a drizzle that seeped into Milton's clothes, but it gradually gained strength until it was a powerful downpour. The heavy cover from the canopy overhead kept them reasonably dry, but, as they picked their way farther south, the big trees became less frequent and then their shelter disappeared completely. The deluge sluiced across his face. The others bent their heads to it, each step a trudge through fresh mud.

Milton brought them out of the wilderness at the same point where they had started, the tall field of corn swaying angrily in the strong, wet wind. They marched in single file through the gap between the crops, thunder rumbling overhead.

Ellie's Escalade was where they had left it.

"We won't get them all in the car," she said.

"Me and Arty could go into town and get the sheriff?" Mallory said.

Milton shook his head. "I'd rather we stay together until it's done. We might as well just keep walking."

He stayed at the back of the formation as they finally trekked back into Truth. He was tired, and his feet were sore, but he was used to feeling like that, and in a perverse sort of way, it was reassuring.

They crossed the railroad track and entered the outskirts of town. The weather was awful, but there were plenty of people around. Milton had told Mallory to lead them to the Sheriff's Office along the quietest route possible, but even so, they had to pass along the main street for a stretch. Johnny's Bar was busy, and after they were seen approaching by a customer who was outside smoking a cigarette, the bar emptied out, and the drinkers gaped as they walked by.

Milton had known that this would be the most difficult part of the journey. The four fugitives were well known from their mugshots, and it didn't take long for a small crowd to gather, following just a few steps behind them. Some of the crowd had joined from the bar, and some of those were drunk. Ellie dropped back so that she could speak to him without being overheard.

She looked anxious. "I don't like this."

Milton looked back at the crowd. "Neither do I."

"Some of the people we spoke to up here, they saw those boys as modern-day Robin Hoods. Taking from the rich, giving to the poor, all that nonsense. They don't seem to remember that guard they shot and killed, the family he left behind."

"Doesn't fit in with the story," Milton said.

"Hey," someone shouted out. "You let them boys go. They ain't done nothing wrong."

"Who deputised you?" another called. "That ain't right, marching them in like that."

Milton felt an itchy sensation between his shoulder blades. He tightened his grip on the shotgun.

"It's not far," Ellie said. "Five more minutes."

"We'll be okay."

They had turned off Main Street when Milton saw Lester Grogan running towards them. He had a rifle clasped in both hands, the gun swinging left and right and bouncing up and down as he pumped his legs. His cuffs jangled on his belt. He slowed to a walk as he approached, his mouth dropping open.

"Well, I'll be damned," he said.

Mallory spoke first. "I told you," she said with a faint hint of accusation. "I told you they were up there with my brother."

"You did," he said. "Looks like I owe you an apology. Where were they?"

"The old mine up by the Lake of the Clouds."

"Jesus," he breathed out. "How…?"

"Can we get them in a cell, please, Sheriff?" Ellie said. "I'd feel much better with them locked up."

Lester nodded. "All right, folks," he called out to the crowd. "There's nothing to see here. Go about your business."

"Come on, Lester. That ain't right, bringing them in like that. Man's innocent until he's proved guilty, ain't that right?"

Lester looked over at the speaker, a big man in a check shirt, and nodded his agreement. "That's right, Morris, and these boys haven't been convicted of anything yet. That's a matter for the FBI now."

"Sheriff?" Ellie pressed.

The sheriff rested his rifle against his shoulder and pointed down the road. "Let's get going."

Chapter 18

LESTER UNLOCKED the door at the back of the Sheriff's Office and went inside. Milton waited in the yard, the shotgun aimed ahead, his finger settled loosely around the trigger. Callow, Chandler, Sellar, and Sturgess followed the sheriff inside. The crowd had disbanded a little, but there were still a handful of hotheads who had followed them, and Milton was pleased to go into the building himself. He shut and locked the door behind him.

Lester looked at him with an expression that said he wanted to know everything that had happened, but knew that his questions would have to wait. He opened the door to the corridor and went inside, leading the way down into the basement and the single cell. The four men followed him down, Ellie bringing up the rear.

Mallory waited. She still held her brother's hand.

"Are you all right?" Milton asked her.

"Yes," she said. "I just wanted to say thank you."

"You don't have to do that. I'm happy to help."

"You were the only person who listened to me."

"You caught me in a good mood." He nodded down in the direction of the basement. "I'd had a good night's sleep in there. I'm not normally so friendly."

She looked up at him and smiled. Happiness seemed to be a rare emotion for her, and he was pleased to see it.

"I'm going to get a taxi and take Arty home," she said. "It's been a long day. It's been longer for him, being stuck up there, and he's tired. I'm tired. Is that all right, do you think?"

"Yes," he said. "I expect so. Ellie will want to speak to you, though. And Arty, too."

"That's fine."

"Where can she find you?"

There was a stack of flyers on the shelf next to Mallory. She licked her finger and separated one from the pile, took a pen from the desk, and wrote her address down. "We've got an RV," she explained. "There's a trailer park west of town, you drive through there and we're right out back, next to the woods."

"I'm sure she'll find it."

She paused there awkwardly for a long moment.

Milton put his hand on her arm, leaned down, and kissed her on the cheek. "I'll see you tomorrow, Mallory. Get a good night's sleep."

She smiled at him again, the bobbing of her larynx betraying the fact that her throat was choked with emotion. Milton went across to open the door so that they could get outside. The crowd had gone, the show over for the day. Milton watched as they stepped through the yard and walked to the town's only taxi office. He shut and locked the door and went downstairs.

Lester had unlocked the door to the cell and stood aside as the four men filed through.

"It's going to be a little squashed," he said. "Sorry about that."

Callow was the last one in. He paused at the door and turned back. He ignored Lester and looked straight across the room to Milton. "You just made the biggest mistake in your life," he goaded. "You're going to pay for it in full, you'll see. All of you, you're all going to pay."

"That's enough, son," Lester said, putting his hand on the young man's shoulder and gently pushing him inside.

"You know your scripture, Milton?"

Milton turned his back.

"Let's leave these boys to stew," Lester said, ushering Milton out.

"If you do wrong, be afraid, for he does not bear the sword in vain."' Lester shut the door, but Callow raised his voice, shouting the words so that they were still audible. *"For he*

is the servant of God, an avenger who carries out God's wrath on the wrongdoer.'"

"You've got more patience than me," Lester said. "If he kept talking like that long enough, I would've knocked some sense into him before we were halfway home."

Milton frowned. For all Callow's bluster, there was something about him now that he hadn't noticed before. He couldn't put his finger on what it was, but he knew it was important.

Lester locked the door, pocketed the key, and indicated the stairs back up to the ground floor. "Let's go," he said. "You've got a story to tell, and I'm practically dying to hear it."

LESTER BOILED the kettle and made coffee for Milton, Ellie, and himself. They took their mugs into his office and sat down. He reached up to his shelf and took down a bottle of whisky that Milton hadn't noticed there. He brought it around the desk to where they were sitting.

"Want a little something extra?" he asked.

Milton held his hand over the mug. "Not for me."

"You sure? Something to warm you up?"

"No, thanks. I'm good."

He shrugged. "What about you?" he said to Ellie. "You going to join me for a pick-me-up?"

She held her mug up for him. "If you insist."

Lester poured a generous measure and then poured another into his own mug. Milton looked away and tried to ignore the sharp, acrid smell of the alcohol.

"You want to tell me what happened up there?"

"We brought them in," Milton said. "Not much more to say."

"Two of you, four of them. How'd that play out?"

"They were a little lazy. They weren't expecting us."

"They were just camping out?"

"That's right."

"Come on, Milton. Throw me a bone. How'd it go down?"

Milton told the story quickly and efficiently. He had no interest in the limelight. Ellie filled in the gaps.

Lester leaned back in his chair and rested his boots on the desk. He looked at Ellie and nodded in Milton's direction. "He ever tell you what he used to do back before whatever it is he's doing these days, all the wandering and shit?"

"Vaguely. He's very coy about it."

"SAS," he said with an appreciative nod. "Special Air Service. I served with those boys before, when I was in the service myself. Hard as nails."

"That was a long time ago," Milton said, waving it off. "Another lifetime."

"You don't forget it, though, do you? Those lessons are for a lifetime."

"Evidently," Ellie said.

Milton took off his wet jacket and hooked it over the back of the chair.

Lester shook his head. "Four young men like that, barely more than boys. What a waste."

Milton slotted his rifle into the rack on the wall and sat down. He would go back to the hotel and take another night. He was getting too old to sleep out in the open without feeling the consequences the following day. It was ridiculous. He'd slept under the stars for weeks on end when he was in the army, and the younger him would never have credited the aches and pains he was feeling now. It was embarrassing. He was getting old and slow and soft.

Milton was brought back from his reverie by a knock on the door. Lester took the shotgun from his desk and went outside to the main room. Milton and Ellie followed.

"Yes?"

A muffled voice answered, "It's Morten and Lars."

The sheriff turned back to Ellie and nodded. "It's all right," he said. "Two of my men."

Ellie nodded her approval and Lester unlocked the door. The two men came inside, rain dripping off the brims of their hats. They took them off, the water running down onto the floor. Milton recognised Morten Lundquist from before. The other man, thick set and with a soft, blubbery face, was introduced as Deputy Lars Olsen.

"What is it?" Lester asked.

"The Stantons," Lundquist said.

Milton stepped forwards anxiously. "What's happened?"

"There's been an accident."

"What?"

Olsen took over. "They were in Joe's taxi, got blindsided by a pickup, smashed up pretty good. I was first on the scene."

"Are they all right?"

"They were lucky. She's got cuts and bruises. Looks like he broke his arm. Could've been worse."

"Where are they?"

"On the way to the hospital."

"But they just left here," Milton said.

"It was just outside Joe's office. Road's wet, slippery, the pickup skidded, couldn't stop... like I say, they were lucky."

"Where's the hospital?"

"Wakewood."

"Twenty miles."

"Give or take," Lester said. "You want to see them?"

"Yes," he said. "I'll get a cab."

"That won't be easy," Lester said. "Joe's taxi is the only one in town and he's not going anywhere. You'll have to call Wakewood and have them send one to get you. Hell, I'd take you myself, but I've got to stay here until those boys are taken care of. You want me to get you a number?"

Olsen pointed back to the door. "You want, I could take you?"

Milton looked over questioningly at Ellie. "I'm all right," she said. "You should go."

"Yes," Lester said. "Go. I'm not going anywhere."

"It's no problem," Olsen said. "Got my car outside."

Milton took his jacket from the back of the chair and put it on. "Thanks," he said. "I appreciate that."

"No problem at all."

"Lester—can I leave my pack and my rifle here?"

"Course. Hope they're all right."

Olsen opened the door, tilted his hat against the rain, and stepped outside. Milton followed him.

ELLIE TOOK off her wet jacket and went through into the restroom to get some towels so that she could mop the water from her face. Her hair was sodden, plastered against her forehead and down the back of her neck. All she wanted was a shower, to let the hot water run across her skin and get rid of the chill.

No, she thought, *strike that. I want a long, indulgent bath.*

She scraped her hair back with her fingers and stared into the mirror. She looked a terrible mess. She thought of Milton. What did he mean, dinner? In Truth? Or was he going to come back to Detroit with them? He hadn't mentioned it today, but, she reminded herself, today hadn't been the occasion for small talk. He had been focused on the four prisoners, following behind them, alert and vigilant from the first minute until the last. She had been nervous before they had started, but that feeling had not lasted very long. There was something reassuring about being with him. He was, she decided, relentlessly able.

And then she thought of Orville. He would have complained about the weather, about the chiggers and the insects that had buzzed around them, the mud on his clothes and the sheer inconvenience of being out of town, so far from his car and cellphone coverage and—

Shit.

Orville.

She should have called him. She had broken a bunch of rules already, and she had allowed the fact that she was off the reservation to blind her to proper procedure. First up, she needed to clear out the civilians. At least the Stantons had gone home, but there was Milton to think about, too. He would need to go back to the hotel.

And then they would need to speak with the marshals. It was their responsibility for moving the prisoners, getting them back down to the city. They would send a truck to pick them up. Orville could sort all that out.

She could be in trouble for what had happened. A stickler for the rules, someone like Orville, they could go to town on her for what she'd done. A single agent going after four armed fugitives was stupid to the point of being reckless. She should have insisted that they come back down from the lake to call for backup. She should have gotten the civilians out of harm's way. But, she knew, she would only have gotten into hot water if something bad had happened. There was a big difference in breaking the rules and coming up empty and breaking the rules and bringing the bad guys back. She figured that she would be okay.

She patted her pockets for her phone. It was in her jacket. She took another handful of tissue paper and wiped it against the back of her neck, mopping up the last of the moisture, dumped it in the trash, and went back into the office.

Lundquist and the sheriff were talking.

"You feeling more human?" the sheriff asked.

"Better."

"Pretty fierce out there," Lundquist offered.

"Tell me about it."

"We get all sorts of weather up here, right, Lester? And it changes, blink of an eye. The number of times we've had to go up there and help folk out who got surprised when it dropped twenty degrees in six hours, you wouldn't believe it."

She went across to her jacket. "I need to make a call."

"The bureau?" Lester said.

She nodded.

Lundquist uncrossed his legs. "You haven't called this in yet?"

"No. No signal up there, and then I forgot." She took out the phone and switched it on. "It's okay. I can do it now. They won't get up here until tomorrow now, anyway."

She turned her back on him and scrolled through the address book for Orville's number.

"Don't."

"Sorry?"

"Put it down."

It was Lundquist. His voice was quiet and firm.

"Morten?" came Lester Grogan's surprised voice.

Ellie turned back to them.

Lundquist had drawn his pistol, and he was aiming it square at her.

"What are you doing?"

"You're not calling anyone. Put it on the chair."

She stared at the gun. "What are you *doing*, Deputy?"

"Morten! Have you gone mad?"

"Put the phone down right *now*."

Ellie looked into his eyes and saw grim certainty there. He wasn't playing. This wasn't a prank. She looked down at the round opening at the end of the barrel, the narrow black hole ringed with chrome, and raised her hands slowly and carefully in front of her chest.

"Okay," she said. "I'm putting it down. Relax."

"Take off your gun."

She unhooked her holster and draped it over the back of the chair.

Lundquist waved at the wall, away from the gun rack. "Get over there."

She did as she was told.

Lundquist's sleeve had ridden up a little, and Ellie saw a tattoo on the inside of his wrist. The sleeve fell back down again and obscured it before she could look at it properly.

"What are you doing, Morten?"

"Get up, Lester."

"What?"

"You heard me. Up. Now."

"What's gotten into you?"

Lundquist jabbed the gun at them and his sleeve rode up again. Ellie saw the tattoo.

1:3.

She remembered.

The four robbers in the cell downstairs all had the same tattoo.

What?

The sheriff did as he was told.

Lundquist moved around, stepping between them and the gun rack and the door. "That fucking guy. Why didn't you make sure he stayed out of town? None of this would've happened if he wasn't here."

Lester's face switched through confusion to a slow, and shocked, realisation. "Please don't say you're involved with those boys?"

He chuckled bitterly, without humour. "Yeah, you could say that. You've got my son downstairs, Lester."

"What?"

"Michael. He's my blood."

"You never—"

"It was a long time ago. You and me, that time we went to Green Bay, remember?"

"The girl behind the bar?"

"I'm not proud of it, but he's my boy. My son. That means something to me, having a boy, you know it does."

"So don't do something stupid that'll get both of you arrested."

"It's not just that. Those boys you've got downstairs are soldiers. They're patriots, Lester. They're fighting against the tyranny," he spat the word, "that people like that bitch over there represent."

"What are you talking about?"

"I'm their commanding officer, and there's no way in hell I'm going to sit here and let the federal government get hold of them, swallow them up, and make them disappear for fifty years."

"They *killed* a man, Morten."

"This is a war, Lester. You make an omelette, got to break a few eggs."

Lester's face darkened with anger.

"Take it easy," Ellie warned him, but his anger just kept deepening, and he didn't hear her. She looked at Lundquist. "Put the gun down, Officer. Nothing has happened yet that can't be straightened out."

"Listen to the agent," Lester said.

That was a mistake, and his eyes flashed with fury. "The day I listen to an agent of the federal government is the day I die."

Lester moved fast, before Ellie could stop him. He rushed across the room, closing the gap between him and Lundquist so quickly that the older man didn't have time to react. They slammed into one another, Lester's momentum carrying them both across to the far wall, crashing together, his hands going for Lundquist's right wrist and the pistol. They wrestled, evenly matched, until Lester's youth started to show, and he pushed Lundquist's arm down towards the floor. The older man grunted with exertion, but his arm was straightened out and then pinioned against the wall. Lester reached his fingers down to the pistol, trying to prise it loose. Lundquist bucked off the wall, sending the two of them stumbling in Ellie's direction.

She stepped into them both, wrapped an arm around Lundquist's chest, and tried to restrict his range of movement. He shifted his stance, and Ellie lost her balance, stumbling into Lester and breaking the hold that he still had on Lundquist's wrist. She fell to the floor.

Her gun. It was on the chair, six feet away.

Lundquist brought his arm up in a flash of desperate motion and fired.

The room went quiet.

Lester staggered back until he bumped up against the edge of the desk. His face was eloquent with surprise, a dawning realisation and then, finally, a wash of pain. He put his hands to his chest, holding them there for a moment as he settled down against the desk, and then, as he pulled them away and let them drop loosely at his side, Ellie saw that they were red with blood.

Lundquist looked dismayed. "Lester," he said. "I… Oh, shit. Why did you have to do that?"

Lester slid down, his back slithering against the side of the desk until he was sitting on the floor, leaning against it. His shirt front was swamped with blood, and his face had been leeched of colour.

"Why did you have to do that?" Lundquist repeated.

Ellie pushed herself to the chair and her gun.

"Don't you move," Lundquist said, swinging the pistol around in her direction. "This is your fault."

"Don't do anything stupid."

"*Your* fault," he shouted, nodding at Lester. "*Yours*. You should have gone home with your partner. None of this was necessary. He didn't have to get shot."

"I'm a federal agent. You're a cop. You know what that means, right?"

"Like that means anything up here? You're in my town now. You're under my jurisdiction."

"It doesn't work like that." She pointed down at Lester. His right hand was fluttering over his wound. "You need to call 911. He's going to die if he doesn't get help."

"It's too late for that."

Her words seemed to have jarred him out of his shock. He aimed the gun at her, steady and true, and gestured for her to get up. She did, reluctantly, and allowed him to back her around against the far wall of the room. He went to the chair, took her pistol from its holster, and slid it into his own. He went across to the front door and turned the key in the lock.

"He's dying, Deputy."

"No," he said. "You call me lieutenant colonel. And men die in war." He pointed to the door. "Downstairs."

THE FOUR suspects were packed tightly in the cell. They must have heard the commotion from upstairs, and they were looking over at the door with a mixture of fear and expectation. Ellie came down the stairs, Lundquist directly behind her with the gun pressed tight into her spine.

"Pops," Michael Callow said. "You all right?"

"I'm fine."

"I heard a shot."

"The sheriff."

Callow's face twisted into a sneer of pleasure. "You shot him?"

"That's right," Lundquist snapped.

"He had it coming."

The others whooped.

Lundquist reached through the bars and slapped the heel of his hand into Callow's forehead. "Shut up, Michael. If you hadn't been so stupid and got yourself caught, if this bitch hadn't stuck her nose where her nose doesn't belong, if that fucking Englishman had passed on through town, like he should've done, it wouldn't have been necessary. But you fucked up, she did, he didn't, and it was. The operation's changed. We need to be getting out of here."

Callow stepped back, rubbing his head. The others settled down, Lundquist's anger quelling their jubilation.

"Are we clear, Privates?"

"Yes, sir," they said, in unison.

Lundquist took the key for the cell and unlocked the door.

Callow came out first. "Sorry, Pops," he said quietly.

"Get upstairs. We've got work to do."

The four men went up first, and they followed. Lundquist had his left hand on Ellie's shoulder, the gun in his right still pressed into her back.

They had only been out of the room for a few minutes, but the atmosphere had changed. Ellie looked down at Lester. He had died while they were downstairs. His body had slipped further down the desk, his legs were splayed, and his neck was at an angle. The blood had washed out of the wound all the way down his chest down to the line of his belt. His eyes were open, staring, eerie.

Ellie felt a wave of nausea, but closed her eyes and forced it back down again.

No weakness, she thought. *Not in front of them.*

"Look at him," Reggie Sturgess said. "Deader than disco."

"Shut up, Reggie," Callow said, anticipating another blast of irritation from his father.

Lundquist had gone over to the gun rack. Aside from Milton's excellent rifle, there were three semiautomatics and two shotguns. "Arm yourselves," he said.

"What are we going to do with her?" Tom Chandler said, looking at Ellie.

"I'll take her to the farm. She can go in the barn."

Callow straightened out the kinks in his neck. "What do you want us to do?"

"Tidy up that mess you made. Go get Leland. He knows Mallory Stanton. Maybe he can make this easier.

Get over to the RV now, pick her and her idiot brother up, take them to the farm."

"Now?"

"Yes, Private," Lundquist snapped. "*Now*."

"Yes, sir."

Chandler pointed at Lester's body. "And him?"

"The Englishman did that. Lester arrested him the day before yesterday, before he went up to the lake and rounded you idiots up. We'll say he came back, looking to settle the score."

"So where is he now?"

"Olsen's taking care of him. He won't be a problem for much longer."

Chapter 19

"THIS WEATHER," Olsen said, gesturing through the windscreen. The rain was thundering onto the glass and drumming against the cruiser's roof.

They passed out of town and kept going west.

Milton looked across at him. "So what did you say happened?"

"They were in the taxi; the car didn't stop and sideswiped them."

"The car?"

"Yes. What?"

"You said it was a pickup."

Olsen nodded, just a little too quickly. "Yeah, a pickup."

"Did you speak to them?"

"A little. He was in a lot of pain. Mallory was better."

"Did she say anything?"

"Just wanted to know her brother was all right."

"Nothing else?"

"I'm sorry, Milton. I'm just telling you what happened."

Milton looked at him again. He was trying to behave normally, but there was something about him that Milton noticed, something vague and indefinable, but something that nagged at his awareness like a torn fingernail.

And then he saw it. Olsen's shirtsleeves were rolled up to the elbow and, inscribed on the inside of his wrist, was a tattoo.

1:3.

Milton's stomach flipped.

"So," Olsen said. "You went and got those boys down from the lake?"

He hid it. "That's right."

"You got a history in law enforcement?"

"Army."

"Army. Right."

They drove on, passing the campsite where Lester had dropped him the day before yesterday.

Milton watched Olsen in the dim reflection of the windshield. He had his left hand on the wheel. His right was in his lap, fidgeting, fingers twitching, and he was casting furtive looks across the cabin at him when he thought he wouldn't notice.

"What does the tattoo mean?"

Olsen brought his arm up a little so that Milton could look at it, and then, as if suddenly aware that he had done something unwise, he hurriedly put his hand back on the wheel and turned his wrist so that it was facing down, putting the tattoo out of sight.

"What does it mean?"

"Oh, it doesn't mean anything."

"It must mean something."

His brow puckered as he worked out which of his meagre, unimpressive selection of lies he should use before he said, "Got it when I got out of high school."

"What is it? A Bible verse?"

He shrugged.

"The four men we brought down from the lake today all have the same tattoo."

Olsen swallowed, his larynx bobbing in his throat. "You pay an awful lot of attention to the way a man looks," he said, trying to sound flippant, but the words were undercut by anxiety, aggression, and fear.

"The business I used to be in," Milton said, "it paid to be observant."

"The army."

"No. Something I did after that."

"Yeah? I was going to say, you get a man paying that much attention to how another man looks, you get to fixing that other man might be a homosexual."

He turned his head and looked at Milton as he delivered that riposte, his lip curling in ugly pleasure, the barb a decoy to try to deflect attention from his hand as it drifted down to his holster, the retention strap already loose and the .45 calibre semi-auto ready to be pulled out and used.

Milton jabbed his left elbow into Olsen's gut, hard. The officer grunted in surprise as he pulled the gun, catching the bump of the pistol's rear sight on the holster, yanking it again and freeing it just as Milton swept his hand sideways into Olsen's face. The man might have been stupid, but he was cunning, full of adrenaline and primed for action. He brought his right hand up to block the blow, their wrists clashing, and then, just barely managing to keep the car on the road, he drove the point of his elbow into Milton's face. The bony joint connected with Milton's cheekbone, sending a coruscation of pain into his brain, distracting him just long enough for Olsen to jerk his hand again and bring the gun out of its holster.

He tried to aim.

Milton blocked Olsen's gun arm, but then his seat belt caught, restraining him. Olsen had leverage on him.

There was no time for anything else.

With his left hand, Milton stabbed down at the base of Olsen's seat, his fingers jabbing into the seat-belt mechanism and releasing it, and then he pulled down as hard as he could on the wheel, clockwise, turning the cruiser against the direction of travel.

The rubber bit on the wet road even as the momentum of the big car continued along the road. There was more than enough force to skid the back end out, and then, the wheels now perpendicular to the direction of travel, the rubber bit again and the cruiser flipped over onto its side and rolled.

Milton braced his arms and legs as his seat belt pulled for a second time. His head smashed into the side window as the airbags deployed, the car striking down onto its roof and then rolling over a second, third, and fourth time. His knees were crushed against the dashboard, and shards of glass cast over him as the front and side windows crashed over him.

The car rolled again, the momentum draining away, finally coming to rest on Milton's side.

Milton found that he had closed his eyes. He felt a heavy weight against his shoulder, and when he opened them, he saw that Olsen had been thrown out of his seat and, eventually, on top of him. His face was a bloodied pulp, with tiny fragments of glass peppering his wounds. His head, when Milton worked his shoulder away from underneath it, flopped loosely on a snapped neck.

He braced Olsen's body and looked around. The interior of the cruiser had been badly damaged and was covered in glass, but he had known that a modern car like this would have been built around a steel alloy safety cage with crumple zones that would absorb the impetus of the roll. All seven airbags had deployed, and the talcum powder that kept them pliable was drifting down, coating the dented chassis and flattened roof in a soft white snow.

Milton reached his right hand down through the remains of the window and braced it on the asphalt as he released his seat belt. He took his weight on his arm and right leg and worked his way to a crouching position. He dragged Olsen's body down with him until his shoulders were square to the road and his legs pointed back up towards the sky. Milton kicked out the rest of the front windshield and slithered clear.

He looked back for Olsen's gun, but it wasn't obvious where it had fallen, and he knew he didn't have the time to make a careful search for it. It might even have been thrown clear of the car. Probing his body with his fingers, scouring it for pain that might signal a problem, he started to jog back to town. When all he felt were the aches and pains of incipient contusions, he picked up speed.

He was suddenly, and certainly, very afraid indeed.

THE CAR had crashed a mile out of Truth. Milton ran back, eventually coming up on the big houses that were set in spacious plots on the outskirts of town. The first house he reached had a pair of metal gates and then, behind them, a wide driveway with a Ford Explorer parked next to a closed garage. Milton tested the gates, noted that they felt secure, and so, rather than trying to force them, reached up to the top bar and hauled himself up and over. He dropped down onto the gravel and triggered a security light, the bright white flooding the driveway and the fringes of the garden.

The Explorer was locked, so he took a stone from the garden and used it to punch through the window. He opened the door, swept glass off the seat, and slid inside. Working as quickly as he could, he pulled off the plastic housing and hot-wired the engine.

Lights flicked on in the downstairs windows, and then the owner of the house threw open the door and rushed out into the driveway, his dressing gown flapping behind him.

There was a remote control stuck to the dash, and Milton pressed it, the gates splitting apart. He spun the wheel, sliding the car onto the road and punching the gas. He saw in the mirror that the homeowner had followed him out into the road. The man disappeared behind him as he raced away into town.

Milton tried to guess what must have happened. Olsen had intended to take him out, that much was clear. Why? He thought of the tattoo that he shared with the men in the jail. They must all be connected. He had been right: they *were* getting support from the town.

Did it stop with Olsen or were the local police complicit, too?

Lundquist?

That seemed likely.

Lester?

He would have to assume that they were all swept up in it until he knew better.

And that would mean that the young men were free or were about to be freed.

So, choices.

He could go back to the Sheriff's Office.

But they would be armed, and he had left his rifle behind.

Ellie?

What about her?

It might be too late to help.

And then he thought of Mallory and Arthur, alone and oblivious to what was happening.

If the conspirators were intent on taking him out, the Stantons would be next on their list. If there was a conspiracy, Mallory and Arty were witnesses to it. They would need to be put out of the way.

He fumbled in his jeans pocket for the address that Mallory had given him.

The field out back of a trailer park.

Milton pressed the pedal all the way to the floor, the dial touching sixty and still climbing.

Ellie.

She was tough and smart. She wouldn't do anything stupid.

He would go back for her as soon as he had brought the Stantons to safety.

And if they had hurt her, he would make them pay.

He prayed he wasn't too late.

MORRIS FINCH arrived in his van five minutes after Lars had taken Milton away to dispose of him. Finch opened the door and Lundquist pushed Ellie Flowers into the back. They had cuffed her in the office and taken her out the rear exit, out of sight, just in case someone was walking by. He considered himself a quick thinker, but people in town knew that Flowers was an FBI agent, and he wasn't sure he would be able to come up with a good reason why he had her in custody. Much better to keep it all on the Down Low.

Finch was a big man, red faced, and heavy around the waist. Checkered suspenders strained to hold up his jeans. A huge scar zigzagged across his bald head. The pockets of his plaid western shirt bulged with pens, his spectacles, and packets of More cigars.

"You ready, Lieutenant Colonel?"

"Yes."

"Up to the farm?"

"No," Lundquist said. "Change of plan."

"Where to?"

"The Stanton RV. Head over there. Don't know what I was thinking. I don't trust Michael as far as I can throw him. He gets excited, and then he's not liable to think straight. Same thing goes for his boys. I should have gone there in the first place, got those kids my good self."

"Right you are. You coming in the van?"

"I'll take my cruiser."

Lundquist looked back at the office as he pulled out into the street. He thought of Lester's body laid out on his back, his eyes still open. That was that. He loved the History Channel and he especially loved their shows on old battles. He thought of how Caesar led his army across the Rubicon, leading them beyond the point of no return.

No retreat for him and the militia now, either.

Whatever came next, they were committed.

No turning back.

Chapter 20

MALLORY STANTON cracked four eggs into a bowl, added milk and cheese, and whisked them together. She hadn't eaten properly since the morning, and she was hungry. Arthur said that he was hungry, too, that the boys only fed him now and again when they felt like it. She was in the galley, and she turned to look down into the RV's salon. Her brother was sitting on the bench, staring intently at the Packers game on the small TV that sat on the table. She felt a sudden blast of love and affection for him. He had no one apart from her. She had no one, either.

She would do anything for him.

She took a loaf of bread from the cupboard. It was stale, only barely edible, but she figured it would be better once it was toasted. She dropped two slices into the toaster and pulled down the slider when there was a knock on the door.

"Mallory?" Arthur said nervously.

"You expecting anyone?"

"No."

"Perhaps it's Mr. Milton."

She wiped her hands on a dishcloth and went to the door. She opened it. Leland Mulligan was standing there. He was holding a large flashlight, and his first movement was to bring it up and point it at her. She shielded her eyes and looked away. "Fuck's sake, Leland, point that thing somewhere else."

"Sorry, Mallory," he said, with that same awkwardness that she had always found so irritating.

She had never quite gotten used to the idea of Leland Mulligan as a sheriff's deputy. She was no expert on such matters, obviously, but she would have imagined that a man like him was about as useful for keeping the peace as lips on a duck. Leland was four years her senior, but Truth was a tiny town, and it was inevitable that their paths would cross. Mallory had been to high school with Leland's younger brother, Kurt, and it had become something of a standing joke between her and her limited circle of friends that the older boy had a crush on her. From what she had been able to gather, Leland had been a poor student, disruptive, something of a bully and not particularly bright. He had graduated with no qualifications and had worked in his father's autorepair shop for a year, spending his wages on booze, smokes, and a collection of the most awful tattoos that Mallory had ever seen. And then he had joined the police.

He was wearing his uniform tonight, and it looked, as it always did, both ill-fitting and incongruous.

"What do you want, Leland?"

"I need you to come with me," he said.

"Don't be stupid."

"I'm serious. I need to ask you some questions."

"You need to?"

"That's right."

"About what?"

"Your brother. What he saw, those fellas he was up there with. It's him I really need to talk to, but, the way he is, you know, I guess I probably need you to come, too."

"The way he is?"

He picked his words carefully. "You know. The retardation."

"Arty's not the retard, Leland."

The barb flew right over his head. "I'm trying to be sensitive, Mallory. To his needs. I don't want him to be frightened."

"He's got nothing to be frightened of. And anyway, it's irrelevant because he's not going anywhere tonight. We just got back. I don't know if you heard, Leland, but we just trekked down from the lake in this shitty weather.

We're both cold and hungry, and we just want to get something to eat and go to bed, all right? If you need to speak to him, we'll come by the Sheriff's Office tomorrow morning."

Irritation flickered across his face. "No, Mallory, not all right. You need to come right now. I'm not asking you, understand? I'm speaking as an officer of the law."

She laughed in his face. "Oh, fuck off, Leland. You can't get us to come tonight, and you know it."

The colour in his face darkened, and she was reminded of the bully in him. He was ready to insist again when he was shouldered out of the way. He dropped the flashlight onto its end, and the light fired straight up for a moment, throwing a sick yellow glow up onto the face of Michael Callow. The batteries spilled out and the light went off. Callow reached up into the doorway, grabbed her wrist in a strong hand, and yanked her out and down to the ground. She caught her toe on the paving stone they had in front of the door and fell onto her hands and knees. Callow yanked on her arm again, throwing her behind him. Her face splashed through the mud, and when she looked up, she saw Callow climbing into the RV and the three other men in his gang coming towards her.

"Arty!" she screamed.

There was the sound of a scuffle inside the RV, something falling to the floor and shattering, and then raised voices.

"Arty!"

"Shut up," Eric Sellar said, knotting his fist in the fabric at the back of her T-shirt and hauling her to her knees. He was tall and gangly, with a dramatically cleft chin; thin, slicked-back hair; and long sideburns.

She heard Arty's voice from the RV, angry, and then the sound of an impact and a heavy weight dropping to the floor, squeaking the suspension. Callow reappeared in the doorway, backing out, his arms wrapped around Arty's chest. Callow dropped him outside into the muck and jumped down after him.

"Arty!"

He was dazed, his eyes swimming.

"He hurt my fist," Callow said, shaking out his fingers. "What's he got in that spastic head of his? Sand?"

Sellar put his hands under her shoulders and lifted her to her feet. She struggled, broke free for a moment, and cracked him in the jaw with a right cross. She stepped backwards, knowing she should run. Maybe, if she sprinted now, as fast as she could, she might even get away. But then she looked at her brother unconscious in the mud, and the strength faded from her legs. Sellar rubbed his jaw and then swarmed at her, wrapping both his arms around her, pinning her to his body. He smelled of sweat and cigarettes.

"She's feisty," he called out to the others. "And she hit me, you see that? Right in the mouth! I say that puts me right at the front of the line. Teach her some fucking manners."

"Seems reasonable," Reggie Sturgess said. "She ain't my type, anyway. No meat on her. Too scrawny."

"What the fuck, Leland?" Callow was saying. "What the fuck? You said you could get them both to come outside without any of this nonsense."

"She ain't rational," he complained. "She never has been."

"Not rational because she don't want anything to do with you? Sounds perfectly rational to me."

She screamed out, but Sellar clamped a hand across her mouth, picked her up so that her feet were off the ground, and carried her into the rain.

Chapter 21

MICHAEL CALLOW watched as Reggie and Eric dragged Mallory Stanton away from the RV into the deeper darkness behind it. Girl sure did have a lot of fight about her, kicking and screaming like that, and it took both of them hanging on tight to stop her from breaking free. She probably had an inkling about what was going to happen next. Michael would have struggled too, if it had been him in that particular predicament. He would have struggled for all he was worth.

Leland Mulligan was covering Mallory's brother with his pistol. Arthur Stanton might have been simple in the head, but he was a big brute, and he had realised what was about to happen, too.

"Cuff him," Michael said to Leland.

Leland nodded as Tom forced Stanton to the ground, wrapping his arms around his chest and wrestling him down. Leland unhooked his cuffs from his belt, fastened one bracelet around his right wrist, then had to sit down with his knee in the boy's back and use both hands to pin his left arm close enough to his right so that he could cuff that wrist, too.

"Bring him over here," Michael said. "I want him to see this."

Michael smoked his cigarette down to the nub and flicked it into the wet grass. All that time they had spent up in the woods, there hadn't been the chance to get with any female company. There were women in the militia, a few of them, and he knew from the way that they looked at him that they thought he was fine. He was fine, too, he reminded himself. He was tall and good looking, with powerful arms that he spent hours pumping up, the best sleeve of tattoos that he had ever seen, and the confidence that came with being good with the girls all the way through school. He'd quarterbacked the school team, was good at it, too. There'd been word of him getting a scholarship to Michigan until he'd run into trouble with the police for smoking dope, and that had been the end of that. He'd been bitter about it, bitter and twisted about his dumb luck for years afterwards, but now he was older and wiser, he could see that God had just chosen a different path for him.

He moved in mysterious ways, after all.

Michael had enlisted into the army just as soon as his old man had decided that was the right thing to do. His momma had no time for him, and there wasn't anything else for him to do. They shipped him out to Iraq, and that was where he had met Tom, Eric, and Reggie. They saw things out there, things that brought focus and clarity to thoughts they had all been having. They shared the same view of their country: government was interfering with things it had no right to interfere with, chipping away at their God-given constitutional rights. Being so far away made it all so obvious. Fuck, they had a *Muslim* as their commander-in-chief, and how could that be anything but a calamity for their country? Michael had worked on them for hours, preaching the word of the Lord until they were converted. They had talked about it for hours as they dodged bombs and bullets in Baghdad, and when they got back, they had taken the decision to desert together. Michael had brought them back to Truth with him. They had all leapt at the chance to join the militia.

Four soldiers ready to sign up to the only army that could do anything to stop the country from going all the way to Hell.

He adjusted his hat, hooked his thumbs into his belt, and followed the others behind the RV.

MILTON MADE two wrong turns, cursing as he had to reverse out of dead-end streets, but eventually he found the trailer park. Mallory had explained that the Stanton RV was all the way out the back, so he sped along the access road, cut through the park at fifty and rushed out the other side, following the half mile of extra track to the secluded spot where their RV was parked. There was an open gate in a fringe of wood and then a slope down into a hollow. Milton could see the lights from the Winnebago right down at the bottom.

He killed the engine, and the lights, and rolled up to the gate.

He saw a pickup truck, both doors open, its lights shining out onto the RV.

Milton gritted his teeth.

Too late?

He opened the door, stepped down onto the sodden earth, and keeping low, he hurried towards the pickup.

The vehicle was empty.

The rain lashed into him. He shielded his eyes from the streaming water and looked out beyond the truck. Mallory's Pontiac was parked next to the Winnebago. The door to the RV was open, and there was a light glowing from the inside. The old vehicle hadn't moved for months. The wheels were on chocks, and there was bindweed all the way up to the axles.

He clenched and unclenched his fists. He wished he had taken ten minutes to search for Olsen's weapon.

He heard the sound of angry voices from somewhere behind the Winnebago. He sprinted ahead, reached the vehicle, and pressed himself against the side. He heard another shout, and then the sound of a punch or a slap, and then a male voice shouting out, "Leave her alone!"

He edged around, itching to run, but unable to shake off his instinctive caution. Size up the situation and then act. That had saved his life more times than he cared to remember.

He reached the corner of the RV and peered around it.

A faint glow was leaking out from the window at the back, just enough to cast a parcel of yellow light out towards the woods at the bottom of the slope that marked the boundary of the hollow.

Milton saw seven people.

Reggie Sturgess, Eric Sellar, and a uniformed cop he didn't recognise were restraining Arthur Stanton. The boy had been cuffed, but even so, it was taking all three of them to hold him back. Sturgess, Sellar, and the cop were armed.

Ten feet ahead of them, where the light from the window was almost swallowed by the darkness of the wood, were Michael Callow, Tom Chandler, and Mallory Stanton. Chandler was straddling her, his knees pressing down onto her arms at the elbows. Callow was crouched down behind them, trying to grab hold of her flailing legs. He was laughing, telling her to take it easy, that it would be better if she relaxed and just took what was coming to her. "Hell," Milton heard him call out, "you might even enjoy it."

Milton felt a sensation, like a switch flicking in his head.

Old memories opened up, a past life that he had tried to bury but couldn't.

He went back to the RV and went inside.

The light he had seen from the window was in the main living area, a small standard lamp on the table that was bright enough for him to see all the way to the driver's seat to his right and then a little way to his left, to the back. The toilet door was closed. The main bedroom was at the rear, and that door was closed, too, with a crack of light visible beneath the door. He went to the galley. A pan of scrambled eggs was burning on the stove. Two slices of toast poked out of the toaster.

There was a dirty kitchen knife in the sink. Milton took it.

MORRIS FINCH led the way to the spot where old man Stanton had parked his Winnebago before he had drunk himself into his early grave. A Ford Explorer was in the road before the gate, blocking the way ahead.

Finch pulled up and stepped out of the van.

"What the hell?" he said, gesturing to the Explorer. "That's not their car."

Lundquist lowered his window. "No."

"Want me to go around it?"

"No."

He opened the door and stepped outside, the rain swamping across him. He reached back inside and grabbed his rifle. Finch looked across at him expectantly. Lundquist pointed back to the rear of the van. "Get her out and bring her down there with you."

He skirted the Explorer and descended the hollow. He went around Leland Mulligan's pickup, the lights still on, shining down onto the Winnebago and Mallory Stanton's Pontiac. There was enough illumination for him to see Michael and the others around the back of the RV, standing in two loose groups between it and the front of the trees. The first group, nearest to Lundquist, had four people in it. He recognised Leland from his uniform and Arthur Stanton from his bulk. Stanton's wrists were cuffed.

Michael and Tom Chandler were twenty feet farther on, nearly at the fringe of the wood, dim in the faint glow from the lights. He saw Mallory Stanton on the ground, pinned down beneath Chandler, and Michael struggling to hold her legs still.

An angry rebuke came to his lips. He had known they were not to be trusted. He had given them something simple to do, collect two kids, take them to the farm, and they did *this*. He should never have trusted them. Was this the discipline the army taught its soldiers these days? No wonder the country was in the state it was in. It wouldn't stand, not for men under his command.

He tightened his grip on the wet barrel of the rifle and was about to start down towards them when he looked back at the RV and saw the figure of a man emerging stealthily from the open door.

He dropped to a crouch.

The man pressed up tight against the side of the RV and edged along to the corner.

Milton.

He had a knife in his hand.

MILTON STEPPED back into the rain. He made his way along the side of the RV to the corner. He peeked out again. The group of four nearest to him were still turned away. They were watching the second group. Sellar and Sturgess were holding Arty up, forcing him to watch what was about to happen to his sister. Milton heard a whoop of excitement and then the sound of encouragement.

Milton lost himself in red mist. It fell over him, deep and blinding. He worked hard to keep it away, tied it down somewhere at the back of his brain where he could try to forget about it. He never could forget it, though, not properly, and it didn't take very much for him to summon it again.

Like now.

He held the knife loosely in his fist, left the cover of the RV, and made straight for the larger group.

Arty Stanton bucked hard and forced Sturgess to let go of him. The man was spun around, just enough to see Milton walking straight at him through the pouring rain.

"Fuck," he said.

Milton kept coming.

"Michael!"

Callow had secured Mallory's ankles, his shoulders braced as he pressed her feet down onto the ground, and he didn't turn around.

Sturgess took a half step back, unsure whether he should stand his ground or run.

"*Michael!*"

Sturgess looked down and saw the knife.

Milton drove it all the way up to the hilt, the blade buried in the soft folds of flesh above the boy's belt buckle, and then tore it up to his ribcage and left it there.

The young cop who Milton didn't recognise had seen what had just happened.

His fingers fumbled for his pistol.

Milton closed the distance between them in three paces, took him by the shoulders, and swept his legs. The man went down, landing square on his shoulder blades, and Milton drove his left fist into his gut, winding him.

Down by the trees, Callow grasped Mallory's legs and turned his head to the abrupt commotion.

Milton reached down to the cop's belt and tore his pistol from his holster.

Callow saw what was happening, fear replacing the cruelty in his face.

He let go of Mallory's legs, and she gave an almighty buck, Tom Chandler barely able to hold her down.

Eric Sellar let go of Arty and took a step towards Milton, raising his fist.

Milton shot him in the face.

Sellar toppled backwards and thumped down onto the grass.

Sturgess stumbled over to him, his hand fixed around the hilt of the knife.

Milton fired again, the shot blasting a gory void in Sturgess' face. He tripped over Sellar and fell down onto his backside, dead before he hit the ground.

"Drop your weapon!"

Milton turned to look across the hollow at Michael Callow. The boy had drawn a pistol, yanked Mallory to her feet, and jammed the muzzle up against her temple.

Milton breathed in and out, regulating his pulse. "Are you all right, Mallory?"

She nodded, her larynx bobbing up and down in her throat. Her eyes were wide with terror.

"She ain't fine!" Callow called back. "You look here, son. She's far from fucking fine. Put that gun down now. *Right* now."

Milton ignored him. "Arty, are you all right?"

"They want to hurt Mallory," he said, still struggling with the cuffs.

"They're not going to hurt her," he said, loud enough for Callow and Chandler to hear him. "No one is going to hurt either of you."

"You're not listening!" Callow shouted. "You don't put that gun down and I'll blow her brains out."

"And what will you do then, Michael?"

Milton started to walk across to them.

"Stay where you are!"

"What are you going to do when you've shot her?"

Milton held his aim steady. He had two choices: Chandler was standing in the open, an easy shot, but taking him out now would probably spook Callow into firing. He couldn't risk it. The second choice, the harder choice, was to take the shot at Callow.

Mallory was slight, much smaller than the man behind her, and she only offered a partial shield for him to hide behind. Milton had a good view of part of his head, his right shoulder, and his right leg. He was fifteen feet away, the light was poor, and the rain was in his eyes.

None of those factors helped his accuracy.

He assessed.

Sixty percent. He would make the shot more times than he missed it.

He held his arm steady and adjusted his aim.

Callow was panicking now. He pulled Mallory closer to his chest and started to back away to the trees.

"I'm not bluffing."

Milton breathed: in and out, in and out.

"Drop that fucking gun!"

Milton's finger tightened around the trigger.

CRACK.

The bullet struck him in the left arm just as he heard the report of the rifle from behind him. The impact sent him stumbling forward two paces, his gun arm jerking up for balance and his right hand opening involuntarily, dropping the gun. Pain raced up his arm and into his shoulder, a great bellow of it that dropped him down to the ground just as a second shot whistled above his head. His instincts took over and, ignoring the shriek of agony, he rolled away to his right. A third shot slammed into the earth just ahead of him, throwing muddy sod into his face. He scrambled for grip, his boots sliding on wet grass as he pushed off and threw himself behind the RV, out of sight of whoever it was who had shot at him from the other side of the hollow.

Callow was on the same side of the RV as he was, though.

He shoved Mallory away from him, took aim, and fired.

Milton ducked.

The window above him shattered, glass falling down onto him.

He ran to the driver's door, praying it was unlocked.

If it wasn't, Callow was going to have a clear shot at him.

MICHAEL CALLOW aimed and fired, but he was too hyped up, and the shot went high again, popping the window of the door as Milton yanked it open. He forced himself to draw a deep breath and took aim for a third time, but Milton hurled himself inside the open driver's door and shut it again before he could get the shot off.

"Fuck!"

He looked back up the slope beyond their pickup and saw a figure jogging down the hill at them. He passed through the headlights, and Callow saw that it was his father, a rifle in his arms, the muzzle pointing forwards.

Mallory was on the grass, trying to get to her feet. Chandler intercepted her, wrapped her in his arms, and hauled her off the ground and away to the side.

Michael's eyes were drawn to the two bodies on the ground. Eric was still. Reggie's leg twitched, up and down, up and down. They were dead or as good as dead. Milton had taken them out.

Milton.

He swung the gun back to the RV, trying to remember how many times he had fired and how many shots were left in the magazine.

"Where is he?" his father yelled out over the drumbeat of the rain. Michael realised that the old man wouldn't have been able to see as Milton had thrown himself inside.

"In there."

"Did I hit him?"

"In the arm."

"Did you?"

"No."

"Dammit, Michael."

Callow grit his teeth in frustration. "I was—"

"Keep him penned in," Lundquist shouted out. "I've got this side."

Callow pounded his fist against his thigh. All he wanted to do was impress the old man, but whatever he did, it seemed he always fell short.

"Leland, Morris is parked at the top. Go and help him bring Flowers down here and get a rifle from the van while you're at it."

"What about him?" he said, pointing at Arthur.

"Chandler, if that boy moves, you shoot his sister and then you shoot him."

"Mallory!" Arthur cried out.

"Don't move, Arty," the girl called back. "Do as they say, you understand?"

Michael flicked his eyes to the side again and watched as his father walked slowly down the final slope into the bowl of the hollow. He had the rifle raised now, pointing at the RV.

"Milton," he yelled out. "You've got nowhere to go. You hear me? Come out and get this over with. Maybe the girl and her brother don't need to get hurt."

Michael gripped his pistol tight. He took a step forwards and took dead aim at the open doorway. If Milton came out that way, he was going to plug him.

"*Milton!*" his father called out again.

The voice that answered from inside the RV was muffled, but still distinct enough. "I've got a shotgun. You touch either of them, and I swear to God, I'll do to all of you what I just did to Sellar and Sturgess."

"He's bluffing!" Michael yelled. "He ain't got shit in there."

"You sure about that?" his father said.

"I didn't see no shotgun."

"But are you *sure?*"

"I'm not sure—"

"Christ, Michael."

Callow saw Morris Finch and Leland Mulligan coming down the slope. There was a third figure between them, head lolling between her shoulder blades and her legs dragging behind her as they hauled her along. Looked like the FBI bitch had taken a bit of a beating. Michael grinned at the thought of that, remembering her attitude as she and Milton had shepherded them through the forest and back to Truth. She didn't have that same attitude right now, did she? Her and Milton, both of them, they were going to be sorry that they had put their noses into the militia's affairs.

Chapter 22

MILTON PRESSED himself against the foot of the sofa bed that took up one wall of the RV's salon.

There was no shotgun. He didn't even have the cop's pistol.

He had heard Michael Callow, and he was right: he *was* bluffing.

He was breathing heavily, and every beat of his heart sent a fresh pulse of pain through his body. He took off his jacket, biting his lip as he withdrew his left arm from the sleeve. He looked down at the wound. The sleeve of his sweater was already soaked through with blood, and he could feel the warm stickiness of it as it slid down his ribs to his belt. He had been lucky: his arm had been at his side and, if the bullet had hit just ten inches to the right, it would have punched through his lung. That would have been that.

"Milton," Morten Lundquist barked out again, "you're done for, and you know it. Come out, or we'll shoot that RV up so bad it'll look like Swiss fucking cheese, you hear me?"

Milton reached up and back until his fingers had wrapped around the curtain. He yanked hard, dragging it off its hooks and gathering it in his lap. He tore the fabric down the middle, wrapped it around his arm, and knotted it as hard as he could. The beige material spotted with blood at once. He held his arm up above his head and reached around with his right hand, his fingers settling on the pressure point and squeezing, trying to restrict the flow of blood. He wouldn't be able to staunch the bleeding, but maybe he could slow it down until he could treat it properly.

"Milton! I'm going to count to five."

"You can count to a hundred if you like, Lundquist, it'd make no difference."

"You're hit, and you don't have a weapon."

"You sure about that?"

"Aw, shit. Take him out!"

Milton covered his head with his right arm as the sound of concentrated gunfire tore up the night. Rounds sliced through the flimsy walls of the RV, perforating the metal and passing through into the night beyond.

He heard Lundquist bark out, and the barrage ceased. Milton scrambled forwards, grabbed the flex that led to the lamp and yanked it out of the wall, plunging the salon into darkness. He knew of two sure ways into and out of the RV: the open door to the side, facing where Lundquist must be, and the closed driver's door that he had used to get inside. He added the closed passenger side door, hoping it was locked, and, perhaps, another one at the back. He had to cover all of them.

"Fire!"

The gunfire started up again, a roaring blaze of noise.

"That's enough."

Someone kept firing.

"I said hold your fire!"

It stopped.

How many shooters?

Milton thought he could detect four different weapons: two rifles and two pistols, but that was little more than a guess. He could be wrong about that.

Lundquist called out again. "You're outnumbered."

"Why don't you come in here and we'll see about that."

"There are five of us out here, friend. You're not going anywhere."

Five: useful information.

Michael Callow, Tom Chandler, Lundquist, and the cop. Who was the fifth?

"And you're hit, right? I winged you in the arm. I'll bet you're losing blood right now. How long you think it'll take for you to bleed out?"

The light of a flashlight glared through the window and up onto the ceiling of the Winnebago, swinging left and right above his head. Another beam joined it, sweeping in through the open doorway in the side of the Winnebago. Milton shuffled away from it.

"We've got your friend from the FBI."

"She's not my friend."

"You want to see her get shot?"

Milton pressed himself against the wall and scoured the inside of the RV for something, anything, that he could use.

A gun, he thought. *Mallory said that her father was into guns.*

"That's not clever," Milton said, stalling them. "If she doesn't check in with her partner, you'll bring the whole bureau up here. What are you going to do then?"

Where would she have put them?

"We're going to pin it all on you, friend. You came into town, and you caused trouble right from the start. The sheriff sent you on your way, and you didn't like it. You came back and had a brawl in the bar. Plenty of witnesses to that. You got arrested; the sheriff let you out after you cooled off, only you hadn't cooled off, you came back with a gun and took out the sheriff, the FBI lady when she tried to help him, and those two poor kids who were just in the wrong place at the wrong time."

Where were they?

There were slide-out drawers beneath the seats in the salon, and he could get to them without getting to his feet. He kept one eye on the open door and slid across to them, opening them, yanking them off their runners, upturning them. Papers, magazines, clothes, shoes, but no weapon.

"Come on, Pops," Callow said.

"Easy," Lundquist said.

"The fuck are we waiting for?"

Pops? He was Lundquist's son?

"Stand down, Private."

Milton prodded. "I warned you not to cross me, Callow. This isn't going to end well for you. Any of you."

He heard the familiar sear of anger as he replied, "You forget where you are and where we are? You're finished."

"Don't let him rile you up. All he's got left are words."

Milton looked down the darkened corridor to the bedroom door. *She must keep them in there*, he thought. A lockbox beneath the bed or hidden at the back of the wardrobe. Somewhere Arty wouldn't find them. There was no way he could get down there to look. He would have to pass the open door, and he was prepared to bet everything he had on the fact that they had at least a couple of their guns trained on the dark space. As soon as they saw any sort of movement, they'd empty their magazines at it. He was trapped in this half of the RV.

"Come out, friend. We'll do you quick and easy if you play nice."

"I don't think so. First person who puts his head in that door gets it shot off."

He looked up. There were cupboards attached to the walls, but they were above the wide, open window and there was no way he could get to them without presenting them with an open invitation to pump a dozen rounds into his chest.

"Get your ass out here right now," Lundquist said, his voice hardening.

"We've got a stalemate, Lundquist."

"We ain't got shit. Show him, Private Chandler."

There came the deeper, more powerful boom of a shotgun, the echo of the blast, the sound of it being pumped, and then a second boom. The spread was fired at reasonably close range, and the buckshot peppered the thin metal walls, dozens of tiny piercings that appeared just a few inches above his head. The openings admitted tiny splinters of light from the flashlights outside.

If the next shot was aimed lower, he'd catch the buckshot in his head and shoulders.

LUNDQUIST LOOKED at the coil of smoke that was unwinding from the muzzle of the rifle. He had been in a situation like this, years ago, in Vietnam. Another world. Another war about nothing, the government sending poor boys to die. Boys without an earthly idea what they were doing. They were doing it again, now, just the same. Gooks then, ragheads now. He remembered all the way back, damned near forty years, and how it had been raining then, too, the monsoon, raining for a week on end with no let up.

He remembered.

The foxhole, the VC outside.

He couldn't forget.

That was where it had started. His hatred of the government, it had fomented there.

Damned if he was going to let this godforsaken Limey throw a wrench into what God had told him to do.

"The girl," Lundquist called. "Bring her over here."

Morris Finch and Leland Mulligan dragged her across until she was in front of him.

"On the ground."

Lundquist watched as the two men dumped Flowers in the mud before him. She pushed herself out of the muck and onto her knees. He looked down at her. She couldn't have been more than thirty, and maybe she was even younger than that. Scrawny. She had put up a fight, and there had been no choice but to knock her around pretty good. Her right eye was puffed up, and blood was crusting beneath her nose. It had been a bad day for her already.

About to get worse.

"Milton!"

Lundquist looked back at the RV, its flanks peppered with bullet holes and studded with buckshot.

No reply.

"You got until I count to five, and then Agent Flowers is going to get badly hurt."

Nothing.

"One."

Just the sound of the rain.

"Two."

The rain, beating on the roof of the Winnebago, drumming on the brim of his hat.

"Three."

Morris Finch looked over at him with sudden concern.

"Four."

He reversed the rifle, holding it by the muzzle and the receiver.

"Five."

He swung the rifle like a bat, the stock catching her on the side of the temple and knocking her out cold. She was unconscious before she fell sideways, landing with a wet slap.

"You did that, Milton," he called out. "I didn't want to hurt her. That was your doing. It's on you."

Nothing.

"You don't come out of there with your hands up, Milton, the next thing I do, I promise you, someone's not waking up."

When Milton called back, his voice was cool and even. "I'm going to kill you, Lundquist. I'm going to kill you and every one of you out there. No one escapes. That's a promise. You can take it to the bank."

Lundquist felt a shiver pass up his spine, but he knew the others were watching him, taking their lead from his example. He was their commanding officer, and he dare not show any weakness. Instead, he set his jaw and looked over at Leland. "Bring him over here," he said, pointing at Arthur Stanton.

Mallory screamed out.

Leland hauled him across, kicking him in the back of the legs so that he fell to his knees.

Lundquist held the muzzle against the boy's head.

"Your call, Milton. You want this on your conscience? It's up to you."

MILTON CLOSED his eyes and tried to think around the pain. He had heard Lundquist strike Ellie, and he knew that he wasn't bluffing about what he was going to do next.

No doubt about it: Lundquist was in it up to his neck now. He had started to kill, and the only way to see himself clear was to keep on killing. He had nothing to lose. Milton didn't doubt that he had hit her. He didn't doubt that he would kill her, too, if he thought that was what needed to be done. He didn't doubt that he would kill all of them.

Milton opened his eyes, looked down at the bloody fabric knotted around his bicep, and knew that he had to get out.

There was nothing he could do for Ellie, Mallory, or Arty.

He was trapped.

He had no weapon, and he was surrounded by men who did. The second they saw him, they would put a dozen rounds into him.

He couldn't help anyone if he was dead.

Maybe there would be nothing he could do for them.

Maybe they had just struck a rich seam of bad luck.

But if he could get away himself, maybe they would take them somewhere.

Maybe he could come back and help them.

A lot of maybes.

One certainty.

One thing for definite.

He would keep to his word.

He would murder every last one of them.

He grimaced from the effort of propping himself back against the seat. He looked around with fresh eyes, not searching for a weapon, but for a means to escape.

And then he saw it and knew what he had to do.

"Ellie," he yelled out. "Mallory! Keep it together. I won't forget about you."

"Milton!" the girl called out.

"Get *out* of the RV," Lundquist ordered, his voice tight with tension.

Milton crawled on his belly to the front of the RV as another fusillade stitched across the panel to his right, the bullets passing through it easily, leaving jagged blooms of metal in their wake. Rounds ricocheted, pots and pans were struck, ringing out as they toppled from their shelves and thudded against the carpeted floor. A digital clock on the wall was blown off its hook, spinning to the floor and smashing into pieces. A framed picture of Mallory and Arty fell onto him.

He kept slithering, arm over arm, until he reached the driver's seat. A flight of four steps led down to the door at the front of the cabin, but only half of it was panelled with glass. He wouldn't be seen.

The keys had been left in the ignition. Milton had no idea whether the engine would still work. He thought of the bindweed wrapped around the wheels. When had it last been fired up? Had it been cared for? Was there any gas in the tank? If it hadn't, or there wasn't, he was dead. He slithered another half foot, reached his left hand to the gas pedal and then snaked his right up above his head, finding the key and twisting it as he pumped down on the gas.

The engine croaked and spluttered.

Come on.

Now Lundquist knew what he was trying to do.

"Fire!"

A parabola of glass fell onto him as the windshield was blown inwards.

Milton twisted the key a second time.

Come on.

The engine coughed and barked and then fired, a thin rumble that he could feel through the floor. The RV had been left in gear, and it jerked forwards. He reached down with his right hand and yanked up on the handbrake, then punched down on the gas. The RV bumped as the wheels rolled over the chocks and then picked up speed. The firing continued from all sides, rounds lancing in through the denuded window and punching out again through the roof, another shotgun spread blowing out the windows at the rear.

He remembered which way the Winnebago had been left, its nose pointing back up the rough track to the entrance to the hollow. Milton hauled himself to his haunches, bracing himself against the seat to mitigate the lurching roll as the RV struggled out of the hollow. He reached up to sweep the fragments of glass from his scalp and dared to raise his head above the lip of the window. The road into the trailer park ahead was blocked by the Explorer and, behind that, a van and a police cruiser that hadn't been there when he arrived. He swung himself up onto the seat, jagged flakes of glass scratching at his legs, the wind from the open window rushing around him. The engine was screeching in first, and he took the stick and crunched down into second, wrenching the stiff steering wheel just in time to avoid slamming the RV into the gatepost.

He looked in the big side mirrors: the one to his left had been destroyed, but the other one was intact, the men left in the Winnebago's wake following after it on foot. He saw muzzle flashes as two guns fired, the bullets winging into the RV and ricocheting off with metallic pings. Milton crashed into the rear of the Explorer, bouncing it out of the way. He would have preferred to have been in something like that, something with a little more power than this old heap, but there was no time to change vehicles.

He gave himself a thirty-second head start.

He had to make it count.

PART THREE

Chapter 23

MILTON SPED through the trailer park and out onto West McMillan Avenue. He swung the wheel and hauled the RV around to the right, passing the junctions with East Court and West Court Streets before reaching the crossroads that bisected Falls Road. He ignored the stop sign, skidding around in a wide loop and bouncing off the row of parked cars outside the offices of North Coast Realty. Metal crunched loudly and alarms sounded, a pedestrian shrieking abuse at him, as he stamped on the gas again and changed up to third.

Behind him, he heard the sound of a police siren.

He looked down at the speedometer. He was doing fifty, and the engine was already protesting. He might be able to squeeze sixty out of it, if he was lucky, but no more. The RV wasn't built for speed, and what was more, this one had been idle for a long time. It had been a small miracle that it had started at all, and he didn't want to push his luck.

Wind was lashing his face and stinging his eyes. He swerved around two cars waiting for a red light, slaloming between oncoming traffic from the left and the right, a cacophony of angry horns sounding in his wake. He pulled out to overtake a logging truck, trunks lashed down to its bed, and swung in ahead of it just in time to avoid another truck coming in the opposite direction. Two more angry horns sounded as he pulled away.

The northern outskirts of town were marked by the railroad, a single track that led to Marquette to the east and Duluth in the west. The railroad signal ahead was flashing red, and the bells were clanging, and with no other cards to play, Milton counterclockwised the wheel hard and screeched around to the left, teetering on two wheels briefly until the RV straightened out and all four wheels touched down again. Railroad Street ran alongside the tracks for a mile, and Milton followed it, the road dipping down and then climbing again, racing by the cheap prefabricated housing that abutted the line. The siren grew louder and, as he looked back in the mirror, he saw the blue and red lights of a cruiser as it turned off the main road and sped along in pursuit. It was directly behind him. It was coming fast. He would never be able to outrun it and, if he stopped, they would shoot him. He had to go someplace they couldn't follow.

The engine began to splutter. Milton looked down at the dash again and saw that the fuel gauge was showing empty.

Come on.

The asphalt ran out, and the road continued as a bare, unadopted track littered with fist-sized rocks and pocked with cavities that crushed the RV's ancient suspension as it bounced over and through them. He lost speed, but the cruiser did not.

It drew nearer and nearer.

He heard the big train before he saw it, a low, throaty rumble that grew louder until he saw the orange locomotive heading right at him. A triangle of headlamps glowed brightly down the tracks, and clouds of black fumes spewed out into the night. The diesel's horn shrieked as the driver saw the RV barrelling towards him.

Milton gripped the wheel tight and kept his foot down hard, pressing the gas pedal to the floor.

The cruiser was close, twenty feet behind and narrowing the gap, but Milton didn't mind that now. He *wanted* it to be close. It suited what he had in mind.

He swung across to the right of the road, leaving enough space for the car to accelerate on his left. He turned and looked and saw Lundquist at the wheel, the flashing lights pouring into the cab. Michael Callow was in the passenger seat, the window open, a shotgun pointed right at him.

Too close to miss.

Milton waited until the last possible second, so near to the massive diesel that he could see its registration stencilled across its flank and then the angry face of the driver in the lit cab. He heaved the wheel to the right, the RV bouncing up the small embankment until it reached the track, the front wheels buckling as they crashed over the leading rail and skimmed across the second. Its forward momentum, although rapidly retarded, was still more than enough to send it down the embankment, steeper on this side, and the front of the RV buried itself into the ditch that separated the railroad from the field beyond. The sudden impact propelled Milton from the seat, bouncing him off the wheel. His head crashed against the dashboard and his vision dimmed. His ears filled with the indignant roar of the train's horn.

Milton's head swam and, as he opened his eyes, he saw two of everything. He wanted to rest, to let the screeching noise in his head subside, to assess the bellow of pain from his left arm. His hearing corrected itself, and the screeching became deeper, an angry ululation as the train thundered by.

The train… the train…

He came around.

He had only bought himself a little time. The cruiser would be on the other side of the train, Callow with his shotgun, and now Milton had no transport to use to get away from them. He had to get clear and spend the advantage he had won to put some distance between them.

He reached his left hand for the handle next to the door and started to pull himself out of the seat. The pain in his arm intensified. He let go and probed with his right hand. His arm was tender and sore, and the harder he pressed, the worse the pain became.

But there was no time to worry about that.

The Winnebago was tilted forwards at fifty or sixty degrees. The angle pressed his chest against the wheel. Milton turned so he could reach his right hand over the back of the seat and pulled himself back into the salon, grabbing the back of a chair, an open cupboard door, the table's single leg, anything within reach. He didn't have the time to make a proper search, but he knew he couldn't just run. He had already decided that he was going to hide in the woods until he had the chance to assess the situation, but his bag, his rifle and all his gear were still back in the Sheriff's Office in Truth.

He had to find the essentials.

He looked for Mallory's pack, but she must have left it in the Pontiac. No way to get that now. He would have to improvise.

He found a bag in the cupboard. There was a first-aid kit above his head, and he yanked it off the wall and stuffed it into the bag. He grabbed a saucepan from where it had fallen to the floor and shoved that in, too. He found a flashlight in a cupboard beneath the sink, a nylon line that was used to dry clothes, another kitchen knife with a serrated edge, cable ties, a roll of dental floss from the bathroom and a small bottle of alcohol-based sanitising gel.

He yanked the drawstring tight, tossed the bag to the front of the RV, and scrambled after it, pulling himself through the empty window of the driver's side door and dropping out into long grass between the trunks of the trees. He reached in and hauled the bag out after him.

The train was still coming: freight cars loaded with logs and then a line of black tankers, warning notices proclaiming that they were filled with ethanol. The noise was immense, a deafening clatter as the brakes slowly brought the mile-long convoy to rest. That was fortunate. The railroad would have been clear much more quickly if the train had just continued onwards.

Lundquist, Callow, and the others had two choices. If they wanted to keep their vehicles, they would have to drive to either end of the train and cross the track there. Or they could wait for it to come to a complete stop before climbing through the boxcars and coming after him on foot. Either way, it had probably bought him an extra five minutes.

Milton slung the bag over his right shoulder and then forced himself between the small trees and bushes, struggling through the vegetation until coming out the other side. He recognised the wide field of corn although he was a long way from where they had entered when they had started their trek the day before yesterday.

Milton ran into the field, each stride sending a flash of pain up from his arm. He stumbled on a deep rut, righted himself, and kept going. Lightning flashed overhead, and he could briefly make out the line of trees, underbrush, rocks, and, beyond that, the darkest of the deep forest and the slow climb up the flanks of the mountains. The lightning flickered away, and darkness fell once more.

He had to keep going.

The train's diesel engine, half a mile farther down the tracks now, finally wheezed out long and hard as it drew to a stop. The freight cars jangled and rattled as they pressed up against each other.

Milton heard the shouts and exclamations. Lundquist, Callow, Chandler, the cop, and whoever else they had drawn into their conspiracy were out of their vehicles and after him. He concentrated on his footing, his eyes scanning the ground ahead of him, occasionally looking up to measure his progress to the trees. There came the report of a long gun, the whistle of a bullet and the wet thud as it scored a trench in the mud to his left. Another gunshot and another splash of mud, this time to his right, and Milton knew that he wasn't going to make it.

HE JAGGED sharply to the right, ploughing into the corn. The crop was tall and healthy, the stalks reaching up to well above his head. The stems looked like bamboo cane, each bearing the same distinctive, large green leaf. Milton raised his forearms before his face and ploughed ahead. There was another crack from a rifle, but the shooter was aiming blind and hoping for a miracle, and the shot went nowhere near him.

The stalks slammed into his body, lashing against his head and face. The pain in his left arm was worsening with every stride. His foot caught against a rock and he tumbled over, scraping his hands and knees as he hit the ground. He paused, gathering his breath, wiping the sweat from his face. He raised himself to his haunches, staying low, and strained his ears for the sound of pursuit.

He heard the sound of running footsteps, then heavy breathing.

"He's in the corn!" a voice bellowed out.

"We'll never see him."

"Look harder. He's hurt."

"Get to the other end. *Move*. If he comes out, shoot him."

Another huge fork of lightning split across the sky. Milton took advantage of the brief flash, moving silently towards the track. He looked out for a second, no longer than that, and worked out his position and the route he would need to take to reach deeper cover in the forest. He was three quarters of the way along the track, a hundred yards from the end of the field. He could see the figure of a man as he jogged to the trees. He turned quickly and looked behind him. Two other men were at the far end of the field, near to the crashed RV.

They were penning him inside the corn.

The flash of light died.

Thunder boomed.

One of the two men by the RV called out. "Milton!" It was Lundquist. "This is stupid. I know you're hurt."

Milton crept back into the corn, leaving six feet between himself and the edge of the tractor's tracks.

"We can wait here all night if we have to."

He started towards the trees, moving quietly.

"You might as well come out."

He stayed low, parting the crop as delicately as he could, the bag bumping against his back as he moved.

"You're making things worse for that girl. You come out now, maybe we go easy on her. But if you put me in a sour mood, I promise you, with God as my witness, I'm going to take it out on her."

He reached the edge of the crop, leaving six or seven rows between himself and the clear space beyond. Lightning branched overhead once again, and he could see the man who was guarding this end of the field. He was average height and build, dressed in a police uniform, with a pistol in his right hand. It wasn't the cop from whom he had taken the gun. This one must have been summoned during the pursuit.

Milton stayed low, each footstep placed carefully as he narrowed the distance between himself and the man.

The light faded as the thunder roared.

Milton was close enough to reach out and touch the man's leg.

He turned back towards Lundquist.

"I don't see nothing!" he yelled out, the noise loud and sudden. "I'm coming back."

Milton held his breath.

"Stay the fuck down there, George!"

The man started to retort, caught his tongue, and turned to face the trees. He cursed under his breath, barely audible, as he presented his back to Milton.

Lightning flashed. The stalks parted around him as he stood and took a pace forwards, reaching out to grab the man with his right arm around his chest and his left, weakly, around his neck. He heaved backwards, hard enough to send another burst of pain up from his wounded arm, and dragged the man backwards into the crop. The man, George, was startled and he struggled impotently as Milton held him. A deafening thunderclap unrolled overhead as he wrapped his right arm around the man's head, and reaching his right hand all the way around to grasp the back of his cranium, he twisted in a hard, crisp movement. The cop's neck snapped with a loud crack, and his body fell limp.

Milton dropped him to the ground, took his Beretta and frisked him. He found a pair of handcuffs, a handkerchief, and a smattering of change. He pocketed them all, then ejected the magazine from the pistol and checked the load.

Two rounds left.

Unfortunate.

He patted him down for a spare magazine, but he couldn't find one.

Two shots and at least four men still left out there. Milton didn't like those odds at all. It had evened out a little, but he was wounded and he didn't have enough ammunition.

He was still going to have to run.

"George!" Lundquist shouted.

Milton crept to the north end of the field where the crop ended. He parted the stalks and glanced both ways. He saw the rocky fringe, then a hedge line, and, beyond that, the start of the trees.

He paused, waiting for the lightning.

It came, a blinding flash, and then it faded.

He stepped out.

"*Stop!*"

There came a loud, concussive report as a rifle was fired in his direction. The shooter's aim was bad, or perhaps he was frightened or jittery with adrenaline, but the shot landed short, throwing a shower of scree against Milton's legs. He swivelled around and raised the gun. Two men, a hundred feet away, at the eastern corner of the field. How had he missed them? He fired, too far away to hope for a hit, but enough to scatter the two men, both of them throwing themselves into the corn.

One round left.

He scrambled up the shallow incline, dislodging small rocks and a cascade of stones, threw himself through a narrow break in the hedge, and then sprinted for the trees.

He heard shouts from behind him, but he knew he would be able to get away from them now. They were scattered, and now they knew that he had a weapon. They didn't know that he was almost dry. Then they would find the man that he had killed, and that would give them pause once more.

The low scrub scratched and clawed at his legs as he burst through it and started to climb the shallow slope that led into the forest and the hills beyond it. He needed time to collect himself. His arm was still leaking, and he knew that he would need to fix it soon. He needed to think about his next move, too.

Ellie, Mallory, and Arty were in trouble.

Lester Grogan? He was willing to bet that the sheriff was dead.

Milton had tried to persuade himself that he was done with Death.

But Death, it seemed, was not done with him.

It had a habit of finding him, even when he cast himself so far out into the wilderness that he might as well have been in another world. He had been able to bury his old urges and instincts, bury them so deep that he had almost been able to forget them, but Morten Lundquist had roused them.

He would have to account for that.

There would be a price to pay.

The scream in his head was baying for their blood.

And Milton wouldn't be able to rest until he had drowned himself in it.

He knew that Lundquist and the others would keep coming for him. They already outnumbered him. Maybe there would be others, too. He had no weapon, save a kitchen knife and a pistol with one shot in the chamber. He was badly wounded.

But if Lundquist did persevere, if he came after him, he would give him a demonstration that would make him wish he had never been born.

Chapter 24

MORTEN LUNDQUIST stood over the body of George Pelham and shone his flashlight down into his face. His eyes were still open, unblinking into the bright light, but his head had fallen at a loose, odd angle that told Lundquist all he needed to know. George had been the son of George Senior and Patricia, good friends of Lundquist and his wife, who had lived in Truth for years. George Junior, who was barely more than a boy, had been involved in the militia for little more than a month. They had needed a little more manpower to help keep the FBI distracted and off the scent of Michael and the others. He had been glad to join. He was a pious man, like his parents.

Another martyr for the Sword of God.

"What do you want us to do with him?" Leland Mulligan asked, pointing down at the dead man.

"Nothing."

"We can't…"

"We need to call it in."

"And what do we say?"

Lundquist paused as he considered that. Whoever this Milton was, he was either the luckiest man alive, or he knew what he was doing. He had evaded their ambush at the RV and then he had hidden in the corn and picked off the one weak link in the cordon of men who had penned him in. Most people would have run for the forest, and most people would have been shot.

He had heard plenty about the SAS.

Seemed that they were as good as advertised.

He shoved his pistol back into his holster. He had been a policeman for years, ever since he left the army, and he'd never seen anything quite like this. The last man to have been murdered in Truth had been Stephen O'Reilly, ten years back, and he had been stabbed by his wife for messing around with Bill Pascoe's daughter. This, though?

This was something else.

And more importantly, all this havoc was putting their fulfilment of God's word at risk.

The vice president was due in Minneapolis in four days. They couldn't let this drag out, start to affect timings, start to affect what God had told him to do.

Lundquist couldn't tolerate that.

He turned to the men. "Listen up. I'm going to go back to town, and I'm going to raise the militia."

"Everyone?"

"Everyone. But you need to stay here. My best guess, Milton has gone straight into the woods, and he's going to keep going. He'll expect us to come on after him. I want you to form a cordon, five hundred yards between you. You can cover a mile."

"And if he comes out?" Leland asked.

"We shoot him," Michael said.

Leland looked apprehensive.

Lundquist snapped, "He's not going to come out, Private. He's injured. He's going to go deeper inside, and then he's going to hide. But we can't take any chances. That's why you're going to wait out here for me to get back with the others."

"Don't worry," his son said. "We've got this."

Lundquist looked at him and laid on the scepticism. "Really, Private? You think so?"

His doubt stung the boy, he knew that. But Michael needed to be kept sharp. He needed to know that Lundquist had been disappointed by what he had allowed to happen up at the lake, and then at the Winnebago, and that he was going to have to earn his father's trust again.

"If he comes out, I guarantee you, sir, he is *dead.*"

"See that he is."

Lundquist saluted. The men returned the gesture.

Michael grinned. Lundquist could see that the boy was excited. That was fair enough, in the circumstances. Hell, Lundquist felt the buzz of adrenaline himself. Leading out a posse of men to track down a fugitive? That kind of thing didn't happen any more.

LUNDQUIST HURRIED back through the field of corn, passed the wrecked Winnebago, clambered up the embankment, crossed the railroad, and then slid down the other side. He ran to the cruiser, got inside, started the engine, and then set off down the road. He took the radio off the hook and pressed it to his ear.

"State police," he said into the receiver. "State police, this is Truth. Truth to State police, come in, please."

"State police to Truth. Is that you, Morten?"

"Nancy?"

"That's right. What's gotten into you?"

He fed her the story he had prepared: they had a man on the run who had killed three police officers, including the sheriff. He told her that the man had been pursued into the woods north of the Presque Isle River. He explained that he was armed and extremely dangerous.

"Jesus H Christ, Morten. Are you all right?"

"Yes," he said, unable to hide his impatience. He needed to be on the move.

"What do you need?"

"Every available man up here as soon as possible. He's in the woods. We need to set up a cordon to keep him there. We need to set up a box: men on the railroad to the south, the river to the north, and ten miles either side."

"And then what?"

"I'm leading a posse to get him."

Nancy said she would sound the alert, told him to stay safe, and ended the call.

He swung the car onto the road into town. He reached down and changed frequencies.

"This is Lundquist. Repeat, this is Lundquist. Come in."

Seth Olsen answered. "Morten. What in God's name is going on tonight?"

"Has Morris arrived?"

"Not yet."

"All right. Listen up. He's bringing the Stanton kids and the girl from the FBI."

"Want to tell me what for?"

Lundquist ran through what had happened.

"Okay," Seth said when he was done. "I'll put them in the barn."

"You keep them there. You got two dead bodies coming, too. Sellar and Sturgess. You need to get rid of them."

Seth clucked his tongue. "I guess the pigs haven't been fed today."

"Do whatever you need to do. We can't have any trace of them left. As far as everyone else is concerned, they never came out of the woods. The FBI is going to be back up here again and, if they find out they were around, they're going to start to doubt my story."

"Relax. There won't be a scrap. You know what the pigs are like. Those big old gals, they'll eat them from the tops of their heads to the tips of their toes."

Lundquist relaxed a little. Seth was his brigade captain. He had years in the army, too. If he said he was going to do something, he did it, and it stayed done. He was married to Magrethe, another solid recruit to the cause, another person upon whom he knew that he could rely. Lars Olsen was their son. Lundquist knew he should tell Seth that their boy was dead, killed by Milton, but he didn't want to distract him from the tasks that he needed him to do now. It would keep. Better to do it face to face.

"Did you call the men?"

"As many as we could. The phones are down again, cell towers and landlines this time. We must've gotten around half of them before it happened. I'm about to go and get the rest. They've started to arrive. We're putting them in the other barn. Where are you?"

"I'll be there in ten minutes. Out."

Chapter 25

MALLORY STANTON was in the back of a van. It was only medium sized and it was cramped, barely enough space for her, Arty, and Ellie Flowers, plus the two bodies that they had loaded inside. Ellie was next to Mallory, her head resting on her right shoulder. She could feel the woman's breath warm against her throat. Arty was opposite her, slumped across the floor of the van. She could hear the rattle of his breathing. Both of them were unconscious.

Mallory didn't want to look to her left. One of the dead bodies was pressed up against her. She didn't know whether it was Sturgess or Sellar, but, whoever it was, his body was close enough that it slumped closer to her whenever they took a corner. The storm was raging outside and the lightning, when it came, blasted a moment of silver light between the cracks in the rear doors. Mallory had looked, once, and had seen the shape of the bodies, one piled atop the other, the fingers of an upturned hand brushing against her ankle.

She hadn't looked again.

She heard a deep groan from the darkness.

"Arty!"

Her brother had rushed Morten Lundquist after Ellie had been struck, and he had been jabbed, hard, with the butt of the rifle. The blow had knocked him out, and he still hadn't come around.

"Arty!"

He groaned again, but he didn't lift his head.

"Mallory?" Ellie's voice was weak and thin, shot through with pain.

"I'm here."

Mallory felt Ellie lift her head from her shoulder.

"Are you okay?" she said, her voice little more than a raspy croak.

"Yes. I'm fine."

"Your brother?"

"They hit him. He was knocked out."

She didn't respond.

"They hit you, too."

"You don't say."

"How do you feel?"

She heard Ellie exhale. "Not good. Like my head's about to split."

The handcuffs that they had used were loose on her wrists, and Mallory had thought that, if she tried hard enough, she might be able to force her way out of them. She had strained as hard as she could, but in the end, all she had done was to turn scrapes and abrasions into cuts that had quickly become bloody. She could feel a single warm droplet as it ran down the inside of her wrist into her palm.

"There's an opening up there," Ellie said. "Can you see where we're going?"

There were no proper windows in back and the narrow slit in the panel that separated them from the driver was high up. Mallory tried to stand. She wasn't quite tall enough to see through it and her balance was impeded by having her hands secured behind her back. She was quickly thrown against the side of the van as they took a sharp corner. She overbalanced and dropped down onto the bodies behind her. She shrieked, throwing herself off of them.

"Shit, shit, shit!"

"Mallory?"

"Sellar and Sturgess. They're dead."

"What?"

"Milton killed them. He did it like it was nothing. You didn't see?"

"I was pretty out of it. They're back there?"

"Yes." Mallory slid away from them as much as she could and rested with her arms pressed between her back and the side of the vehicle. "What happened to you?"

"They jumped me at the station," Ellie said. "The deputy—"

"Lundquist."

"He shot the sheriff."

Mallory hugged her knees to her chest.

"Where's Milton?" Ellie asked.

"I don't know."

"You better tell me what happened."

She breathed in and out, composing her thoughts.

She told her about Leland turning up at the RV and trying to get her to come to the station.

She told her about Michael Callow.

She told her about how Milton had appeared out of nowhere, how he had killed Sellar and Sturgess just like *that*, as easy as shelling peas. She told her how she had watched him bury her old kitchen knife in Sturgess's gut, yanking it all the way up even as he turned to face Leland, taking his gun from him and shooting Sellar in the head, like it was something he did every day.

She told her how Callow had grabbed her, how Milton had aimed the pistol, and how she had known that he was going to fire.

And then how Milton had been shot.

By Morten Lundquist.

What was happening to them?
What had they run into?

"They didn't kill him?"

She shook her head. "Shot him in the arm. He got the RV started and drove off. The deputy and Callow went after him."

"He's gone?"

She nodded. "You think he's abandoned us?"

"No," she said. "I don't."

Mallory squeezed her legs tighter, crushing them against her chest. She wished she had the same confidence.

"Who's driving?" Ellie asked.

"Morris Finch. He's a plumber. This is his van."

"*Mallory?*" The voice was faint and befuddled. "*Mallory?*"

"I'm here, Arty!"

Lightning flashed, and she saw his head move as he slowly brought it up.

"Are you okay?"

"My head," he mumbled.

"You got your ticket punched. You feel okay?"

"Dizzy."

"Stay down there, then. It'll clear."

"Eric and Reggie are dead."

"They got what was coming to them, Arty," Mallory said, iron in her voice.

"Is Ellie here?"

"I'm here."

Mallory heard her brother shuffle around in Ellie's direction.

"Deputy Morten hit you, Ellie."

"I'm okay. I'll live."

"Why did he hit you? She wasn't doing nothing, was she, Mallory?"

"No, she wasn't."

"I don't understand. Where are we?"

Mallory composed herself. She knew she would need to stay calm or else he would freak, and that would just make things worse. But she would have to say something. "We're in the back of Morris Finch's van."

"Why?"

"Michael Callow and Tom Chandler are angry with us."

"And Deputy Lundquist."

"Yes, and Deputy Lundquist. They're taking us someplace. I think they want to talk to us."

"Why are they angry with us? Is it because of Mr. Milton?"

"Yes," she said. "I think it might be. Just stay there, okay? It'll all be straightened out soon."

"And then we can go home?"

"Yes," she said, trying very hard to hide the fear in her voice.

Ellie spoke for her. "That's right, Arthur. It'll all be straightened out, and then we can go home. Mallory, do you have a cellphone?"

"No, and it wouldn't matter. The storm's taken the network out."

"Really?"

"Was on the news."

"Maybe it's fixed now. It's worth a try. Do you think Sellar and Sturgess might have one?"

Her stomach flipped. "You want me to look?"

"I don't know how easy it'd be for me to get over there."

She swallowed and turned around so that her back was facing the two dead bodies. By leaning backwards a little she was able to reach over to them and pat them down. She felt something in the breast pocket of the body nearest her, reached her hand inside, and pulled out a Motorola cellphone. She turned her back to Ellie and backed into the middle of the van so that she could pass the phone across.

"Thanks."

Mallory saw a faint green glow from the other side of the van. Ellie had activated the cellphone, and the light from the screen glowed.

"No signal."

"It's the whole state north of Wausau."

"That's great."

The van rumbled onwards, taking them farther away from town and into the countryside beyond.

Ellie used the light from the cellphone to look around the inside of the van. Mallory saw racks of plumbing equipment above them, pipes and sockets and screws, and then, before she could stop herself, the confusion of arms and legs that was Sturgess and Sellar.

"Oh, God."

"Mallory, I need you to do something for me," Ellie said.

She closed her eyes, and she could still see them.

"Mallory."

"Yes?"

"If I give you a number, will you be able to remember it?"

She opened her eyes and stared across at the faint outline of her brother. "Arty can. He's great with numbers."

That was an understatement. Arty had plenty of problems. But if there was one thing he was good at, it was remembering things. Mallory remembered the time when she had read aloud a page of the Truth telephone directory and he had recited back the first hundred names, just like that. The doctors they had seen when he was a little boy said that was one of the things that people with his condition could sometimes do.

"Arty," she said, "I need you to pay special attention, okay? Agent Ellie needs you to remember a number. Can you do that for her?"

"Sure, Mallory."

"It's *very* important."

"What is it? I'll remember it. I'm good with numbers."

"I know you are. Go on, Ellie."

"Okay. Ready? 313-338-7786."

Mallory recognised it as a Detroit telephone number. "Have you got it?" she asked him.

"Sure," he said, as if what he had been asked to do, and the circumstances in which he had been asked to do it, were perfectly normal for him.

"Repeat it to me."

"313-338-7786."

"Good."

"What do I need the number for?" he asked her.

"That's my partner's number. Agent Clayton. I don't know where they're taking us, but maybe there's a chance one of us can get away. If we can, we need to call him."

"The phones are down…"

"Maybe they'll be fixed then. He'll be able to help us."

"Okay, Ellie. 313-338-7786. I got it."

Ellie said, "You too, Mallory. You need to remember it too."

"313-338-77—"

"7786," Arty finished for her as she stalled.

"313-338-7786. Got it." She tried to fix it in her mind, but she knew that she would forget.

"Well done," Ellie said. "Now. When we get to where we're going, I want you to do whatever they tell you. No attitude. No lip. Got it?"

"Yes," Mallory said.

"Arty?"

"He'll be fine."

They were quiet. Mallory might not be able to see where they were going, but that didn't mean she was helpless. She made sure she concentrated on everything else: how long they were travelling, the sounds that she could hear, the terrain that they passed over. The surface of the road was smooth for what she estimated was the first five minutes. Then, they rolled over a bump and then another bump, and she recognised the sound that the tyres on her car made when she crossed the railroad at the north end of town. They proceeded on asphalt for, she guessed, another ten minutes. When the van slowed down, the red taillights glowed through faulty housings, their light leaking into the back. They slowed right down, the axle creaking as they negotiated bumpy terrain.

"What happened to Mr. Milton?" Arty asked.

"He left," Mallory said.

"But he'll come back for us?"

"I don't know."

THE VAN continued along the rough track for ten minutes, and then it swung around sharply to the right, the brake lights flashed again, and they slowed to a stop. The engine was turned off.

"Where are we?" Arty asked.

"I'm not sure."

Mallory reflexively tensed her arms against the cuffs, but there was no give there, and all the effort did was make her wrists sore again.

She heard a door at the front of the van open and the sound of feet dropped down onto the ground. She heard footsteps and then voices.

A woman's voice: "You want to tell me what's going on? Seth says we got a problem."

"In a minute, Magrethe," answered a man.

"Seth says you've got two dead bodies in the back plus the two Stanton kids."

"And an FBI agent. So, yes, Magrethe, I'd say Seth was right, we do got a problem."

"Where's Morten now?"

"Busy. Says he'll be here presently. Probably on his way now."

"Then you better tell me what in God's name is going on tonight."

"The agent and another man went up to the mine and arrested Michael and the boys."

"What other man?"

"There was an Englishman in town, got into a brawl at Johnny's a couple nights ago. Mallory Stanton set the whole thing up, the whole expedition into the woods. She roped the guy and the agent into it."

"We know anything about him?"

"Name's Milton. That's all."

"Where is he now?"

"Morten's got it in hand. He won't be a problem."

"But he brought the boys back?"

"That's right. Morten heard it over the radio, went to the jail, and busted them out."

Mallory recognised the man's voice. It was Morris Finch.

"What do you mean, he busted them out?"

"What I said: he busted them out. Lester was there. He shot him."

"He *shot* Lester?"

"No choice, Magrethe. What else was he going to do? If he did nothing, everything would've gone to shit. Everything we've been working for. The militia, God's word. You reckon those boys would've been able to keep their mouths shut if the FBI had gotten hold of them? *Shit*, no. Not because they ain't loyal, but because they ain't the smartest. There was no choice. It was Lester or us, Magrethe. Morten did what he had to do."

Magrethe. Seth. Mallory thought hard about that. Magrethe and Seth. The only Seth she knew had a farm out on the edge of town and, the more she thought about it, she was sure that Seth's wife's name began with an M.

"You know where Lars is?"

"Morten didn't say. You can ask him."

"He got a call before the lines all went down, took off like a scalded cat."

"Morten will know. Come on, we got stuff to do. We got to put the agent and the Stantons out of the way for a bit. You got space in the other barn?"

"Yeah."

"What are we going to do with the bodies?"

"We feed 'em to the pigs," she said.

"Wish I never asked."

Mallory heard footsteps splash through water.

"Do what they say," Ellie hissed.

Mallory reached out with her leg and touched Arty's knee with her foot. "Don't do anything crazy, okay?"

"Okay, Mallory. I won't."

The handle turned, and the door opened. Morris Finch was standing there, water cascading from the brim of the wide hat he was wearing and his raincoat slick with run-off. He brought up a flashlight and shone it into the van. The beam shone into Mallory's eyes, and she turned her head away.

"Out," Finch said.

Mallory went first, getting her knees beneath her and then pushing up to her feet. She shuffled over to the door, stepping over the two bodies. Finch reached up and put his hands beneath her shoulders to help her jump down.

The rain lashed onto her as Mallory took the chance to look around. They were in an open yard. A large oak tree was off to one side, a lean-to beneath the wide spread of its boughs. There was a farmhouse on the other side of the yard, old and in need of repair. There were lights on in the downstairs windows, and a yellow finger stretched out into the yard from the front door, which had been left ajar. Mallory didn't recognise the building, but although it was dark, the place had the feeling of open ground.

On the other side of the yard, opposite the farmhouse, was the track that they had followed to get to the farmhouse. Cars and pickup trucks were parked along the side of the road, and as she looked at them, she saw the lights of another car sweep across the barren fields as the driver turned off the main road. She could see the figures of people, just shadows in the darkness, hurrying through the rain.

Arty jumped down. He stumbled in a puddle and bumped up against her. Morris reached across to steady him.

"Come on," Magrethe said. "I'm drowning out here."

Mallory turned in the direction of her voice and saw her just on the other side of the van. In one hand, she held a child's umbrella open above her head, Minnie Mouse on the pink canopy. It looked ridiculous. In her other hand, she had a shotgun pointed down to the ground, the stock wedged up beneath her armpit.

Finch reached into the van, caught Ellie beneath the shoulders, and pulled her out.

"Come on, Morris," Magrethe snapped. "Let's go."

They walked on. The water drenched her, running down into her eyes and mouth, and since she couldn't use her hands to clear it away, she had to duck her head instead. They went behind the lean-to, along a gravel path, around a waterlogged vegetable patch and then to one of two large barns that loomed out of the murkiness in front of them. One of the barns had been opened up, and a cascade of bright golden light poured out from the door. Mallory could see and hear people in the barn, and the figures she had seen hurrying from the cars in the lane trotted across and disappeared inside. To the side of the barn, Mallory could see the tractor cab of a large Freightliner semi. The trailer, if there was one, was out of sight behind the barn.

Magrethe went to the door of the other, smaller barn and unlocked it with a key that she had in her hand. She opened the door and stood back a step. Finch raised his flashlight. Mallory saw agricultural machinery arranged around the inside of the large barn. There was a riding lawnmower, a plough attachment that would be towed behind a tractor, bags of feed and, wrapped in black polythene wrapping, bundles of silage.

Magrethe levelled the shotgun. "In. Get."

"Can you take the cuffs off?" she asked.

"All right," Finch said.

Magrethe scowled at him. "What are you doing?"

"They're kids, Magrethe. The shed's secure, right?"

"I guess."

"So there's nothing to worry about."

Mallory turned so that Finch could get to the cuffs. He worked at them for a moment, and then the clasp opened and they fell free. He turned to Arty and released his cuffs, too.

"What about her?" Mallory said, looking at Ellie.

"I don't think so."

Finch quickly frisked all three of them. He found the cellphone that Ellie had kept and pocketed it. "Don't do anything stupid," he warned them. "You're out in the middle of nowhere. There's nowhere to go. No one will hear you. You try to get out, we'll just cuff you again, fix you to the wall. Understand?"

Mallory rubbed her sore wrists.

"Now," Magrethe said. "Get into the shed."

Arty hurried across until he was alongside her. "Mallory?" he said.

"It's all right."

"I don't want to."

"What is it?" the woman snapped irritably.

"He doesn't like the dark," she explained.

She rolled her eyes. "You tell him to get in there or we'll throw him in."

Mallory ignored her, the harshness in her voice, and turned to her brother. "It's okay, Arty. I'm here, too. I'll go in with you. We'll go in together."

She saw the fear on his face as he nodded that he would do that.

"Everyone says he's simple," Finch said to Magrethe as they stepped inside.

"Simple?" she said disdainfully. "People walk around on eggshells when it comes to things like that. It's better to call a spade a spade. He's a retard, Morris, that's what he is. A fucking retard."

The door clanged shut behind them, and they were plunged into total darkness.

"Mallory!" Arty exclaimed fearfully.

"It's all right," she said. "I'm here. Stay where you are." She shuffled her feet in the direction of his voice until she bumped up against him. "Here I am."

"It's dark."

"I know it is."

Mallory waited for a moment, willing her eyes to adjust. There was a little grey light that came from the roof, and after a moment, she began to make out the outline of the equipment that she had seen from outside. She stepped ahead carefully, leading her brother, until they had crossed the shed and were up against the wall.

"Mallory?" Arty said plaintively. "Mallory, I don't like it in here."

She waited a moment to reply, waiting until she could control the quaver that she knew would be in her voice. "We'll be just fine," she said. "Sit down next to me."

He did as he was told.

She lowered herself to the ground. It was dry, a minor blessing. She rested her back against the corrugated metal wall.

"We'll be fine," Ellie said.

"You feel okay?" Mallory asked. "Your head?"

"Just a bit dizzy. It's not a problem. You should both try to get some sleep."

Mallory waited for Arty to settle in beside her. He lowered himself so that he could rest his head in her lap, and she stroked his thick, dark curls. She said again, "We'll be fine," although it was under her breath and for her benefit as much as for his.

The trouble was, she didn't believe it.

She wondered where John Milton was.

Chapter 26

SETH OLSEN had two big barns near the house. The Stanton kids and the FBI agent were in the one where he kept his old equipment. They had the spare nitromethane and fertiliser in there, too. The other barn was where Seth usually kept the hay bales, silage and feed, but they had emptied it out two months ago so that it could be used as the militia's gathering space and armoury instead.

Lundquist took Seth and Magrethe to one side. He told them what had happened to Lars. Seth clenched his jaw, the crinkles that appeared around his eyes the only indication of the impact the news must have had. His wife sobbed, just once, Seth reaching out to take her shoulder, but she shook him off. She snapped that she was fine, but the colour had drained from her face and her eyes were filmed with tears that didn't spill. Magrethe was tough. They both were. Lundquist knew the news would set them both implacably to the cause. He led them in prayer for a moment and then made his way inside.

THE BARN had been decorated. A mural of a crowned sword bisected by a Z-like slash, the emblem of the Sword of God, was emblazoned on the wall behind his pulpit. A Nazi battle flag was hung on the facing wall. This church's crucifix was a sword with an Iron Cross on its hilt, the handiwork of a disciple named Kenny Woichek. A portrait of Saint George and the Dragon hung from the pulpit. One of the dragon's horns was topped by the Star of David.

Lundquist had needed a headquarters for the militia, and the farm had been perfect. It was out of town and impossible to approach without giving good warning first. Seth had eight hundred acres of land, a huge expanse that meant that there was plenty of space for them to train without any fear that they would be seen or heard. Lundquist had worked his men and women hard, preparing them for the role that the Lord had prophesied for them. He had turned it into a guerrilla training camp, complete with firing ranges, stockpiles of weapons and ammunition, and accommodation for everyone who needed it. They had built a facility they called Silhouette City, where his soldiers could fire at targets of Barack Obama, Jeh Johnson, and Janet Yellen. There were checkpoints, and a log cabin served as a guardhouse along the only road that offered access.

When the time came, when the final trumpet was sounded, the farm would be an Ark for God's people.

The men and women of the militia were all gathered inside, bundled in ragged clothes and military surplus jackets. The barn was lit by lanterns that Seth had hung from the rafters. The light was warm and golden, the flames flickering this way and that, sending dancing shadows against the walls. He climbed into the pulpit and looked out at them all.

There were thirty of them, and they had turned out with impressive alacrity. That was some good discipline right there, Lundquist thought, complimenting himself, damned impressive. He had drilled them well, made them understand how important it was that they operated as an effective, cohesive unit. He used the things that he had learned himself during his career in the army, and his lessons were being learned. The word of God he had been working to fulfil demanded unswerving, absolute loyalty and obedience. This was as good a demonstration as any that they were on the right track.

The night ahead would present further opportunities to prove that.

He cleared his throat and raised his voice to address all of them. "What we have here is our first real test since the Lord spoke to me. The first test since we started to work on delivering the Word of the Lord, working towards His prophecy to take our country back. We've had the federal authorities in town for a week, and we just about saw them off. We would have done it, too, until a fellow who was passing through got involved, went up into the woods, and brought our boys back down again."

"The Englishman?" Barry Forshaw asked.

"That's right, Barry. The Englishman. His name is John Milton."

"Who is he?"

"We're looking into that." He stared out at the sea of expectant faces, all of them hanging on his words. "Now, I'm not happy with how easy our boys made it for him to bring them back, but that doesn't mean we should underestimate what this fellow is capable of. From what Private Callow and Private Chandler have said, he's extremely proficient. He knows how to operate in the wild, and he knows his way around firearms. That's about all we have on him right now, except to say that he's caused us a whole heap of trouble."

"Is the sheriff dead?" Vernon Smith interrupted. "I heard that he was dead."

"Milton delivered the boys to Lester, and the FBI agent was about to call the marshals to come and pick them up. That would have been an end to our chance of bringing God's word to fruition. Couldn't have that happen, so I took action. What we are doing is more important than one man and, like we all know, there was no way Lester would have understood us and what we are doing. So I shot him. God have mercy on his soul."

One of the men, Percy Fisherton's boy, let out a loud whoop, a few of the others sniggering at it.

"*Quiet*. Lester was a good man, and what had to be done gave me no pleasure. The Englishman should be dead, too, but he killed Private Sellar, Private Sturgess, Private Olsen, and Private Pelham."

The atmosphere changed as if at the flick of a switch. Some of the men went slack jawed. Others mouthed "four" with disbelieving expressions.

"That's right, four. That's how serious this is. How serious he is. He's killed four men, and then he got away into the woods. And we can't let him stay out there. We need to find him."

There were murmurs of angry assent.

"We know he's tough and resourceful, but we also know that he's injured. I put a shot in his shoulder. Now, a man with a wound like that isn't going to be able to cover long distances, plus it's night, and he doesn't know the woods like we do. So, you ask me, what he's going to do is find himself somewhere to shelter from the storm out there, hunker down, try to fix his arm, and then make his move tomorrow. The state police will have a cordon in place by the time he can get to the boundaries, so he's not going to find it easy to get out. He's going to be hiding in hills and woods no more than twenty square miles across. And we're going to have thirty armed men and women who know those woods going in there after him. Bearing those things in mind, you want to tell me how in God's green earth that son of a bitch is going to get away from us?"

No one demurred.

"That's right. He isn't."

"What about the police?"

"What about them?"

"If they get him first?"

"Wouldn't be a problem if they did. I put out the APB, called state, said that he killed the sheriff, Private Olsen, Private Pelham, and the agent. As far as they're concerned, this is a multiple cop killer. Most likely, they shoot him on sight and solve this for us. If they don't, if he somehow manages to surrender, he doesn't know anything about all this"—he waved his hand at the armaments at the back of the barn—"or the truck and what we're going to do with it, so he can't do anything about that. If he denies he killed those men, then it's the word of a drifter who ignored Lester's instructions to stay out of town and then beat up two tourists in Johnny's against the word of the local police. No, sir. How's that going to play out for him?"

"Badly," Forshaw called out.

"That's right, Barry. It's going to play out badly."

The men and women nodded in agreement. Lundquist could see that they were impressed. They knew that he was clever and cunning, and they knew that he was a strong leader. They knew that he was filled with the spirit. They all knew it. Lundquist got a thrill of excitement from seeing their reaction, just like he always did. God had chosen him for this responsibility and the spirit had filled his soul, like water pouring into an empty vessel. He was overflowing with it.

"What about the VP?" Paula McMahon called out.

"What about him?"

"It's soon, right. Three days he's coming. This has got to affect it?"

"No," Lundquist said. "It does not."

The vice president was campaigning in Minnesota over the course of the next week. Lundquist had gotten hold of his schedule from a buddy over in the Minneapolis PD and knew that he was going to be stopping for a photo opportunity at a little truck stop on the outskirts of the city. Mom-and-pop kind of place, lots of open space around it, difficult for the secret service to lock down. The kind of place where it would be almost impossible to stop a man who was full of the Word of God and not afraid of dying.

"I don't want to sound like I'm doubting you, Colonel, but how can you be sure?"

"It's not going to be relevant, Paula. Because we're going to have ourselves a little hunt."

He pointed to the back of the room, where Seth Olsen was bringing out the weapons that they had been assembling with the money that the boys had been liberating from the banks. They had a hundred grand's worth of equipment and ordinance: automatic rifles, carbines, shotguns, pistols. Thousands of rounds of ammo. "Get yourself equipped. We're going to make three squads. Each squad will be led by one of the best woodsmen we got. Jesse Kay?"

Kay was a tracker, short and wiry as a speed freak. "Yes, sir?"

"You take ten men and go west into the woods from South Boundary Road."

Kay saluted him.

"Ben Teale?"

"Yes, sir?" Teale was a park ranger. No one knew more about the woods than he did.

"You take the next ten, go up to Little Carp River Road and then cut in to the east."

Teale saluted.

"Walker Price, you and me get the last ten. We're going in the woods where he went in."

He looked out at them again. They were men and women of God, His Holy brigade, and they were going to do great things in His name. Satan had wrapped his arms around their country and, if left unchecked, he would drag them all down with him back to Hell. Lundquist was not going to let that happen. The thought of their glory, soon to be achieved, filled him with pride, and he swallowed down the emotion that had caught in his throat. He raised his voice.

"In case you need reminding, I'm going to tell you what's at stake tonight. America has drifted far from the Founding Fathers' dream of a white, Christian nation. Jews and non-whites are defiling the Promised Land. Life has become bitter. The farms and factories are closing, small towns are emptying, the fabric of society is shredding. Crime goes unpunished; school prayers are unsaid. Divorce, abortion, drug abuse, and homosexuality threaten our way of life. In the cities, people get rich manipulating paper while farmers are forced to sell their crops for less than it costs to coax them from the soil. The Zionist Occupation Government conspires to rule the earth. The media pours out a steady stream of filth and deception. And they have the audacity to accuse people like us of trying to *overthrow* the government? We just want it back!"

There were exclamations of "Yes!" and cries of "Say on!" A woman, her arms upraised, looked faint. Lundquist felt the sweat on his face, left it untouched and pulled down his right sleeve to reveal his tattoo. He turned his wrist so that it faced the others, clenched his fist and raised his arm.

The others mirrored his salute.

He recited the words of Revelations 1:3 that he had chosen as their mantra: "'Blessed is he that readeth, and they that hear the words of this prophecy, and keep those things which are written therein.'"

The others responded, chanting out the final words: "For the time is at hand."

"'A sword, a sword is sharpened and also polished.'"

The others joined in with him, their left hands pressed over their hearts, reciting the scripture with lusty enthusiasm. "'Sharpened to make a dreadful slaughter, polished to flash like lightning. And He has given it to be polished, that it may be handled; This sword is sharpened and it is polished to be given into the hand of the slayer.'"

"And what did Jesus say?"

"'Think not that I am come to bring peace on earth. I came not to bring peace but a sword.'"

"And who are we?"

"The Sword of God."

"This is the word of the Lord."

"Praise be to God."

"Amen."

"Amen!"

They took communion after that, passing around a tray of shot glasses filled with grape juice and tiny rectangular wafers. When they had finished, there were cheers and shouts of excitement. Lundquist saw the fire in their eyes. They would do their duty by God. They were like a pack of wild dogs, he thought, and he was about to unleash them.

Chapter 27

MILTON HAD entered the forest from a different point than the previous day, and he was soon lost. It was thickly wooded and on a slight incline, a gentle slope that he could soon feel in the back of his calves as he ascended. It was rocky underfoot, ridges that tore out of the greensward and shallow ravines and crevasses that plunged down almost without warning. The land reminded him of Kosovo, of the time he had dropped behind enemy lines with orders to melt into the night until a particular target revealed himself. He would take his shot and be absorbed into the background again.

Milton was comfortable in this kind of terrain. His history with the regiment had included weeks spent living off the land. He had trained in the jungle in Borneo. There was nothing here that was unfamiliar or daunting to him.

He kept running, his legs burning and the pain in his left arm pulsing every time his feet struck the earth. At least it had stopped raining, and above him, the clouds had parted to admit a little silvery moonlight. Not much, but enough for him to see where he was going.

He followed the terrain as it led upwards. He needed to climb, to get as high as he could before he stopped. He needed to gain his bearings. He needed to work out how far he was from the field and which direction he should take.

He could feel the blood against his skin, a wet slickness that had soaked through his shirt, the curtain that he had wrapped around his arm, and into the lining of his jacket. Branches slapped and scraped, brambles gouged him as he ploughed between bushes, his face soon lacerated by a network of tiny cuts. He broke free from the tree line into a space that had been logged, a collection of stumps and trunks that had been stacked, ready to be collected. Ahead of him was a steep rise up to a plateau, a climb on a shifting trail of loose rocks and gravel. He sprinted at it, managed the first few steps until his momentum was halted, and then bent to power up, pushing his feet into the unreliable give of the surface, his hands pressed into the sharp stones to help keep him upright. He churned upwards, an avalanche of scree scattering behind him. The footing became firmer the nearer to the top he climbed and, eventually, he was able to stand again. He stopped, his muscles burning and his breath coming in hungry gulps.

He turned and looked back in the direction he had come from. The forest stretched out beyond him to the east and west, as far as the eye could see in each direction. He knew from his earlier journey that there were fire breaks and small roads cut into the trees, but they were impossible to see from here. The terrain continued to climb to the north, the trees becoming ever more sparse the higher the ground rose. He turned to the south and saw the beginning of the forest, the field of corn beyond it and, behind that, the line of the railroad and the hazy lights of Truth. He squinted to the southeast, but it was too dark to make out the Stantons' Winnebago.

He waited for another minute, his hands on his knees as he filled his lungs with oxygen. He turned and looked north to the shallow hills and peaks that characterised this part of Michigan. He needed to keep moving. He needed to put some distance between himself and Lundquist and his men. He needed to get as far away from the field of corn as he could.

He saw the line of a stream, five hundred yards away to the northeast. He headed for it. The clouds rolled in again, and soon all he could see were the outlines of the larger rocks and the bunched trunks of the trees. The stream was small, little more than a trickle, maybe even run-off that had found its way into an old winterbourne. He stayed close to the water, stopping every now and again to listen, but all he could hear were the noises of the natural world around him: the chirping of crickets, the shrieking call of a nocturnal predator high above, the gentle tinkle of the water as it passed over bedrock. He wondered whether Lundquist would have access to dogs and, assuming that he might, he ploughed through the water, hoping to mask his scent. He leapt out on the opposite bank and pressed ahead.

The terrain descended into a low open hollow, and gravity pulled Milton down in a headlong plunge, his feet sinking to the ankles in the loose shale. He raced at speed into the base of the depression, catching his right foot in an uncovered branch, thrusting out his left and barely managing to scramble away without falling. He was sweating heavily, and his arm throbbed. The stream wound its way through the hollow, and he followed it, the ground becoming soft and boggy underfoot. It turned this way and that until it led up the opposite slope. The incline grew steeper and steeper until the water was passing between two steep shoulders of rock.

There was no point in continuing. This would do. Milton walked to the edge of the water and splashed it across his face for a moment. He was already sodden from the earlier rain, but the water was fresh and invigorating, and it washed the sweat, blood, and muck away.

He looked at his surroundings. The angle of the ravine was steep, but it looked as if there was a trail that picked a path along the more accessible portions. The path ahead was hemmed in by trees, mountain ash, beech and oak, and the cover from the leaves was dense. He walked to the rock face on his side of the river, followed it up and, after twenty paces, found an outcrop that reached out to provide a natural ceiling.

He hurried across to it.

THE BREAK in the storm had been temporary and, now that the thunderhead had rolled back across the moon, the rains were falling once again. He clambered up to the rocky outcrop. The ravine bulged outwards here, and the face was twenty feet from the water's edge. There was a carpet of scree beneath the ceiling that was, at least where it was close to the overhang, reasonably dry. The outcrop itself was sheltered by a canopy of leaves from large red and silver maple trees, and a comfortable nook was fashioned between two large dogwood bushes. Milton decided that the spot was as good as it was likely to get, and besides, he was tired and starting to feel very cold.

And his arm ached. It *really* ached, but he didn't think it was getting any worse. It could wait. His priority had to be shelter and then fire. He needed to get warm and dry his wet clothes. He would risk hypothermia if he didn't.

Shelter first.

He went back down the slope into the trees and located three six-foot branches that had fallen to the ground. They were reasonably straight, and notched with nubs and small branches all the way down their lengths. He took the bag and removed the kitchen knife that he had taken from the RV, using it to saw into the ends of two of the branches, then used his hands to split them apart into shallow Vs. He rested those two branches against the rock wall and slotted the third branch into the grooves that he had cut. He used the nylon cord to lash the central pole to the struts and then stood the frame against the wall at a sixty degree angle, rolling two small boulders to provide stability at the base and a head start on the thatching he was going to have to do. He went back down to the woodland floor and collected a double armful of coniferous branches and large leaves. He started at the bottom of the frame, above the log, and worked up, thatching the smaller branches and then stuffing the holes with the vegetation. He returned to the wood again. A large pine had fallen, and since the wood inside rotted faster than the bark outside, there were large plates of it that could be easily removed and used as tiles. It took him thirty minutes, but, when he was done, he had shelter from the rain.

Now, fire.

He went back down to the trees and gathered tinder: dry grass he found in the lee of a tree, dead cleavers, nettles and parsley, honeysuckle bark, pine needles, fluffy seed heads, dry lichens and mosses. He returned to the outcrop and used the knife to dig out a shallow fire pit, lining it with small rocks and handfuls of scree.

He took the Beretta from his pocket. One round left. Hypothermia was his most immediate danger, and he couldn't waste time waiting for a fire to start. He would have to sacrifice the bullet. He released the magazine, racked the slide, and the round fell into his hand. He gathered up the tinder and fashioned it into a nest and added a squirt of the alcohol-based sanitising gel. He used his knife to prise off the end of the bullet and poured out the gunpowder onto a dry shard of wood. He placed the tinder over the gunpowder and used his fire steel to drop a cascade of sparks onto it. The gunpowder fizzed and spat, and a flame caught hold. He curled his hands around it, feeling the negligible fire on his calloused skin, shielding and shepherding it, and then, as it took better hold, he added bigger pieces of kindling, careful not to smother it, nursing the flame at each step until it was strong enough to take the dry twigs that he had scavenged. It took him thirty minutes, but when he was satisfied, the fire was healthy, and it radiated a strong heat.

All right, he thought. *Now the arm.*

He took off his jacket and sweater and unwound the torn curtain. He set up the flashlight so that the beam played back against him. He could examine the wound more carefully now. The bullet had passed through his bicep and left through his tricep. That was fortunate on the one hand, not so fortunate on the other. While there was no slug to remove, the journey through his skin and muscle had slowed the bullet down, the friction exerting enough force to start spinning it. The entry wound was neat and tidy, a perfect little blackened circle that would heal on its own with no need for any serious ministration on his part. The exit wound, though, the round punching out more slowly and rotating as it did so, was wide and messy.

He went to the water's edge and rinsed out the grit and debris and, for a moment at least, he numbed the pain. He slathered sanitising gel over the two wounds, wincing from the sudden sting. He reached into the bag and took out the sealed plastic container that held the first-aid kit. There was a needle and thread, but he knew the wound was not ready to be sutured yet. It would be better for it to be left open so that if it did become infected, the pus could drain away. As long as it could drain, it was unlikely to become life-threatening, regardless of how unpleasant it might look or smell. He unfolded one of the dressings and laid it across the entry wound. He attached it with a roll of adhesive tape and then repeated the procedure for the exit wound.

Milton spread the remaining ferns on the ground and lay down on them, feeling the warmth on his skin. The smoke from the fire issued out of the chimney he had left against the rock, but he wasn't concerned. It would be invisible in the dark, and the glow of the flames would be masked by the thatch and hidden in the cleft of the ravine. He looked at the flickering glow as it cast patterns against the moss-covered rock, picking out a glittering vein of quartz that ran down from the top and disappeared into the scree. He added more wood, raising the fire to a happy blaze.

He closed his eyes. He hadn't slept for nearly forty hours. He needed to rest. He trusted his body to wake him with the dawn, his habit for twenty years, and then, the fire warm on his face, he was quickly submerged by sleep.

Chapter 28

MORTEN LUNDQUIST saw his son at the same time as he heard the barking from the field behind him. Michael had built a bonfire, and he was sitting in front of it, cross-legged, facing into the woods. He had a rifle resting across his lap. Lundquist tramped on, leading his squad of six men out of the field and down to the fringe of the woods. The fire was warm.

"Morning, Pops," Michael said to him. "Everything all right?"

"All good."

The men settled around it, some extending their hands to the flames to drive away the cold damp of the early morning.

"Any sign of him?"

"He hasn't come out, least not this way."

Lundquist grunted, not ready to start praising his boy after the eternal fuck up he had brought down on them all by letting the Englishman and the agent round them up in the first place.

The sound of barking drew closer.

Michael looked up.

"It's Walker," Lundquist said.

He swivelled and looked over his shoulder. He could see Walker Price coming towards them on the track that cut through the cornfield, his three hunting dogs surging ahead, straining at the master leash. Walker was a lieutenant in the militia, a good and trustworthy man. He was a hunter, too, and a good one. His dogs had keen noses, and he knew that they would be able to track the Englishmen wherever he went. They would give them the advantage in finding him. He supposed that he could have assigned Walker to another team, but, he admitted, he wanted Milton all for himself. God willing, he wanted to be the one to make an example of him. It would be perfect, a chance to underline his leadership just before they started to follow God's word.

Lundquist stretched his arms. He hadn't been out in the open like this for years. Hell, he couldn't recall the last time. He remembered nights that he had spent with his old man, weekends that involved hauling their gear up and down the hills on the other side of the peninsula, days spent outside because the old bastard said he needed to be "toughened up" and this was the best way to do it.

Lundquist came from an old military family. His father said he had been one of Teddy Roosevelt's Rough Riders, that he had run guerrilla units in the Philippines during World War Two and that he had been promoted to lieutenant colonel at twenty-six, a full decade ahead of his army cohorts. "I killed Japs," he bragged. "Plenty of them with a knife."

His father had been a hard, severe man, and Lundquist knew that some of that tough attitude had been passed down to him. That was the reason why he had always been hard on his own kids when they were growing up. It was inevitable, wasn't it? Like father, like son. Michael had been brought up by the slut in Green Bay that he had knocked up on that drunken evening with Lester twenty-five years ago. He had no hand in the boy's upbringing until he had come to his door, five years ago, a stupid expression on his face, his hand held out, saying, "Dad?"

Lundquist remembered that day like it was yesterday.

The sound of the dogs drew closer.

His thoughts settled on the story that he would tell when the authorities came back into town. He knew that it would hold up. There was the record of John Milton's arrest after the brawl with the out-of-towners in Johnny's Bar. Witnesses, too, if he needed them. That was evidence of his violent disposition. Lester had written up how he had picked the man up on the outskirts of Truth and driven him to the other side with the instruction that he keep on walking. Milton had ignored him, evidence of his disregard for authority and, maybe, something else to add to his motive.

Lundquist thought about it, laid the story out, and it all made perfect sense.

What had happened next? Milton had come back to find Lester, shot him, and then fled as Lundquist and Olsen arrived just in time. They had gone in pursuit, and Olsen had found him and had been killed for it. George Pelham ran into him as they had given pursuit, and he had been killed, too. Three policemen dead. Shit, Lundquist would be able to bring the National Guard down on his head if he wanted to.

He took out his tin of tobacco, rolled a cigarette, and lit it.

"What's the plan?" Michael asked him.

"We let the dogs find his scent, and then chase him down."

"Now?"

"No. We'll wait until dawn. A couple hours. I want some light."

"But he could've kept going. He could be halfway to the lake by now."

Lundquist had a speck of tobacco in his mouth; he spat it out. "You see his arm? How he couldn't carry it right? No way on earth he can keep going without stopping to get that seen to. Maybe he doesn't know what he's doing; maybe we find him bled out somewhere."

"He knows what he's doing," Michael said. "He's tough."

Lundquist drew down on the cigarette. "'But they that wait upon the Lord shall renew their strength; they shall mount up with wings as eagles; they shall run, and not be weary; and they shall walk, and not faint.' You know what that means, Michael?"

"Patience."

"Patience. God willing, we'll find him."

"Yes, Pops."

"He tell you anything that might tell us who he is?"

"Nah." Michael shook his head. "He's pretty quiet. But he's good with a gun, and he can handle himself. He took all four of us down, right?"

"Says more about you than it does about him."

"I've apologised for that. Won't happen again."

"Make sure it doesn't."

Lundquist knew that he was riding him, but he knew that it was his responsibility to correct the flaws in his character. He thought of the words in Proverbs: "'*Whoever spares the rod hates his son, but he who loves him is diligent to discipline him.*'" That was a message that he would do well to heed. Michael needed discipline in his life. He was full of the foolishness and stupidity of youth, and Lundquist intended to see that it was all erased. Only when that was done would he feel comfortable in trusting the boy completely.

THE NINE of them sat around the fire, waiting for dawn to break. Lundquist was anxious to start, but it wasn't difficult to remember what Milton had already done to four of his soldiers. The man was dangerous. He would be even more dangerous in the dark.

No, sir, he thought. *This is better. Balance the disadvantage of giving him a little head start against the danger of getting yourself killed. That's not a tough call to make.*

Michael had been chomping at the bit. He tried to persuade him again that they should get going, how they were giving him a chance to get away. He had been persistent, on and on at him for a full five minutes until it had started to look like he was questioning his orders, and Lundquist decided he had no choice but to shut him down. He had made a cruel jab at him about the mess up at the mine, embarrassed him in front of the others, but it had quietened him for the time being.

Lundquist looked through the flames at him now, watched as he hugged his legs to his chest and stared into the fire with a baleful expression. He had the passion of the zealot mixed with the insecurities of a young man who was lost in the world.

He needed guidance. He needed the succour of God's word to help him see the righteous path. Lundquist would help him find that.

He was reminded again of how Michael always tried so hard to impress him. He wasn't a headshrinker, but all his time in the police meant that he had come to see plenty of human life, and he thought he could read people pretty well. Michael was easy to work out: Lundquist had abandoned him as a kid and, now that he had found him again, he was doing everything he could to impress him, show him that he was worthy of his love.

Yeah, well.

That had been useful to start with. Lundquist needed good young men, men who would be loyal and who he could trust, and his own flesh and blood was the perfect place to start. It had been easy enough for him to show the kid where the country was going wrong and who was to blame for it all. He was ready to be persuaded, like a bottle into which Lundquist could pour all of God's teachings. Lundquist showed him what was happening to the country, how intrusive politicians were stripping away their rights, softening them up, getting ready to subjugate them. Fattening them up like hogs for the slaughter. Michael was a willing student. He had seen the truth in it.

The boy had been working at the gas station on the edge of town. There was no profit in that for the militia, so Lundquist told him that he needed to sign up for the army. It would be useful training, he said. And wasn't it kind of ironic, getting the federal government to train the soldiers that Lundquist would use to bring it down? And, he knew, it would be another chance for Michael to see what the politicians were doing to America. It would show him how the government was an evil entity, Satan's puppet, perpetrating violence on its own people and on others abroad.

It had worked.

Michael had been a good soldier. He had served for three years, Iraq for the most part, his commanding officers commending him as the epitome of infantry, but when Lundquist felt his training was complete, he called him home. He had fallen in with the three other boys—Sellar, Sturgess, and Chandler—and recruited them, too, bringing them back to Truth with him. He had left for the war a believer, but he came back again a zealot. He was passionate and hot headed, but with the right direction he had demonstrated that he could be effective. He seemed to exert swing over the other boys in his crew, too. Lundquist had seen the way they all looked to follow his lead, and had seen the way his instinct to violence had kept them in line.

The Sword of God needed money for armaments. Lundquist had been thinking about how easy it would be to hit the banks hereabouts for years. He could use his police credentials to get information on their security set ups that would have been impossible otherwise. He had worked it all out. He would craft the plans, and Michael and the others could carry them out. He ironed out the risks that their inexperience might have created and turned them into a smooth and effective crew. He suggested that they use dirt bikes to get in and out of the towns, following routes that he had plotted in advance to make sure that it was practically impossible to chase them. He knew about the old mine up by the lake and suggested that they should hole up there for a week after each job, at least until the temperature had cooled down.

Michael had not needed persuading to get involved, and he had delivered the others just like he said he would.

The first four heists had been flawless.

Houghton.

Ironwood.
Barksdale.
Duluth.
Then Marquette, and the dead guard.

He should have called a halt to it then, but he had been greedy. Each time they had returned to the mine with sacks full of money.

The money went a long way. Guns, ammunition, explosives. Everything that they needed.

It was difficult to turn the flow off.

So they had dropped down into Wisconsin instead.

Wausau.

Green Bay.

No more problems.

It had been going well.

Until now, and the Stanton kids, the FBI.

Until John Milton.

But Lundquist was on top of it.

All of it.

He would get it straightened out.

MICHAEL WAS tending to the fire, dropping a large branch across the middle of it, the sap spitting and hissing as the wood started to combust. The shadows around the camp were fading, the early dawn light spreading lazily up from the horizon. It would stay dim for another twenty minutes, and then the sun would rise, and the darkness would be pushed away.

Lundquist looked into the depths of the forest. John Milton would be watching the same sunrise. Wherever it was that he had hidden overnight, it would feel a lot less secure with the darkness banished for the day.

The dogs became agitated.

He turned and saw Leland Mulligan approaching through the field. He had sent him back into town earlier to check that everything was in hand.

"About time," he said impatiently when the deputy had reached the fire.

Leland spread his hands helplessly. He was another youngster who had been easy for Lundquist to recruit. His late parents had been God-fearing folk, and they had brought their son up the right way.

"Well? How did it go?"

"Good. The kids and the agent are locked up tighter than a duck's ass. Magrethe and Morris will keep an eye on them. They ain't going nowhere."

"The state police?"

"Just like you said. The men they had available, they sent them out right away last night. They're getting in position right now, stationed just like you said, boxed him right in. They've promised to double the men, gonna bring the late shift in early. He's not going to find it easy to get through the line."

"Good." Lundquist finished his roll-up and flicked it into the fire. "What about Olsen?"

Leland winced. "That was one nasty crash, Lundquist. The fire department had to cut the car in half to get him out. Flipped over five, six times. I'm surprised Milton got out of it in one piece."

"George?"

"Coming to bring his body back to the morgue. You ask me, that there was a broken neck. Whoever this dude is, he ain't interested in love taps. I think he's serious."

"That so?" Lundquist said sarcastically as he rolled another cigarette. "Leave the thinking to me, Leland, all right? It's not what you're good at. What else?"

He indicated the hounds with a sullen shrug. "I found Milton's pack like you said." He held up a large plastic evidence bag into which clothes had been stuffed.

Walker Price brought the dogs over. They strained hard on the leash, barking avidly.

Lundquist took the bag and opened it, pulling out a sweatshirt and a pair of jeans. Neither of them had been washed. He tossed them to Walker, who knelt down as his dogs bounded around him, nudging him with their muzzles, their tails wagging furiously. They buried their noses into the clothes, breathing in Milton's scent, and then turned towards the woods. The lead dog was a bitch that Walker called Blue. She lifted her head, holding the point, her tail held out behind her.

"She got it?"

"She does," Walker said. The other dogs picked up the trail, too, one of them starting to howl. "Look at them. They're practically begging to be let off the leash. I don't think this is going to be difficult, Morten."

Lundquist nodded his satisfaction.

Leland took another large bag and opened it up. Inside were a dozen bacon rolls. The men took one each and ate hungrily. There were two flasks of coffee, too, and cups for them to share. Lundquist ate and drank, the nourishment giving him a jolt of energy.

He looked around at the posse that they had assembled: him, Leland Mulligan, Walker Price, Michael, Thomas Chandler, Larry Maddocks, Harley Ward, Dylan Fox, Randy Watts, and Archie McClennan. Ten of them. That ought to be more than enough. If Milton was still in the forest, and he was sure that he was, there would be no easy way for him to get out. They would pick up his scent and track him down. And there would be no arrest. They would bring him back in a body bag. Milton was a cop killer, after all. They would come back into Truth as heroes.

They would do God's will.

Lundquist felt a buzz of excitement.

This was an old-fashioned manhunt.

Milton was the prey, and he was the hunter.

There was nowhere to hide.

I'm coming for you, you son of a bitch. I'm coming for you, and I'm going to shoot you dead.

Chapter 29

MILTON WOKE. It was dark, he thought, and then he saw that it wasn't, that light was edging in through the gaps in the thatched screen propped against the overhang, obscuring the sun. He closed his eyes for a moment, uncertain where he was and how he had come to be here, and tried to stitch together the fragments of memories that he could recall. The sound of water from the rushing river was audible, a steady musical tinkle, and it all came back to him in a rush. He surged upright, cracking his head against the rocky overhang. He lowered himself again, touching his scalp, blood staining his fingertips.

Wonderful.

The fire had worked its way through the logs and branches and had reduced them to a blackened pile of ash, just a few embers left. Milton swung his legs around and pressed up with his arm. The rush of pain was sudden and shocking, and he remembered the gunshot wound.

He remembered. The crazy rush of last night, the flight in the RV, the train, hiding out in the crop as the police searched for him, the man whose neck he had snapped, the sprint into the woods.

He crouched down next to the pit and blew on the embers to nurse them, gently sprinkling the rest of the tinder across them and then nurturing the flames that resulted, adding the rest of his store of dry vegetation and, when that was alight, the smaller twigs. He had thought that the thatch was thick enough to offer shelter, but he had either miscalculated or the wind had shifted overnight, because now the rocky wall was damp with moisture, and his clothes were wet again. He laid a thicker log onto the merry fire, nursed it alight, and then took off his jacket and trousers and draped them across the branch again to try to dry out the worst of the damp.

He sat back down on his bed and gingerly raised his left arm so that he could look at the damage in the light. He carefully removed the dressings. The entry wound hadn't become infected. The exit wound, though, was different. The jagged gash was unpleasant to look at, and it smelled bad, too. The flesh at the edges was black and rotting, most likely already dead. He would have to do something about it before it got too much worse.

And then he remembered.

Ellie.

Mallory and Arthur.

Shit, he thought. *Shit*.

What had he blundered into?

What should he do?

His instincts told him to get going right now, to flee, to set his back to the sun and just head west. He had the benefit of a decent head start and a detailed training in just this sort of warfare. He would be able to live off the land until he was far enough away to find a town and work out, as discreetly as he could, what had happened back in Truth.

But he couldn't do that.

He couldn't leave them behind.

It wasn't difficult to put it all together. Lundquist had released the four men, for a reason Milton couldn't yet discern, and then he had started to collect the people who knew the fugitives had been caught.

Mallory, Arthur, Ellie, and him.

Lester?

There was a chance that the others were dead already.

But he couldn't leave without knowing.

And he had given them his word.

He would go back for them.

Milton's word meant something to him.

He had made Lundquist a promise, too.

He would kill him and the others who had allied themselves with him.

ONCE HE was satisfied that the fire was properly alight again, he collected the pistol he had taken from the body of the dead cop, and checked the magazine. Empty. He had hoped that he had been dreaming that part, the part where he used his last bullet to start a fire, but clearly not. Practically unarmed, then. All he had was the kitchen knife.

Fair enough.

He stepped around the thatched screen.

He paused for a moment and listened: nothing, save the rustle of the wind through the leaves at the foot of the ravine below him.

He looked up, noticing, with discomfort, that the thin column of smoke rising from the chimney was already visible. Never mind. He wouldn't be staying here for very long. He looked at his surroundings with the benefit of daylight. The rise through the ravine was gentle up until this point, but it became steeper the further it climbed, several spots angling towards the vertical with the water splashing down in small falls and goat trails picking a path upwards. The trees and underbrush on either side thinned out a little, too, but larger trees remained all the way to the top of the ridge.

Milton reached for the overhang and hauled himself onto it, then climbed up another fifteen feet until he was near to the top of the ravine wall.

He crouched down, his eyes fixed to the south, the direction that the police would come from.

He estimated that he had covered two miles last night even though it had felt like more. He tried to put himself into the shoes of his pursuers. They would have discovered the dead man's body, and that would have frightened them. They knew that he was armed, and that, too, would have given them cause for circumspection. If he had been in charge of the pursuit, with the benefit of that limited information, he would have set up a cordon as far along the south side of the forest as he could and then called for reinforcements.

The state police, perhaps.

He would have painted himself as a dangerous fugitive, a cop killer, and flooded the forest with as many men as he could find.

He would have waited until daybreak to start into the trees.

And now he would be coming.

Right now.

The way he saw it, he had two options.

He could run.

Or he could fight.

There was something to be said for running. He had enough of a head start that if he went now and moved as quickly as he could, he would stand a decent chance of getting clear. He expected that Lundquist would have divided the forest into grid squares and then set up a quarantine to contain him within the squares that he could realistically have reached last night. There would be police there already, but the longer he waited, the more there would be. If he went now, he was confident he would be able to break through the cordon and get away.

But Milton knew himself too well for that, and he had already discounted it. There was no point pretending that running was ever going to be an option.

Lundquist had killed the sheriff. The boys he was sheltering had killed a guard during a raid. They had very nearly killed him. They had beaten Ellie. They had taken Mallory and Arthur. There was no telling what they would do to them, and that was assuming that they were still alive. Milton couldn't leave until he had either rescued them or taken revenge in their names.

No. Milton couldn't run.

He looked out to the south, to the wide swathe of green and to the town just visible in the distance. Ellie, Mallory, and Arthur were out there.

Lundquist was out there, too, in the trees, raising a posse and coming after him.

No. He couldn't run.

But he could fight.

Milton clambered carefully down the slope, loose scree skittering ahead of him, and slipped back behind the screen again. He dressed, his clothes still damp. He collected the first-aid kit and pushed it back into the bag. He broke the fire apart, kicking dirt and stones over it until the flames died, and then stepped back outside and started to climb.

He would head north and find somewhere to make a stand. He would take out his pursuers, one by one, and he would get the information that he needed.

What was happening in Truth?

Where were Ellie and the Stantons?

And then he would go and get them.

Chapter 30

THEY BROKE camp and left soon after the dogs had arrived. There was no sense in waiting any longer. Lundquist thought there was a decent prospect that they might be able to run Milton down by the end of the day, and he wanted to get started as soon as possible to put this whole sorry mess behind them.

The terrain sloped gently up, heading to the hills and modest mountains that provided a natural margin between the land and the shores of the Lake of the Clouds. It was still reasonably level down here, and Walker Price guided the dogs onto a path that Lundquist knew would be easily passable for the next mile. It was clear enough to jog, and he found that he was quickly covered in a sheen of sweat.

"You remember the last time we chased someone out here?" said Walker between breaths.

"Sure do."

"Not that different to this, was it?"

"Same thing."

That set him to thinking. It had been half a dozen years ago. The man, Lundquist remembered he was called Gus, he had a trailer in the park next to where the Stantons had parked their RV, and the word was that he was into little girls. When the Lattimers' daughter didn't come home from school one afternoon, Lester had gone around to Gus's trailer to talk to him, hopefully to cross him off his list. He had driven off, followed pretty much the same route as Milton had, and had gotten into the woods before they could stop him. Lester had raised a posse, all of the deputies plus Walker and his dogs and another ten local men, and they had gone after him. They had tracked him six miles north to the lake. They had found his body slumped against the trunk of a tree, his shotgun in his mouth.

The little girl had come home two days later. Turned out that Gus had nothing to do with it. Lundquist hadn't wasted too much time thinking about it. He had been running from something.

Guilty conscience.

That was good enough for him.

"How far do you think he's managed to get?"

"Not far," he said.

It *couldn't* be far. Milton was wounded. He would have had to find somewhere to stop if only to treat the wound to his arm. How far would he have been able to travel? Say he kept going until midnight. That would have been a two-hour head start. Lundquist added another hour onto that to be charitable. Give him three. A man who didn't know these woods would struggle to head in a consistent direction. There were ravines and draws you could go into that couldn't be exited at the other end. There would be dead ends and double backs that would neutralise some of that advantage. He had no food and no drink, so that would slow him down. And then there was the gunshot wound. Lundquist figured that a healthy man with a knowledge of the paths and trails around here would have been able to move at two miles an hour. But Milton, with all those disadvantages, he would have struggled to keep half of that pace. If he was right, the maximum Milton would have been able to travel before he stopped for the night was two miles.

Two miles was nothing to Walker's dogs. They had a great spoor from the clothes in the bag, and their noses were so sensitive that Milton would never be able to lose them. He could be ten miles away, but, for all the good that would do him, he might as well be just behind the next tree. The hounds were anxiously tugging the leash, yapping to each other in excitement, and if they were to be released, Lundquist didn't doubt that they would sprint right to him like arrows to a target.

The path wound left and right and up and down, skirting the trunks of bigger trees and sending them through the middle of the underbrush. Lundquist was older than the others, but he made a point of keeping himself in shape, and his habit of taking a run first thing in the morning was starting to look pretty smart now. He settled into an easy stride, his waist angled down and forwards a little so that gravity could give him a friendly boost in the right direction. Even Michael and the other younger men were beginning to blow, but Lundquist knew he would be able to keep going for another half an hour without having to think about stopping to catch his breath. That brought a smile to his lips.

They reached a stream that ran through a small meadow. The leash went slack as the dogs stopped and started to circle, their noses to the ground.

"What are they doing?" Tom Chandler asked.

Walker reached down, unfastened Blue from the master leash, and handed her off to the younger man.

"They've lost the scent. You ask me, he went through the water to put them off." He pointed to the other side. "Take Blue over there."

"Aw, Lieutenant, do I have to?"

"Get over there," he snapped.

Chandler did as he was told, splashing through the thigh-high water with the dog swimming determinedly beside him. They emerged on the other side, and Blue immediately put her nose to the ground, scuffled at the grass with her paws, and then started to bark.

"She's picked it up again."

The other dogs were agitated, keen to follow their sister over to the other bank, and Walker led them into the water. It was icy, the current was strong, and the footing on the bed was treacherous. Lundquist stepped carefully, submerged deep enough at one point that his balls were in the water, the cold taking his breath away, and then he was out. The dogs clambered after him, shaking their coats dry and then pulling urgently at the leash.

They set off again. The terrain started to climb, and they slowed their pace.

Lundquist jogged alongside Leland.

"This guy is serious, isn't he?" the younger man asked.

"He's military."

"How do you know that?"

"He told Lester. British Special Forces."

"Shit, Morten."

"So what? There's ten of us."

Leland didn't reply.

"You get anything else on him?"

"I ran the prints that Lester took when he had him in overnight."

"And?"

"Got one hit. He was arrested in Texas three months ago."

"For what?"

"Assault. Another bar brawl."

Lundquist clucked his tongue against his teeth. "You'd think he'd learn his lesson."

"Maybe not."

"They get anything else on him?"

"File said that the feds came and claimed him the day after. This is where it gets real interesting, though. The sheriff down there, he wasn't on duty when Milton was arrested. He came in the next day, heard the story about the FBI and why his deputy had let him out of his custody, thought he'd check it over, and called the local office down there. Turns out there was no record of Milton on any of their active cases. When he described the female agent who got him out, they said they didn't have anyone there who even halfway fitted the description."

Lundquist shook his head. "What are we dealing with here?"

"I'll leave the thinking to you," Leland replied. "It's not what I'm good at."

"Enough with the sass," Lundquist said, but he was too intrigued to be irritated for more than a moment. "Maybe he works for the government?"

Leland jogged on, breathing heavily.

The government? Maybe he did. Wouldn't that be something? Did it change anything? Only if they let him get out of the woods alive, and Lundquist did not intend to allow that. Perhaps there were complications involved here, but, at the end of all of it, they would just say that John Milton had killed Lester Grogan, Lars Olsen, George Pelham, and the agent. He had killed them, fired on the rest of them, and then run.

What else were they supposed to do? Let him go?

God had placed John Milton in Lundquist's path. A final obstacle to clear. A final test before the glory of what He had instructed him to do.

The dogs pulled harder on the lead, and Walker's arm was soon pulled straight, parallel with the ground. "Good dogs," he called down to them. "*Good* dogs. You take us to him."

Chapter 31

JOHN MILTON RAN.

He stopped only to drink from the river and to eat. He saw an elderberry bush, and he stopped next to it, plucking off a handful of berries and stuffing them hungrily into his mouth. The juices were sweet and acidic, the tang making his mouth water. He hadn't eaten properly since the venison two nights ago. That was going to have to be remedied sooner rather than later. He wouldn't be able to run forever on an empty stomach.

He took off his shirt and wrapped it around his waist. He wanted to let some air get to the wounds on his arm. The pain was still there, and he had been reminded of it by the jolt that greeted every upward swing of his arm. He turned back and tried to assess how far he had travelled. Two miles in the last hour? The arm had compromised his stride. He was covering much less ground than he would have liked.

He set off again, pushing himself harder, gritting his teeth to ignore the pain. After another twenty minutes, though, the pain got worse. He couldn't ignore it.

He stopped by the water's edge, dunked his face, and then took off his jacket and sweater and examined his arm again.

The entry wound in his bicep, neat and circular, was healing. He had plucked out the worst of the debris. That wound would heal without the need for too much intervention, at least for the next few days.

He turned over his arm. His tricep was worse. Much worse. The flesh around the edges of the hole had become blackened and necrotic. It was dead, and unless he did something about it quickly, he would develop a fever, and that would stop him dead in his tracks. Worse, if left untreated, the wound would eventually become gangrenous, and he might lose the arm. He had to deal with it.

HE SMELLED the deer before he saw it. The body was just a short distance from the path, slumped down in the brush with a large bite taken out of its hindquarters. A wolf, Milton thought. It reeked of rot and decay, and he had to fight the urge to gag. He covered his mouth with the sleeve of his jacket and crouched down next to the body. He looked at the sticky, fibrous remains. A mess of white and brown maggots, each of them the size of half a fingernail, wriggled and seethed.

Maggots. Milton knew his battlefield medicine, and he knew his military history. It had worked for injured soldiers in the Napoleonic Wars. Maybe it would work for him. And, he knew, maggot therapy had gained credence recently. Doctors were using them again to clean the gangrenous feet of diabetics, saving them from amputation. The cleanliness in those circumstances couldn't have been much more different than this, but beggars couldn't be choosers. He didn't have much choice.

Milton plucked out a couple of them and held them in the palm of his hand. They looked like blowfly maggots. That would do. He reached back down to the carcass and picked out twenty of them, held them loosely in his fist and then rinsed them in the river, shaking them gently to clean them as best he could. They were far from sterile, but that was out of the question today. He'd risk the *possibility* of infection against the *certainty* that things would get worse if he let the wound continue to fester.

He winced at the thought of what he was about to do, chided himself for his squeamishness, and dropped the maggots into the wound. He fixed the dressing and wound the bandage around it again.

Chapter 32

LUNDQUIST LOOKED up into the sky and knew, with a local's sure and certain knowledge, that the storm would be back again before the hour was out. The clouds were the deepest and angriest blacks, solid blocks of ink that gathered at the horizon and then rolled at them as though they were the outriders of a hurricane.

"Where is he?" he said in frustration, louder than he had intended.

"Can't be far," Michael said.

Lundquist ground his teeth. He had been saying that since they had started.

The dogs had stayed on his scent all morning. There had been no obvious attempt to lose them. His track led them along the banks of the little river, climbing ever upwards into the slopes that led to the larger hills and then, eventually, to the shallow peaks. There had been no more attempts to go through the water to lose the dogs. It was if he had stopped caring.

Yes, Lundquist had been surprised that Milton was still ahead of them. He was wounded, and they had moved quickly, barely stopping. The men had been running with their weapons ready for the last two hours, kept alert by Lundquist's barked exhortations should their focus waver.

Milton had killed four men already.

Damned if he was going to kill any more.

They had been following the gentle upward slope, and Lundquist was feeling it in his legs and buttocks. Leland Mulligan had been blowing hard for the last hour, and Walker Price was damp with sweat. Michael was the fittest of them all, though. He had loped ahead of them, outpacing the dogs on occasion, diverting a few feet from the path in the event that Milton had left a more obvious sign that he had passed through.

The path dropped into a hollow that was bordered by slopes of loose shale. They followed a stream up the other side, the incline becoming steeper and steeper, the water sheltered by the steep shoulders of a ravine. The dogs pulled harder, and Lundquist recognised in their agitated behaviour that they were close.

"Weapons ready!"

Lundquist looked around. He knew the woods, and he remembered this spot. They called it the Whitefish Trail. The climb that faced them was steep, but there was a narrow path that cut upwards that could be accessed without too much difficulty.

He tightened his grip on his rifle.

Tom Chandler was up front. "Hey!" he cried out. Walker hauled the dogs back onto their haunches.

The dogs had led them to the face of the ravine on the right hand side. They had found an outcrop that reached out from the rock wall.

Lundquist hurried across. There was a thatched screen propped against the rock face. Chandler was on his haunches behind it, poking at the remains of a fire with a stick. Walker settled down next to him and looked.

"What do you think?" Lundquist said.

"Yes." Walker nodded. "Look at that. He's been here."

Milton had dug a fire pit and lined it with rocks. The pit was full of ashes, and there were the unconsumed remains of a larger log that had been pushed away to die down. Walker disturbed the ashes all the way down to the bottom of the pit, but there was no sign of life at all. The fire had died out two or three hours ago, but that didn't matter.

Milton had been here.

Lundquist stood, his knees complaining a little, and turned back to the others. They were gathered around the outcrop.

Lundquist was about to speak when there came a tremendous thunderclap. He looked up: the black clouds had sealed off the last square of blue sky and now rolled black and unending as far as he could see. The temperature had plunged, and then, just as he crammed his wide-brimmed hat onto his head, the rain started again.

"All right, men," he called out, watching as they prepared their clothes for the change in the weather. "This is where he camped last night."

"How's he stayed so far ahead of us?" Michael called out.

"Pay attention!" Lundquist called out. "The dogs have a good scent. They've had a good one all morning. Maybe he stayed here for less time than we thought he did, maybe he's just ahead of us. Maybe he isn't as badly hurt as I think he is. I don't know. It doesn't matter. What I do know is we are going to find him, and, when we do, we're going to make him wish he didn't drag us out in this weather."

"What are we doing now?"

"We stick with it. We keep going until we find him."

Tom Chandler groaned.

"What?" Lundquist said. "You want to stay? You forget what he did back in the field before we came after him? Think it'd be a good idea to wait here on your own? Don't be so stupid."

Chandler looked away, chastised. Lundquist adjusted his hat, working the brim down, and nodded to Walker Price. The dogs leapt to follow the spoor again. Milton's scent might as well have been painted on the path in fluorescent paint. He wasn't far ahead, Lundquist knew it.

Chapter 33

HE KEPT RUNNING.

A large ridge loomed up out of the trees, a sudden protrusion of sixty feet of bedrock granite that cut through the green with no obvious way around. Milton kept running towards it, pounding across the boggy trail. He heard the sound of the water from half a mile away, a shushing hiss that grew in strength the nearer he came to it. It became louder: a murmur, to a groan, to a roar. The trail cut through a stand of trees. Milton followed it, tracing a path around a gentle oxbow to the left and then to the right, and then he came to the waterfall.

He stopped and looked up.

He found himself in a little hollow, the river pooling in the bottom before draining away in the direction that he had come. It was verdant and fresh, with stands of ash and fir gathered on the shallow slopes. The ridge shot up ahead of him, more of a sheer cliff now that he was closer to it, blocking his way. The river rushed over the top. The falls consisted of two separate drops spaced about two hundred yards apart. The upper falls dropped about sixty feet; the lower about forty. The soft, layered, river rock was worn and sculpted, finished almost to resemble hand-rubbed pewter. It was formed into a number of channels, ledges, potholes, and other unique configurations. The river was funnelled between two sheer rocky lips and then was sent gushing out over the steep drops to crash against the rocks below.

There was no obvious way to go on.

Milton followed the river right up to the falls, treading carefully on the slippery, lichen-crusted stone. The ridge on either side of him was steep, too difficult to scale. He looked up. The falls offered a sheer drop into the plunge pool and the rocks that encircled it, mist and spray swirling around him.

He turned and looked due south, out over the slopes of the hills, high above the terraces of trees below, and tried to place himself in relation to where he expected his pursuers to be. They would have started to follow him by now. He guessed that he had a lead on them, but he couldn't guess how long that lead would last. Not long, surely. He was injured. He didn't know the terrain, and he didn't have a map. They would have none of those disabilities.

Could he retrace his path and find another way around?

And then, just audible in the quiet of the morning, he heard barking.

They were tracking him with dogs.

Milton allowed himself a wry smile. He had expected it, but it was hardly fair.

Unless he was able to throw the dogs off, he knew that they would follow him relentlessly until they had him. He wondered what they were using to give them his spoor, and then he remembered his pack back in Lester Grogan's office. He chided himself. He should have taken it with him when Lars Olsen had offered to drive him to the hospital. Apart from making it more difficult to track him, his pack had everything that he needed to stay out in the woods. Was he getting rusty? Should he have expected trouble? Leaving it behind had been negligent. In a situation like this, that could very easily be fatal.

The dogs barked again. They made up his mind.

He couldn't turn back.

The hounds would have taken Lundquist north, following his trail. They had probably reached last night's camp by now. They would keep coming. He only had a short lead on them now. How long could he stay ahead?

Not long.

And if he was going to make a stand, this wasn't the time or the place.

He turned back to the waterfall again. He needed to put a barrier between him and them that would slow them down.

The dogs would lead Lundquist right up here, but that would be as far as they could go.

He would give Lundquist two choices: either leave the dogs and send his men up the cliff in pursuit or retrace his steps and find another way to ascend the ridge.

Milton had to climb.

HE WENT right up to the rock and laid his hands out flat, feeling the moisture, the slickness, the damp air below him reaching all the way up to his head and beyond. He shrugged the bag from his shoulder. He wouldn't be able to climb with it safely.

He considered his ascent. His left arm was sore and weak, and wouldn't be much use. The rocks would be slippery and wet, too, and there were only a few decent handholds that he could identify from below. He would have to hope that he was strong enough to support himself, and that he would find enough suitable grips as he climbed up. It was a gamble. If he was too weak or if there was no suitable path, he wasn't sure that he would be able to climb back down again.

And he might fall.

He took a deep breath, and bracing his hands on two suitable handholds just above him, he bore his weight. His left arm screamed with the effort, more than he was expecting, and the sudden pain dimmed his vision for a moment. He found a handhold above, and then another, and then another, slotting his feet into nooks and niches, jamming his toes onto narrow ledges.

Thunder boomed.

Ten feet.

Twenty feet.

His arm collapsed, and he lurched backwards, his feet cycling helplessly through the air. He shot out his right hand, and his fingers lashed around the roots of a sapling just up above, anchoring himself there until the pain cleared. He breathed in and out, sweat washing into his eyes, and gathered himself.

Thirty feet.

Halfway.

He tried to find another foothold. The toe of his right boot jarred against the face. He angled his foot and jammed it into a crack. Then, trusting that his foot would hold, he let go of the trunk and reached his right hand up. His fingers fastened around a spur of rock, and he heaved up again. The spur was wet and slick, but his fingers found their grip, and he collected his balance again.

Forty feet.

He looked down and saw the pool below him. It looked even farther down now from his lofty perch, but the jagged rocks looked bigger, hungry teeth ready to devour him, distorted by the spray and the hurried glance that was all he dared risk. He remembered the climbs he had undertaken during Selection, up and down more challenging rock faces than this one.

But, a contrary voice reminded him, *you were younger then. You were in your twenties. It wasn't raining like this. You weren't injured. You had two good arms.*

He reached up as far as he could with his left hand and found another grip. He jerked his head around to the right and looked up again, identifying what he hoped might be another suitable grip. He closed his eyes, trusted his judgment, opened his eyes, released his handhold, and pushed up. His right foot slipped off the rock and dropped down, and he fell. His right hand missed the grip. He had a split second to anticipate the pain as his left arm had to bear all of his weight, but knowing that it was coming was only a minor assistance, for the pain, the incredible depth of it, drowned him in a tide so complete that he was only barely aware of the yell of effort that was impossible to suppress. His consciousness dimmed again, but his fingers knotted around the rock and held firm, his left foot sliding down the wet rock until his ankle clashed against something raised and sharp. He swung from his left hand, his fingers beginning to slip, and scrabbled up again with his left boot, ignoring the pain in his shin and ankle until his toes were wedged in a cleft and his right hand had found a trailing vine.

Fifty feet.

Nearly.

He stopped there for ten seconds, pressed against the damp rock face, breathing in deeply, the pain lighting up his left arm and all the way down the side of his body. The water boomed angrily from the plunge pool below him, spray billowing up at him. He craned his neck to the right again and saw another handhold five feet across the face and, above that, a narrow shelf that would fit his boot perfectly. He didn't allow himself the time to question his decision. He yanked hard on the vine and pushed off with his left foot, scrambling across the face before gravity clutched at him and tore him down, his right hand brushing against the grip and missing it, his boot crashing onto the shelf. He reached up again and found the handhold, his fingers fastening around the sharp rock so tight that he cut himself, pressing gratefully against the rock again.

He heard the dogs again, but they were louder now, much louder.

It sounded as if they were right below him.

The gunshot cracked out from the woods below, and the bullet winged off the rock a few inches below him.

He had misjudged the sound of the dogs. They had been much closer than he had guessed.

"Fire!" he heard Lundquist shout. "Bring him down!"

Another round cracked off the rock face, breaking off sharp little fragments of flint and drawing sparks.

He was helpless.

He blinked sweat out of his eyes and looked straight up.

It was easier from here. The face was pocked with small niches and nooks, and he found that he could ascend with just one arm, reaching up to secure himself before stretching out with his legs until his feet found the places to bear his weight. He quickened his ascent, salty sweat covering his face and dripping into his eyes and mouth. The water crashed and roared as if frustrated that he had managed to negotiate the climb.

Every second that passed was another that he expected to be shot.

Another round went just wide, slamming into the wall.

He hauled himself up the final five feet, found another foothold halfway up, and then clambered the rest of the way, pulling himself over the lip of rock and rolling clear. He was breathing heavily, and his arm was livid with pain. He closed his eyes, catching his breath for a moment, before he slid back to the lip and risked a half-second glimpse below.

Lundquist was down there, staring up at him. He saw Michael Callow, Thomas Chandler, and the other cop who had been at the Stanton RV. He saw another six men, counting them instinctively. Three dogs, rearing up on their hind legs, howled at him. Lundquist had his rifle raised, and he altered the aim quickly, loosing off a wild shot that flew high and wide and handsome. The other men raised their weapons and fired, but Milton was out of sight behind the lip of the cliff and safe.

"Cease firing!" Lundquist yelled.

The firing continued.

"*Stop!*"

The firing stopped, memorialised by the brief echoes that played out as the reports bounced back off the rock.

"Milton!"

He stayed where he was, on his back, taking deep gulps of air into his lungs.

"*Milton!*"

He rolled over onto his belly and shouted down, "I'm here."

"You can't run from me."

"I've done all right so far."

"You can't *keep* running."

"I'm not going to run, Lundquist. I told you what I was going to do. I'm going to kill all of you."

"No," he yelled back. "You're *not*." His voice was ragged with sudden anger and frustration. Milton was pleased to hear that. He could be manipulated.

"The man I killed in the field. You find his weapon?"

"George was an idiot. Never carried spare mags. Whatever was in the gun, that was it. You've already fired at least one round. How many you got left? Five? Six?"

"Climb up and find out. I'll wait for you."

He crawled backwards, away from the edge.

"You think that's the only way up the ridge? We'll loop around. The dogs have your scent, and we've quarantined the whole area. You're trapped. You can't run. Give up. Toss the gun and then come down after it."

Milton pushed up to a crouch and then stood, the blood rushing from his head. He was dizzy for a moment, bobbing down again until the weakness had passed.

"Milton!"

He stood and started to jog to the north, following the slope as it climbed away from the plateau.

"Milton!"

He picked up speed. He kept on going.

"*Milton!*"

Lundquist's voice was lost amidst the rush and roar of the water, baffled by the rise of the cliff, but even as he ran, Milton could still hear his anger.

Chapter 34

SPECIAL AGENT Ellie Flowers slept for an hour at most. It was cold and uncomfortable in the shed, but it wasn't the discomfort that kept her awake. It was the apprehension about what might happen to them when the sun came up.

She knew that dawn would be early. It was too dark to see her watch, so she waited impatiently for the hours to pass. Arty fell asleep in his sister's lap, snoring lightly. Ellie talked to Mallory for a little while, both of them keeping their voices low so that they didn't disturb him. There was something about their predicament that demanded the hush of a conspiratorial approach, too. It was as if Morris Finch or Magrethe Olsen or any of the others who were involved in the plot stood on the other side of the wall, eavesdropping on their conversation.

They spoke about what had happened to them and about what might happen next. Mallory suggested that they would be able to have a better look around the shed when it grew light. Perhaps they would find something that would enable them to cut through Ellie's handcuffs. Then, she said, maybe the three of them would stand a chance of overpowering their captors and getting away.

Ellie wasn't optimistic. Mallory was barely more than a girl, and her brother, although full grown, was too easily distracted to be relied upon. And she was still cuffed.

Their conversation had moved onto John Milton. Mallory said that she had heard Finch and Olsen talking, that Morten Lundquist was going to deal with him. On that score, Ellie had more confidence. Milton was tough and, even in the short time they had spent together she had seen that he was cunning and savvy. And he had killed two men. He was dangerous.

Would he leave them?

She didn't think so.

But then, as they fell quiet and the hours drew on, she began to doubt herself. Even if he had been able to get away, where was he now? Why would he come back? What was there to stop him from getting to safety himself? He didn't know them, not really. He didn't know her. The night by the lake might just have been sex to him. He didn't owe her anything.

Eventually she persuaded herself that their position was hopeless. Mallory must have been the same, too. Ellie knew that the girl was awake, lying quietly against the wall next to her, but she, like her, could no longer see the point in talking about something in which she invested no hope. There was no point in pretending otherwise: they were in a terrible, terrible position.

Eventually, Mallory slept. Ellie heard her breathing change. She dropped off herself soon after, but the sleep didn't last.

Thin shafts of sunlight started to lance into the shed through tiny holes in the wall and the ceiling. Mallory had been resting against Ellie's shoulder and she raised her head.

Ellie moved around so that she was sitting on her right leg, got her feet beneath her and pushed so that her back slid up the wall. Her muscles were tight and sore, kept in the same position for so long, and she stretched out to try to loosen them up. She looked up at the walls and ceiling. The light was coming in from loose joins between the planks that had been assembled to form the walls. The gaps could only have been a few fractions of an inch wide at most, but when the light that they admitted was aggregated, there was a dim illumination that was enough for her to explore the space. She edged away from the wall.

The shed was twenty paces in length and ten paces in width. There was a large lawnmower parked up against the wall in the middle of the space and, next to it, a plough that was still caked in dried mud. There were several barrels and boxes, the light too dark to make out the stencilled words that might have identified their contents. There was a strong smell emanating from them, ammonia perhaps. Fertiliser? They were on a farm, after all. She looked for tools, something that they could use to work at her cuffs or the lock on the door, but there was nothing. She walked to the wide door that they had arrived through and pushed at it with her shoulder. There was a little give in the lock, but she could feel the door butting up against something outside. She had seen the brackets out there when they had thrown them inside and guessed that the door had been locked *and* barred. It felt secure. She turned to look for another door, but there was none. She looked up to the ceiling for a trapdoor and saw nothing. There was nothing in the floor that might suggest a cellar.

She sighed in frustration. It wasn't surprising. They had taken off the cuffs on Mallory and her brother. They were hardly likely to do that if there was an easy way out of the shed. There was nothing else to do but to face facts: they were stuck.

"Anything?" Mallory called out softly.

"Not that I can see."

"Look at these."

Mallory had found a box of pamphlets and poorly printed newsletters. The light had strengthened enough to read the titles: The Plot Against Christianity, The Thirteenth Tribe, You Gentiles, White Power, The Talmud, The New Jewish Encyclopaedia, The Christian Patriot Crusader, The Klansman, Aryan Nations' Newsletter, the Christian Vanguard Newsletter.

"What is this all about?"

"I don't know," Ellie said, although she was starting to get a pretty good idea.

It was almost too late by the time she heard the noise from outside. There came the rattle of a metal bar being drawn through the brackets and then the click of the lock. Mallory stuffed the leaflets back into the box, and they hurried back to the wall and dropped to the floor beside Arthur.

The door swung open, and light swamped the darkness.

Ellie blinked furiously, trying to adjust to the sudden glare.

Morris Finch was silhouetted in the doorway. He was holding a shotgun.

"Morning," he said. Was he aware of how foolish his good manners sounded? "Did you manage to get some sleep?"

Ellie stood again. "You want to think very carefully about what you're doing. I'm a federal agent. You know the penalty for the murder of a federal law enforcement officer is death, don't you?"

"No one's talking about murder," he said uncomfortably.

"No, but we *are* talking about kidnapping, right?"

"You just need to help us out."

"Let us out. Let me have your van. I'll see to it that you're treated leniently."

"Can't do that. Too much has happened for that."

"What then? It *is* murder, then?"

"No…"

"What else is there if you won't let us out?"

"It's not my decision to make."

"Who, then?"

"The colonel," he said, looking away. "He's in charge."

"Who?"

"Lundquist."

"What do you mean, the colonel?"

Finch shrugged uncomfortably. The man's eyes were dead, his pale face expressionless. Ellie stared at him and he stared back.

She tried again. "What do you mean?"

"He's in charge."

"Of *what?*"

Finch didn't answer.

"Where is he?"

"In the woods."

"Why?"

"Your friend, the Englishman, he's out looking for him."

Ellie felt a buzz of hope. "What happened?"

Finch took a step into the barn. He was morbidly obese, an enormous gold and silver belt buckle holding up jeans big as spinnaker sails. His doughy face became visible from out of the shadows. "He got away last night," he said, his voice a whisper. "The colonel and the other men have gone to track him down."

"You have to let us out, Mr. Finch."

"How do you know my name?" he said, and then, looking at Mallory, he added, "She told you."

He was a little simple, Ellie saw. She noted that for future reference.

"Milton will go and get help. If you haven't freed us by the time the FBI gets here, there won't be anything I can do to help you. You'll be treated just like the others. Kidnapping of a federal officer, at minimum. You know how long they'll lock you up for that?"

Finch seemed not to hear her. "Morten tricked him. He said they were in a car crash. He was going to be driven out of town and shot, but it didn't go down like that. He worked it out, somehow, and he got away."

"I know they tricked him. I was in the office when they left." Ellie looked at Finch and saw the faraway look on his face. "Are you listening to me, Mr. Finch?"

He wasn't listening. "There's something you need to know. The officer who took Milton out there was Lars Olsen."

"So?"

"You met his mother last night. Magrethe. Her and his father, Seth, they live out here."

"And?"

"Milton killed Lars. There was a wreck up on the road out of town. They had to cut Lars out of it. He's dead. Magrethe was all for coming in here and shooting all of you. She would have done it, too, except I managed to persuade her that it wasn't a good idea. But I don't know how long I can keep that up. What I'm saying is, you have to do what we want you to do. If you don't, there won't be anything I can do to help you. We have work to do, God's work, and I won't let anything stop that from being done, but I'd rather you didn't have to die for it."

"You can let us out," Ellie repeated, but then they heard the sound of footsteps approaching the barn, and Finch looked at her with urgent eyes, imploring her to be quiet.

Magrethe Olsen arrived before she could press him any further. She was carrying another shotgun in the crook of her left arm, and she had a fierce expression on her face. She stepped inside, reached out for a light switch and slapped her hand against it. There were two naked bulbs suspended from the ceiling high above, and they flickered on. She shut the door and turned back to them.

"The man you were with in the woods. John Milton. Who is he?"

"I don't know," Ellie said.

"It'd be better if you played ball," Finch warned them, his newly assertive tone more for Magrethe's benefit than for theirs.

Mallory stepped forwards. "Why do you want to know?"

"Tell me."

The girl had a gloating tone to her voice. "Giving you trouble, is he?"

Finch frowned at her. Ellie turned and gave the tiniest shake of her head. She could see from Finch's discomfort and Magrethe's anger that it was true, Milton was still out there, and for the first time in hours, she felt a flicker of optimism that maybe they were not completely lost.

Mallory didn't take the hint. "He'll give you more trouble by the time he's through."

Magrethe slapped Mallory across the face with the back of her right hand.

"Hey!" Arthur started to his feet, but Magrethe turned the shotgun towards him, and Mallory, panicked, reached for his sleeve and yanked him back behind her.

"We don't know who he is," Ellie said, trying to get the woman to turn her attention back onto her again.

Magrethe swung the shotgun around and aimed it straight at her chest. "You want to know what your friend Mr. Milton did last night? He killed my son. So you want to think very carefully, give it a lot of thought, how much lip you want to be giving me. I guess you found out plenty about him when you were out in the woods going after the boys. So you better tell me, right now, exactly who he is. What is he doing here?"

Ellie looked at the gun pointed right at her, and swallowed. Finch's warning had not been gratuitous. There was an iron resolve behind the grimace of wrath that animated the woman's face. She *would* shoot her. Ellie had seen that look before. It wasn't a bluff. She had to give her something.

"He's an outdoorsman. He said he's been trekking through the countryside."

"He's more than that. He killed Lars, and then he got clean away into the woods."

"He said he was a soldier."

"Special Forces," Mallory added gleefully.

"Shut up, Mallory," Ellie said.

Magrethe jabbed forwards with the shotgun. "And?"

"She's right. British Special Forces. He didn't tell us anything else. He's quiet."

"You must have more than that."

"No, that's it. He's private. Believe me, I was interested in knowing more about him after I saw how he brought in Callow and the others, but he wasn't much into talking about himself."

Magrethe frowned. "What you think, Morris?"

"I think she's telling the truth," he said, a little too quickly.

"And I think you're getting soft in your old age, soft as shit. You want to remember what's at stake here. This little bitch, she knows enough to put us all away for the rest of our lives. Shit, they all know enough. We've got God's work to do, and, I don't know, I been thinking about it overnight, and I'm not sure if I can think of one good reason why I don't put bird shot in them right now and feed them to the pigs. You think of a reason why we better not do that?"

Ellie felt an emptiness in her gut. Again, she doubted it was a bluff.

Finch shuffled uncomfortably. "We don't want to do that yet, do we? We got their friend running around in the woods, the Lord knows where he is, but it might be that we need them if he keeps causing trouble. What you'd call leverage. We shoot them now, and we don't have any cards to play. If the colonel wanted them dead, he would've said, right?"

The woman's frowned deepened into an irascible scowl, but he had persuaded her. She took a step back, to the door. "You get to live a little longer, but I'm telling you, if I hear so much as a mouse's fart from in here, I'm going to come back and shoot all of you. I'll be honest with you: I was going to do it this morning. Maybe I still will. You don't want to push your luck." She stepped back outside. "Morris, get your fat ass out here."

The man looked into Ellie's face, his expression eloquent with warning, and then he left the barn, too. Magrethe shut and locked the door, and then they heard the sound of the metal bar as it was slid into its brackets, sealing them inside.

"DON'T PROVOKE THEM."

"I wasn't," Mallory said.

"You were. If you push it too far, they'll shoot us."

Mallory didn't reply.

"I'm *serious*."

"What's happening?" Arty asked plaintively.

"I don't know," Ellie said. "Did they say anything to you when you were at the mine with them?"

"They talked about God a lot."

"What about him?"

"They read out of the Bible at nights."

"Can you remember what they said?"

"Some of it," he said, his face brightening. "I got a good memory, everyone says so."

"Tell us."

"'And I saw heaven opened, and behold a white horse; and he that sat upon him was called Faithful and True, and in righteousness he doth judge and make war.'"

"Anything else?"

"'These shall make war with the Lamb, and the Lamb shall overcome them: for he is Lord of lords, and King of kings: and they that are with him are called, and chosen, and faithful.'"

Arthur was ready to go on when they all heard the low rumble of a big, powerful engine.

Mallory hurried across to the wall that faced in the direction that the noise was coming from.

"What are they doing?" Ellie said.

"The truck. Come and look."

Arty helped Ellie to her feet, and they went across to the gap in the wall that Mallory was looking through. She put her eye to the wall and looked out into the yard.

The big Freightliner had been driven into the space between the two barns. There was a trailer, a forty-foot unit, with four men working around the back of it. A collection of large metal drums and barrels had been delivered to the yard on a tractor trailer. The Freightliner's loading panel had been lowered, and the men were heaving the drums from the trailer into the semi. The drums were the same as the ones that she had seen in the barn.

"What are they doing?"

"I don't know," Ellie said.

She didn't know, not for sure, but she had an idea.

"What's in those barrels?"

"Can't tell."

She walked across to the barrels that she had seen earlier. Now that the light was better, she could make out the words.

NITROMETHANE 99.5% MIN
FLAMMABLE LIQUID

"What is it?"

"Fuel."

"Why are they loading it into the back of the truck?"

She didn't say, but she could guess. The Oklahoma City atrocity had been part of the syllabus she had studied at the academy in Quantico. She remembered reading the testimony from the trial of the bombers, and in particular, she remembered how they had constructed their massive truck bomb.

They had used a Ryder rental truck, a sixteen-foot City Van with a six thousand-pound capacity. The explosion that they had triggered was so big that it had turned a city block into a war zone.

The Freightliner outside was forty feet long. Nearly three times bigger. What was the capacity? Five times more? Ten times?

"We've got to get out of here," Ellie said.

Chapter 35

MILTON RAN for another five hours, hardly stopping. He didn't know how long it would take Lundquist to find another way up the ridge. He hadn't seen an obvious path before he had made the climb. He worked on the assumption that the ascent and his bluff from the top had bought him another hour or, if he was lucky, another two. Lundquist would find his way up eventually, and those dogs would pick up his spoor again.

But that was all right.

He wanted them to.

He wanted Lundquist to follow him.

His path bisected the old railroad tracks that they had followed on the first journey to the mine. It was only the day before yesterday, but it already seemed like much longer ago. He passed the Little Carp River and the wreck of the Model A, and then after pounding uphill for another hour, he made the top of the rise and looked down at the Lake of the Clouds. It lived up to its name this time. The cloud bank was low, a carpet of greys and blacks that provided a ceiling just a few thousand feet over his head. Patches of mist and wispy cloud were lower still, almost on the water itself, and rain lashed into him. Visibility was limited.

That was all right, too.

If he could have had his way, it would have been even more limited.

They thought they were hunting him, but they were wrong.

He started down the slope.

THE ENCAMPMENT did not look as if it had been disturbed in the time that he had been away. The remains of the fire were undisturbed, cold ash that had been rendered into muddy sludge by the rain. The doors to the huts were still shut tight, and when Milton opened them, the insides were just as he remembered them. Nothing had been moved in the two days since he had been here.

The inside of the store shed was gloomy, and he squinted into the murkiness as he assessed the contents. He remembered seeing a green first aid box and it was still there. He opened it: there were fresh dressings, bandages and, best of all, two bottles of pills and a tube of ointment. The first bottle was labelled Amoxi-Boll. It was amoxicillin trihydrate, a broad-spectrum antibiotic that he knew would help with his arm. The other bottle contained ibuprofen. The tube was labelled Bactroban. It contained mupirocin, an antibacterial ointment.

There was a cardboard tray of mineral water, the bottles still sheathed inside their plastic covering. Milton stripped it away, opened a bottle and drank down a handful of the amoxicillin and the painkillers, then finished the water.

He stripped to his waist and, moving carefully so as not to tip out the maggots, he peeled off the dressing. The maggots wriggled inside the wound, always moving. It was difficult to say how much good they had done but, as he looked at it, he thought that there was less of the blackened, decaying flesh. He tipped the insects into his hand, washed out the wound with another bottle of water, and then applied the mupirocin cream. When he was done, he tipped the maggots back in and covered them with a fresh dressing, binding it tight with adhesive tape.

He looked around again.

One wooden crate caught his attention. He heaved it away from the wall. Stencilled letters on the side read CORPS OF ENGINEERS – US ARMY. He knelt down and used the kitchen knife to loosen the tacks that fixed the lid to the frame. He worked two of them out, slipped his fingers into the gap and yanked back, splintering the pine and tearing the lid off.

Sticks of dynamite sat inside, packed neatly. Twenty sticks, forty percent nitro. He guessed that Callow and the others had stolen the explosives for their bank jobs, just in case they needed to blow a vault door to get at their spoils. It was good fortune that it was all still here. Still dry, too, still ready to be used.

Maybe his luck was changing.

There was a box of safety fuses slipped inside the crate. Each fuse ended with a nonelectrical blasting cap. He emptied them out onto the floor and attached one to each stick. He guessed each fuse would burn at the standard rate of a foot every thirty seconds. Plenty of time for what he needed.

He took eight of the sticks and shoved them into his pockets, four in each.

Now, he was going to need a fire.

There was plenty of tinder in the shed: old newsprint and the brown paper that had been packed with the dynamite. The crate that had stored the dynamite would be easy to break into kindling. There was plenty for what he had in mind.

The compound bow was still hanging from the nail on the wall. He took it down and inspected it. It was an expensive piece of kit, at least a thousand dollars. It used a levering system comprised of cables and pulleys to bend the limbs and tighten the bowstring. The bowstring was applied to cams, each of which had cables attached to the opposite limb. He drew back the string, causing the cams to turn. The set-up required less force to bend the limbs and tighten the string than a recurve bow or a longbow.

Considering the state of his arm, that was fortunate.

He stood the bow on the floor. There was a quiver with eight arrows inside. He took that, too.

Now, he needed to eat.

How long did he have?

Not long. He would have to be quick.

The remains of the deer were out of the question. It had decayed badly, and it was infested with maggots. He looked at the shelves and found packets of trail mix, fruit roll-ups, a box of energy bars, crisp breads and tins of beans. He needed calories, so he ate everything he could find, opening the cans with his utility knife and using it to spoon the beans into his mouth. He washed it all down with another bottle of water.

He felt a little better. The painkillers had numbed the pain from his arm, and his belly was full.

Better.

He was ready.

He gathered the things that he needed and hurried across the camp to the adit that led into the darkened maw of the mine. As he reached the steps, he fancied he heard the sound of a dog barking.

He hurried inside.

Chapter 36

THE DOGS yelled and yammered and dragged Walker Price down the slope. Lundquist and the other six men followed behind them. He felt his pulse racing until he could feel his heart slamming in his chest. Milton was here. The dogs knew it.

He knew it.

"Eyes open," he called out. "This is one slippery bastard."

He had decided that it was too dangerous to try to climb the falls. There was no way of knowing if Milton was still up there, waiting at the top with George Pelham's gun. He couldn't have many rounds left to fire, but he wouldn't need many. As soon as a man popped over that lip, he was liable to have the top of his head shot off. Lundquist wasn't prepared to take the risk.

He had split the party. He had ordered Randy Watts and Archie McClennan to stay back and guard the falls in case Milton decided to wait for them to leave and then tried to climb down again and slip behind them. Randy and Archie were good men, solid and reliable, and Lundquist had sent them back into the tree line so that they wouldn't be visible from the top. If Milton did try to descend, they would shoot him.

He had led the other seven men as they had retraced their steps. Walker Price knew the terrain, and he had directed them east, following the line of the ridge for a mile until they reached a draw that cut up through the ridge all the way to the plateau on the top. It was still steep, and Lundquist was sweating at the end of it, but at least they were up. The diversion had taken them ninety minutes. Lundquist was frustrated, but it had been necessary. Price had assured him that there was nothing else like the falls between here and the lake, no other feature of the landscape that Milton could use against them. They doubled back to the falls, but the dogs caught the scent before they got there, dragging them back up to the north.

To the old mine.

Lundquist knew that was Milton's final destination.

It had to be.

"Michael," he called out.

His boy jogged across to him.

"Yes, sir?"

"The mine. What did you boys have up there?"

"What do you mean?"

"Guns."

"Shotguns. Milton used one to cover us on the way back."

"Does he know that the others are there?"

"Found them all."

"So he'll have one?"

"Won't be able to use them." He grinned. "He disabled them. Took the barrels off."

"Anything else? You have a rifle? A handgun?"

"No."

"Nothing with longer range?"

"Didn't need anything like that."

"Ammo?"

"Just shotgun shells."

All right, he thought. *Assume that all he has is a handgun and a limited number of rounds.*

There were eight of them. They were all armed. Lundquist had a rifle. Michael had a rifle, too, and the army had trained him to be an excellent shot. He'd had plenty of practice, out there in the sandpit, and he had been given a medal for one shot in Iraq, plugging a raghead from a thousand yards. They would stay behind in the tree line and cover the others going in. It would be a turkey shoot. The men would flush Milton out of cover, and him and his boy would pick him off at range.

The trail led them down and around, and then the trees thinned out, and he saw the lake and the old mine buildings laid out before him. The old place hadn't changed in forty years. He looked out at the lake, the wind curling the surface into spume-topped breakers and the rain hammering into it. There were the two huts backed up against the tall shoulder of bedrock that hemmed in the lake on its western border, one of them overwhelmed by the water. The buildings were almost hidden by the trees and underbrush around them, a smothering blanket of vegetation. He saw the fire pit that the boys had been using.

"Stop," he called out.

The men did as they were told. The dogs yipped and growled, frustrated to be held back so close to their quarry. Lundquist gestured that the men should gather round.

"You sure he's down there?" he asked Price.

The man nodded down at his dogs. "*They* are. Look at 'em. That's good enough for me."

"If he is," Lundquist said to the others, "this is the end of the road for him. He's got the cliff to the west and the water at his back. There's nowhere else for him to go."

"What are we going to do, sir?"

"Me and Michael will stay up here with the rifles. The rest of you, you go down into the camp and find him. Search the huts, the trees at the back, all the way down to the water. He's in there somewhere."

"With a gun."

"A handgun, with maybe a couple of rounds. He pops up, I promise you he'll get shot. I can shoot, and Michael was a sniper in the army."

"That don't fill me with confidence," Larry Maddocks said, "the mess he's made of things already, dragging us all the way out here in weather like this."

Michael faced up to Larry and took a step closer to him. Lundquist put a hand on his shoulder. "Enough, Larry. And calm down, Michael. You know what Milton can do. You think we stand a better chance if we start bickering among ourselves?"

"Yes," Larry said. "I do know. That's why I'd be much happier if it was me staying up here and you and him going down there."

"That's the way we're going to do it. You got a problem with it, Private?"

Larry sighed in frustration. "No, sir."

"Where are your bikes?" Lundquist asked.

"Around back," Tom Chandler answered. "There's a grove. We put them in there."

"Does Milton know where they are?"

"Probably. He had a good look around."

"Well, you need to keep that in mind. He might run."

Michael took his rifle. It was a lever-action Winchester Model 94, and he already had a cartridge in the chamber. "If he gives me a clear shot, I guarantee you, I will hit him."

MILTON SAW them come down the slope. There were six of them. The man with the dogs was in the lead, his animals pulling hard at their leash. Tom Chandler was behind him, a shotgun aimed out ahead, and behind him came another four men. Milton had counted ten of them when he had looked down from the top of the falls. Lundquist must have left some of them back there in case he tried to double back. How many, though? Two? Three? Four? And where was he? Had he given himself that duty, the safer option? Lundquist hadn't struck Milton as craven, but maybe he was more bark than bite. In Milton's experience, it happened that way sometimes. You never could really tell until the chips were down and the bullets started to fly.

Didn't matter.

Milton would find him wherever he was.

The lead man slowed at the fringe of the tree line, pulling back to halt the dogs.

Deep breaths. Milton picked up the bow and held it in his left hand. He stood at a right angle to the target, his feet shoulder-width apart with his back foot slightly forward. He slipped an arrow into the rest, pushing it back until the nock clicked into the bowstring. He straightened his bow arm, raising it until it was parallel with the ground, and, using his upper back, drew the bowstring straight back. The effort of holding his left arm stiff sent a shudder of pain across his numbed muscles, and the bow jerked off to the right. He gritted his teeth, tried to ignore the pain, corrected the aim, and pushed his arm out to the target.

They were still in cover, just among the trees. Milton watched as another man came into view, just for a moment. The man had a rifle. Visibility through the rain was dreadful, but Milton recognised the bulky frame.

Lundquist.

He disappeared again.

The dogs barked excitedly.

The man with the lead started forwards, the hounds drawing him down the slope at an easy jog. The five other men followed.

Shotguns.

Pistols.

Milton held the bowstring up against his cheek and nose and aligned the sight with his target.

He opened his hand, and the arrow raced free.

LUNDQUIST LAY flat on the slope, the rifle laid out ahead of him so that he could sight down the barrel. Michael was alongside him in a similar position. He thought he had imagined the flash of movement. It was so fast and so stunningly quiet that he didn't register what it was until Walker Price tottered backwards, his hands clutching the long shaft that had suddenly appeared in his chest. He released the leash, and the dogs sprang away, then stopped, confused. Price weaved around until he was facing back up the slope. Lundquist saw the fletching on the shaft and realised, with horror, that it was an arrow.

Michael had seen it too. "Oh shit," he gasped. "Oh *shit*."

"*What*, Michael?"

"I forgot that."

"You forgot *what*?"

"My bow. He's found my bow."

"You had a *bow* down there?"

"Sure. We were hunting."

"You didn't tell me you had a bow!"

"I didn't—"

"You didn't what? You didn't *think*. You *never* think."

Walker collapsed onto his knees, and his dogs scattered, howling.

The other five men were halfway between the safety of the tree line and the shacks that made up the camp. Walker had been in the lead, so they had all seen what had just happened to him. They were a little closer to the camp. They should have made for shelter there, but they all assumed that Milton was in that vicinity, and their instinct was to go back in the direction from which they arrived. At least they knew that there was safety there.

Lundquist knew that was wrong.

"No!" he screamed. "Keep going! Get into the camp!"

Larry Maddocks broke first. He turned, but as he tried to push off, his foot skidded through a sheet of mud, and his leg flew out from beneath him. He splashed into the mud, face first, and, as he pushed himself up and scrambled on hands and knees, a second arrow streaked through the air. His slip saved his life. The arrow missed him by fractions, flying into the trees.

Someone shouted out a strangled, "Fuck!"

Maddocks ran for cover.

Thomas Chandler, Leland Mulligan, Dylan Fox, and Harley Ward were in the open.

"Get into the camp!" Lundquist yelled as loud as he could.

Michael stared down the sight of his rifle, sweeping it left and right. "You see him?"

"Get into the camp!" he screamed at the men. "He can see you there!"

Tom Chandler turned first and headed the other way, going for the shacks. The other three followed.

Lundquist stared into the slanting rain and saw a quick flash of movement.

"There!" he said. "In the mine."

They both fired, again and again. Lundquist held his Ruger .223 steady, pulling back the bolt handle in his open hand, the jacket ejecting past his right ear, pulling the trigger, repeating, the rifle always held against his shoulder. He fired until he was dry.

"Did you get him?" he yelled out as he fished in his pocket for another magazine.

Michael was more selective, pulling and firing until the hammer clicked down on an empty chamber. "I don't know," he said, using a stripper clip to reload the magazine.

Lundquist's hands were shaking. "Keep him penned in. The others can flank him."

MILTON PRESSED himself against the rock wall. The barrage from Lundquist and Callow peppered the walls and ceiling of the adit, but he had moved out of sight, and now he could just wait for them to run dry. At least one of them was firing wildly, indiscriminately, and he was happy to see them waste their ammunition. He was badly outmatched in that department—he only had another four arrows clipped into their slots on the bow, plus two "specials"—and if their hysteria brought them nearer to parity, then that was to be welcomed.

But the firing stopped.

That second arrow had only missed by two feet, but it had missed. A moving target, at medium range, in these conditions, with a bow and arrow? It would have been a difficult shot to make if he had been healthy. The pain in his arm was affecting him badly, even with the ibuprofen, and it had been all he could do to ignore it and hold his arm straight enough to fire. But he had missed, and that meant at least nine of them were still alive: Lundquist, Callow, the five survivors who had come out of the trees and the two men who must have waited for him at the falls.

The noise of the rain was all he could hear. He glanced back down into the corridor. The tiny fire that he had set was burning, the smoke sucked down towards a vent in the wall at the end.

Milton had seen Chandler, the young cop, and the two other men sprint ahead, to the camp.

He had expected them to do that.

He had *hoped* that they would do that.

Lundquist would try to pen him here and send his men to flank him. If Milton allowed that, he would be at their mercy. There was no way out.

He didn't plan on allowing it.

He had another arrow notched and ready to fire. Running to the cover of the shacks had bought them just a few extra moments to live. He would have picked them off otherwise.

A temporary reprieve.

The two shacks were fifty feet away from him.

There was a natural shelf in the corridor at the same height as his head. It was sheltered and dry. He unnotched the arrow that he had readied, reached across and took the first of the two modified arrows that he had left there. He had used medical tape to fasten a stick of dynamite to the shaft between the fletching and the arrowhead. He had balanced it as well as he could, but it was ungainly, and it would fly with poor accuracy, but that was acceptable.

He didn't need it to be accurate.

Thunder boomed outside the entrance to the mine. The clouds were down low, right overhead, and the clap was louder than Milton could remember.

Rain cascaded down, the run-off pouring down from the rocks above the adit, screening him.

He reached down with the arrow and held the short fuse in the flames until it hissed and popped and fizzed.

He quickly notched it, drew the drawstring back, aimed it, and let it go.

The arrow arced out of the entrance, a graceful parabola, reaching up and then curving back down as gravity clutched it.

The rifle fire started up again. He pivoted back into cover.

LUNDQUIST FIRED and worked the bolt, fired and worked the bolt, but before he could run dry again, he saw a third arrow launch out of the darkened entrance and slide through the rain, apparently aimless.

But it wasn't aimless.

It landed on the roof of the first shack, the arrowhead piecing the rotten old shingles, the shaft quivering. Lundquist stared at it. Something was wrong. He saw the tiny pinprick of light alongside the fletching, swaying back and forth as the arrow oscillated.

Oh no.

A second arrow was loosed from the mine, landing between the boards of the wall of the other shack.

That one, too, looked strange.

"*Run!*"

The first stick of dynamite exploded with a massive boom, a sudden cloud of dark grey smoke and debris billowing out. The shack was blown apart, the planks and shingles and the wooden frame torn into a million fragments and scattered for a hundred feet in all directions.

Lundquist pressed his arms over his head and pushed his face down, his mouth and nostrils in the wet muck.

The next stick detonated. This shack was closer to their firing position, and the shards of broken wood pattered around them, larger fragments caught in the branches of the trees overhead.

Lundquist looked up. Harley Ward and Dylan Fox had been right behind the first shack, and there was no sign of them anymore.

Tom Chandler had seen what had happened and had sprinted away from the second shack just before it, too, was destroyed. The blast must have picked him up and helped him on his way, for he had been flipped around and thrown down to the water's edge. He was rolling onto his belly, slapping the sense back into his head.

Lundquist could smell gunpowder, heavy and acrid, hanging in the wet air.

There was a crashing through the undergrowth, and Lundquist swung the rifle around, his finger ready to pull back on the trigger. Leland Mulligan appeared from out of nowhere, his clothes and hair scorched from the explosion, and fell down beside Larry Maddocks.

"What the fuck!" Leland gasped, the words gushing out and fear obvious in his wide eyes.

Michael had saucer eyes, too. "Pops?" he asked. "What do we do?"

He pressed himself to his hands and knees, mud dripping from his face. He held onto his rifle with shaking hands.

"Run," he yelled. "Run!"

Chapter 37

MILTON CAME out of the dark entrance to the adit.

They had fled. He had watched them scramble back up the slope, heading for the ridge and the long run back to the south and the relative safety of the town.

Milton grimaced.

What had they been thinking? That this was going to be a simple manhunt? Chasing a one-armed man up here until he ran out of places to hide, put a bullet in him, and be done with it all? Lundquist had probably expected that this would be easy.

More fool him.

Other people had made that mistake before.

It was a mistake you only made once.

Lundquist would know that he had changed tactics. He wasn't running any more. He had lured them up to the mine and trapped them. They had been fortunate. Three of them had been killed. More of them should have been dead. Lundquist knew a little more of what Milton was capable, and what he was prepared to do. He would know, too, that he was coming for them. That would make things more difficult. There would be no more complacency.

Now he was going to go after them and hunt them down.

The man with the dogs had dropped his shotgun, but it had fallen in the open, and Milton dared not risk trying to retrieve it. They might have doubled back, ready to pick him off. The two men behind the first shack had been carrying weapons, too, but the explosion had thrown them so far away that he might be looking for hours before he found them. He would have to rely on the bow.

He stayed off the path, climbing the slope in the cover of the trees and brush. It slowed him down, but he couldn't risk a more direct approach. They still had their rifles and, if he got close, their shotguns and pistols. There was a swathe of long grass between the trees and the lake, but he dared not stray into it for fear that he would leave a path that Lundquist would be able to see from farther up the slope. The trees grew sparser as he started to reach the top of the slope. He moved more carefully, lying flat in the mud, propelling himself farther by digging his toes into the muck and pushing.

THE RAIN became a deluge. Larry Maddocks scrambled up the slope to the ridge, slipping and sliding through the slop and the mud, driven ever onward by the thought that Milton might be coming after them.

What had just happened?

Oh man. He was scared. Was he ever scared.

Maybe the colonel would decide that the time was right to put a lid on things, at least for a while until things calmed right back down again. Maybe now wasn't the right time for what they had been planning. Maybe God's word could wait. Too much heat. Getting out of this in one piece was a sign. Larry was a devout man, like they all were, and he knew an omen when he saw one. There was no point in pushing things further than they were ever meant to be pushed. God had given them a message.

You need to be waiting.

He decided, right there, that he would bring it up with Lundquist the next chance he had.

They crashed and clattered through the trees. Larry gasped with the effort, hardly daring to look back, and then his leg snagged on an outstretched root and he fell into the mud.

The impact jarred the rifle out of his hands.

When he got up, he couldn't see it.

He couldn't see the others.

Shit, shit, *shit*.

Where were they?

He looked up into the sky, the midnight black, and saw a seam of lightning as it spread out for miles on either side.

He didn't want to call out, but he didn't want to stay silent, either, and have them carry on without him.

"Hey?" he called tremulously. Then, louder, "Hey?"

Dammit!

He looked down at the long grasses and underbrush, scouring it for his gun. He needed his gun. He couldn't just leave it here.

He didn't see Milton until it was too late. He came out of the darkness that had gathered beneath the canopy of branches, the light all gone, blanketed by the gloom from the storm. He had been hiding in the underbrush, and as he loomed up and took a quick step towards him, Larry noticed that his face and throat had been smothered with thick black mud. His whole head was daubed with it, just his pale blue eyes visible as he punched the serrated kitchen knife he carried in his right fist into Larry's chest. He bent double, right over the knife, feeling the metal inside him as it probed and pressed in between the long slither of his intestines. The man pulled the knife out, and Larry felt his blood follow after it, a gush that splashed out onto the grass, red droplets that diluted and dispersed in the rain.

He felt light-headed, only vaguely aware as strong hands took fistfuls of his jacket and hauled him off the path. He was dumped in the undergrowth, face up, and he was still awake when he saw those cruel blue eyes again and then the knife, sheathed in his blood, the jagged edge descending to his throat and swiping across and up.

"LARRY?"

Lundquist cursed him again. The man was a liability, always had been. He wasn't taking this seriously. Maybe he would when he was locked up, or dead, but it would be too late by then.

"*Larry?*"

The rain hammered down, sliding off the brim of Lundquist's hat and washing down to join the quagmire that had formed where the muddy path had been.

They couldn't wait for him.

"Keep moving," he called out.

They climbed towards the ridge, their boots slipping on the wet muck underfoot.

"Lundquist, come in… Lundquist, do you copy…"

He had put the radio into his pocket when the rain started to fall again, and he heard it crackle into life. He reached inside, took it out, and put it to his ear.

"This is Morris Finch. Are you there?"

"I'm here, Morris," he said between gasps.

There was a blast of lightning and a hiss of static that obscured Finch's next sentence.

"What was that? Please repeat."

"Said that there's someone… wants to talk to you."

"Who?" More static, more gasps for breath. "Jesus, Morris, I can't hear shit."

The line cleared, and a different voice became audible. "Officer Lundquist, this is Lieutenant Colonel Alex Maguire from the Michigan National Guard. Can you hear me?"

"Yes, sir," Lundquist said, gasping again.

"I'm the commander of the troops assigned… help you find… fugitive."

"Glad to hear your voice, Colonel."

"You were lucky… at Fort Custer normally… up at Nicolet for manoeuvres… jumped onto a truck… over here."

"How many men?"

"Five hundred, plus equipment… couple of Black Hawks… come in handy… reinforcing your cordon… advance and flush him out."

"Come now. We've got three men down, maybe four!"

There was another squall of interference, and when it cleared away Morris was talking again.

"… and it's all going to be fine."

"Morris! Tell them to come now! He's killing us up here!"

Another flash of lightning; another fizz of static.

Morris Finch didn't respond.

Lundquist had to fight the urge to fling the radio into the trees. He put it back into his pocket.

He looked back.

Still no sign of Larry Maddocks.

Leland was running next to him.

He heard the *crack* of the rifle over the sound of the falling rain. Leland ran on for another two steps before he fell forwards, ploughing a furrow through the mulch. He pressed up with his arms and looked down in dumb incomprehension at his belly. The bullet had burrowed through his back, sliced through his guts and exited through the front of his raincoat.

Lundquist stopped running. For a moment, he stood there paralysed, his mouth hanging open.

Lightning flashed like the sun.

"Pops!" Michael screamed over the slamming of the water.

Lundquist thought he saw something moving in the undergrowth.

"Pops! He's here!"

LUNDQUIST SQUINTED into the murkiness, his hands shaking with the sudden torrent of adrenaline.

Milton was behind them.

Close.

Walker Price was dead.

Leland Mulligan was dead.

Larry Maddocks.

Harley Ward.

Dylan Fox.
Dead.
Dead.
Dead.
There were only three of them left.

"Get behind the trees!" he yelled out to his son and Chandler.

Michael didn't hear him. He brought up his rifle and loosed off a round into the bushes, then another, and another. His rifle cracked out against the sound of the rain.

"Stop firing!" Lundquist shouted, not daring to take his eyes away from the bushes where he thought he had seen movement. "Get into cover!"

Michael fired again, his eyes bugged out with fright. His finger pulled and pulled, spent shells ejecting and new ones chambering, the recoil juddering against his shoulder.

"Stop firing! Save your ammo!"

Michael heard him this time. He looked over in his direction, and Lundquist saw how terrified the boy was.

"Come on," he shouted, starting back up the slope. There was a stand of large hemlocks, and he pressed himself behind the trunk of the nearest. Michael arrived a moment later, the barrel of his rifle trembling. He squeezed next to his father, aiming out around the side of the tree. Thomas Chandler sheltered behind another tree.

"Shit," Michael said. "He shot Leland."

Lundquist nodded. "Probably got Larry, too."

"Oh fuck." Michael's larynx bobbed up and down in his throat as he tried to swallow the fear away.

Think.

Milton had changed tactics. He had stopped running.

Think.

Lundquist looked up at the sky. The thunderhead was low and as black as pitch. It could be midnight for all the difference that would make. The rain was coming down as hard as ever, and visibility was reduced to twenty or thirty feet. The rainwater fell to join the spate that was forming around his feet. Lundquist picked his shirt away from his chest, but it sucked back again, stuck to his skin, drenched through.

"Listen to me," he said to them both, his voice low and urgent. "We can't stay here. He'll just circle around and pick us off. We need to get moving."

"Where?"

"Back home."

"We'll never make—"

"I know the terrain around here better than he does. We—"

"*Lundquist.*"

They both heard the shout over the clamour.

Lundquist felt his heart jackhammer in his chest. He swallowed hard, feeling the anger starting to surge. He channelled that, instead, and the fear receded, if only a little.

"What do you want?"

"You know what I want."

The voice was coming from below them, down the slope.

"The National Guard will be here soon," he called back. "You know that, you son of a bitch? Five hundred soldiers. You've got no chance."

"We'll have to disagree on that, won't we?"

Lundquist looked across to his son. Michael was gripping the rifle tightly in both hands.

"You asked what I used to do. Do you still want to know?"

"You were a soldier."

"An assassin, Lundquist. I killed people for my country. I killed one hundred and thirty-six men and women."

"Bull*shit.*"

Milton didn't answer. Lundquist looked around the edge of the tree, trying to see him. There was nothing.

"And now you're out of your depth," Lundquist said, trying to get him to speak again.

"Doesn't look that way to me."

"How's that arm of yours?"

There was a short pause. "It's been better. But I don't need both arms for what I'm going to do to you."

"You think you can take us out with a bow and arrow?"

"I've got a rifle now."

"You're still outnumbered."

"I've done all right so far. Only three of you left, plus those two you left behind at the falls. Or maybe I already took those two out, who knows?"

Lundquist tried to pinpoint the direction of Milton's voice. He was a decent distance away and maybe off to the right, maybe moving between sentences, but it was difficult to be sure. The sound bounced around the tree trunks, and the rain deadened everything. He took his hand off the barrel of his rifle and scrubbed water from his eyes.

"Milton!"

Milton didn't answer.

"Want to know the way I see it?"

He didn't answer.

"We outnumber you, and you have one arm. There are five hundred soldiers coming into these woods right now. They've got helicopters, too, probably already on their way. If I were you, I'd come out of there with my hands up right now and hope to God that I'm feeling disposed to bringing you in alive."

"Don't think I'm going to be doing that."

He turned to Chandler and Michael and hissed, "We need to move. You ready?"

Michael's eyes were wide. Chandler's face was bloodless. Lundquist glared at them both, nodded up the slope, and said, "You two go first, and I'll cover you. Get up to those trees, see them?"

They nodded.

"Then you cover me when I come up. Okay?"

"Yes."

Lundquist looked up into the sky, allowing the rain to wash off his face for a second.

He took a deep breath and tightened his grip on the rifle.

"Now!"

Lundquist crouched and swung around the edge of the tree, the rifle aimed into the forest where he thought Milton's voice had come from last. Michael and Chandler ran liked scalded deer, their feet slipping and sliding through the mud and the cataract of water that was coming down the slope from above. He thought he saw a shimmer of movement from within a stand of hardwoods. There was the sharp retort of a rifle. Lundquist swung the rifle up and aimed at the spot, firing two rounds in quick succession. He stared hard into the underbrush, straining his eyes and ears, but there was nothing. He glanced up the slope and saw Michael at the top, turning back to him and crouching down behind a fall of rocks, aiming back down into the woods. Chandler's head appeared around the trunk of a large oak.

Milton had missed.

He closed his eyes for a moment, remembering his scripture.

The Lord is my light and my salvation. Whom shall I fear? The Lord is the strength of my life.

He opened his eyes and ran. He pulled his boots out of the quagmire, each step splashing in the torrent as he ran as hard as he could to his son. He stared fearfully at Michael's face, terrified that it would register the sight of Milton below him, the preface to the bullet that would find him between the shoulder blades, but Michael's face remained intent with concentration. The bullet didn't come.

"Did you get him?" the boy cried out as he slipped into cover behind him.

"I don't know," he said. "Maybe."

Tom Chandler hurried over to them.

"What do we do?"

"We need to get as far away from here as we can. We need to keep running."

Chapter 38

THEY HAD made it to the top of the ridge and then the uplands beyond when the radio crackled with static from the lightning.

Lundquist put it to his ear and tried to press it there as he ran on.

"We… helicopters… too… thunder."

"This is Lundquist. Say again. Repeat, say again."

"Dangerous… lightning… on foot."

"I can't hear you."

The radio buzzed and fizzed and popped, and when the static dissolved, the voice wasn't one he recognised, and he couldn't even be sure it was meant for him.

"Dammit!" He was gasping from the hard running. "This is Lundquist. We are under attack. Men down, repeat, men down. We need help."

The lightning crackled again, lighting up the uplands, and then the thunder rolled over them, on top of them, so loud that it felt like his ears were ringing. Lightning flashed again, and Lundquist suddenly worried how wise it was to be out in the open when the storm was directly overhead. The whiteness stained a lattice against his retinas, and he blinked it away, squeezing the water out of his eyes, and then it was gone and the uplands were dark again.

"They're not coming," Michael gasped out.

"I don't know… this weather…"

"We're on our own," the boy said, his eyes still bulging.

Lundquist knew that they had to hurry. The land around here was horribly open. Milton wouldn't need to track them; he would be able to *see* them. He remembered the creek that they had followed earlier, cutting through the uplands, down the rise and then into the thicker forest. But where was it? He couldn't remember. What about the falls that Milton had climbed to get away from them? If they could find the river, maybe they could climb down there and get back to Truth. If they could keep Milton behind them, there was no reason why they wouldn't be able to get to help in one piece.

"Dad?" Michael called.

"We're going to be okay," he shouted over the roar of the storm. "I know a way down."

"What about—"

"He's behind us, right?"

"Yes."

"We keep him behind us. He's been shot. We're halfway home, boys, you hear? We just have to keep on going."

Rain pelted his face. He reached up to wipe his eyes when a gust of wind swept across them, snagging the brim of his hat and tearing it away. It jerked up into the sky, twenty feet high in an instant, and then spun away behind them.

Lundquist was past caring.

They started off, rushing out of the tree line and onto the wide-open space of the uplands. They covered the first hundred feet without incident but then Chandler turned and started to trot backwards so that he could look behind them, with his eye off the path ahead. His left leg plunged down into a rabbit hole, and he overbalanced, his leg buckling with a stomach-churning crack as he fell to the left, the leg still planted in the hole. Chandler screamed.

MILTON DIDN'T think it would be possible for it to rain any harder, but he had been wrong.

It was.

He reached the top of the ridge and held himself still, listening hard. He heard nothing. His breath coming thick and heavy, he poked his head up and surveyed the terrain. The upland was as he remembered it: broad ridges with rounded summits and wide, shallow valleys. There were rough grasslands, scrub, and pockets of trees. Plantations of conifer came in geometric blocks and formed hard, angular lines across the rounded slopes of the ridges. Patches of scrubby woodland, pastures, and marsh added to the mosaic.

He saw the three men in the near distance. Five hundred yards? They were running and, as he watched them, Chandler turned around to look for him, trotting backwards and tripping. He dropped down onto his side, and Milton heard the scream even above the thunder and the ululation of the rain. He watched as Callow stooped down to him. He heard another scream of pain. Chandler stayed on the ground as Lundquist turned and knelt, his rifle sweeping the ridge as he tried to find Milton.

He pressed himself down into the wet ground and watched.

Callow slipped his hand beneath Chandler's shoulders and hauled him upright. Another scream as his left leg was freed from the hole into which it had jammed. They started towards the south again. Chandler was hopping on his right leg, Callow was trying to support him on his right hand side, Lundquist was jogging ahead then turning back to cover them.

Knee ligaments?

A broken ankle?

A broken *leg?*

Milton calculated.

The odds had swung further in his direction, but he was still outnumbered and outgunned. The magazine of the rifle that he had taken from the dead man had been almost empty, with just the two rounds left in the chamber. They were gone now. The young cop had fallen in a spot where he wouldn't have been able to get to him without getting shot himself. He wondered whether he should go back now and look for his weapon. He decided against it. He didn't want to give them any more of a head start. The bow would have to do.

He squinted out into the rain. He knew that he wouldn't be able to take them if he followed them out into the upland. They had long guns, and as soon as he came out of cover, they would be able to start taking potshots at him. He could make himself difficult to hit, and the weather would mean that they would need luck to make the shot, but, at the very least they would be able to keep him out of range. It would be a stalemate, apart from the fact that he didn't know how long he would be able to survive out in the open in the middle of the storm. They were better equipped than he was. Better dressed. They would be able to last out the weather. He didn't know if he could.

He stopped beneath the shelter of a pin oak and tried to remember the map.

He needed a way to get ahead of them.

LUNDQUIST STOPPED, turned, and raised his rifle. He was looking back into the wind, a constant gust that seemed impossibly freighted with rain. He narrowed his eyes to slits, then scooped the water away, squinting so hard that the muscles in his brow started to ache.

No sign of Milton.

Where was he?

A wounded deer must feel like this. Injured, helpless, the hunter stalking it, sighting it, waiting for the proper time to finish it off.

"Come on! Too slow! We need to go faster!"

"This is as quick as I can manage," Michael yelled out over the noise. "His leg, Pops... Jesus."

Chandler moaned. The boy had snapped the tibia in his left leg. Lundquist had heard the crack, loud as a gunshot. His leg had been wedged up to the knee, and the sudden shift had torqued the bone too much. A compound fracture. The bone had sheared in two, one sharp half slicing through the skin at his shin. The colour in his face had disappeared completely now. He looked like he was about to faint.

"We're going to have to leave him."

"We can't."

"He's going to get us killed."

"No," Michael shouted at him, suddenly angry. "No man left behind. You know that as well as I do."

Dammit.

Be on your guard; stand firm in the faith; be men of courage; be strong.

Lundquist turned back to the south. He could leave them, he thought. He *should* leave them. He had God's word to consider. He had been chosen by God to do His will. Michael and Chandler would give Milton something to think about, buy him enough time to get all the way clear. There was backup ahead, Randy Watts and Archie McClennan, the two men he had left at the falls. He could run back to Truth and leave this whole sorry mess to the National Guard.

He could.

But…

Michael was right. No man left behind.

Dammit.

He raised his rifle again. The wind blasted him and the rain soaked him to the skin, but there was still no sign of John Milton.

Come on, you bastard. Show yourself.

MILTON HEADED across the upland, following a path through a shallow depression that would shield him from Lundquist. He ran as hard as he could, tripping and falling three times, but, after each fall, he scrambled back to his feet and kept going. He ran for a full hour and, by the time he arrived at the creek, he was dizzy from the pain.

The river was in full spate now, swollen by the cloudburst, and the water had flowed over its banks. A great torrent swept down from the hills, sweeping over the goat track and surging around the trunks of the trees that had sprouted in the rich soil.

Ahead of him, the water reached the fall that he had climbed earlier and piled over the edge, the cacophonous barrage competing with the sound of the rain and the thunder.

Milton lowered himself down a slope of scree and onto the gently cambered wall of the creek, and then he saw them.

Fifty feet behind him, laboriously clambering down the side of the creek, the rushing water springing at their feet.

He dropped low, scuttering down the scree, pebbles clattering around him as a tiny avalanche was pouring down into the water. There were slabs of rock stacked up along the edge of the river. Milton slid between them and lowered himself into the water. My God, it was cold. The fierce current tugged at his legs, jerking him downstream. There were straggles of thick root from the bald cypress tree that grew on the bank, and Milton knotted them in his right fist, the fingers of his left hand pressed into a rocky cleft.

The water was freezing. He wouldn't be able to stay in it for more than a minute or two.

He heard them approach, bickering, their footsteps clattering across the loose rocks, and he lowered his head beneath the surface. The water was so cold that it seemed to sting his brain, and he gasped, sucking a mouthful into his nose and the back of his throat. His eyes bulged, and his every instinct was to drag himself to the surface, but he squeezed his eyes shut and counted to five, then pulled up against the roots and took a deep, hungry breath.

He heard their footsteps and muffled voices right overhead, and he ducked down again, praying that they would keep walking, praying that they didn't stop, praying the bow across his shoulder wasn't poking out of the water.

He prayed they didn't see him, helpless, below them.

The water closed over his head, and time became a concept impossible to quantify.

One minute?

Thirty seconds?

Ten seconds?

He surfaced, gasping for breath again, and saw the back of Michael Callow's head as it disappeared beneath the line of the bank ten yards downstream.

Milton reached out with his right hand, fastened it around a rock, and used it as an anchor, tugging up and slithering out of the water and onto the bank. He pressed himself to his feet, took the bow, notched his second-to-last arrow, and pulled back on the string. He knew before it happened that he was going to fall. Blood rushed away from his head, and he quickly became dizzy, his balance awry, and he stumbled across the flooded path until he tripped and went down to his knees. The water splashed around him, and he must have groaned, because Chandler, who was being dragged sideways by Callow, now turned his head and saw him.

Chandler had his pistol aimed down and to the side, into the river, and he was swinging it around when Milton let go of the string.

The arrow hit the boy in the gut. He fell backwards, breaking free of Callow's supporting grip, slumped against the rocky wall, and slid down onto his backside.

Now Callow turned.

Lundquist heard the commotion, and he, too, turned.

There was no time to notch another arrow, so Milton clambered up and charged them. He crashed into them both, all three men pitching onto the rocks. Callow tripped and slammed down backwards onto a large boulder, gasping as the wind was punched out of his lungs. His rifle was jarred out of his hands, and it spun away into the river and disappeared.

Lundquist felt solid and muscular, and he knew that Milton couldn't use his left arm. He rolled on top of him, concentrating his weight on Milton's right arm, squaring his forearm and striking down with the elbow. It drew a glancing impact against Milton's forehead, enough to dim his vision for a moment.

"I'm going to kill you," he snarled.

He tried to use his elbow again, but Milton jerked his head aside.

"Michael! *Help!*"

He tried to strike down again, but Milton pressed his feet flat and pushed up, bucking Lundquist away from him.

Callow was still on the ground.

Lundquist and Milton staggered up and stumbled farther down the path. It bulged upwards for a short stretch, lifting it above the swollen river, a drop of a few feet on the right hand side with spume spraying up from where the water clashed against the rock. The falls were close now.

They closed again and Lundquist threw a punch that Milton blocked. He reached in with his right hand and grappled the older man closer to him. Lundquist forced his rifle up, pushing until the gun was held vertically between their bodies, pointing at the thunderclouds. Lundquist's right hand was pressed against Milton's chest, his fingers still looped through the trigger guard. It was just at the right height for Milton to reach across with his left hand. He grimaced from the blast of pain as he grabbed Lundquist's fingers and started to bend them backwards, one by one. The hand came away from the trigger, but he still had his left fastened around the barrel.

Milton butted him in the nose.

Lundquist relinquished the long gun and stumbled backwards.

Milton had the rifle now. He swung it at him, one handed, the stock slamming into Lundquist's left shoulder.

The older man reached the end of the path overlooking the falls as the water rolled over the edge and crashed down sixty feet to the plunge pool below. He tottered on the edge, his arms windmilling comically, before he took another backward step, his foot pawing the air, finding nothing.

He overbalanced and fell into space.

Milton dropped to his knees and crawled to the edge. Lundquist hit the water on his back and disappeared underneath the surface.

"*Pops!*"

Callow shoved Milton out of the way and leapt straight out from the lip of the cliff, turning in the air and hitting the water in an untidy dive.

He was swept beneath the surface, too.

Milton reversed the rifle and aimed down at the river, watching the frothy torrent, but there was no sign of either of them. He remembered the two men, who he guessed must have been left here, but there was no sign of them, either. The water roared, loud and angry and hungry, and still there was nothing. The current must have been strong, an underwater riptide that might have kept them below the surface or dashed them onto the rocks.

Milton waited for another ten seconds, staring down onto the roiling surface, tons of water crashing down every second, and finally, he saw them.

The river had carried them fifty feet away. Lundquist was on his back, Callow with his arm wrapped beneath his father's shoulders. Both of them were kicking against the pull of the water, slowly sliding across to the opposite bank.

Milton raised the rifle. He tried to sight it, but he could barely raise his left arm to brace it, and the barrel twitched to the left and right. He fired anyway, the round drilling into the rocks on the side of the bank.

He fired again.

The shot landed short, throwing a jet of spray into the air.

He fired again.

Wide to the right.

Callow must have noticed that they were being fired upon, for instead of fighting the current, he submitted to it. They were drawn back into the centre of the river, the water picking up speed. The two men, treading water to try to keep their heads above the surface, were spun backwards, sucked downstream, and borne out of sight.

Milton closed his eyes and rolled over onto his back.

He drifted into unconsciousness, woken by a boom of thunder like the sky being ripped asunder. He raised his head. He couldn't stay here.

He had to get down.

Had to follow them.

He went back to Chandler's body. He had died, his hands grasped uselessly around the shaft of the arrow that was still planted in his gut. He searched his body, found a packet of trail mix and three energy bars, and stuffed them into his pockets. There was nothing else of use.

He went back to the lip of the cliff and tossed the bow down. He slung the rifle over his shoulder, and then slithered over the edge. He remembered the first few handholds from before, but he was weaker now, much weaker, and his feet slid off the ledges and out of the niches that should have offered an easy start to the descent. He almost fell twice, both times saving himself with his right hand, and, as he swung out from the rock, his fingers burned as they clawed the roots and handholds as if they were functioning independently of the fuzz in his brain.

He made it to thirty feet down, halfway, and then somehow slid and scraped down another fifteen feet. He had neglected to plot a route, and now he found himself above a particularly sheer stretch of the face. He knew that there was no way that he would be able to find the strength to go back up again, or even to shimmy across so that he could get to the easier part of the face.

Nothing else for it.

He closed his eyes and pushed himself off, a fifteen-foot drop with an impact strong enough that his legs buckled, and he slammed back down onto his chest.

The crash and boom of the falling water was like white noise, and before he could fight it, he lost consciousness again.

Chapter 39

MILTON TRIED not to close his eyes, but they were intolerably heavy, and he couldn't resist.

His tiredness engulfed him like floodwater overwhelming a levee.

HE COULD hear the thunder of the waterfall and voices and the sound of a car and then the long boom of a jet's engine. The sound of a door opening softly. The sound a magazine makes when it clicks home, the sound of a bullet being pressed into the chamber. He heard the sound of children's voices and a plastic ball bouncing against the ground, but it was faint and peaceful, and it did not disturb him. He was on a motorbike. He was wearing the uniform of a motorcycle courier. He was in a *favela*, but he couldn't remember where, and then he wasn't, he was somewhere else, and he heard a doorbell. A finger pressed the doorbell, his finger, and then he heard the sound of the door being unlocked and opening on hinges that needed oil. He saw a face, a man who didn't know him, but a man that he knew.

SOMEONE FAMILIAR laid her hand on his shoulder and pointed to the dark square of a grave and said, "We need to dig a little deeper," and she lifted a shovel and sank it into the soft earth. She had a tattoo on the side of her torso, eight bars of black. He was holding a pistol. Now he was on a wide road next to a river he recognised. A car crashed into a tree ahead of him, a man ran from the car, and Milton knew that he was supposed to follow the man. Someone familiar was holding another pistol. He saw blood: splatters of blood on the walls, blood on his shirt, blood on the floor. He was Death, come to drink his fill.

He saw a group of children in the *favela* playing with their ball. He saw more blood. He saw a woman. She was young and pretty and scared. He saw the pistols, both of them, and saw them turn to the woman, and then there was the sound of a click and then an explosion and then—

MILTON AWOKE to the sound of crashing water. He was lying on the ground, on a hard rocky floor, sharp edges pressing into his back. He opened his eyes into complete darkness. He closed them and then opened them again. Still dark. He reached out with his left hand, tried to put pressure on it, and felt the now familiar throb from the bullet wound in his arm.

He remembered being shot.

He remembered the men he had hunted down.

Six men.

Six more dead men on his ledger.

He remembered Morten Lundquist and Michael Callow going over the edge of the falls, disappearing into the pool and then being borne away on the swollen current.

He had been wrong, though, about the dark. It wasn't complete. He rolled over onto his right side and saw how it lightened, just a little, in the direction that the sound of the falling water was coming from. He made out the irregular, jagged mouth of a cave.

He saw a fire, an arm's length away, damp wood spitting and fizzing.

A small pile of firewood sat next to it.

Who had made the fire?

Had *he* made it?

He tried to keep his eyes open, but he couldn't. Sleep swept up at him from behind, and despite his attempts to keep ahead of it, it was faster than he could ever hope to be.

He closed his eyes.

WHEN HE awoke again, the storm had passed. He could still hear the crash of the water from the fall, but there was no thunder and, as he listened to the quality of the noise, he couldn't hear the beat of the rain. He opened his eyes, and the cave was brighter, too, faint sunlight entering the chamber and reaching halfway inside, where it was eventually consumed. Milton was lying on a bed of springy ferns. They were damp, but not wet, and more comfortable than the naked stone of the floor. He was close to a small fire, a lattice of branches that had burnt about halfway through.

He had no idea how long he had been asleep.

He had no idea where he was.

He had been feverish, he knew that, but it seemed to have passed. His head felt clearer than it had for a long time.

He gingerly brought his left arm around so that he could look at the injury. He felt pressure in the wound, and when he touched his fingers to the dressing, he felt the soft, gentle motion beneath. He carefully peeled it back. He looked at the maggots, white and fat, twisting and turning as they finished the work that they had started. The wound was clean and beginning to heal. They had done an excellent job. The dead, necrotic flesh had been eaten, and the blood that gathered at the edges as he abraded them was fresh crimson. He poked the new, pink flesh and felt a prickle of discomfort. Another good sign. It was healing.

He tipped his arm over and shook it, the engorged maggots falling to the ground. They lay there for a moment, bloated and stunned, before they started to wriggle and crawl away.

He would wash the wound in the water outside, use the ointment in his pocket and—

He heard voices.

He held his breath, straining his ears.

He heard a voice, a man's voice, and then the squelch of static.

What did that mean?

Lundquist?

No.

He remembered: the National Guard.

Lundquist had warned him.

Five hundred men.

He crawled to the entrance to the cave and looked out.

The opening was nestled in the face of the cliff, screened by underbrush.

There was a patrol of four men at the foot of the fall. Ten feet away from him. They had stopped there, one of them operating a field radio that he wore on his back. The falling water obscured the conversation too much for Milton to be able to eavesdrop, but the occasional word was audible: "sector," "nothing," and an enquiring sentence that concluded with "orders?" The operator listened to the inaudible reply, nodded his satisfaction, and put the radio away. His comrades gathered around as he faced away from Milton and relayed what had been said.

Milton had no choice but to stay where he was. If they came any closer, they wouldn't be able to miss the mouth of the cave. They would look inside, see the signs of his habitation, and find him. If they did that, he wouldn't resist. They had done nothing to him. They were just following their orders. He could imagine how Lundquist had painted him. It was possible that their orders were to shoot him on sight.

Milton would have to accept that.

But they did not come in his direction.

Instead, they turned to the east and set off into the underbrush, following the line of the ridge.

Milton realised what had happened. The soldiers had carved the area into sectors. Each team would have been given a group of sectors to investigate. He had been fortunate; he was in the seam where one sector ended and the next one began. If there was a team from the uplands atop the falls above him, then they must have been tasked with the path down the face. Or perhaps the face was the boundary, and they had neglected to check it. These four boys were being routed away to continue the search in the adjacent map square.

Milton had enjoyed very little luck since he had arrived in Truth. This was luck. Perhaps it marked a change in his fortunes.

He knew that he would have a narrow window within which he could drive home his advantage. The search teams were likely to advance in a rough line so as not to leave gaps that he could slip through. That meant that the team that was adjacent to the one that he had just seen was most likely to turn east at the same time, and that they would be at the fall before too long. The cordon behind him, from the uplands heading south to his position, would also be moving. But the path directly to the south was open now. It had been searched and would have been reported as clear.

If Milton moved quickly, he might be able to slip between them and get out of the woods.

He hurried back to the fire, broke it apart, and returned to the mouth of the cave. He scoured the tree line again, but he could not hear or see anything. He emerged into the sunlight and trod carefully on the wet rocks, reaching the still swollen river that had carried Lundquist and Callow away, and then followed it to the south.

PART FOUR

Chapter 40

MORTEN LUNDQUIST and Michael Callow had been swept downstream. Lundquist was sure they were going to drown, such was the ferocity of the current as it was swamped with more and more water from the falls, the spate supercharged by the torrential deluge of the last few days. He had struggled to stay afloat for as long as he could, but he was old and tired and the water was cold, and he had started to feel himself slide beneath the surface. The water had pressed into his nostrils and then his mouth, and he was ready to submit to it when his son had surfaced next to him, grabbing him around the shoulders and holding him up, kicking for the quieter waters at the edge of the swell.

The current had spun him around so that he was looking back at the top of the falls. He had seen Milton on the lip of the rock face, trying to aim his rifle with one working arm, the barrel kicking as he had fired. The round passed harmlessly overhead, striking a rocky outcrop. He fired two more times, both shots harmless, and Lundquist realised that they were going to make it. The river would carry them out of range. Tom Chandler was still up there—he was dead, Milton had killed him, obviously—and they didn't have to worry about him slowing them down any more. Milton would take time to climb down the falls, if he even could, and by then the river would have swept them out of his reach.

They were swept downstream for two miles.

Michael swam them across to the bank when the fierce downstream tug of the river had finally abated. They clambered out, shivering in the cold, the rain a foolish irrelevance now.

"Where are we?" Michael asked.

Lundquist looked around and tried to gain his bearings. "A good way to the south."

"How far to town?"

"I don't know. Three hours?"

"We made it. Praise the Lord."

"Amen," Lundquist muttered.

He couldn't stop shivering.

"Do you have the radio?"

The radio! He had forgotten he had it. He reached up to his pocket and patted where it should have been, but there was nothing there, just the damp squelch of his jacket.

"Where is it?"

"Must have lost it… the river…"

He felt a sudden wash of helplessness. If he could have used the radio, he would have been able to call for help, send an SOS to the National Guard and have them send men or a helicopter or something, anything, to get them down out of these godforsaken hills and back to civilisation again.

He dropped to his knees. He was done.

"Come on, Pops," Michael said. "We have to keep moving."

"I'm tired."

"We have work to do. God's word. He spared us for a reason."

His chin slumped onto his chest. He didn't have the strength.

"Remember the scripture: *Be strong and of good courage, do not fear nor be afraid of them; for the Lord your God, He is the one who goes with you. He will not leave you nor forsake you.*"

"Deuteronomy 31:6," he mumbled.

"If we stay here, it's all finished. Think of all the work you've done. We can't let that go to waste. We are the Sword of God. We have a duty. You preached it. These are the End Times, right? We need to strike the first blow."

Lundquist nodded. The boy was right. He thought of the truck and the load that they had put together. All the effort it had taken. He thought about what they could achieve with it. The original plan, as he had conceived it, was dead. Milton had seen to that. But perhaps that plan was not God's will. Perhaps he had another use for them. For Lundquist.

He grabbed Michael's coat and used it to help drag himself to his feet.

"Come on."

They set off, both of them aware that Milton was somewhere behind them. Lundquist was cold, and he knew that he needed warmth and dry clothes. Michael, too. Hypothermia didn't take long to take hold, and if it did, Lundquist knew that they would be in trouble. Done for, most probably. He had seen plenty of hikers caught out by the weather, stumbling around in the woods with no idea where they were or even, sometimes, who they were. He trusted God to keep them safe.

They followed the camber down into the forest.

"Who is he?" Michael said. "Milton. Who *is* he?"

"I don't know," Lundquist admitted. "A soldier."

"What he did… I mean…"

"Maybe he is what he said he is."

"An assassin?"

"Maybe."

"He's not an assassin," he said, although there was doubt in his voice.

"He's killed…" Lundquist tried to remember how many people Milton had killed. Four? Five? He couldn't remember. Seemed like there was a lot of blood and death all of a sudden. The dead flashed through his mind: a knife, the arrows, the detonations as the two shacks were blown to kingdom come. How many? No, it wasn't five. He had forgotten Sturgess and Sellar. Stabbed and shot. Seven, then? No. More. What about Randy Watts and Archie McClennan? Where were they? He must have killed them. There was Pelham, too, his neck snapped and his body dumped in the field for them to discover. And Lars Olsen, who had to be cut out of his crushed car. Twelve. He had killed twelve men.

Twelve.

Lundquist felt fuzzy headed, and as they stumbled ahead, a memory appeared through the haze. It was a face, grizzled and dirty, a man with evil in his eyes, and Lundquist remembered that this man had been a member of his patrol in Vietnam, a vicious man with no regard for human life and a particular talent for death. Lundquist could remember his eyes, icy blue and devoid of any flicker of humanity, as if the things that he had seen and done had burnt the compassion from them. Lundquist thought of that man many times through the years and, since his conversion, he had become certain that he had looked upon the face of Satan.

He had looked into Milton's eyes as they had struggled with the rifle atop the falls, his eyes just inches from Milton's eyes, and he realised that those cold blue orbs were just the same.

He doddered onwards, only half aware that he was leaning on Michael for support, when he felt his son stop.

"Hands up!"

Michael stiffened. "Pops…"

"What?"

"Hands where I can see them, *now*."

Lundquist grabbed Michael's shoulder and raised his head. There were four uniformed men blocking the trail ahead of them, two of them with automatic rifles raised and pointing straight at them.

Praise God, Lundquist thought.

LUNDQUIST EXPLAINED who they were and what they were doing in the wilderness. One of the soldiers radioed their descriptions while the others stood guard. Their identities were confirmed, and the men escorted them the final mile south. They had blankets in their packs, and Lundquist wrapped himself in one, the shivering gradually easing. He was still in soaked clothes, though, and still cold. He needed to get changed. A hot drink. A long bath would have been nice, but that was out of the question. He didn't have time. He had so much to do. He didn't know if he could afford to stop.

They broke through the tree line into the fields of corn that fringed the northern border of the town. An olive green Humvee was waiting for them there. Two more soldiers were in the Humvee. They disembarked as the patrol brought them out of the trees.

"Lundquist?"

"Yes."

"I'm Lieutenant Colonel Alex Maguire. We spoke on the radio."

"I'm glad to see you."

"I bet you are. Are you injured?"

"No, Colonel. Just cold."

"We'll get that straightened out. You want to tell me what's been happening up there?"

"It's a massacre."

"How many?"

"Ten. Maybe twelve. He killed them all."

He thought of those men, Christian soldiers ready to fight for the cause, and he felt a wave of nausea.

"Jesus. We knew it was bad; that's why the governor sent us up here, but... well, *Jesus*. Who is he?"

"I have no idea."

"You never spoke to him?"

"He said he was an assassin. I thought he was joking, now I'm not so—"

Lundquist felt the nausea rise up from his gullet, and before he could do anything to stop it, it was in his mouth. He bent double and let it pour out, splashing into the furrowed mud, spattering over his shoes and the bottom of his pants.

Michael put his hand on his shoulder. "Pops?"

Lundquist pushed his hand away, overwhelmed with embarrassment at such a show of weakness. It was ridiculous. It was pathetic. He had seen dead bodies before, many more than he'd seen today. The VC had been every bit as ruthless as Milton, and more inventive with the ways that they dealt death. And Uncle Sam had killed freely, too. He remembered foxholes full of dead gooks, a line of smoking corpses after an engineer with a flamethrower had flambéed a trench full of the bastards. What was this in comparison to that? It was nothing. And, he chided himself, what else did he expect? This was war. The word of God that they were about to fulfil, the culmination of years of planning, of course there would be blood spilled by the time he was done. Innocents would suffer. You could take that to the bank.

"Are you all right?"

"I'm fine. Tired. And I need to get warm."

"Yes, deputy, in a minute. One more question. Do you know anything else about him? I mean, he obviously knows what he's doing up there."

The question lit him up. "Are you serious? He's killed the sheriff, three deputies, an FBI agent, and the men I took up there to apprehend him. He very nearly killed me and my son. So, yes, I'd say he knows what he's doing."

"Yes," the man said, embarrassed to have asked. "Of course. I can see that."

"What are you actually doing to find him?"

The soldier flinched defensively. "I've got five hundred soldiers up there and, now that the storm's passed, we've got Black Hawks in the air. He won't be able to hide much longer. And you say he's wounded, too?"

"I got a shot off. Hit him in the arm."

"There we go, then. Matter of time, Lundquist. Just a matter of time."

Chapter 41

ARTHUR STANTON didn't want to go.

"I don't want to leave you here," he said to Mallory as she untangled herself from his embrace.

"I don't want you to, either," she said, "but you have to. I'm not tall enough or strong enough to climb up there and get out. Ellie can't do it, either. But you can, Arty. You can do it."

She looked up at the pitched roof of the barn. It was an awfully long way up. Arty liked to climb, and he was good at it, but she knew he wouldn't have chosen to try a climb as difficult as this. It was only because she had asked him that he had said that he would, but now that he realised what she wanted him to do when he got to the top, he didn't want to go.

"Mallory…"

She took his shoulders and squared him up so that she could look right up into his face. "Listen to me, Arthur. You have to get up there, and you have to get out. If you don't, they are going to shoot all three of us. Do you understand?"

"Why do they want to do that?"

"Because we know what they did to the sheriff. You remember that?"

He nodded.

"And what they tried to do to Mr. Milton. That's what they'll do to us if we don't get out."

"But you and Ellie aren't getting out. It's just me."

"I know that, Arty. You climb out, climb down and then try to open the door."

"But what if it's locked?"

"Then you run back into town. You're not to stop for anyone. We're at the Olsen farm. You remember where that is? It's four miles south of Truth. You need to get back into town as fast as you can, and then you need to call the number Ellie told you in the back of the van. You remember it?"

"313-338-7786."

"That's right, Arty," Ellie said.

"What if the phones are still down?"

"They'll be fixed now."

"What if they're not?"

"You'll need to turn around and go south," Ellie said. "Get someone you trust to drive you until you find a phone that works. Or all the way to Detroit if you can't find one."

"Who do I speak to?"

"You just need to tell them that you were with Agent Flowers and that she has been abducted. They'll ask you for more details, but you tell them they have to come to Truth, and they have to come to the Olsen farm."

"They have to come to Truth, and they have to come to the Olsen farm."

"That's it."

Mallory leaned in to him again, wrapped her arms around his chest, and hugged him.

"I love you, Mallory."

"I love you, too." She untangled herself for the second time. "Now, go, Arty. Go, right now."

The roof was eighteen feet above them. It was supported by a series of oak posts and cross braces, each brace supporting a frame that met at the roof. One of the posts was next to the old plough, and Arty scrambled onto it, grabbing the metal teeth, his fingers breaking the dried muck off into his hands, and hoisted himself onto it. From there, he was able to pull himself onto the first girt that split off from the post at a diagonal. He reached up and heaved, clambering high enough above the beam to reach up for the brace that ran parallel with the floor. His boots scrabbled for grip on the dry wood, but he negotiated the short climb until he was on it.

The damaged section that they had noticed was on the other side, only accessible if you used the beams to traverse across.

The next part was the most difficult. Mallory watched with her heart in her mouth as he stepped out carefully, one foot following in the path of the other, until he was out in the middle of the beam. There was a sigh and long creak as the old wood complained at the addition of his weight and then a judder as it dropped down, almost coming loose, slotting back securely in position just as he was bracing for the long drop to the floor below. He kept going, one foot after the other, until he was on the other side of the barn next to the damaged roof.

"Can you get through it?" Mallory said, just loud enough for him to hear.

A piece of tarpaulin had been fixed to a space between the rafters where the asphalt shingles had come away. Arty reached up for it and pressed his hand against it, noticing the tacks that secured it in place. They had been driven in from the outside. He ran his fingers along the edge of the tarpaulin and the rafters until he found the weakest spot; then he curled his fingers between them and yanked. One of the tacks came free, loosening the tarpaulin and giving him more to tug, and after another minute he had pulled it away from all the nails in one rafter, peeling it back so that it hung down freely.

"I got it," he called down.

"Quietly," his sister chided. "Can you get through?"

"I think so."

"Go on, Arty. Be careful."

He looked down at Mallory.

"Go on."

He reached out until his fingers locked into one of the vents set into the ridge beam. He swung his leg up and through the hole, then pulled the rest of his body out and into the dark night. Mallory looked up through the opening. The sky was hidden behind a shroud of thick, black cloud.

"He knows what he's doing, doesn't he?"

"You can trust him," Mallory said, a little defensively.

They heard a bang and then the noise of Arty's feet skidding on the wet shingles. Mallory held her breath until she heard him dig the heels of his boots in and arrest his slide. There was a pause, and then they heard the sound of his feet as they banged on the wall and then, finally, the wet splash as he dropped down to the ground.

Mallory closed her eyes. She found that she had crossed her fingers.

She heard the sound of his footsteps as he came around the barn to the door. Her heart hammered in her chest. What if they were out there? Magrethe Olsen and Morris Finch. What if they had posted a guard? She felt sure that she would hear the boom of a shotgun, the sound of his body slamming into the ground. She felt sick.

There was no boom.

Instead, she heard the scrape of the metal bar as it was pulled through the brackets.

She hurried across to the door as Arty tried to pull it open. The lock caught, rattling in the frame. Arty pulled again, harder this time, but the lock held firm. There was a crash as he threw his shoulder into it, but, still, it didn't move. There came another slam, even louder, with the same result.

"Arty!" she said through the door. "Stop."

"I can't open it," he said, his voice frantic with panic.

"Don't worry."

He was crying. "I'm sorry, Mallory."

There came another crash as he threw himself at it again.

"Tell him to stop," Ellie said urgently. "They'll hear him."

"I tried, Mallory, but it's too strong. I can't open it."

"*Stop*, Arty."

"What do I do?" he sobbed.

"Go to Truth. Just like we said."

"I don't want to go."

"You have to, Arty. The sooner you call that number, the sooner we'll see each other again."

"313-338-7786. I got it." There was a moment of silence, just the sound of the rain on the shingles, and then she heard him again. "Okay, Mallory. I'll do it."

"I love you, Arty."

"I love you, too."

She heard his footsteps, coming quickly as he ran, and she pressed her ear to the knotted wood until she couldn't hear them anymore. Her cheeks were wet with tears.

Chapter 42

MILTON HAD been on the move all day. He could have reached the edge of the forest more quickly, but he was still as weak as a baby, and he knew that he needed to move carefully. For all he knew, the Guard had a second perimeter team sweeping up after the first one. If that was true, he didn't know what he would be able to do. The thought of going back into the deeper forest again was not something he was happy to contemplate. He knew that he didn't have the strength.

He didn't have the time.

Ellie and the Stantons didn't have the time.

He moved carefully through the trees, staying low, and then, when they petered out, he scrambled from bush to bush until he was at the edge of another field. This one was not full of corn. It had been allowed to go fallow, restoring its fertility for a crop the next year. Milton estimated that it was a full mile across the field to the railroad on the other side. He guessed that he had exited the forest two miles to the west of the point that he had entered.

A mile. He would normally be able to cover that in a flat run in five minutes. He was injured and tired, though, so call it seven minutes, maybe eight.

He set off into the open field, feeling naked as he left the cover of the leafy canopy overhead. The field had been ploughed, and his feet caught against the ruts and jammed in the troughs, slowing him down. He fell for the first time when he was a quarter of the way across, getting his legs beneath him again and pushing on. He fell for the second time when he was two-thirds of the way across, landing heavily in a muddy puddle.

He had started to raise himself when he heard the sound of an engine. He dropped to his belly again, pressing himself down amid the mud and the mulch, and held his breath. The engine drew nearer, and then he heard the bounce of a suspension as it crossed the railroad track and started to work across the field. He watched as a Humvee came into view, springing up and down across the uneven field. It went by less than fifty feet away from him, and Milton was sure that he must have been spotted. He saw two men in the vehicle, a driver and, next to him, a soldier armed with an automatic rifle. The driver swung the Humvee around so that it was facing into the forest.

Away from him.

They hadn't seen him.

Milton got up and ran.

He heard another engine, louder than the Humvee, and when he risked a glimpse into the blackened sky, he saw something that made his heart sink.

A black dot was approaching from above the forest to the north, low and fast, the sound of its engines growing louder and louder as it drew nearer. He recognised it as it cleared the edge of the field: it had the distinctive shape of a UH-60 Black Hawk.

He was at the edge of the field now, the steep rise of the railroad embankment above him and the unruly thatch of scrub directly ahead. He dived head first into the vegetation, rolling deeper inside and praying that he hadn't been seen.

He turned back and looked.

The Black Hawk swept on, flaring as it approached the parked Humvee, the pilot gently guiding it down onto the rutted field twenty feet away from it. The doors slid open, and soldiers started to disembark. Milton counted fifteen. A hand signal was relayed from the ground to the pilot, and the engines roared powerfully again. The chopper lifted back into the air, the forward landing wheel rotating slowly as the nose dipped. The pilot swooped over the trees and executed a sharp turn to port, hurrying back to the north.

Milton stayed where he was, praying that his position was obscured by the vegetation. The fifteen men unslung their packs and prepared their weapons. The passenger in the Humvee jumped down, stepped across the field to the senior man amid the new arrivals, and gave him his orders. The soldiers formed up in two squads and tramped across the field. Milton watched as the two squads deposited a pair of men every half a mile. They were setting up a cordon.

Milton waited there until his breathing returned to normal.

He had been lucky.

If he had been five minutes longer in getting out of the forest, he would have been trapped. A cordon to the south and patrols in the forest all around. Two pincers that would have caught him above and below, gradually narrowing his freedom to move, until he had nowhere to go. He would have been helpless.

But now he saw that he had a chance. They thought he was still in the forest. They were concentrating the search for him there.

He crawled through the bracken and thistle until he reached the start of the embankment. He turned back again to make sure that he was not observed and then clambered up it. The railroad was ahead of him, the thick sleepers at eye level as he lay prone next to them. Beyond that, in the near distance, was Truth.

Milton pushed himself up to his haunches and then, unsteadily, to his feet. He crossed the rails and slid down the other side until the rise of the embankment shielded him from the soldiers in the field.

He started to walk and then to jog, and then he started to run faster and faster until he was sprinting towards the town.

Chapter 43

THE NATIONAL GUARD arranged for a Humvee to drive them back into town. Lundquist told them that they lived out at Seth and Magrethe Olsen's farm, so they took them there. He had them stop at the end of the driveway, before the gate and the guardhouse, saying that they would walk the rest of the way. The last thing he wanted was a couple of soldiers nosing around. The Freightliner was parked up in the yard. They might wonder what a vehicle like that was doing on a farm, and if they looked inside...

He needed to avoid that.

They waited until the Humvee had started to turn around, and as it slipped and slid across the muddy track back to the main road, they walked around the gate and made their way across the yard to the farmhouse.

Lundquist knocked on the door. There was the sound of hurried activity inside and then footsteps. The door opened. Magrethe Olsen was standing there, Morris Finch behind her, his arm resting on a French dresser with a pistol clasped in his hand.

"Morten," Magrethe said, "we thought you were dead."

"You should have more faith."

He bustled past her, Michael tailing in his wake.

"What happened?" Finch said, putting the pistol back into a holster that he was wearing on his belt.

"The Englishman," he said. "Milton. He happened."

He suddenly felt dreadfully tired, exhausted right to the marrow of his bones. He went over to the sofa with the quilted cover and slumped down into it.

"The others?"

"All dead."

Finch blanched. "What do you mean?"

"You want me to spell it out for you, Morris? Milton killed all of them." They both just stared at him. "God is testing us. He wants to be sure that we are worthy for the task that He has set before us."

All he wanted to do was sleep, but he was cold and, anyway, he knew that particular luxury was for other men. Weak men. He needed to get warm, think about what he needed to do, and find a moment's peace where he could work it all out without being bothered by his son or Magrethe Olsen or Morris Finch or anyone else.

HE WENT upstairs to the bathroom. There was a shower over the tub, and he cranked the water on, twisting the faucets around until the water that cascaded down was almost too hot for him to stand under. He undressed and stood there for ten minutes, letting the heat seep into his skin and bones, scrubbing it into his scalp, almost scalding himself in an attempt to drive out the cold from the icy rain and their soaking in the river. He let it run down his face and into his eyes and mouth and ears, kneading his cheeks and his forehead with his knuckles, until he felt red raw.

He was tired. His mind started to drift, and he couldn't stop it.

He thought about what he had seen all those years ago.

Thirty-five years ago.

His vision.

God's word.

He had been in the jungle. An eighteen-year-old conscript thrown into the deepest circle of Hell. It was sweltering, so hot that his brain felt as if it was boiling inside his skull. His rifle company was in pursuit of the enemy, but the VCs tricked them and led them into an ambush. Machine guns, grenades, knives to finish off the wounded. It was a turkey shoot, and most of his platoon had their tickets punched that day, but he had been spared.

A miracle, by any definition.

He squeezed his eyes shut as the water ran over his face and tried to remember.

There had been a glowing light through the trees. When he followed it, he was led to safety. Praise be to God. He couldn't remember much of what happened next. Even in the immediate hours afterwards, all he could recall were fragments: the glowing lights that seemed to rise from the ground; the beautiful music that was everywhere and nowhere, all at once; the calm and strong voice that talked to him. The memories merged into one as the hours became days and then weeks and months and years.

He couldn't remember the words, but the message had been imprinted on his consciousness.

These were the Last Days.

The End Times.

The government would be taken over by the antichrist.

He would be responsible for firing the first salvo in the Last Great War that would wipe the stain of its evil from the Earth.

The Lamb was coming.

He had asked when.

You will know.

What would he have to do?

You will know.

Time passed, he had waited, and now it was upon him.

He *did* know.

The time was now.

He opened his eyes, turned around, and let the water fall onto his shoulders and back.

He knew that there was no way God's word could be put into effect the way he had planned, not now, not now since there was so much heat in town. The National Guard, for one. The FBI would be back once they were notified that one of their own had gone missing, presumed murdered. The ATF might get involved, too. Lundquist didn't need to be reminded what they had done at Waco.

John Milton had brought down the full might of the federal government onto Truth and had slammed the lid shut on what he had worked so long to put into place.

Lundquist had worked everything out. Years of planning until the operation was perfect. A series of attacks all across Michigan and Wisconsin, happening all at once, Holy Christian soldiers going forth to do battle against Satan.

The assassination of the vice president would have been the first salvo.

That wasn't going to be possible now.

He needed to adapt.

The hot water came down, and Lundquist closed his eyes and prayed for guidance.

MAGRETHE HAD laid out a set of Lars's clothes, and Lundquist changed into them and went downstairs. If the woman thought anything about seeing him in her dead son's check shirt and jeans, then she didn't say anything. She was in the kitchen preparing a pot of hot coffee. Morris and Michael, who had showered in the downstairs bathroom, were waiting for him in the sitting room. Magrethe brought the coffee inside and shut the door behind her. There were cups on the table, and Finch went to work, pouring the coffee and distributing the cups.

They sat quietly for a moment, sipping at their drinks.

Michael was the first to speak. "What are we gonna do, Pops?"

"We're going to relax."

"It's all gone to shit."

Lundquist felt his temper flare. "No, it hasn't."

"My boy is dead," Magrethe said. "George Pelham is dead. The others you took up there, they're dead, too. I don't know, Morten. I don't much like agreeing with your boy, but, you ask me, he's right. It's exactly what's happened. This can't be what God had planned for us."

"Obstacles are sent to test us. We could've died up there with the others, and we didn't. What does that say to you?"

They frowned. No one answered.

"Michael?"

"Says we got lucky. Falling in the river says that saved us from him."

"No, it says the Good Lord spared us so we could continue to do His work."

Magrethe shook her head. "It don't look that way to me."

"Where's your faith, Magrethe? You don't remember your Bible? 'Jesus said unto him, if thou canst believe, all things are possible to him that believeth.'"

She looked down, abashed. "I know that."

"Hand on my heart, none of what's happened so far has changed my dedication to our cause a single bit. This is a war. We are fighting Satan and all his minions. Men die in war. Men *have* died, and I'm going to make damned sure that they didn't shed their blood in vain. You remember what Jefferson said? 'The tree of liberty must be refreshed from time to time with the blood of patriots and tyrants.' I'm going to make sure that their sacrifice refreshes that tree. I'm going to make sure that people see them as patriots and our foes as tyrants. I'm going to make *damn* sure that happens even if it kills me to do it."

His vehemence struck them dumb and, for a moment, all they could hear was the rain hammering against the kitchen window.

Magrethe couldn't look at him. "So what are we going to do?"

"We got to think on our feet. Things change. Plans need to be adapted. We have to move tonight."

"But the VP?"

He shook his head. "He got lucky. We don't have time to wait. We'll pick another target."

"But we're not ready. Some of the men who were going to fight are dead."

"That doesn't mean that we can't start without them."

"How we gonna do that, Pops?"

"I've been praying to the Lord for guidance, and He has showed me the way. There's the federal courthouse down there in Green Bay. They've got a lot of things they need to be apologising for: abortion, for a start. You want to get me started on the blood that they've got on their hands? What about the Second Amendment? They try to put restrictions on semiautomatic weapons. You confident they wouldn't take everything away if they thought they could? What you say I drive that truck right up to the front doors and blow that place to kingdom come?"

There was a pause as the others absorbed his words. Lundquist would have gone ahead without them, but he found to his surprise that he needed their approval.

Michael stood. "I'll come with you."

Lundquist had already anticipated that Michael would want to do that. He had dismissed it. He didn't need him and when you came down to it, this was something that felt like it needed to be done alone. He knew that he wouldn't come back alive and, even if he did, he was ready for the government to kill him so that he might get the chance to spread his gospel far and wide. He wanted some time to himself. Michael would be in his ear the whole time and, even if he was quiet, Lundquist knew that he wouldn't be able to pray.

"No."

Michael shook his head. "I can't let you do that on your own."

"I need you here, Michael. We've got three witnesses in that barn. One of them is a federal agent. They need to be shot right away. Should've been shot already. Once they've been shot, they need to disappear without a trace. You, Morris, and Magrethe need to take care of that."

He looked at the woman, and she gave a firm, sure nod. Magrethe was a hard woman. She wasn't squeamish, not like so many people were these days. Seth had always left it to her to euthanize the cattle that couldn't be saved. She would take them out around back and put a bullet in their brains. Lundquist knew that he could rely on her to see that the job was done.

"Can you do that, son?"

"Sure. I can do it."

"What about Milton?" Finch asked.

"We have to assume that he's coming."

"How could he know we're here?"

Lundquist had thought about that. How *would* he know that? There was nothing to say that he would, but he might have spent a little extra time with Tom Chandler, or any of the others he had killed, and maybe he would have been able to get the information out of them. He was resourceful. They couldn't assume that he would be ignorant.

"He's coming. You need to be ready for him. You need to take him down."

LUNDQUIST OPENED the door of the trailer and pulled himself up and inside. He took out his flashlight and played the beam over the large barrels of ammonium nitrate, diesel, and nitromethane. The blast would be triggered by four hundred pounds of Tovex Blastrite Gel. A time-delayed fuse led from the cab to a dozen blasting caps. The explosion would be enormous. Volcanic. What a statement it would be. Like the Israelites sounding their horns and the walls of Jericho coming crashing down.

The other militias would come to their side.

The country was like a powder keg. All it needed was a spark.

The start of the Holy Revolution.

The return of the Lamb, riding at the head of God's army.

He jumped down onto the wet yard and closed the door up nice and tight.

Michael was waiting for him at the door to the tractor cab. He had an M16 in his hands.

"I'm sorry, Pops."

"What for?"

"If we'd been more careful up there. The other day. If… I don't know, maybe this wouldn't have happened the way it has."

"It's God's will," he said. "Do what I told you and we'll still make history."

"You think?"

The boy's doubt was pitiful. The same for his need for Lundquist's approval, but, as much as it irritated him, he couldn't deny that he had affection for him.

He extended his hand. Michael took it, and Lundquist gripped his hand hard.

"You've done well, son. I'm proud of you. Maybe we see each other again when this is all said and done, maybe we don't, maybe we have to wait until we're both in Heaven, but you take care of things here and then I guess you've done everything I could have expected from you. Can you do that?"

"I can do it."

"I can't ask for any more."

Lundquist let go. Michael's eyes were damp. He proffered the M16 and Lundquist took it, sliding it into the cab.

He reached for the rail and hauled himself up.

"Good luck, Pops," Michael called after him.

"Ain't nothing to do with luck, son. 'Trust in the Lord with all thine heart; and lean not into thine own understanding. In all thy ways acknowledge him, and He shall direct thy paths.'"

"Amen," Michael said.

"Amen."

Lundquist turned the ignition, and the truck's engine rumbled. He pressed down on the gas, feeding it revs. Michael looked up at him, his eyes still wet, and slammed the door shut. Lundquist put the truck into first gear and rolled slowly out of the yard.

He figured he could make Green Bay in four hours.

Chapter 44

MILTON WAS slow and cautious as he made his way back into Truth. He knew that the focus of the search would be up in the wilderness, that the Guards would not have expected him to have been able to slip through the cordon, and, even if they could have anticipated that, they would not expect him to head back into town again. They would expect him to take a car and drive away as far and as fast as he could.

That had never crossed Milton's mind.

He had made promises, and his word meant something to him.

He had promised to kill Lundquist, and he would.

He had promised to come back for Mallory, Arty, and Ellie, and he would do that, too.

The town was eerily quiet. The storm was unabated, and that would have been more than enough to clear Main Street of pedestrians, but there was no traffic on the road, either. The stop lights at the junction flashed red, amber, and green, reflecting on the wet asphalt, but there were no cars to observe them. Perhaps the residents were frightened. Soldiers were abroad, and men had been killed. A maniac was running amok. Perhaps they were all hiding indoors.

Milton moved from cover to cover. He was absorbed into the welcoming darkness of an alley, and then he rushed to hide in the lee of a big industrial bin. He ducked down behind the wing of a car and pressed himself into a doorway.

He heard the grumble of an engine, deeper than a car, and ducked down behind a bus stop. A Humvee, olive green, with a fifty-calibre machine gun mounted atop it, rolled at a medium pace right down the middle of the street.

Milton waited until it was out of sight and then hurried on.

HE WAS passing a takeaway that he had seen when he had first come into town when he saw him.

Arthur Stanton.

He was inside, using a payphone that was fixed to the wall. Milton stood in the doorway for a moment, assessing the place, and then stepped inside.

There was a table and a couple of chairs just inside the door, and Milton sat down so that his back was facing the door. Arty had the phone pressed to his ear and a frown on his face.

"I told you," the proprietor called out to him from behind the counter. "Everything's down. Storm's knocked the whole thing out."

Arty put the receiver back onto its cradle and turned to the door. His face was anguished, pale, and it looked like he had been crying. He was distracted and he didn't notice Milton until he reached out and took his sleeve.

"What—" he said, his face twisting with fright.

"It's me, Arty. Remember? John."

The disquiet seemed almost to worsen.

"It's Mr. Milton."

He stopped. The shock lifted to be replaced instead with upset.

He gestured to the seat opposite. "Sit down."

He swayed from foot to foot, unsure what to do, but, with a softer "Arty," Milton gently tugged on his sleeve and he sat.

"I don't know what to do," he said.

"Where are Mallory and Ellie?"

He didn't hear the question. "I got out. I climbed up, got out through the roof. I tried to open the door, but it was locked. Mallory said I was to call a number, 313-338-

7786—I remembered it, see—but they say the telephones aren't working, and I can't do what she wanted me to do. She said I had to go south, to Detroit, but I don't know how to get there."

"Arty. You have to tell me where they are."

"In the big shed," he said, his face open and surprised, as if that was something that surely Milton must have known. "On the farm."

MILTON FOUND a car on a back street, put his elbow through the window and unlocked it from the inside. He got inside, with Arty in the passenger seat next to him, hot-wired the ignition and drove away. It took less than a minute, and it didn't look as if he had been seen.

"Which way?"

Arty pointed to the south. Milton turned onto Main Street and drove carefully, wary of attracting attention.

"How did you get away?"

"I climbed out. There was a hole in the roof."

"And then?"

He repeated himself. "I tried to open the door, but it was locked. Mallory told me to run into town, so I did. But the telephones don't work and now I don't know what I'm supposed to do."

He was getting agitated again. "It's okay, Arty. Don't worry. I'm here now. We'll soon have this sorted out."

"But what are we going to do?"

"Fix it."

Milton drove on. "How many people did you see there?"

He screwed up his face. "There was a woman and Mr. Finch, the plumber. We saw them most of all. There were a lot of people in the other barn the night they took us there but they all disappeared. We didn't see any of them again."

"Did anyone have any weapons? Guns?"

"The woman and Mr. Finch—they have shotguns."

"Anything else?"

"No. I didn't see anything."

"Well done, Arty. You've done very well." Milton cleared the outskirts of the town and put his foot down. "Hold on."

MILTON KILLED the lights a mile out and rolled up to the start of a long drive that led towards farm buildings. He switched off the engine and rolled to a stop, water splashing beneath the tires as they passed through deep puddles.

"I want you to stay here," he said to Arty.

"What about Mallory? And Ellie?"

"I'm going to go and get them. But you have to stay here. Do you understand?"

He shuffled awkwardly in the seat.

"Arty—you have to stay here. Do you understand?"

"I just want to help."

"I know you do, but I don't need help. And you'll get in my way. Stay here."

Arty grunted that he would. Milton opened the door, exited the car, and slipped into the cover of a clutch of fir trees. He crouched down, flexing his sore arm, and assessed the terrain ahead.

The farm was encircled by a fence. Thirty yards behind the fence was a log gatehouse that reminded him of a frontier stockade. A log was lowered across the dirt road like the arm of a highway toll booth. An oblong of light stretched out from the side of the gatehouse, a door that Milton couldn't see. The oblong was split in half by a shadow; someone was in the booth and had come to the doorway.

The farmhouse was at the end of the road, lights glowing in the downstairs windows. There was another light above the porch, swaying in the wind. Surrounding it were sagging sheds, bungalows. There was a bunkhouse, probably added as farm and family grew. Now the house was empty and silent, huddling under cedar and pinon trees. He saw other buildings: a tall grain silo, two barns. Faint light glimmered from a number of ramshackle constructions he could see in the distance. There was a long line of vehicles parked along the shoulder of the lane between the guardhouse and the farm.

Save the lights, there was no sign of life.

And then there was.

He heard the sound of a powerful engine. He ducked right down as a pair of high beams swung out from behind one of the barns. A truck, a big eighteen-wheeled semi, crawled slowly out of the yard and rolled through the gate and onto the lane. He saw the figure of a man in the yard, but he was much too far away to be able to identify him. The truck bounced along the potholed track towards him, the lights stretching out across the furrowed fields until they were interrupted by the trunks of the fir trees, casting inky black shadows for a dozen feet behind him. He couldn't make out any detail through the darkness and the rain and he stayed down low as the semi drew nearer. The brakes sighed as it reached the end of the track, the tractor swinging onto the main road and the trailer following after it.

Milton was close enough now to make out the driver.

Lundquist.

The engine growled again as Lundquist fed it more power. The truck was old and in bad shape. It rumbled away, passing the car with Arty inside and heading southeast.

Milton worked his way around the boundary of the property until he had enough cover between himself and the buildings to make an approach without being detected. This stretch of the fence was old and in need of repair, and Milton was able to duck down and slip between the top and bottom rails. He stayed low, sliding through long grass, moving quickly to a grove of black gum trees with a tangle of young buttonbush beneath their boughs.

He was halfway to the barns. The figure he had seen earlier was still there. It was a man, but he was facing away from him. His silhouette was slender. There was a line of chokeberry and cinquefoil ahead, and he was about to make out for it when another person emerged from the farmhouse. A woman. She was carrying a double-barrelled shotgun, the action open. The first man turned as she approached, and the light from the porch fell onto him.

Michael Callow.

Milton felt the jolt of adrenaline and felt his lips as they pressed tight against his teeth.

Milton heard the sound of a door creaking on rusty hinges. Callow and the woman turned to one of the barns. Two people emerged.

Mallory.

Ellie.

A third person followed them outside.

A man he hadn't seen before. Big, obese.

Ellie's wrists were cuffed.

He waited for them to turn away from him, but, before they could, he heard the sound of someone approaching from behind him. He turned his head back towards the car and saw Arthur Stanton's large figure, moving low and quickly, headed towards the yard.

There was nothing he could do. Arty hadn't seen Milton or, if he had, he was deliberately avoiding him because he knew what he would say. He was thirty feet away to the right, heading towards another clump of buttonbush. He couldn't call out or Callow and the others would hear him. But if he stayed silent, what would Arty do?

Milton knew. It would be bad.

He clenched his teeth. Helpless.

Callow stepped in front of Ellie and said something to her, his harsh laugh sounding like a bark as it rang around the yard.

He put his hands on her shoulders and pushed her down onto her knees.

The man standing behind Mallory did the same to her.

The woman closed the shotgun.

Milton couldn't wait.

If he left cover, if they saw him… a spread from the shotgun, medium range, it would pepper him.

But if he didn't…

Chapter 45

ELLIE TRIED the cuffs for the thousandth time, and they still held firm. Her knees and legs were inches deep in a thick slop of mud. She looked across to Magrethe Olsen's boots, smothered with the same mud, and then followed her legs up until she was looking into the barrels of the shotgun aimed straight at her. She had imagined dying in service, like her father before her, but it had always been an abstract idea. The kind of thing that happened to other people. Now, though, it was horribly, awfully real.

She was going out, kneeling in mud and pig shit in some backwater hick farm. She found herself thinking of Orville. If she ever got out of it, ever told him what had happened, she knew that he would find it hilarious.

But she wasn't getting out of it.

"I'm a federal agent," she said, again, knowing that it wasn't going to help them here.

"You know what's going to happen tonight?"

"Why don't you tell me."

"That truck, that's the biggest bomb this country's ever seen. It's going to make Oklahoma City look like powderpuff."

"So why don't you tell me where it's headed?"

She laughed. "Don't think so. All you need to know, when that bomb goes off, it's going to start the war to end all wars. All the Jews and the niggers and the wetbacks, the liberal intelligentsia, the sickness in the federal government, they're all going to get swept away. All of it. The Messiah is on his way. The Second Coming. Tonight is the start of it."

Ellie saw, in the corner of her eyes, that Mallory had closed her hand around a large stone.

Callow was just behind her. "Just get on with it."

Magrethe raised the stock and pressed it into her shoulder.

Ellie started to close her eyes.

There was a sudden blur of motion.

She looked up.

Arthur Stanton.

He came running out of the undergrowth. He moved with a clumsy gait, but he was big and strong and he bellowed with fury. Morris Finch was between him and Magrethe. Arty drew back his fist and pummelled the man in the side of the head with enough impact to spin him around on his standing leg, flipping him so that when he landed it was face first, out cold even before he splashed down into the mud.

Arty headed right for Magrethe.

There was ten feet between them.

Too far.

He roared at the top of his lungs.

She swivelled quickly, too quickly, the barrel swerving away from her and at him.

Her aim was quick, inaccurate, but the shotgun was loaded with buckshot.

She pulled the trigger and fired a spread.

Arty screamed, his legs collapsing beneath him as he slammed down to the earth.

Mallory shrieked.

"*Arty!*"

MALLORY SCREAMED.

Milton crashed out of the chokeberry, put his head down, and pounded the ground. There were twenty feet that separated him and the woman with the smoking shotgun, and she was facing Arty, a quarter turn away from him.

She hadn't seen him.

He sprinted, his muscles burning and adrenaline surging through his veins.

Callow saw him and shouted a warning.

The woman started to turn, her attention straying away from Ellie and Mallory for a moment.

Long enough.

Mallory bounded to her feet. She had a rock in her hand.

Callow made a move on Milton, trying to block him.

The woman turned back, too late, and saw Mallory.

Milton lowered his shoulder and barrelled into Callow, wrapping his arms around his waist and picking him up, driving him backwards, slamming him into the barn wall.

Mallory swung her arm, the stone clasped in her fist, the impact thumping into the woman's temple, dropping her backwards.

Callow grabbed Milton's shoulder, trying to draw him down onto the ground with him, trying to hold him there. The young man was strong.

The woman dropped the shotgun. It landed at Mallory's feet.

Milton raked Callow's eyes. The younger man gasped with pain, but held on. Milton butted him, then prised his fingers open. He leaned away just far enough to strike down with his right hand, putting his shoulder into it, trying to punch straight through his head into the muck beneath him. Callow groaned, and his eyes rolled back into his head.

Mallory stooped to collect the shotgun.

Milton scrambled up, his fist tingling.

The woman was on her hands and knees. Blood was running freely down her temple.

Mallory aimed the shotgun at her.

"No, Mallory," Milton said. "Give it to me."

Mallory shook her head.

The gun looked too big for her, almost too big for her to hold the fore-end with her left hand at the same time as the index finger of her right hand was up against the trigger.

"*Mallory.*"

Milton saw the emotion in her eyes: fear and anger. He recognised it. Knew how powerful it could be. He had tapped the same combination many times before.

"Mallory, please. You don't have to do that."

She shook her head. "I do."

"It won't make you feel any better."

"Ellie," Mallory said, "is Arty all right?"

Ellie hurried across to where the boy was thrashing on the ground, his hand pressed against his thigh.

The woman moaned, put her hand to her temple, drew it back, and looked at her bloody fingers.

"It's not as bad as it looks," Ellie said. "Flesh wound."

"Look at me," Mallory said to the woman. Her voice was cool and drawn.

"*Mallory.*" Milton took a step closer to her and extended his hand, palm out, ready to take the gun from her. "You'll hate yourself forever. Trust me."

"Listen to your friend," the woman said. Her voice was dazed, but there was scorn in it.

"I don't think so."

"You ain't gonna shoot me."

"No?"

"What's her name?" Milton said.

"Magrethe Olsen," Ellie said.

"That's right, and you killed my son. You are going to burn in eternal hellfire for what you've done."

Milton really couldn't disagree with that. "You need to shut your mouth."

She cackled. "Eternal damnation, that's what you've got coming to you."

Mallory took a step back so that she could cover her properly with the spread.

Magrethe shook her head, ridding herself of the cobwebs. "I knew your daddy, girl. You know that?"

Mallory did not reply. She bit the corner of her lip instead.

"That's right. I did. Before he went off the rails. He was a good man. I'd say he got dealt a shitty hand in life, I'm thinking about your mother and your brother being born the way he was, retarded and all—"

"Don't say that," she cut across her.

She carried on, "But all things considered, your old man was a stand-up fellow. I was older than he was, a few years, who's counting, but we knew each other like everyone knows everyone else in this town. And I'll tell you something, Mallory, he'd be proud of how you've turned out."

Magrethe struggled up onto unsteady feet. "I'll tell you something else, Mallory."

"Mallory," Milton said, "give it to me."

"He would've been proud of how you've looked after your brother. A retard, I mean, that's not—"

Mallory's eyes opened wide at that, and she said, in a voice that should not have been misunderstood, "I told you, don't call him that."

"What? A retard?"

"Say that word again."

"And what? You'll shoot an unarmed woman? No. You won't do that, Mallory. Now, enough of this nonsense."

"I'm warning you."

"Don't be so foolish. It's just a word. You call him special; everyone else calls him a ret—"

The boom was deafening. Magrethe caught the blast at close range, and it tore her to shreds, flinging her backwards, her face and scalp gouged by the buckshot into a raw, pulpy mess.

Mallory looked at what she had done. She stood there for a long moment, stock-still, and then she carefully placed the shotgun on the ground and went over to her brother and Ellie.

Chapter 46

THE BODY of Magrethe Olsen lay face up on the ground, shot to pieces. Ellie looked down at her and felt nothing.

Mallory hurried across to her brother, took his hand, and hugged him close.

Milton put out a hand and steadied himself against the side of the barn.

"You all right?"

"I'll be honest. I've been better."

"What happened?"

"I went back into the hills. They sent a posse after me."

"And?"

"And I'm here and they're not."

"What does that mean?"

"They're dead, Ellie."

"How many?"

"I stopped counting at five."

He said it without emotion or inflection. Like it was business. "Are you hurt?"

"Took one in my arm. Lucky shot. I've cleaned it out. It'll need to be treated, but it's fine for now."

The rain kept coming down, but Ellie thought that she could hear something else. "We have to stop Lundquist."

"I saw him, in the truck. Where's he going?"

"I don't know. They do, but they won't say."

"They'll say," he said grimly. "You know what's in the trailer?"

"It's a bomb, Milton. They had it parked outside. I watched them load it. Barrels of fertiliser, fuel, explosives, too, I think. They're planning to blow something up. You get the registration?"

"It's a white Freightliner. BDH 5578."

"My partner," she said, "when he hears this…"

The noise in the rain came again, clearer now. They both swung around and stared into the darkness, but they couldn't see it yet. Ellie knew what it was: a helicopter, the distinctive *whup whup whup* of the blades, the bird coming in low and fast from the north.

"Ellie," Milton said, "you have to listen to me. It's the National Guard."

"So they'll help us."

"No, they won't. All they know is what Lundquist told them. They think I'm a murderer." He gestured down at the shot-up woman. "They'll see her body and shoot me on sight."

"I won't let them. I'll explain—"

"You got any ID?"

"No. They took it away."

He shook his head. "Then we don't have time. Lundquist is already on the move, and I need to get after him. We need to get Callow into the house."

Mallory helped Arty to his feet and supported his bad leg, helping him hobble across to the farmhouse.

Milton took Callow beneath the shoulders and dragged him, face down, after them.

The Black Hawk swooped over the tree line and roared over the roof, the rotor wash sending up a cloud of spray and terrifying a coop of chickens. They ducked their heads in the sudden storm of debris and the clattering, terrible noise.

Inside. The door led into a hallway with three doors. There was a large French dresser that held a collection of plates and other crockery. Milton ushered them all inside and then went back to the dresser. He heaved it around, plates toppling off it and smashing against the floor. He dragged it until it was flush against the door, blocking the way inside.

"You sure that you know what you're doing?" Ellie said.

"If we let the Guard take over here, we'll lose any chance we have of getting to Lundquist."

"They'll contact the bureau."

"Yes, and they should, but we'll have to wait for them to realise that's what they need to do. We don't have *time* to wait. The bureau has no idea what's happening. They don't even know what happened to you. How long would it take your partner to get out here?"

"Hours."

"And it'll be too late by then. Lundquist could have driven to Green Bay, Detroit, Minneapolis, Cleveland, Chicago… He could've driven anywhere. If you're right, if it *is* like Oklahoma, think what he could do with that truck."

"I know. It's all I *can* think about." She frowned. "It's not going to be easy to mobilise. The storm's taken out the local phone lines and cell towers. Everything north of Wausau. It would be a nightmare to try to organise the response."

"So we don't have any choice, do we? We *have* to do this ourselves. It's on us."

He was right; she knew it. "So what do you need?"

"I've got to interrogate Callow."

"You want to tell me what that means? *Interrogate?*"

"You really want to know?"

Ellie bit the inside of her lip. She knew exactly what he meant and, despite everything that the militia had done to them and everything they might go on to do, the prospect still sat uncomfortably with her.

"We don't have the time to be pleasant, Ellie. I need to know everything he knows."

"You'll… you'll kill him?"

"It's tempting, but no. I'll leave that to the government."

"What do I have to do?"

He nodded, his face a blank and inscrutable mask. "Keep the Guards off my back. I need five minutes with him and then as much of a head start as you can manage."

"How am I going to do that? I don't have my ID."

"I don't care how you do it. Be persuasive. Five minutes, that's all."

"What are you going to do?"

"Stop Lundquist."

MICHAEL CALLOW woke up to the sensation of his feet scraping along the floor. He felt strong arms looped around his chest, hands clasped over his sternum. His head felt unbelievably sore, as if he had been hit with a jackhammer just behind his ear. He felt dizzy and nauseous, and, as he opened his eyes he saw the ceiling of a room he partly recognised above him. He remembered what had happened in the yard outside and felt the first explosive eruption of vomit launch from his gullet, up his throat and out of his mouth. It ran over his chin and into his nostrils, and splattered all over his shirt.

Callow felt as if his head was full of smoke.

They were in the kitchen of Seth and Magrethe Olsen's farmhouse. He recognised the beadboard on the walls, the soapstone counters, the tin splashbacks, the ceiling panels painted light blue, the big iron range. He saw the baking station. The eighteenth-century mustard-painted Quebecois bar. The antique dining table where they all had pledged their allegiance to the Sword of God, swearing it over his father's Bible.

John Milton walked over to him and looked down. It all came back to him in a terrifying flood of images and sounds, the chaos that this man had wrought. He tried to tell his legs to move, to get him away from him, to get him anywhere but *here*, but his brain was fuzzy and his legs weren't listening.

Milton put his right shoulder beneath the edge of the dining table and straightened his back a little to raise it from the floor. He arranged two piles of Magrethe's thick cookery books beneath each leg, raising them up and sloping the angle of the table.

He came back to him.

Callow tried to struggle, but Milton was strong. He grabbed him beneath the arms and hauled him to the table. Callow tried to hook his leg around the cabinet, but Milton yanked him away. He kicked and bucked and tried to plant the heels of his boots on the floor, but all he succeeded in doing was to leave a track of scraped rubber across the wide wooden planks.

Milton pushed him onto the sloping tabletop, grabbed both his shoulders, and hauled him the rest of the way up. He took a nylon washing line and lashed his legs and shoulders to the board, arranging him so that his head was lower than his heart. The dim fog in Callow's head started to disperse more quickly, but the confusion was replaced by panic, and all he could do was squirm and wriggle. It was useless. The bonds were too tight. He squeezed his eyes as tightly shut as he could.

He started to protest, trying to find the words that would persuade the man that this was unnecessary, but, before he could tell him any of that, a towel was draped over his face, his eyes and his nose and his mouth, blocking out the light. On top of the hood, which still admitted a few flashes of random light to his vision, layers of cloth were added. Total darkness absorbed him.

Milton's voice was muffled. "Michael, I need you to tell me where your father has gone."

"I don't know," he said, his voice muffled, the exhalation of his breath gathering against the towel, with nowhere to go.

"He's driven off in the semi. He's going to detonate it. You need to tell me where he's going to do that."

The panic cut through his dizziness like a hot knife. Awareness came plunging back.

He blinked furiously against the fabric, remembering what his father had told him as they sat around the kitchen table. He remembered the story of John Wilkes Booth and the words he had shouted after he had assassinated Abraham Lincoln.

He shouted them.

"Sic Semper Tyrannis!"

Thus Always to Tyrants.

He waited, his breathing clotted and difficult through the weight of the cloth above his mouth, and wondered whether Milton had been able to hear his words or whether they were too muffled to be intelligible. Then he felt the wet slap of water as it was poured over his head. He felt a slow cascade of water going up his nose.

He held his breath for as long as he could, but then he had to exhale and inhale, the damp cloths brought tight against his nostrils, as if a huge, wet palm had been suddenly pressed over his face. He couldn't tell whether he was breathing in or out, whether he was breathing in water, whether his nostrils and mouth and lungs were engulfed with it or whether it was all in his imagination. Lines blurred. Reality shifted, became slippery. The water kept slapping down onto him. He thumped his fist against the side of the table.

The wet towels were pulled away from his face. He blinked furiously into the sudden light, spluttering water from his nose.

"Where is he going?"

"'Therefore do not fear them. For there is nothing covered that will not be revealed…'"

"Where?"

"'… And hidden that shall not be known.'"

"Want to try again?"

He gasped for air, his pulse racing. "You can do what you want. I'm not saying anything."

He heard the doubt and fear in his voice and cursed himself for his weakness. He prayed for strength.

"I barely washed your face that time," Milton said as he dropped the sodden, heavy cloth over his face again.

He heard footsteps moving away. He heard water sloshing into a vessel. He heard footsteps approaching. Water was poured over him again. Callow tried hard, fighting the wave of nausea and terror, but it was a hopeless task, his gag reflex overwhelming him, filling him with abject terror, *primal* terror, and he slapped the table again.

The wet cloth was pulled away for a second time.

Milton was leaning over him, looking down into his face. Those *eyes*, so cold and pitiless. The eyes of the Devil. Callow sobbed out, his breath racing in hungry gulps, and then he looked into those eyes, and he knew that this was not a man from whom he could expect clemency or mercy. Milton would kill him.

"Where is he, Michael?"

"'Be merciful to me, O God, because of your constant love. Because of your great mercy, wipe away my sins. Wash away my evil and make me clean from my sin.'"

Milton raised the cloth and held it above his face, water streaming from the sodden fabric and falling onto his face. *"Where is he?"*

"Green Bay. The federal courthouse in Green Bay."

Chapter 47

MILTON PLACED the pewter jug on the floor and left Callow trussed up on the table. He hurried into the sitting room. Ellie had found a bunch of keys on the table, and one of them fit her bracelets. She looked up at him, concern on her face.

"It's Green Bay."

"Where?"

"Federal courthouse. A bomb that big, though… it'll do a lot of damage."

"What do you want me to do?"

He nodded to the cuffs. "Put those on Callow."

"And then?"

"Explain to the soldiers what's happened. Everything. Tell them about the truck and that he's probably taking it to Green Bay."

"*Probably?*"

"Callow wasn't lying, but maybe Lundquist didn't tell him the truth. Can't say for sure. They'll need to block all the major roads out of the Upper Peninsula."

"And you?"

"I'm going after him."

Milton paused, looking at her. Her eyes flickered down to his arm. He looked down, too, and saw fresh blood spotting on his sweater.

"John, you can't. Look at you. You're hurt."

There was no point in pretending otherwise. "There's no choice. If he gets stopped, he'll blow up the truck. An explosion like that will take out everyone within a hundred yards of it. If he can't kill feds, he'll make do with soldiers. Maybe I can stop him before that happens."

He wouldn't be dissuaded, and Ellie quickly saw the futility in trying. Instead, she came to him, put her hands on his shoulders, and stood on tiptoes, placing a soft kiss on his cheek.

"Good luck."

"I'll be fine."

"You still owe me dinner."

He allowed her a smile, squeezed her hand on his shoulder, and then gently disengaged himself. He turned and left the room, following the hall to the parlour at the back of the house. There was a wide picture window. The lights in the room were off, and Milton approached it carefully, seeing his own reflection looking back at him as he stared out into the darkness of the yard beyond.

He couldn't see anyone.

The turbines of the Black Hawk whined as the chopper powered down on the other side of the house.

He heard voices.

He slid his fingers beneath the bottom sash and pulled it up, grimacing as the wood squeaked in loud protest. He pulled again, his arm complaining from the effort, and then, when he had opened it far enough, he pulled himself through and dropped down onto the muddy lawn beyond.

More voices.

He ran across the backyard to the porte cochère that had been built on the eastern side of the house. There was a dirt bike propped up there, a Honda CRF450R, a light and powerful bike that Milton knew would pack a punch. That was good.

The keys were in the ignition. Milton pulled it away from the wall, surprised that it was so light, straddled it, and then twisted the key. He fired the engine with the kick-start, hearing it growl and whine as he fed it revs, and then held on tight as it bucked out from beneath the shelter and started across the yard.

Two uniformed soldiers were right in front of him.

"Stop!"

Milton swerved around them both, the back wheel sliding out, the tyre cutting through the sludge until it bit on the mud beneath. The unexpected jerk almost unseated him, and the effort of clasping hard with both hands sent a blast of pain up his damaged arm.

Milton settled his balance again, not daring to look back, and aimed the bike for the fields that spread out to the south of the farm. More corn, tractor trails bisecting the field right down the middle. He heard the sound of the warning shot fired just above his head, ducked down and squeezed out more revs. The bike shot ahead at forty and then fifty, raced through an open gate and leapt off a furrowed slope, slamming down onto the uneven surface of the field ten feet farther on. Milton was sprayed with mud as he fought to control the bike. He squeezed the brakes until he was comfortable and then aimed for the passage between the crops.

He raced between the tall shoulders of the stalks, deeper and deeper into the field.

ELLIE RUBBED her sore wrists and crept low to the window, daring a quick glance outside. The Black Hawk had come down in a field to the west of the farmhouse, the branches still shaking and the tremendous noise rattling the panes of glass. A bright searchlight swung around from the open doorway of the chopper, a blinding yellow light that played across the farmhouse, fixing on the window and lighting up everything inside, the darkest shadows painted on the wall behind them.

"What are we going to do?" Mallory asked fretfully.

"You heard what Milton said. We need to let them know we're not the bad guys."

"How—"

"Let me talk to them, Mallory. Stay here with Arty. We'll need to get him some help. Make sure Michael Callow stays here, too."

She went to the hallway. She put her shoulder behind the French dresser and pushed it aside so she could open the door wide enough to squeeze through.

She walked out into the yard.

The searchlight played out through the trees, throwing spectral shadows against the walls of the farmhouse. She saw the silhouettes of men crouched down low, running away from the field where the Black Hawk had landed. The dark figures parted, some going to the left of her and some to the right. They spread out around her, adopted firing positions, and aimed their rifles at her. The searchlight jerked around again, finally fixing on her, and she had to raise her arm in front of her eyes so that she could see.

"Put your hands up!" a harsh voice called out.

She raised her left hand, the light flooding into her face again.

"Who are you?"

"My name is Ellie Flowers. I am an FBI agent."

"On your knees!"

"I'm FBI."

"Do it now!"

She lowered herself to her knees.

One of the soldiers took a step in her direction. He had a pistol in his hand, and it was aimed straight at her head.

"Identification?"

"No, sir. It's been taken from me."

"Name?"

"I just told you: Ellie Flowers."

"Field office?"

"Detroit. 477 Michigan Avenue. My partner's name is Orville Clayton. Call him."

"Anyone else in that house?"

"Yes," she said. "Mallory and Arthur Stanton. They're local kids. Arthur has been shot and is going to need a medic. There's a man tied to a table in the kitchen. His name is Michael Callow. You'll want to speak to him."

"You want to tell me what in the name of God is going down here?"

"Secure the area, soldier. I'll need to talk to your C.O."
"Where's John Milton?"
"I need to talk to your C.O."

Chapter 48

MORTEN LUNDQUIST was shrewd, an old soldier, and Milton guessed that they would make similar tactical assessments.

So he considered what he might have done had the roles been reversed.

Time, first. How much time would he have as a head start? Milton would have assumed that the situation would mean the compromising of his headquarters and with that, his plan. That would have told him that he only had a limited amount of time. Not long enough to gamble with a safer, but slower, journey to the south on quieter roads. Speed would be very important.

Milton's first assumption: Lundquist would follow the quickest route south.

Milton remembered the map and plotted a route from Truth to Green Bay. He would have driven to Stannard and then picked up the US-45 to the south.

How much of a start did he have? A new Freightliner was a big, powerful semi with 450 horsepower, turbocharged engines which would top out at, what, eighty miles an hour? He had seen the truck, though, and it was old and tired. The engine had sounded worn, and that would mean that it would lose compression and, thus, power. So reduce the top speed by twenty miles an hour: call it sixty. And the load was unstable. Too many bumps and jolts might make for an unfortunate accident. Milton settled on fifty-five, a little less if the roads were bad.

He pictured the map in his head. A thirty-minute head start, fifty to fifty-five miles an hour, that might give him a lead of twenty or twenty-five miles.

The bike was comfortable at sixty, but Milton cranked out more speed, bringing it up to seventy.

Lundquist was probably in Union Bay right now. In an hour, he would have swung to the south and would be on US-64, maybe down in Bergland.

After an hour, Milton ought to be able to make it to Iron Mountain.

He should be able to catch him around there.

He held the throttle wide open, almost maxing it out until he thought the piston was going to blow through the head. He backed off a little, racing around the side of another big eighteen wheeler hauling freight, the trucker pulling down on his air horn as Milton went by him in a blur.

THE HUMVEE had arrived soon after the Black Hawk had touched down and soon after that, another two parked alongside. The soldiers had secured the perimeter of the house and had started to fan out into the outbuildings. A shout went up as they reached the barn and found the body of Magrethe Olsen.

Ellie was taken to the first Humvee. A soldier in soaked olive fatigues dismounted.

"I'm Lieutenant Colonel Alex Maguire," he said, extending his hand.

Ellie shook it. "Special Agent Ellie Flowers."

"I'm sorry for the confusion."

"You've confirmed my ID, Colonel?"

"Yes, ma'am. We've raised your partner on the radio. He wants to speak to you."

Ellie took the handset that Maguire offered her and put it to her ear.

"Orville?"

"Ellie?"

"Yes."

"Jesus, Ellie, what the fuck is going on up there?"

"I'll explain. Just—"

"You find those boys?"

"Yes, Orville. I did. Just listen to me, please, for once. I need you to listen very, very carefully."

There was a pause on the line, a clatter of static. When he finally spoke, he sounded abashed, even with all the interference. "Okay. Go ahead."

Ellie ran through what had happened as quickly as she could. The colonel was listening, too, which was good; it would save her telling the story twice. She left out the details that were unimportant, like the treatment she had received. That, she knew, would just inflame Orville's guilt and that would mean she'd have his paternalism to deal with, and she could do without that right now. She left out anything about her and Milton because his jealousy would be just as bad. Instead, she told him about the arrests of the gang, the murder of Lester Grogan, how the bank jobs had been funding the militia, the truck bomb, and that Morten Lundquist was driving it to a target right now.

The colonel waved for his number two, anxiety all over his face.

"Jesus," Orville said. "You know where he's going?"

"I think Green Bay. The federal courthouse."

"You think? Be specific."

"That's what one of the militia told us"—she paused, searching for the right euphemism—"in circumstances that suggest he wasn't lying when he told us."

"What the hell does that—"

"That's the most likely," she cut across him, "but it could be anywhere within a four- or five-hour drive. Your guess is as good as mine where he might go."

He swore. "I need to make some calls. Can you handle the Guards? They need to find him."

"Don't worry, Orville. I'm on top of it."

"Christ, you know what'll happen if he gets that truck into a built-up area?"

"He won't."

"How could you possibly know that?"

"Someone's already gone after him."

"Who?"

"Milton."

"Who the hell *is* this guy?"

"Never mind. Make your calls. We'll speak later."

She handed the radio back before he could press her any further.

The colonel looked concerned. "That all true?"

"I'm afraid so."

"I'm sorry about before, ma'am. I kind of feel we're three steps behind on this."

"It's all right. I know the feeling. How did you know we were out here?"

"We picked up a couple of fellas in the woods. Watts and McClennan? You know them?"

"No."

"They were part of the posse that went after this Milton guy. Their stories didn't tally. Watts told us if he got out of the woods, he'd come down here."

"They'll be a part of all this."

"They've just been put in custody. But this Milton guy, you want to tell me whose side he's on?"

"Ours," she said.

"For sure?"

"He saved my life. And he's gone after Lundquist now."

"You should see the mess he's left up by the lake. Dead bodies left and right. Police are going to have one hell of a job working that out."

"I'll explain it in the air."

He gaped. "I'm sorry, ma'am?"

She nodded in the direction of the Black Hawk. "Can you give me a ride?"

Chapter 49

MILTON SAW the truck as the lights of Watersmeet were visible on the horizon. The US-45 was long and straight, cutting between the green shoulders of birch and fir that clustered on either side. There had been almost no traffic, just a few trucks making early deliveries and the cars of hunters heading up into the woods so that they could get started at dawn.

He had hammered the bike as hard as he dared, but now the engine was beginning to strain a little. It was running up at seventy, and, at that speed, it was as skittish as a frisky colt. He had been riding with the headlamp off so as not to betray his approach, and that made it even more challenging. The asphalt was decent, but there were patches, now and again, that were littered with potholes. There had been moments when he had passed across them with no warning, sure that the front wheel was going to jerk out of control and that he would be thrown from the seat. He managed to hold on and keep the bike pointing down the road. His left arm throbbed from the continued effort of grasping the handlebars, and his right wrist was sore from twisting the throttle all the way around to its stops.

He saw the lights of the truck when he was a mile behind it. It was too far away to be sure that it was Lundquist, but he was travelling faster than it was, and he closed rapidly until he was three hundred yards away and could recognise the livery in the light of the wan moon. He was driving carefully, observing the speed limit, nothing out of the ordinary.

They passed isolated houses and businesses as they approached the town, and then the buildings started to come closer together. There was a crossroad, where US-2 met US-45, and there were gas stations on both sides of the road, a diner, a strip mall. Milton throttled right back. If Ellie was right and the truck had been loaded with explosives…

He had seen truck bombs go up before, and remembered one blast in particular in Kunduz, the Taliban detonating a dump truck that was smaller than the semi. The neighbourhood had been levelled, scraped off the face of the Earth, and what had been left had been a field of rubble and debris so bleak and desolate as to be almost lunar.

He let the truck pull ahead.

MAGUIRE LED Ellie to the chopper, approaching from three o'clock to avoid the forward tilt of the rotors. She was pelted with mud, sticks, and leaves from the wash and, without a step to help her into the waist-high doorway, she accepted Maguire's helping hand. She took one of the canvas-covered seats and locked herself into the four-point harness.

Maguire handed her a pair of headphones and indicated that she should put them on.

The turbines throttled up, and the chopper lifted into the air, whipping the branches of the trees as it climbed above them.

Maguire's voice came over the headphones. "You think south?"

"That's right."

"We'll follow Highway 28 and then the US-45," the pilot said as he dipped the nose and the Black Hawk pulled away from the farm. "When did he leave?"

"Half an hour ago."

"So he couldn't have gotten far. We can push this all the way up to one hundred and fifty knots. It won't take long to catch him up."

"If he is going south," Maguire said, looking at Ellie.

"Green Bay," she said. "That's what we were told."

Maguire nodded. He looked ill at ease. His orders had changed radically over the course of the last hour, and he looked a little uncomfortable with the new responsibility that he had been given.

"Is this helicopter armed?"

"Sure," Maguire said. He nodded to the belted machine guns that had been fitted on either side of the Black Hawk. "We got two 7.62mm machine guns up here. We use them for suppressing fire normally, but they'll make a mess of anything we point them at."

"You have orders to use them?"

"I've got orders to take a look, and flexibility to act based on that."

MILTON PICKED up speed again and started to close the half mile that he had allowed to develop between him and the truck. He was halfway there when he heard the engine start to rev harder, and the truck started to accelerate.

Lundquist must have seen him.

He twisted the throttle all the way, the engine firing out at maximum, and the distance closed again.

Four hundred yards.

Three hundred.

Two.

One.

The truck was laden down, riding down low on its axles, and Lundquist either couldn't, or dared not, try to run any faster than he was.

Milton closed right up next to the rear doors. He balanced himself across the bike, stood up on the foot pegs and leaned forward. He reached up, his hand fastening around the locking handles.

The brake lights flashed a sudden red and the truck lurched right back at him. The front tyre bumped against the frame and then caught beneath it, the wheel buckling and the rear of the bike bucking upwards, propelling

Milton out of the seat and over the handlebars, into the door.

He slammed into it, his hands fastened around the handle as his legs crashed down onto the road with the toes of his boots scraping against the blacktop. The sudden friction tore him backwards, but he held on.

He held onto the handle, his right boot wedged against the rear underride guard, and then brought his left foot up alongside it.

The front wheel came free, and the bike somersaulted away behind him.

There was a meaty thud as something bumped up against the doors from inside the trailer.

Milton shuffled across the guard so that he was behind the left-hand door, but close enough to reach the locking mechanism for the right. He anchored with his left hand and stretched out with his right, flicking off the safety latch and rotating the handle. He yanked back just as Lundquist stamped on the brakes again. There was another heavy bump from inside, and then the unlatched door suddenly swung open. A large plastic barrel teetered on the edge and, as Lundquist accelerated again, it overbalanced and tipped out of the back, crashing down onto the road and tumbling over itself, crazy cartwheels that sprayed diesel across the asphalt.

The door swung as Lundquist negotiated a gentle left-hand turn, and as it fell open, Milton got a clear view inside. Ellie had been right: the truck was packed with large plastic barrels of many different colours, together with distinctive "sausages" of explosives that had been fastened onto them with tape.

He wrapped his fingers around a wooden pallet that had slipped down to the lip of the trailer bed, and used it as an anchor to help him slither ahead.

Lundquist braked again. The wheels locked this time, leaving rubber on the road as the trailer fishtailed left and right. Milton slid back again to the edge, his fingers clutching the pallet so hard that he felt splinters digging into his flesh, but he just squeezed harder, his grip the only thing that was preventing him from falling from the trailer.

The pallet slid backwards, too.

Another of the barrels teetered back and forth and, as they swerved again, it fell. More diesel sloshed out of it, flooding out of the back, pouring over Milton. It rushed over his hands, then his wrists and arms and over his torso.

The barrel rolled around on its side, straight down the centre of the cargo bay at him.

THE BLACK HAWK's navigator worked off a paper map that he held open over his lap, relaying instructions to the pilot. They flew fast and close to the ground, following the route that Lundquist was most likely to have taken. They started due east on Highway 28, the trunkline that bisected the Upper Peninsula east to west.

They reached Stannard Township and swung sharply to follow the 28 south.

Ellie looked down over Bond Falls State Park, the canopy of dense foliage, the road stretching ahead and behind them.

They rocketed over Watersmeet at three hundred feet above ground level.

"There!" the navigator said.

Ellie strained forwards against the restraints that held her in her seat. She craned her neck so she could see through the open door.

"That it?" Maguire asked her.

It was the same truck that she had seen earlier. "Yes. That's it."

They drew closer, still staying well back in the event that a blast was triggered.

The truck started to swing wildly to the left and right, as if Lundquist was trying to throw someone off.

Milton.

One of the doors was open, flapping as the truck swerved.

"Holy crap," the gunner said.

They edged a little closer, and she could see him. He was half in and half out of the trailer, grabbing onto a wooden pallet that was wedged against the closed door.

Her headphones squelched with static, and then she heard the voice of the pilot. "Hotel two-six, Crazy Horse one-eight. Have the target in range. Request permission to engage."

The next voice was distant, without the clamour of the turbines, someone in a command post somewhere. "Roger that, Crazy Horse. We have no personnel close to your position; you are free to engage. Over."

"Okay, we'll be engaging."

"Hey!" Ellie yelled.

The gunner covered his throat mike with his hand. "Permission to fire?"

"Roger, gunner, go ahead. I'm gonna... I can't see it now. It's behind those trees."

"Hey!" Ellie shouted, louder this time.

She reached down and started to fumble with the clasps on her belts.

"Ma'am," Maguire said.

"Tell them to hold their fire!"

"Don't try to get out of your seat, please."

MILTON DUCKED his head as the barrel bounced over the sill at the edge of the truck, spun high into the air, and cleared his trailing legs by a few spare inches.

He reached with his right arm, slowly hauling himself into the trailer. He assessed it quickly. There was a strong, cloying odour of ammonia and diesel. It was pungent, and Milton quickly felt a headache developing. He would not be able to stay inside the trailer for long. It was forty feet long and two-thirds full. He saw barrels of different colours, hundreds of pounds of explosives marked with TOVEX, and thirty PRIMADET blasting caps. There were an additional twenty fifty-pound bags of fertiliser lashed up against the right-hand wall. Milton knew enough about explosives to know that if those blasting caps were ever detonated, they would trigger a blast strong enough to shake the heavens.

He started to feel light-headed from the fumes.

He looked back to the open rear end. The door was still swinging to and fro, given fresh momentum every time the trailer turned through a corner or bounced across an uneven surface. The trailer was twice Milton's height and the ceiling was a good four feet above him. He went to the nearest barrel and wrapped his arms around it, grunting with exertion as he moved it, inch by inch, towards the rear. When it was close enough to be almost directly beneath the overhang of the ceiling, he clambered atop it, almost losing his balance on more than one occasion, and then reached up to fasten both hands around the edge of the roof. He boosted himself up, scrambling with both feet against the right-hand wall, heaving with every last scrap of strength until he had managed to wedge his torso over the edge, bringing up his right leg and pushing until he was all the way over.

The wind whipped at him, stinging his eyes, and he had to lay flat and clasp the edge of the trailer to stop himself from being blown off. The trees rushed by on either side, and when he wriggled across to the edge, he looked down to see the asphalt unrolling like a long and unbroken black ribbon.

He reached forward, grabbed at the edge, and pushed with his legs.

He reached forward and pushed.

Again.

Again.

LUNDQUIST JERKED the wheel left and right, feeling the huge mass of the trailer as it swung across the road. He knew that he had to be careful, that tipping the rig over would be the end of it all, but by the same token, he couldn't allow Milton to interfere.

He had seen him earlier, racing down the road.

He reached across to the passenger seat and pulled the M16 closer so that he could easily reach the trigger, and yanked the wheel again.

He thought of what David said to Solomon.

Be strong and courageous. Do not be afraid or discouraged, for the Lord God, my God, is with you. He will not fail you or forsake you until all the work for the service of the temple of the Lord is finished.

He stomped down on the gas and swerved the tractor in the opposite direction.

"YOU CAN'T FIRE," Ellie said. "The truck's loaded with explosives."

"And that's why we have to," Maguire shouted into his mic. "If we detonate it out here, all we'll do is knock over some trees and make a mess of the road."

"You'll kill Milton."

"We don't know who he is."

"He's the only reason we've got a chance to stop this."

"I've only got your word for that, Agent. I've got clearance to take that truck out at my discretion."

"Then *use* your discretion. Give him a chance."

"We let him drive on, we risk him triggering a blast in a town or a city. Can't take that risk."

"He'll stop him," Ellie shouted back. "You don't need to shoot it."

The headphones squelched again with the pilot's voice.

"Man on the roof of the truck."

The gunner looked out. "Okay, confirmed, we got a guy climbing up on the roof."

"That's Milton!" Ellie yelled.

"I'm gonna fire," the gunner said. "Okay?"

"Once you get on, just open up," the pilot said.

"Give him a chance!"

Maguire looked at Ellie. He bit his lip and then said, "No, this is Maguire. Hold on."

"Sir?"

"Get ahead of it and then come around. We'll see what he's going to do. Position?"

"Six miles out of Iron River," the pilot reported.

"Get ahead of the truck. If it's still rolling three miles outside town, take it out."

MILTON HAD seen the Black Hawk as it swooped ahead of them a hundred yards to the left. They wouldn't get too close, just in case the trailer was detonated and the blast caught them, too. It raced away to the south. Milton doubted that they would let them pass into another town.

He would have jumped and left the chopper to blow the explosives, but the semi was going too fast. He didn't much like the odds of walking away if he leapt from it onto the road.

That, and he had made a promise to Lundquist that he meant to keep.

The wind tore at him as he clambered across the full forty feet of the trailer. He gripped onto the lip of the roof and dropped down onto the catwalk behind the tractor. The handle to release the fifth wheel was an arm's length beneath the trailer and he didn't know whether it would be too far for him to reach. He lowered himself to his belly, his head pointing to the back of the trailer, and slid further until he was resting on the wheel guard, almost wedged beneath the tractor and the leading edge of the trailer. He looked over the side: the big Yokohama tyre rumbled just inches below him, across asphalt that seemed almost close enough to touch. Spray churned up and over him; he had to blink furiously to clear his eyes and then he had to grip hard with both hands as they turned into a sharp lefthander. The trailer pivoted on the fifth wheel and, for a moment, he thought he was going to be crushed beneath it.

It brushed his shoulder. The edge pressed into his deltoid, smearing thick black turntable grease, and then it straightened out again. Milton slid further beneath the trailer, the last few extra inches that he could manage, and then reached out his hand until his fingers closed around the locking handle.

It could only be pulled out at a perpendicular angle to the tractor.

He yanked it.

Nothing.

He had poor leverage.

Another inch…

He stretched out further until his muscles were taut.

He yanked again.

The handle rattled, and then slid out.

He backed up, clambered onto the catwalk, and braced himself against the cab.

Lundquist gave the engine a jolt of gas and the sudden surge separated the king pin from the fifth wheel. The road ascended a shallow rise and the connecting plate that fastened the trailer slipped out.

It started to fall away.

The airlines and the electrical cable stretched out, went tight, and then were yanked out of their couplings.

Without air, the trailer's spring brakes automatically locked.

There was a huge crash as the front of the unit slammed down onto the road, sparks flying in a crazy cascade behind it, smoke pouring from the locked tyres.

It jerked left and right.

Milton flinched, expecting a blast.

Nothing came.

It gouged a track down the middle of the road, somehow staying upright. After fifty feet, it ground to a halt.

The tractor, shorn of its weight, raced ahead.

He anchored himself with the broken airlines and stepped onto the side of the tractor. The eight drive tyres turned, the spray flaying him. He reached the corner and stretched out, his fingers fixing around the handle of the storage compartment. He stepped onto the fuel tank, his feet sliding against the bulbous shape of the wet metal, and then he lunged ahead and took the grab handle. The exhaust stack chugged, fumes pouring out into the darkness. He caught sight of himself in the mirror, ducked beneath it, and hopped from the tank to the step.

He raised himself above the line of the window, looked inside…

… and saw the M16.

He let go of the handle, dropped below the line of the window, and swung away.

The automatic gunfire blew out the window, a sparkling parabola of glass that arced outwards and scattered behind him.

He held onto the handle of the storage compartment with his right hand, his right foot on the fuel tank, and swung back to the rear of the tractor.

He didn't know what to do.

If Lundquist had spare ammunition, and Milton knew that he would, there would be no way he could get into the tractor cab before being shot.

He tightened his grip on the airline.

He was stuck.

"SIR?"

The pilot had given them a lead on the semi and then turned back to face it. Ellie had watched with fear and admiration as Milton had uncoupled the trailer. The road ahead was straight for three miles, and they had seen it scrape to a halt. It hadn't detonated, not that it would have mattered out here.

Now all that was left to deal with was the tractor.

Denuded of its trailer, it had raced ahead.

She had watched Milton clamber around the side of the cab and had seen the muzzle flash and the sparkle of glass as Lundquist had fired at him. She had watched as he held on with one hand and then swung back around the back. She found that she had been holding her breath.

The tractor was two miles away from them now and it was closing fast.

"Sir?" the gunner said. "What are your orders?"

"When it's in range, shoot it."

"What more can he do?" Ellie protested.

"We don't know if that maniac has explosives in there with him. Can't take the chance. If your friend has got any sense in him, he'll jump and get clear."

The tractor kept rolling.

"Jump? He'll kill himself."

"Give him a warning," Maguire said.

The gunner settled in behind the M-60 and squeezed the trigger. A dozen rounds tore through the darkness, the tracer describing a diagonal trajectory that blew up the road twenty feet in front of the speeding tractor.

Lundquist kept coming, the tractor rushing over the fresh potholes and through the cloud of pulverised asphalt.

Maguire looked at Ellie, his expression apologetic, then at the gunner.

"Do it."

Chapter 50

MORTEN LUNDQUIST looked at the Black Hawk. The chopper was hovering above the road two hundred yards away, directly ahead of him.

He didn't know how he had done it, but Milton had decoupled the trailer. The airlines must have been torn out. Every time he touched the brakes he would be depleting the air tanks, and, when they were empty, the spring brakes would stop the tractor, too.

So he didn't brake.

He accelerated.

Sixty.

Sixty-five.

The chopper waited for him.

He closed.

One hundred and fifty yards.

One hundred yards.

It was no good.

The game was up.

He had been mistaken.

Maybe he hadn't been listening.

God's word?

It wasn't what he had thought it was.

He had a different plan for him.

Thy will be done.

He could see it now, everything that he had done wrong. He had let Milton distract him. He had allowed him to fill his thoughts, his voice drowning out God's voice.

It was obvious, now.

Milton *was* an agent of Satan.

And Lundquist needed to stop him.

Perhaps that was what God had always wanted him to do.

He looked up at the helicopter as its powerful searchlight swung across the road and raced towards him, filling the cab with its blinding glow. He blinked, taking his hand off the wheel and shielding his eyes with it just as the muzzle of the big machine gun sparked a vicious starburst.

The rounds detonated into the asphalt and then reached up into the chassis of the truck, shredding the hood, pulverising the radiator and the engine. Flames leapt out, and then a thick pall of black smoke started to rise up.

Lundquist yanked the wheel to the left.

The disabled tractor was doing sixty as it left the road.

ELLIE GRIPPED the side of the chair as the rattle of the machine gun overlaid the roar of the turbines.

"Shit!" the gunner cursed.

The tractor passed out of sight.

"Pull up," Maguire said. "We need a better view."

They gained altitude, opening up the dark vista of the woods. The forest around here was crisscrossed with the same access roads and firebreaks, and it was one of these into which the tractor had plunged. She could see the glow of its headlamps pulsing orange through the trunks of the trees. The pilot kept the chopper behind the tractor, and they watched as it gradually decelerated before it smashed a path through the trees that fringed the road and came to a sudden stop.

"I can't set down there, Colonel," the pilot reported. "There's nowhere to land."

"Keep us on station and call in our position. How far away are the units on the ground?"

"Ten klicks."

"How long can we stay here?"

The pilot checked his dials. "We've got a quarter tank. Fifteen minutes if we want to get back again."

The searchlight shone into the darkened trees. The operator trained it on the wreck of the tractor and then gave out a shout of surprise. "There he is!"

Ellie squinted down.

The figure of a man. Bulky, moving slowly, awkwardly. The spotlight tracked him, moving in a northeasterly direction as he struggled through the undergrowth away from the wreck.

"Is that Lundquist or Milton?"

"Lundquist," she said.

"Fire at will."

The gunner fired a barrage, and as he did, the searchlight lost the man. "Dammit."

Maguire gritted his teeth. "He's going to get away."

Ellie looked back at the tractor.

Where was Milton?

THE TRACTOR had bounced and leapt, crashing through the smaller trees and tearing the scrub up by the roots. The firebreak was just barely wide enough for it, and then it had turned away and the tractor had kept going in a straight line, slicing through a stand of newly planted fir. The windscreen had shattered as the tractor splashed through a stream. It had eventually slammed to a dead stop against the trunk of an ancient oak.

Lundquist had been thrown around the cab like a puppet, and the final impact had crashed his head against the wheel. The jolt had made him bite clean through his lip, and now blood was running into his mouth and pouring down his chin. The seat belt had cut into the fleshy parts of his neck, and he could feel the bruises forming on his sternum, chest, and pelvis.

He had taken the M16 and kicked the door open. His foot slipped on the step and sent him crashing into a bush bristling with thorns.

He took a pause to catch his breath.

The tractor's shattered engine ticked, its heat gradually dissipating.

Shards of glass fell like teeth from the broken maw of the window frame.

He looked up as the tremendous clatter of the Black Hawk came from directly overhead.

He ran.

The big machine gun opened up and rounds tore through the canopy overhead, stitching jagged holes in the sodden greensward. He tumbled out of the way, the splashing, muddy impacts stretching away from him and terminating in the trunk of another oak, sending a storm of splinters in all directions.

He scrambled up, burrowed deeper into the undergrowth, and then paused.

The forest was disturbed, filled with the complaints of birds and animals that had been roused by the tractor's plunge through the trees.

The helicopter was somewhere overhead, close, its turbines roaring and the rotors cutting noisily through the air.

He heard something, saw a flash of movement.

A deer.

He saw the white-tail bob as it pranced out of danger.

Another noise?

He swung up the M16 and fired a burst into the bushes.

Blind fear, the searing white heat of terror, burned through his mind so fast and so fiercely and so thoroughly that he almost forgot his own name.

He remembered one name.

John Milton.

He stumbled forwards, the thorns ripping at his flesh, scratching his face and his hands and tearing his clothes, none of that as important as putting distance between himself and the tractor.

Between himself and the Black Hawk.

Between himself and Milton.
He ran.

Chapter 51

MILTON PAUSED. Lundquist had barrelled across a space that had been cleared of trees. In spite of his urge to rush after him, he knew that he could not. The Black Hawk was overhead, the searchlight glaring down at them, its twitching light illuminating the space so well that there would be no way for Milton to pass through it unobserved. He had to wait until the chopper had passed over. Lundquist might not have been sprinting away; maybe he was pressed down on the ground, the M16 laid out before him, aiming.

Milton heard a metallic, amplified voice. "Morten Lundquist! This is the National Guard."

Milton looked up. The Black Hawk was hovering fifty feet above the tree line.

"Lundquist! You need to surrender."

Milton knew that there was little they could do. The clearing was much too small for them to land.

There came the strobe of gunfire from the other side of the clearing, and he saw the sparks of impact as bullets struck the helicopter's fuselage.

The chopper slid away to the right and the clearing was plunged into darkness. Milton heard the crash of movement through the bushes and ran low and fast in pursuit. He stopped and listened and heard, not far up ahead, the sound of something crashing through more thick underbrush.

He followed, staying low. Lundquist wouldn't run forever. There would come a point when he would grow tired or impatient, and then he would stop. He would try to lay out an ambush, and Milton had to be wary of that. But the noise kept coming, the rustling of the undergrowth and the sound of boots splashing through mud, and as long as he could hear him moving, he knew he could follow safely.

When the noise stopped, he stopped, falling to the ground and inching forwards on his belly, his eyes searching ahead for any sign of Lundquist's passage. The Black Hawk came back again, the searchlight probing for them, the solid shaft of its light absorbed by the canopy overhead, so bright that Milton could see the veins of the leaves lit up from above. He heard the sound of a curse, and then the running started again, so he got up and ran, too.

It must have been fifteen minutes before the noise stopped for a second time. Milton dropped back into the brush. He waited there, controlling his breathing, vigilant.

He looked around, recognising his surroundings.

Lundquist had been running in circles.

The noise of boots slapping through water came from up ahead, and he followed again. The pursuit continued through a dense thicket of trees and across another open patch of ground. Lundquist led him to a long stretch of dogwood, crawling beneath the branches through the dirt and the muck, and then down a loose slope of scree to a stream, across that and then along the opposite bank. Milton stayed within the margin of vegetation. It would have been faster to run through the water, but he would have made too much noise and would present a target that would be impossible to miss.

He would be patient.

Lundquist was losing it.

Wouldn't be long now.

THE SLEEVE of Lundquist's jacket snagged on the thorns of a bush, and the fabric ripped as he tore it loose. He ducked down and cursed, not because of the jacket, but because he was beginning to feel desperate. The Black Hawk was still overhead, the searchlight questing for him, but he could stay ahead of it, and he knew that eventually they would run low on fuel and have to leave. It wasn't the helicopter that he was worried about.

It was the sure and certain knowledge that John Milton was behind him.

He pushed up and tried to scramble away. The brambles, which he had forgotten about, lashed him in the face. Their spikes scratched into him, tearing the skin on his cheeks and throat. He covered his eyes and pushed through them, feeling the blood on his skin and ignoring it.

He just needed to keep going. He had waited twice, settled down in deep cover, and turned the M16 to face the direction that Milton must surely be coming. But he did not come. The forest was full of noise, loud with panicked birds and animals and the noise of the Black Hawk overhead, but there was nothing that sounded like a man in pursuit. It was as if he had a sixth sense. Whenever Lundquist stopped, Milton stopped.

Or maybe he was wrong, maybe he was paranoid, maybe Milton wasn't following him after all?

Lundquist stopped for a moment to catch his breath. He was winded, his knees were watery, and he had no idea where he was. He thought of just turning and firing in a wide arc, emptying out the magazine and trusting God, but he couldn't do it. It would be suicide. He could fire for a week, and he wouldn't hit him. And the muzzle flashes would just give him away.

He set off again, following the course of a stream to the south, but his legs felt empty, and he had no strength left. He dragged his foot, and his ankle was snagged by a bare root, his momentum arrested as he slammed down onto his hands and knees. He dropped the M16 and tried to withdraw his foot, but he was panicked, and every yank and jerk seemed to jam it in ever tighter.

Finally, he managed it. He scrambled backwards, to his rifle.

Now, he thought. Now he would make his stand.

He swallowed compulsively, his stomach an empty pit. He fumbled the M16 and aimed back down the stream, sweeping into the trees on the left and on the opposite bank to the right.

And fear not them which kill the body, but are not able to kill the soul.

He listened, but he couldn't hear anything. Something was different. He realised what it was: the helicopter was gone. It wasn't just away from him, for he would have been able to hear the engines from miles away, it was gone.

It was just him and Milton now.

But rather fear him which is able to destroy both soul and body in hell.

He heard a crashing sound from the other side of the river, swung the rifle in that direction, and fired.

The noise was terrifyingly loud, the echoes cracking around the trees, and he got to his feet and ran again. His foot slipped off a moss-covered rock, and he went flying through the air, legs flailing, and then he pounded back down on his back. His head smacked against a rock, and his vision fluttered, then dimmed. The stream ran around him as he lay there, his eyes squeezed tight. He could feel the sharp pebbles on the bottom digging into his back.

And he said to them, 'This kind cannot be driven out by anything but prayer.'

He couldn't breathe. He closed his eyes and prayed, again, for strength. He gulped for air, but his stomach muscles wouldn't push out.

He tried to roll over. He couldn't.

He couldn't move at all.

He opened his eyes and saw that John Milton was on top of him, his knee pushed into his chest and his arm braced across his throat.

He tried to free himself.

Milton was too strong.

Lundquist looked up into his face, about to beg him for mercy, but he saw his cold blue eyes, and the words died on his lips.

Milton grabbed him by the lapels of his jacket and hauled him further out into the stream. It was shallow at the edges, but a narrow channel in the centre was deep enough to reach up to Milton's knees as he tugged him out with him. Lundquist started to float, no longer able to feel the pebbles against his back. The water splashed over his throat and onto his face, into his mouth and nostrils.

He closed his eyes for the last time as Milton shoved his head below the surface. The water was icy cold, and Lundquist's skin prickled with it. He felt, finally, shockingly alive just as he opened his mouth and drank it all in.

Chapter 52

SIX-THIRTY AT NIGHT, a snowstorm kicking eddies against the windows, and the restaurant was emptying out. It was on Lombardi Avenue, close to Lambeau Field, and the Packers were home against the 49ers. There were groups of stragglers at several of the tables, fans in Packers gear finishing their meals before bundling themselves up in their winter gear and heading out for the short walk to the stadium. The restaurant was a local destination, that was what Ellie had heard, a popular stop on the way to the stadium. There were signed pictures on the wall: Bart Starr, Brett Favre, Aaron Rodgers. A large portrait of Vince Lombardi had pride of place behind the bar, above the racks of bottles and the cash register. A sign above the portrait read TITLETOWN. Half a dozen TVs were tuned to the local FOX affiliate, the pregame shows well underway.

She went to the bar and sat down.

Green Bay. What the fuck.

The five men at the nearest table to her were loud and irritating. She gathered from their conversation that they were in town for the game, a corporate box, a chance to shake hands with an old Packers alumnus in return for some astronomical payment. Lawyers or accountants, she guessed, cutting loose now that they had managed a night away from their wives. She'd noticed that they had stopped talking as she had walked past the table, and then, when they started up again, their tone was a little lower, conspiratorial, snide little chuckles and guffaws as they looked over at her.

Like she wouldn't figure out they were talking about her, or couldn't guess what was coming next.

She almost got up again and left. She wasn't in the mood. But she decided to stay. She needed a drink and a change of scenery. She'd been staring at the same four walls for hours, the same bland conference room in the same bland federal building, and she was about to lose her mind.

She had been practically breathing the case all week. The National Guard had found Lundquist's body face down in a stream that ran through the woods. Drowned. An animal had started to make a meal of the soft tissue on his face. She had seen the autopsy photographs. Pretty grisly, his eyes gone, half of his nose, cheeks burrowed out. No definitive evidence of foul play, the pathologist said; he could easily have fallen into the stream and drowned.

Ellie knew better than that.

John Milton had been picked up on the road walking back in the direction of Truth.

Orville had been predictable. He had done exactly what she had thought he would do: he swooped into town, flashed his badge like he was the director, made the calls, and started to look so busy with it all that people who didn't know any better might have thought it was his bust rather than hers. He had made a ham-fisted attempt at a reconciliation, but his heart wasn't really in it, not enough to give him the backbone to push on when it became obvious that she hadn't changed her mind about what she'd said, and after she blew him off when he had suggested dinner so that they could "talk," he had punished her by sending her to Siberia, otherwise known as Green fucking Bay.

It happened fast. There had been no opportunity for her to speak to Milton.

The media had the story by the time she arrived in Wisconsin. It was a big deal. The director went on the air and laid down the edict that the militia was going to be completely squashed. The US attorney lost no time filing charges against the twenty men and women they picked up in the forest, plus Morris Finch and another ten who were involved. They were looking at trials for attempted bombing, plus conspiracy and weapons offences.

Milton was key to the case.

Orville had decided to do the interview himself. Ellie would have loved to have been in the room for that. She had been given the play-by-play by another agent with whom she was friendly. Orville had put Milton through two solid days of interviews. Word was, he had tried to turn him into a cooperating witness, tried to persuade him that he had to testify. He hinted that charges against him were being stayed on the basis that he cooperated. It sounded like a threat, and she guessed that threatening Milton was not likely to be productive. And so it had proved. His answers became clipped and then monosyllabic, much to Orville's evident irritation. Eventually, he just stopped answering, saying he would only speak to her. When Orville refused that, Milton had insisted on a phone call.

What happened next had been plain bizarre.

Whoever it was Milton had called, it had blown things up. The director had scurried to meet with him personally. There had been the suggestion of a medal, which Milton had rejected outright, and then a fulsome apology from Orville for the way in which he had been treated. The suggestion was that Milton had agreed to cooperate with the investigation on the condition that he was made a confidential informant. He wouldn't be asked to testify, but he would share his knowledge of the militia without any risk of being charged. Ellie had even heard that the bureau and the attorney's office were working on creating the fiction that Milton was working for them as an informer all along.

After that, he was told he could go.

He was last seen walking out of town, his pack and his rifle slung over his shoulder.

And then, it got even weirder.

Ellie had been called by the director. He told her that she was in line for a nice bump in salary. She said great. He said you've done well, but this is on two conditions.

First, she had to play ball with the big media campaign they were planning. It was hazy, the details all to be confirmed, but it sounded like they wanted to make her into a heroine. Magazine interviews, morning television, the whole nine yards.

The second condition?

Milton's involvement in the affair was not to be mentioned, under any circumstances.

She knew how the game was played, and she didn't know how she felt about it. Her dad would have told the director to shove his media plan up his ass, but Ellie was more practical. He had been jaded, plus he was a man. Ellie was still fresh and keen, and she had found not having a dick was an impediment to quick advancement. She could see the benefits in playing nice.

One phone call from Milton had done all of this?

Who did he *know?*

She told the director she would think about it.

SHE LOOKED out of the window. She could see her reflection in the glass, the smart suit and the sensible shoes, and staring at herself, she remembered the trek up through the wilderness to get to the Lake of the Clouds.

It felt like another world.

A man detached from the table of five and came over.

"Excuse me. Mind if I sit down?"

Ellie waved her hand absently. "Free country."

She was distracted. Orville and one of the bureau's rising young stars, this fresh-faced ingénue flown over from Quantico, had spent several days shouting at the suspects. They had extracted leads, most likely wild goose chases, but they all had to be followed up anyway, just in case there was a grain of truth to them, some other wacko waiting in the shadows with a truck full of fertiliser and racing fuel. They had been told that there was another militia in Wisconsin, brave Christian soldiers waiting for the first sign of the Second Coming, ready to start the war. Ellie had been told to find them.

These people who almost certainly didn't exist.

In Green fucking Bay.

"Get you a drink?"

"No, thanks," she said.

"I'm Frank."

He was wearing a Packers jersey with FRANK across the back. It was brand new, and he had forgotten to take the tags off.

The barman passed her a bottle of beer.

"Put that on our bill."

"No," Ellie said. "I'll buy my own drinks."

The man shuffled a little awkwardly, but Ellie could see that his friends were watching the show, and she knew that he wouldn't give up after the first brush-off.

"You here for the game?"

"No."

"Business, then?"

"Something like that."

"What kind of business?"

"This and that."

"Mysterious." He laughed.

She ignored him.

"You going to ask what I'm doing here?"

"No."

He went on as if she hadn't spoken. "There was a charity auction, the Make-A-Wish Foundation, my law firm bid for a box. I'm a partner there. It wasn't cheap, never is, but we figured it was for a good cause, so why not, right?"

"Right."

She noticed the small details: expensive shoes, designer denim, Rolex that probably cost the same as a small family car. "Listen," he said, "if you're around tonight and you've got nothing planned, we've got a spare seat. We'd be delighted to have your company."

Ellie was about to tell him to take a hike when she paused, the words dying on her lips. She saw the indistinct outline of a man standing outside the entrance. He was peering in through the glass, maybe looking at the menu they had there to tempt diners inside, maybe looking into the restaurant, she couldn't be sure. There was a lattice of frost across the glass, and it was difficult to make out the details, but something about the man said that she knew who he was.

"So?"

She realised he had continued to speak. She hadn't heard a word of it.

"What do you say?"

She stood quickly, her stool clattering back against the bar.

Frank rested his hand on her elbow, blocking her way forward. "So, you gonna come and have a good time with us?"

The man at the window turned and faded away into the falling snow.

"Excuse me, Frank."

"Come on, don't be like that."

"I'm not interested in your company. It'd be best for everyone if you just took your drink and went back to your table, okay?"

He still didn't get the hint.

"What's your name, honey?"

She reached into her pocket, took out the leather wallet that she used to carry her badge, flipped it open and held it up so that he could see it. "Special Agent Ellie Flowers," she said, angling her torso a little so that her jacket fell back enough that he could see the glint of the Glock 22 on her belt.

He looked down at the badge, wide-eyed. "You're FBI?"

"That's right. And I've had a hell of a week, and I'm not feeling all that sociable, so go on, go back to your buddies and enjoy the game. Give me a fucking break, okay?"

The man did as she asked and went back to the table.

She hurried to the door and threw it open, the cold air rushing in to embrace her. The snow fell softly, the cars crunching across compacted ice. The road was busy as fans meandered towards the stadium and two blocks over the big floodlights threw up a corona of golden light that reached up into the dark, snowy night.

There were too many people. The man she had seen had been absorbed into the crowd.

She went back inside. Frank's friends welcomed him back with amused expressions on their faces that said his pride had taken a bit of a slap.

She finished her beer and decided to have another, taking it to a table next to a window. She looked out at the snow again, whipping up against the window, and, beyond it, a cityscape carpeted in white.

JOHN MILTON adjusted his pack across his shoulders so that it was more comfortable and trudged on through the snow. The sidewalk was busy with people in Packers' green and 49ers' red and white, crowds of fans enjoying good-natured banter, their expectation for the game buzzing in the air. The convivial atmosphere was different from the equivalent back home, he thought. It was better than it had once been, but you could still get a fat lip for wearing the wrong colours on the wrong street.

He paused at a crosswalk, just one man within the crowd. Faceless and anonymous, just how he liked it. The traffic hurried ahead under the green light. The light went to red, and a mounted cop edged forwards, marshalling the crowd.

He had been in town for three days. He had located Ellie on the first day without too much difficulty: a call to the Detroit field office under a pretext provided the information that she had been sent to Green Bay. A brief stop in an Internet café revealed a host of stories about how the FBI was investigating reports of copycat militias in Wisconsin. It had been trivial to find the bureau office and stake it out until he saw her. He had watched her. She was staying in the Marriott, room two-twelve. On the second day, he watched her eat breakfast at six, saw her take a cab across town to the office, and then it picked her up again at eight when she finally finished for the day. He had been close to going over to her, asking her out, seeing if she wanted that dinner. It was cheesy, but he knew it would work.

So why had he backed out? What had stopped him?

He had waited outside her office again today. It was six o'clock when she had finished, stepping out into the cold with a thick winter coat wrapped around her. She had deviated from her routine, and he had followed fifty feet behind her as she had walked, alone, to the restaurant.

That meant something.

He had walked around the block to ensure that he wasn't being tailed, old habits, and, by the time he had made it back to the entrance she was with another man. He was dressed for the game, Packers colours, but he had the look of an agent: short, well-trimmed hair, anonymous clothes, good quality. Milton had watched as he had laid his hand on Ellie's elbow. They looked intimate. They were going to the game. He must have been her date.

She hadn't mentioned whether she was seeing someone but come on, seriously, there had to be someone, right?

What did he think? That they were going to have a relationship? She was an FBI agent, and he was who he was. As far as Milton was concerned, a relationship could only work if it was built on a foundation of total honesty.

He felt that very strongly, and it was something he would never be able to offer. Secrets were toxic and he had a million of them. And even assuming that he *could* be honest, assuming that he *could* ignore the legal and moral implications of telling her about the things that he had done, it would poison the way that she saw him.

How could it ever have worked?

It couldn't.

He had been stupid for even entertaining the notion.

Best to leave it as it was. They had their moment.

Ellie would be better with someone from the same world as her. The guy in the bar. They would be a better match.

He thought about mortgages, credit cards, consumer goods. He thought about children and nine-to-five jobs, about medical insurance and dental plans, about pensions and savings accounts, and he knew he was making the right decision.

It was time to move on.

And so he walked on, heading west. There were seven hundred miles between Green Bay and Minneapolis. That would take him three weeks to walk in weather like this. He would have to hitch a ride to make it in time for the gig. He would hike out to the WI-29, get to a truck stop, and see if he could find a driver who wanted some company.

Milton took his battered headphones from around his neck and put them over his ears. He reached into his pocket, took out his iPod and scrolled through his playlists for the one he wanted. He settled on The Smiths, pressed play and nodded his head a little as the distorted guitar riff from "How Soon is Now?" started to play. He took a woollen beanie from his pocket, pulled it over the headphones and then put on his gloves.

He set his face to the west, the icy blast of the wind lashing against his cheeks, his breath clouding before his face, and started to walk.

GET TWO FREE BEST-SELLERS, TWO NOVELLAS AND EXCLUSIVE JOHN MILTON MATERIAL

Building a relationship with my readers is the very best thing about writing. I occasionally send newsletters with details on new releases, special offers and other bits of news relating to the John Milton, Beatrix Rose and Soho Noir series. And if you sign up to my no-spam mailing list I'll send you all this free stuff:

1. A copy of my best-seller, The Cleaner (116 five star reviews and RRP of $5.99).

2. A copy of the John Milton introductory novella, 1000 Yards.

3. A free copy of my best-seller, The Black Mile (averages 4.4 out of 5 stars and RRP for $5.99).

4. A copy of the introductory Soho Noir Novella, Gaslight.

5. A copy of the highly classified background check on John Milton before he was admitted to Group 15. Exclusive to my mailing list – you can't get this anywhere else.

6. Later this year, a copy of Tarantula, an exciting John Milton short story.

You can get the novels, the novellas, the background check and the short story, for free, by signing up at http://eepurl.com/1ab6H

IF YOU ENJOYED THIS BOOK…

…I would really, really appreciate it if you would help others to enjoy it, too. Reviews are like gold dust and they help persuade other readers to give the stories a shot. More readers means more incentive for me write and that means there will be more stories, more quickly.

ABOUT THE AUTHOR

Mark Dawson is the author of the breakout John Milton, Beatrix Rose and Soho Noir series. He makes his online home at www.markjdawson.com. You can connect with Mark on Twitter at @pbackwriter, on Facebook at www.facebook.com/markdawsonauthor and you should send him an email at markjdawson@me.com if the mood strikes you.

ALSO BY MARK DAWSON

Have you read them all?

In the Soho Noir Series

Gaslight

When Harry and his brother Frank are blackmailed into paying off a local hood they decide to take care of the problem themselves. But when all of London's underworld is in thrall to the man's boss, was their plan audacious or the most foolish thing that they could possibly have done?

The Black Mile

London, 1940: the Luftwaffe blitzes London every night for fifty-seven nights. Houses, shops and entire streets are wiped from the map. The underworld is in flux: the Italian criminals who dominated the West End have been interned and now their rivals are fighting to replace them. Meanwhile, hidden in the shadows, the Black-Out Ripper sharpens his knife and sets to his grisly work.

The Imposter

War hero Edward Fabian finds himself drawn into a criminal family's web of vice and soon he is an accomplice to their scheming. But he's not the man they think he is - he's far more dangerous than they could possibly imagine.

In the John Milton Series

One Thousand Yards

In this dip into his case files, John Milton is sent into North Korea. With nothing but a sniper rifle, bad intentions and a very particular target, will Milton be able to take on the secret police of the most dangerous failed state on the planet?

The Cleaner

Sharon Warriner is a single mother in the East End of London, fearful that she's lost her young son to a life in the gangs. After John Milton saves her life, he promises to help. But the gang, and the charismatic rapper who leads it, is not about to cooperate with him.

Saint Death

John Milton has been off the grid for six months. He surfaces in Ciudad Juárez, Mexico, and immediately finds himself drawn into a vicious battle with the narco-gangs that control the borderlands.

The Driver

When a girl he drives to a party goes missing, John Milton is worried. Especially when two dead bodies are discovered and the police start treating him as their prime suspect.

Ghosts

John Milton is blackmailed into finding his predecessor as Number One. But she's a ghost, too, and just as dangerous as him. He finds himself in deep trouble, playing the Russians against the British in a desperate attempt to save the life of his oldest friend.

Salvation Row (summer 2014)

In the Beatrix Rose Series

In Cold Blood

Beatrix Rose was the most dangerous assassin in an off-the-books government kill squad until her former boss betrayed her. A decade later, she emerges from the Hong Kong underworld with payback on her mind. They gunned down her husband and kidnapped her daughter, and now the debt needs to be repaid. It's a blood feud she didn't start but she is going to finish.

Blood Moon Rising

There were six names on Beatrix's Death List and now there are four. She's going to account for the others, one by one, even if it kills her. She has returned from Somalia with another target in her sights. Bryan Duffy is in Iraq, surrounded by mercenaries, with no easy way to get to him and no easy way to get out. And Beatrix has other issues that need to be addressed. Will Duffy prove to be one kill too far?

Blood and Roses

Beatrix Rose has worked her way through her Kill List. Four are dead, just two are left. But now her foes know she has them in her sights and the hunter has become the hunted.

Standalone Novels

The Art of Falling Apart

A story of greed, duplicity and death in the flamboyant, super-ego world of rock and roll. Dystopia have rocketed up the charts in Europe, so now it's time to crack America. The opening concert in Las Vegas is a sell-out success, but secret envy and open animosity have begun to tear the group apart.

Subpoena Colada

Daniel Tate looks like he has it all. A lucrative job as a lawyer and a host of famous names who want him to work for them. But his girlfriend has deserted him for an American film star and his main client has just been implicated in a sensational murder. Can he hold it all together?

ACKNOWLEDGEMENTS

I am indebted to the following for their help, all above and beyond the call of duty: Lucy Dawson (for her early edits and direction); Martha Hayes and Pauline Nolet; Detective Lieutenant (Ret'd) Edward L. Dvorak, Los Angeles County Sheriff's Department, and Joe D. Gillespie (for their advice on weapons and military matters); Senior Inspector John W., US Marshals Service; Julian Annels (for advice on semi trucks); and Robert Lass, for working with me on the ending.

The following members of Team Milton were also invaluable: Lee R, Nigel F, Frank W, Gary P, Brian E, Bob , Mel M, Phil P, Charlie, Matt B, Edward S, Desiree B, Don L, Barry F, Corne vdM , Dawn T, Paul Q, Carl H, Chuck H, Don, Bernard C, Julian A, Charles R, Michael C, Grant B, Rick Lowe, Randall M, Steve D, Chris O, Mike S, Rick S, Pat K, Dale M, Robert L, Bill D, Rob C, Ian C, Chris G, Jared G, Roman P, Cecelia B, David S, Caleb B, Louis P, Sonny dC, John H, Matt B, JKP, Richard S, Bev B, Dave Z, Steve C, Christian B, Daniel C, Debra K, George W, Linda F, Mark G, Phillip S, John O, Melinda D, Janet H, Lynn E, Tim A, Steve H, Martin W, Kent, Mark D, Jack O, William L, Dale V, James F, David, Alan, Daniel O, Reid W, Robert T, Reid W, Robert T, Thom L, Andrew G, Tom C, Cindy S, John C, François D, Delbert L, Paul L, Robert D, Craig M, Nick B, Keith R, Bob U, Daryl, Andrew H, Lewis B, Jim C, Tim H, Iain A, Larry C, Byron M, Charlie, Ann B, Jeff B, Jim B, Bev G, Pete P, Mark D, Sanjay K, John L, Anton P, Andy W, Bob T, Shawn H, Mark F, Steve P, Kirk I, Terence A, Gene K, Dean Y, Houston H, Joe T, Edward H, Julia W, Hank H, Glenda W, Mark D, David V, Randy S, Piet dP, Lisa P,

Virginia W, Charlotte M, Milton, Skip W, Peter G, Patrick F, Bob C, Stuart R, Rob, Jesse, Amanda L, Tony M, Monte H, Peter B, Vinnie V, Jay, John, Nigel E, Victoria W, Steve U, Maxine B, Maurice G, Claire, John H, Pete B, FR, Andras N, Len F, Mike M, Terry, Jami C, Jim A, Robert W, Genevieve L, Ralph W, Steven, Casey P, Jay J, Jim E, Bill M, Brad, Rory, Billy, Ann W, Michael G, Keith B, Walter K, Jeff R, Andy W, Mark, John C, Buzz B, Steve G, Doug C, Bill W, Stephen C, Bruce C, Greg G, Cynthia M, Bill N, Alana F, Randall B, Philip E, Allen M, John G, Morris D, Chris W, Paul M, Hendrik

Printed in Great Britain
by Amazon